Dear Reader,

Are you like me? Do you have 'reading moods'? Sometimes I like a story with an element of mystery in it, on other occasions I enjoy a sexy read; there are times when I love my romance novels spiced with a little humour and others when I look forward to a warm and involving family-centred story. How about you?

Each month, I work hard to provide a balanced list for you, to ensure that every *Scarlet* reader's taste is catered for. As you can imagine, this is quite a difficult feat, particularly as I may suddenly be offered four similar stories – four tales of romantic suspense, for example, all at one time. So far, from your letters and questionnaires, it seems that we're getting the mix just right. But do let us know, won't you, if there is anything you particularly want to see more of on *your* list. Or is there something you think is missing from the *Scarlet* list? In the light of the current interest in Jane Austen, would you like *Scarlet* to include some Regency romances?

Keep those letters and questionnaires coming, won't you?

Till next month,

Sally Cooper

SALLY COOPER,
Editor-in-Chief – *Scarlet*

TINA LEONARD

NEVER SAY NEVER

Enquiries to:
Robinson Publishing Ltd
7 Kensington Church Court
London W8 4SP

First published in the UK by Scarlet, 1996

A copy of the British Library Cataloguing in
Publication data is available from the British Library

ISBN 1-85487-715-1

Printed and bound in the EC

10 9 8 7 6 5 4 3 2 1

To my grandmother, Isabel Cather Sites, for suggesting I dust off my writing skills

To my husband, Tim, for supporting my efforts

To my six-year-old daughter, Shelly, for never passing up a wishing fountain without dropping in several pennies so the wishing star would choose her mother's book to buy

And my two-and-a-half-year-old son, Dean Michael, who carried a magazine to us one day, pointed proudly at Nora Robert's picture and announced, 'Look, it's you, Mommy!'

Luckily for me, everyone in my family is a dreamer.

CHAPTER 1

Last week Jill McCall had thought her world was in a fairly secure orbit. Today, she felt like she'd been hit by Halley's comet.

What a shock to discover that she'd been downsized by the company that had hired her fresh out of college. Downsized, as her boss kindly explained, meant that the company was laying off workers in an attempt to become more financially stable.

Tell that to her apartment manager, Jill snorted. The company might be more fiscally healthy, but being laid off right after Thanksgiving meant it was going to be a very slim Christmas for her. So much for that bonus she'd been counting on.

To add to the feeling of being torn loose from the universe, only last week she had broken off her engagement to her fiancé. The relationship, she'd realized, was comfortable, but missing something. It was sadly lacking in fire, and in passion, she had decided. At least it had seemed that way before a note had been dropped on her desk at work, revealing that

Carl had enough passion to go around – and around and around.

He hadn't even bothered to deny it when she'd questioned him about his apparently popular stamina and expertise. This was a side of Carl she personally had never experienced.

Well, she had plenty of excitement in her life now. No job, no boyfriend. Jill eyed the newspaper she had laid out in front of her on the kitchen table. If the cosmic forces of life were telling her anything, it was that she needed to make some changes. However, making changes could be difficult when there were no funds in one's purse. Her gaze roved over the paper one last time, discounting the unappealing ads she'd circled.

Then, a small box caught her interest.

WANTED: HOUSEKEEPER FOR RANCH HOUSE. *Cleaning and meals for a man, young boy, and an elderly woman. One hundred miles away from nearest big city; mall-dwellers need not apply. Good salary, three thousand dollar bonus one year from hire date. 1133 Setting Sun Road, Lassiter, Texas.*

Jill quickly scanned the words again. Country life would almost certainly be a positive change from her not-so-exciting routine. The bonus was tempting, and she could be gainfully employed while sending out resumés for another corporate position. Jobs like hers as a marketing manager, didn't grow on trees. It would take time to explore the market.

Surely this rancher couldn't be very demanding, Jill mused. He was probably out a lot, tending to cattle or whatever it was that ranchers did. Nor should an elderly woman be too great a problem. Handling a young boy might prove to be a challenge, but she'd had siblings as well as having done tons of baby-sitting. It couldn't hurt to call and inquire about the position, could it?

She started to circle the phone number, then realized there was only a mailing address. Jill checked her watch, then reached for a map out of a kitchen drawer. Lassiter, Texas, was located a little over a hundred miles north from where she lived in Dallas, and her mother's house was thirty minutes in the same direction. She could journey to Lassiter to check out the ranch and see if she could glean any information from the locals about the owner, then she could drive back to her mother's for the night. It was a lot of travelling for one day, but it would also give her a chance to decide whether she really wanted to apply for the job.

If she didn't like what she saw or heard about the ranch inhabitants, she could move on to searching for employment in the city. These days, a woman couldn't be too cautious. Without further hesitation, Jill called her mother and set the plans. Throwing a few things into an overnight bag, Jill took one last look around her apartment before walking out the door.

There was an old saying that a man could not serve two masters. Wryly, Dustin Reed acknowledged that

3

this was true. The cattle herd he had started building two years ago – replacing the dairy cows that had been on the ranch since his parents had owned it – took all of his time. Since the ranch made him a lively income however, perhaps it was only fair that it should be a demanding master.

Still, the anger Dustin kept burning inside him was a draining and unforgiving master. There was no release from the rage he felt at the speeding, drunk driver that had killed his wife, Nina, leaving him to raise their son, Joey, now three-and-a-half. Like a slow-burning torch growing steadily hotter, Dustin was angry that Nina's parents had filed a custodial suit for Joey, and he feared they just might win. The judge who was presiding over the case was sitting squarely in David and Maxine Copeland's silk-lined pockets. Though his lawyer had filed for a change of venue, the request had been denied.

But the greatest anger burning inside Dustin was that it was the start of the Christmas season, the first since Nina had died, a fact which time was pushing inexorably into his mind. Now it was only a matter of days until either he or the Copelands won custody of Joey, and though he was going to fight like hell, something inside him was frozen when it came to his son. Maybe it was that he didn't have any practice with small children, and had let Nina do most of the rearing.

Of course, that was when he'd been living under the assumption that he had all the time in the world to learn to be a good father.

4

Time had run out on him.

The frozen part of him couldn't thaw for the wrenching fear that Joey was going to be taken from him. Dustin hadn't expected Nina to be taken. Now he couldn't seem to relax around his son, knowing that in a few short days, they, too, might be separated.

The anger grew, becoming Dustin's master and selfishly, perhaps, he found he needed to ignore the marching of time, and so this year, he was having nothing to do with the spirit of the season. It seemed the only way he could take the edge off the anger was to ignore Christmas. There would be no festive lights in his home this year, no Christmas tree. To wake up on Christmas morning, with no pattering of small feet in the house, to face a tree that needed no presents because the child wasn't there – Dustin feared the agony of it would kill him. So it would be a small spiritless gathering for holiday dinner, just him and his mother, Eunice, who lived at the Regret Ranch, too. Until the judge made his decision, Dustin was going to protect his emotions. But if the judge ruled in his favour, Dustin was going to launch a major decorating assault on his house. Until then, it simply didn't feel safe.

He scanned the north for signs of breaking clouds, knowing that his pet name for the Regret Ranch symbolized his acceptance of that insidious master thriving inside him. This place where he was standing, this large stretch of property fit primarily for running herds of beef cattle, had been the Reed

Ranch since his grandparents' time. But since the last two letters in Reed had fallen off the metal sign at the entrance to the ranch, he'd renamed it to suit himself, and had avoided rehanging the letters.

The faster the Christmas season passed, the faster people stopped saying 'Happy holidays!' to him and sending him cards he instantly tossed in the trash without opening, the faster life might return to normal. Yet he had a feeling that the well-meaning merriness in the town was only going to escalate as Christmas approached.

A blue flash at the south end of his property suddenly caught Dustin's eye. He squinted, wondering if a blue-jay was foraging red berries off the yaupon bushes.

There was the flash again, only the blue looked more like denim this time. If he didn't know better, he'd think that flash was a trespasser on his ranch.

Dustin walked to his truck, reaching inside for the shotgun off the rack and some shells out of the box. Silently, he crept down the hill, watching as the denim-wearing intruder appeared to be sneaking toward the house.

He thought of his mother, home alone with Joey, with only the aid of a cane to protect her. The arthritis in her hips and back that plagued her regularly was acting up now and he knew there was no way she could escape from an attacker. For Dustin, this was the last straw. Enough bad things had happened this year. A trespasser he knew how to deal with – swiftly.

The denim paused, and now Dustin could see the person wasn't large, perhaps just a teenage boy out for a prank. The big-horned steers that ran on Regret Ranch were an awesome sight, and the boy likely couldn't resist a chance to spy on them. However, he'd have had a better chance at getting a tour if he'd rung the front bell. A good scare now would keep the young prowler from trying this trick on Dustin's property again.

He moved to the next pecan tree, just behind the trespasser. With one hand, he reached out, clamping his hand down in a vice-like grip on the boy's shoulder.

'Aiee-ee!'

Dustin grinned at the terrible shriek of fear. The boy whipped around to see what had grabbed him, and the first thing Dustin registered was what large, darkly lashed blue eyes the boy had.

The second thing Dustin saw was that he wasn't gripping a boy at all. It was a woman, a woman so adorably cute that she took his breath away faster than the nippy air did.

'How dare you?' the woman gasped. 'Take your hands off of me!'

She saw the shotgun and her eyes became huge and round. She started backing away. 'Don't touch me. Don't even look at me. I'm going right now.'

The look on her face told Dustin that the woman thought she was in grave peril. He would have smiled, but he was still too shocked by what he'd bagged on his own land.

7

'Wait,' he said, holding up a hand. 'I didn't mean to scare you so badly. I thought you were a trespasser.'

'I am,' she asserted. 'Well, I guess I am. But I'm leaving now!'

He wanted to tell her that she wasn't a *bad* trespasser. He definitely wasn't going to shoot the lady. Her voice, he'd noticed, was light and sweet, even though she was frightened out of her wits. Her full mouth trembled, and the nostrils in her dainty nose flared. The cap she'd been wearing had fallen off when she swung around, revealing shiny, chin-length blond hair. She was definitely the prettiest thing he'd laid eyes on in a long time.

Jill had never been so petrified in her life. If this was the man who'd run the ad in the paper, then she'd been very smart to come out here and check out the situation. He was *crazy*. That shotgun he was holding looked like it meant business, and she wondered if the cowboy always carried that thing around like an ordinary billfold.

Just several more steps, she thought, and she'd be at her car. Jill turned, dashing that way.

'Wait!' the crazy man called.

'I can't,' she said on a gasp, fumbling in her purse for the keys. Drat them; they fell from her nervous fingers into a deep wheel rut in the dried mud. She got down, scrambling to find them, all the while glancing nervously back up at him.

He was the most handsome crazy man she'd ever seen.

8

'I've got to go,' she told him. 'If you'll give me a second, I'll – '

He knelt down beside her, retrieving the keys which had taken an unlucky bounce toward the other side of the tyre where she couldn't see them. 'Here.'

'Um . . . thanks.' Jill brushed hair from her eyes and tried to look like she wasn't impressed by the man's size. Or that he smelled wonderful, all outdoorsy and warm. Of course, this whole area had quite a different scent than what she had become accustomed to in Dallas. Lack of pollution, for one thing. Growing vegetation, for another. 'I'll be going – '

'Why are you here?'

'Ah – ' Jill tried to glance away from the question in his brown eyes, and failed. Would she sound ridiculous if she admitted that she hadn't really been trespassing, but had been coming to enquire about honest employment when those big ugly cows roaming his land had side-tracked her into wanting a closer look? That, for the sake of curiosity, she'd wanted to see what the house where she'd be working looked like? 'I . . .'

The sound of something crying snapped both their heads around.

'Did you hear something?' he asked softly.

Oh, Lord, there was something besides herself wandering around his ranch. Jill shivered, tucking herself closer into her coat. 'It was probably just a bird or something,' she said. 'Nothing you can't take

9

care of with that.' She gestured toward the shotgun. 'And since you appear well-protected, I'll be on my way.'

The sound wafted on the air again, louder and more intent, yet still threadlike, as if the creature wasn't very large. Jill froze where she was beside the big man.

'I can't figure out what that is,' he muttered.

Jill was intrigued, too. 'If I didn't know better, I'd think that was a baby,' she whispered.

His eyes met hers in a shared instant of co-conspiracy. 'A baby!' he whispered back. 'What kind of baby? Kitten? Dog?'

She shook her head, unsure. But the next time the sound came, they stepped forward together. They had gone about fifteen yards when Jill saw pink at the trunk of a barren tree.

'There,' she said, pointing down at the dull fall leaves on the ground, serving as a sort of nest for a swaddled infant.

The man beside her was suddenly very quiet. Jill walked forward to the pink bundle, squatting down beside it. A little round, pale face with roses in the cheeks from the cold, screwed itself up for another call for dinner, or perhaps a protest at being left to the elements, although its body seemed warm and well-wrapped. Gently, Jill picked the infant up, cradling it in her arms.

The man stared, his mouth open, first at the bundle, then at Jill. 'I can't believe you came to my ranch to dump your baby,' he said.

10

'*Dump my baby*!' Jill was outraged. 'Dump my –
Have you lost your *mind*? How could you think I
would – no, no,' she paused, shaking her head at him.
The baby let out a squall between the two comba-
tants. 'I can't believe you'd be so careless as to leave
your baby lying on the ground. Did you forget to pick
her up instead of your gun? That's a man for you,
always forgetting responsibilities. Here.' She thrust
the well-covered infant at him, but he stepped back
cautiously.

'Uh-uh. I don't want it. It's angry . . . and it isn't
mine. You take it right back wherever you came
from,' he said righteously.

Jill's mouth dropped open. She couldn't *leave* with
this baby, just because he thought it was hers. 'This
is not my child,' she said stubbornly.

'Looks like you.'

'No, it doesn't! I mean, what an idiotic statement!'
Jill was getting madder by the moment. 'What do you
think you see that possibly resembles me in this
child? The fact that it has two eyes and a mouth?'

'A loud one,' he said agreeably.

'Look,' she said, striving hard for patience, 'even if
this was my baby, I wouldn't have been driving
around with it in my car with no car seat. Do you
understand safety precautions?'

He appeared to mull over her statement. The baby
had quieted for a few minutes, but was showing signs
of anxiety in Jill's arms by thrashing in the silence.
After a tense moment, the man strode down the hill.
Jill followed, wondering if he intended to leave her.

Stopping in front of her tired old car, he peered inside. 'No car seat.'

'I said that already,' she said through gritted teeth. It was the last of Jill's patience. 'Put that damn gun down,' she commanded. He didn't look like he was going to, so she said, 'If you don't, I'm going to . . . scream.'

She wouldn't, but she felt like it. He must not have liked the idea, worrying that she might upset the baby or bring somebody running to witness their dilemma, because he leaned the gun against a tree, tossing unused shells beside it. She thrust the yelling bundle at the crazy man, which he took this time, maybe realizing she was at the end of her tether.

'I came here to inquire about the housekeeper's position, but I can see that would be a mistake.'

She marched to her car and opened the door.

'Why didn't you say you were here about the job?'

'You've given me precious little opportunity,' she ground out.

The infant appeared to be at the end of its tether, too. Jill paused. 'You'd better take her up to the house and see if she'll take some warm milk. Oh, wait a minute. Here,' she said, returning to the man's side. 'Someone thoughtfully provided you with a panic bottle.'

She withdrew a small, four-ounce bottle from inside the pink wrapping, where it had popped up due to the infant's agitated movements. 'It even has directions on it, and the brand name.' She gave the rancher a delightedly saucy grin. 'You'll probably

12

have just enough time to feed her that and run to the store and buy some more before she demands her next meal.'

She had turned to go again when his voice stopped her.

'Hey,' he said, his voice suddenly softer and less angry than it had been in the five minutes they'd been together, 'I'm sorry I've upset you. I'm pretty freaked out myself. Do you think I could talk you into coming up to the house with me, while I feed her? Then maybe keep an eye on her, while I call the police? I feel a little overwhelmed by this . . . early Christmas present.'

His voice had softened when he'd glanced back down at what was in his arms. It *was* a Christmas present of sorts, Jill thought. After all, how often was a baby delivered to your house, with blanket and bottle and instructions?

But he'd accused her of dumping the infant, charging her as the abandoner. Jill shook her head. 'I don't think I can, I – '

The unhappy baby let out a wail. Jill looked at it, forcing back latent motherly instincts she hadn't known she possessed.

'Will you come up to the house with me?' he asked again. 'My mother is there, but I'm not sure how much help she'll be with a newborn. She has bad arthritis which the cold seems to aggravate.'

The man had a mother inside the beautiful old ranch house. She'd forgotten that part of the advertisement. Jill nearly sighed with relief. She could go with him, and keep an eye on the baby while the proper authorities were called. Her conscience would feel much better.

'On one condition,' Jill said, staring him down so he'd know she meant it.

'Now what?'

'You have to put the gun away. I'm not used to men running around waving armaments.'

'Lady, this is a *ranch*.'

'Well, this is a *baby*,' she replied, mimicking his sarcastic tone. 'And where I come from, guns and babies are not said in the same breath.'

'You're a city girl.'

The statement was made without any rancor. Jill nodded. 'Down to the underwear I bought at Macy's.'

'You said you'd come to answer the ad! I specifically said *no mall-dwellers*,' he said, in a now-I've-got-you voice. '*If* you were really interested in the position, like you claim.'

'I bought them several years ago, when I got my first real job. They might fall off of me any minute. Satisfied?'

His sudden silence made her think perhaps he was. Jill took the baby from him.

'I'll carry her, you dispense with *that*,' she said with an imperious nod toward the gun. 'Poor little baby,' she murmured, walking toward the house with the delicate package wrapped securely in her arms.

Crackling leaves told her the man was following fast behind her. Jill smiled, hugging the baby to her

14

chest. He was a little crazy, but she had an idea he was also pretty harmless.

After all, she'd been watching the way he'd held the baby in his arms. Those big, flannel-covered arms of his had been holding her quite protectively. He might be grouchy, but he also cared.

After the man and the woman had walked to the house, Sadie eased to her feet. Her legs were cramping from staying still so long. Her eyes burned from the tears she longed to shed. But it wouldn't do to be caught on Dustin Reed's land – not since she'd just left the thing she loved most in the world in his care.

Sadie stumbled away, silently begging the tears not to fall. Mr Reed was handsome, though he was so big and frightening that Sadie had wondered if her mother had told her the right thing to do. But the lady who was visiting him, now, she was something else. Sadie had watched the pretty lady carefully hold her baby and sweetly try to soothe it. In that moment, that lady had become Sadie's angel, so that Sadie could rest a little easier with the trial she had to bear. Maybe Mr Reed would marry the lady and then one day, Holly would have a real family.

Just not her real mother. But that couldn't be helped. Sadie had learned tough lessons in her nineteen years, and one of them was that raising a family without enough to eat was difficult. If trading motherhood for the chance for Holly to be protected, and to have enough food – healthy food – to eat was the only way, then she would make that painful sacrifice.

Stealthily, Sadie pulled her bike from behind the tree, staring down at the basket where her baby had been just a little while ago. Then she peddled away, making certain no one saw her leave the ranch.

By the time Sadie reached her house, the night sky was falling rapidly. Dark blue clouds covered the moon, making everything seem darker. As if anything could seem darker than her life was now. Sadie put her bike away, thinking her house appeared very tiny and dingy, compared to Mr Reed's ranch. Thank goodness he'd come outside, so she hadn't had to go up and leave Holly on the porch, the way she'd planned. She'd been terrified enough as it was by the big steers meandering along the fence, and the overwhelming size of the house. It was like creeping up to a castle.

She went inside her house, to be greeted by the smell of greens cooking and the sound of the television blaring. Her mother looked up from shelling pecans she would sell at the roadside stand.

'Did you do it, gal?' her mother asked.

Shamed and regretful, Sadie bowed her head. 'I did it, Mama.'

Even though the TV was loud, there was a silence between mother and daughter that was even louder, and more intense. Her mother put down the bowl and the pecans and held out her arms.

'Come here, gal.'

Sadie rushed into the comfort of her mother's

arms, trying desperately not to think about never holding her own daughter in hers.

'You did the right thing. You know you did.'

'But it was hard, Mama! I felt awful, listening to her cry and not being able to go to her!'

Vera Benchley drew soothing fingers through her daughter's hair. 'I know. I know. But think for a moment. Won't you feel better knowing Holly has enough to eat? Has warm clothes to wear in the winter? Gets regular doctor visits and shots?'

'Yes, but . . . but she's mine,' Sadie whispered. 'I love her. I feel like I've given away my heart.'

'Sh, sh, now,' her mother comforted. 'You'll know you've done the right thing when you see Holly going into church, wearing shoes that fit and pretty dresses, gal. When you come home to another dinner of greens and not much more tomorrow, you'll feel much better.'

'But they can't love her the way I do.' Sadie turned anguished, dark eyes on her mother. 'And he seemed so mean. He was kinda yelling at this woman while I was there.'

Her mother thought about that. 'I can't speak for Dustin. He's a different man since his wife died. But, Sadie, Miss Eunice is there, too. She may be older now and a bit frail, but the Homecoming queen I went to high school with had more heart in her than any of those other silly rich girls. Almost more heart than anyone I ever knew.' She was quiet for a moment. 'And you know we had to do it, to keep Holly safe.'

Sadie laid her head down in her mother's lap once

more, closing her eyes in deep misery. Of course her mother was right. She thought about the pretty lady who'd yelled at Mr Reed to put the gun away. A little peace stole into her heart.

If the pretty lady could make Mr Reed mind, then maybe he wasn't that bad after all.

CHAPTER 2

Dustin opened the door so the woman carrying the baby could walk past him into the house. 'Mother!' he called. 'We've got company!'

The lady eyed him a bit peevishly before walking into the parlor off the hall. He watched in amazement as she sat down, settled the baby in her arms, and popped the cap on the bottle. Testing it deftly on her arm, the woman shrugged, then put the bottle to the baby's lips. The infant started sucking greedily. It was a relief, though the baby's fussing hadn't really been that loud. He just hadn't been able to bear knowing that the minuscule person was hungry. Tiny gulping sounds in the antique-furnished parlor made Dustin smile.

But not as much as the sight of the woman cuddling the infant to her breast, close and secure, as she murmured soft, comforting words to it.

A large piece of the past suddenly lodged in Dustin's throat. His wife, Nina, had wanted their baby so badly. And although even the baby hadn't been enough to keep Nina's unhappiness at bay for

19

long, she'd been a good mother. She had to be turning in her grave to know that her parents were trying to wrest Joey away from his home.

'We have company, Dustin?'

His mother's voice interrupted his musings. Dustin turned to see Eunice making her way slowly from the kitchen to the parlor.

'You should use your walker, Mother,' he said quietly. But he knew what her instant reprimand to him would be.

'I don't in front of company, Dustin,' she reminded him. She drew near him, peering around into the parlor. 'Oh, my,' she murmured. 'Introduce me, please, son.'

'Mother, this is – ' he paused, staring at the woman who was looking up from her task with delicate, questioning brows – 'I'm sorry. I don't think I asked you your name. I'm Dustin Reed, and this is my mother, Eunice.'

Boy, his manners left a lot to be desired. His legs had been knocked out from under him with the woman's appearance, and it seemed his brain had taken a vacation.

'Hello,' she replied calmly. 'It's nice to meet you, Ms Reed. I'm Jill McCall, from Dallas.'

'How nice of you to visit us all the way from Dallas,' Eunice said, stepping into the parlor and slowly making her way to a chair in front of the fireplace. Dustin hurried to help his mother ease gingerly into the chair. He noticed she chose the seat to give her the best vantage of the feeding session.

20

'You have a beautiful baby, Jill,' Eunice commented.

'Oh, it's not mine. We found it,' she corrected, nodding toward Dustin.

'You found it! Dustin?' His mother turned astonished eyes on him.

How to make this situation sound less incredible than it was? 'I saw Ms McCall, and thinking she was trespassing, I . . .'

No, no, that wasn't what he meant to say. 'She's come to ask about the housekeeping position, except then the baby . . .' No, no, that wasn't right, either. 'Tell you the truth, I don't know what the hell's happened, Mother. All I can tell you right now is that the baby is sucking on what Ms McCall called a panic bottle, which means I've got to hurry out to the store. I think.' He sat down heavily in a chair, wondering how a peaceful afternoon examining the pecan trees on his property had turned out so complicated.

His mother glanced at Jill, whose attention was solely on burping the baby. 'You found the baby on *our* property?'

'Yes.' Dustin's nod was brief. And unhappy.

'Hm. I don't know anyone in town who's been pregnant,' she said thoughtfully. 'I wonder whose baby it could be?'

'I have no idea,' he said tautly.

Jill looked up briefly.

'Well,' Eunice said. 'So, you've come to apply for the housekeeping position. Isn't that fortunate for us? We've had such difficulty keeping someone.' She smiled at Jill to make her feel comfortable.

Dustin was having trouble covering both subjects, but it seemed his mother was switching back and forth between strange matters with ease.

'Did you bring your credentials, or references, dear?'

Jill shook her head. 'I hadn't really intended to apply or interview today. I thought I was being smart by coming to check out what the ranch was like before taking up your time with my application.'

She noticed Eunice and Dustin looked rather worried. Realizing they might have taken her explanation to mean she wasn't interested in the job now that she'd seen the ranch, she said hastily, 'From what I can tell, this would be a very nice place to work.'

Eunice pursed her lips. 'Thank you, my dear.' She leaned back, obviously deciding not to interfere further. The baby burped loudly, breaking the tension in the room.

'Now, you should have room for more dinner,' Jill said to the baby.

The infant seemed content to finish the rest of the bottle, blissfully unaware of her unusual circumstances. Dustin caught his mother looking at him calmly, waiting for him to take the lead. He wished he could somehow telepathize with her to go ahead and take over, because he was totally lost. What the heck was he supposed to say to a sexy-as-hell woman who'd said that she was wearing underwear that might fall off at any time?

Except, please, please, stay and keep my house for me?

'We haven't had much time to explore the job possibility,' he said tensely. 'I do know Ms McCall shops at Macy's.'

Dustin closed his eyes. Boy, it had been too long. This woman with the unlikely story, and perhaps the stray baby, too, was forcing him to think about things he didn't want to resurrect from the past. Like sex. And the wife he still missed occasionally, who had tried to be a good mother. Had tried to be a good wife, though it had been a strain for both of them.

And then he thought about sex again. Particularly with Ms McCall, from Dallas, Texas. Before he got himself into trouble, Dustin decided he'd better get a move on.

'Well, if you ladies will excuse me, I suppose I'll go call the police. And then head to the store.'

'The police!' His mother's shocked exclamation startled the baby, which shifted unhappily in Jill's arms. Whispering, Jill soothed the little one back into stillness. But Jill's eyes immediately pulled back to Dustin's. He could tell the first thought in her mind was that he might be calling the police about her for abandoning the baby on his property.

'Somebody left this baby here. It's not ours. We can't keep it,' he said. 'The police need to be alerted that someone has tried to get rid of their baby. And in a very unfortunate way, too. What if Ms McCall hadn't been – ' he paused, about to say, 'trespassing,' when he corrected himself. 'What if she hadn't come to apply for the position? The baby might have been down there for hours.'

'Oh, dear,' Eunice murmured. 'I suppose you're right.'

'She hadn't been there long,' Jill said hurriedly.

Dustin stared at her. Her lashes dropped to cover her eyes. 'I just meant that, when I picked her up, the blanket felt warm to me. Like she hadn't been outside long.'

'Oh.' It sounded plausible. And surely, if the baby was Jill's, she wouldn't let him call the police to take it away.

'Oh, for heaven's sake, Dustin. Anyone with two eyes can see what you're thinking,' his mother complained. 'This is not Jill's baby. It's a new-born, honey.'

For the first time Jill smiled, a warm and friendly expression that tugged at Dustin's heart.

'I know I had a time of it when I had Dustin,' Eunice continued. 'Took me months to lose my pregnancy weight.'

'My mother says the same thing. Although you can't tell by looking at her that she had four of us.' Jill held the baby closer. Dustin saw the child was just about to fall asleep, enjoying the woman's warmth and soft voice, no doubt.

Lucky baby.

'I hope you don't mind that I dropped in on you like this,' Jill said to Eunice. 'I *am* interested in the position, if it's still available.'

'I see,' Eunice replied. 'Dustin?'

24

His mother looked so pleased that Dustin scowled. 'Well, I don't see. Can we get on with finding this child's parents and save the social amenities for later?'

It was lack of sex, pure and simple, that was making him irritable, Dustin decided.

'But what will happen if you call the police?'

Dustin met his mother's eyes. 'I'm sure they'll take the baby with them until someone from Child Protective Services can be reached.'

His mother was quiet for a moment. 'I really hate for this little orphan to be taken somewhere right before Christmas, Dustin. Don't you think we should keep her, just over the holidays?' At Dustin's astonished expression, Eunice hurriedly clarified, 'By all means, notify the police. But maybe you could just offer that, until the mother is located, we can take care of her.'

Dustin shook his head slowly, looking first at his mother, then at Jill, who appeared interested in his reaction to these plans. 'How in the world are we going to care for that baby?'

'I can,' Eunice replied calmly.

'How?' He stopped himself from reminding her that sometimes, when the arthritis flared up, it was all she could do to walk, never mind care for a tiny and fragile infant – and Joey was a handful besides.

'My hands work just fine, Dustin. Hand me that little angel, please, Jill.'

Gently, Jill laid her in Eunice's arms. The infant made the transition without opening her sweet, shell-shaped eyelids. Dustin's heart clenched. Eunice had held Joey that same way many times. Would it hurt anything to give her one last chance to love a baby, while she still could?

Shaking his head at the thought that maybe this wasn't the best idea in the world, Dustin said, 'I could mention it to them, I suppose. But they may not let us have her.'

He'd meant to warn her, but Eunice shook her head. 'By heaven,' she said with spirit, 'we should be able to get our way on this one thing, Dustin. If we have to fight for our own Joey, and believe me, we are going to fight Maxine tooth and nail, then we should be allowed to keep this little bundle of joy for the holidays. It seems like we deserve this one bit of good fortune.'

Jill's eyes had widened. Her gaze traveled from his mother to him. Questions were there, but Jill lowered her gaze without asking any of them.

He had to give Ms McCall some credit: she was handling the whole strange situation with a lot of cool. The uncanny thought hit him that she approved of Eunice's wish.

Slowly, Dustin nodded. 'Maybe you're right, Mother. I'll mention that we'll be willing to keep the infant until her parents can be located. The police will have to take it from there.'

'I should think that there would be few places as nice as this one for her to stay,' Jill said. 'Maybe she will get to remain here for Christmas.'

She stood, glancing down at the sleeping infant in

26

Eunice's arms. 'What if I go get some formula, and diapers and wipes, while you're talking to the police?'

Pride had started flowing through Dustin at Jill's compliment. She liked the ranch and his home, maybe even his mother, and him, but her offer to get supplies pricked the pride instantly. 'I don't think that's a good idea. Since you helped find this child, I think you should be here when the police arrive.'

How stupid did she think he was, anyway? Whether it was her baby or not – and he tended to think his mother was right, because Jill's body was too melted into those jeans to have recently birthed a baby – the police were going to want to question her. She and the baby appearing at nearly the same time was too coincidental for even Lassiter's easygoing sheriff to ignore.

'Fine.' Jill sat back down. By the disgust written on her face, Dustin knew she'd guessed his ulterior motive in keeping her there.

'Must we have the police, Dustin? Can't you just talk to Marsh and see what he thinks we should do?' Eunice asked.

'That's probably the best idea. I'll go call him now.'

The baby grunted in Eunice's arms. He saw his mother cast an amused glance at Jill.

'I suggest you hurry and get those diapers, Dustin, since you won't let Jill do the errand for you. I think this little darling's giving you an early Christmas present,' Eunice said with a too-innocent grin.

* * *

27

'So, what makes you interested in the position, Jill?' Eunice's question pulled Jill's gaze away from surreptitiously watching Dustin talk to the sheriff who had arrived a few minutes earlier.

'Stability,' she answered. 'The idea of living in one place for a year is very appealing.'

Jill thought about her answer, knowing that there had been more that had pulled her out to the ranch on Setting Sun Road. Meeting Mrs Reed's eyes, Jill said honestly, 'The bonus at the end of a year was an incentive also.'

Eunice nodded. Jill watched as the baby opened her mouth in an angelic yawn. 'Although I suppose you weren't counting on both of us joining you for the holidays. Will you have enough room?'

'Space isn't a problem at all. I rather like the idea of a house full of people during Christmas. It's been somewhat lonely around here. If we can agree on the position, then your coming here is very fortuitous. We'll need help with this baby, of course.'

'Hello, Ms McCall,' the sheriff said, coming over to introduce himself with a big smile. 'I'm Sheriff Tommy Marsh. Go by Marsh, 'cause Dustin's too lazy to yell more than one syllable at me.' He paused, giving her a moment to digest that. 'So, you're the one who found this early Christmas delivery.'

She glanced uncertainly at Dustin. 'Well, we both did.'

'I see.' Marsh nodded, writing something down in a note pad. 'And you were coming out to answer Dustin's ad for a housekeeper?'

28

'That's right,' she said. Dustin was listening carefully to her answers. She sat up and ran a smoothing hand over her hair.

'And your current employment situation?'

Eunice and Dustin both waited, as did the sheriff. 'I don't have one,' she said quietly, uncomfortable with the admission.

'Are you married?'

'No. Although I was engaged until recently.'

Why she had added that, she wasn't certain. It seemed important that these people not think she had no place else to go, that she was some kind of society reject just because she was interested in a job out in the sticks.

Dustin looked surprised – and there was another expression in his eyes, one Jill couldn't define. She didn't take her gaze from his. The pull between them was mesmerizing and intense, and caused her to further qualify her answer.

'My ex-fiancé and I parted on fairly amicable terms.' It was a blatant untruth, but did she have to pour out the disastrous events that had led her to leave her fiancé? 'Since I have no job at present, this position would give me a fresh start in a new place.'

'Ah.' The enlightened sound was from the sheriff. 'I'm afraid that this changes the equation,' he said kindly. 'If the two of you decided not to get married for whatever reason, it stands to reason you might have felt desperate enough financially to try to give away your newborn baby. Without a father figure in the picture to help with the expenses and you without employment . . .'

'I don't think so,' Jill shot back. 'I am looking for a job, which is not the same thing as being desperate enough to give up my own flesh and blood.' She stood, spearing Dustin with angry eyes. 'I'm sorry someone picked you to take care of their little angel, but it's not my problem.'

Taking a deep breath, Jill looked around at the people crowded into the Victorian-style parlor. 'And now, if you don't mind, I've stayed long enough. I do have some things in my life to tend to.'

Like giving notice on the new apartment she and Carl had rented to move into after their marriage. It was wonderful and homey, but she wouldn't be able to hang onto it without a job, or the extra income. She and Carl had been able to swing it with both their salaries. Now there was neither.

Jill gave Mrs Reed an almost sad smile. The old lady appealed to her. She could easily envision the two of them becoming friends, and she sensed Eunice would be a great deal easier to care for than Dustin.

'Thank you for your hospitality, and for considering employing me more seriously than these . . . men,' she told Eunice. Jill barely stopped herself from saying 'immature men'. Insulting an officer of the law would not be a good thing to do on her way out of town. So, she gathered up her wits and her determination and after kissing the baby on the back of her little downy head, marched to the front door.

Fury kept her warm all the way to her rundown

car. It was a good thing she'd come to Lassiter to check out the ranch, because it was definitely not the place for her. She and her would-be employer had gotten off on the wrong foot, to say the least.

Perhaps worst of all, she sensed a disastrous ringing in her hormones when she looked at Dustin Reed that signaled trouble.

That disastrous ringing had sounded when she'd met Carl. Having heard it before, Jill was determined to avoid it at all costs. No more ringing hormones for her. Next time she fell for a man, he was going to be a model of responsibility, an honest-to-goodness family man.

Not a man like Dustin, who didn't know the difference between size-four jeans and I'm-still-wearing-my-maternity jeans.

Jill sighed, turning the car on to let it warm up. The window fogged up from the warmth of her breath, so Jill used her sleeve to wipe the side window clean. Glancing into the back seat, she looked for a tissue or old paper towel to rub across the front windshield.

When she turned back around, a face was peering through the side window. Jill nearly jumped out of her skin.

Seething, she rolled down the window. 'You startled me!'

'I tried not to,' Dustin said. 'I didn't knock on the window so you wouldn't be.'

'Thanks a lot.' She couldn't help sounding a little sarcastic. 'What do you want now? Fingerprints? A forwarding address, where you can send the little bundle just as soon as you Harvard-types convince yourselves further that that actually *is* my baby?'

Dustin shook his head. 'No. I was going to offer you a cup of hot chocolate and a place to spend the night. There's a storm moving in, the sheriff said, only about twenty minutes west of here and moving fast. He doesn't think you can outrun it. In the interest of *safety precautions*, which I know you're concerned with, my mother and I would like you to phone your mother and spend the night with us.'

He paused for a moment, weighing his next words carefully. Jill couldn't take her eyes from the firmness of his jaw, nor the fullness of his lips as he spoke. 'And in *our* interests, my mother says I'd be nuts not to hire you immediately. You're not the type of housekeeper Mother and I had agreed upon to hire, but – ' he lowered his voice in a confidential whisper that fascinated Jill – 'she didn't like either of the previous help, so her vote for you makes you something special.'

'In spite of my lack of resumé and references.'

Dustin shrugged. 'Mother makes the point that you are here and want a job, and that makes you a bird in the hand. She says you seem to be doing just fine with the baby now, and that Joey will probably adore you after the two iron-clad housekeepers we had. And though it may seem underhanded, I should admit to you that Marsh radioed in your license plate number. Right now, we at least know you don't have any outstanding traffic citations.'

'Oh, and that's an excellent statement on my character, I suppose.' Jill put the car back in park, turning it off, all the while wondering who was crazy now. 'Okay. Talk salary, talk benefits. Then tell me why you've run off two previous housekeepers.'

Dustin snorted at her demand. He leaned his forearms on the open window, all the while looking in the car at her.

'Apparently, it's somewhat isolated at the ranch. That's what the other two women claimed, that the silence drove them mad. That there wasn't enough to do, no one to talk to.' He jutted his chin in a wry gesture. 'I don't know if you noticed or not, but my mother is very independent.'

'Yes, I noticed,' Jill murmured.

'I am, too,' he continued. 'Maybe we don't chit-chat as much as we should. But you won't have quite as much time on your hands, since the sheriff has agreed to let us keep the baby through the holidays, until her mother can be located.'

'Oh, good!' Jill exclaimed. At Dustin's questioning look, she said, 'For the baby, I mean. She needs to stay where she's wanted for a while.'

Dustin nodded. 'That's what the sheriff said. Mother reminded Marsh that she's had foster children in the past and is already approved. Marsh doesn't think CPS will have a beef with that, considering it would be difficult to find a better place than here to live during the busy holiday season, not to mention that it's the Friday after Thanksgiving and the offices are closed. Nobody's going to want to be rustled up from their holiday when that baby's more safe and secure here than anywhere.'

He lowered his voice. 'And Marsh seems to think that our ranch was chosen for a specific reason, that we weren't a random choice. If the baby stays here, the mother may try to sneak back to check on her periodically. They're going to keep a look-out for anyone hanging around.'

'I see.' Jill was concerned for the mother. 'I hope the sheriff will be more sensitive with her than he was with me.'

'Don't mind him,' Dustin said. 'Marsh's heart is in the right place. We've just never had anything like this happen in Lassiter before. He's checked all the hospitals, and a baby hasn't been born in two weeks. They're going to take her down to a doctor, to have her weighed and examined, but none of us think she's older than a week.'

'At the most,' Jill agreed. 'Her eyes still don't want to open very much. And she smells new.'

'Hm. I don't remember,' he said softly.

And suddenly, Jill knew he wasn't talking about the baby, but possibly about the little boy she'd seen smiling from pewter-framed photographs on the parlor's mantel. Dustin looked a bit forlorn, and she thought she saw sadness in the depths of his saddle-brown eyes. His mind had definitely traveled somewhere else.

'I'll spend the night tonight. Further, I'll give you a one-week trial period to see whether all of us can bear living under the same roof.' She paused, not wanting to seem like he was the reason she was staying. 'I think your mother and I will get along fine.' She gave the excuse easily, telling herself it was the truth.

Just not all of it. She'd like to get along with Dustin, at least enough for them to find some equal ground to stand on. She would love living at the ranch, if she and Dustin could ignore the way they'd started out.

Dustin emitted a grunt of what could have been sarcasm – or satisfaction. 'I'm glad you and my mother have taken such a shine to each other,' he said blandly. Then he named a salary and some benefits that made Jill's eyes blink.

'You're being very generous,' she said.

'You're being nice to give us a second chance, considering the circumstances. A baby will take up a lot of your time.'

Jill thought about that. Tiny snowflakes began falling, blowing into her eyelashes. For some reason, she smiled at Dustin, and he smiled back.

Maybe, with a Christmas miracle, it would be too cold for her hormones to ring. But she'd need to stay on her guard, unless she wanted to find her hormones ringing in the New Year.

Moments later, she had followed Dustin up the lane in her car, parking where he pointed. Then she walked in the house with him, telling herself she could leave any time if things got any more crazy.

Marsh and Eunice were both quiet, Dustin noticed immediately. 'Is everything okay?' he asked. 'I've brought Ms McCall back like you suggested.'

'I was changing the baby when I found a note,' Eunice said. 'It seems her name is Holly, and she may be in danger.'

Dustin could smell bad news a mile away. 'What kind of danger?'

Eunice shook her head, thoughtfully running her finger along an embroidered design of a crown at the edge of the blanket. 'Apparently, the father is over-interested in the child. The mother believes the man's purpose is evil-minded.'

'Oh, for crying out loud. Give me that.' Dustin looked over the paper before glancing up at Jill. She was very still on the sofa. 'Guess this clears you, Ms McCall,' he said rather meanly. It wasn't that he felt that way toward Jill, because Marsh, Eunice, and he had already come to the conclusion that there wasn't any way the baby was hers. But he was starting to feel like somebody had hit him from behind. 'I suppose you'll change your mind about the job now that there's a possible risk involved.'

Jill shrugged. 'Please feel free to call me Jill, Mr Reed. And since you seem to routinely greet visitors with a loaded gun, I think we'll all be safe enough.'

Oh, he could tell she'd enjoyed jabbing him back. The moment of ease they'd shared outside had evaporated. 'Marsh? Are we in over our heads with this?' Dustin asked gruffly.

The sheriff shook his head. 'Jill will actually be extra protection, because there'll be another person to keep an eye on the baby at all times. The story we should stick to is that Jill is a niece of yours, Eunice, visiting for the holidays with her new baby. It all wraps up nicely.'

Dustin didn't know what to say. On the one hand, it was great of Jill to tackle this job. On the other, he didn't know if he should endanger his mother, or Joey. The Reeds had enough on their plates without adding this worry. But if his mother thought they were doing the right thing, and Marsh agreed, and Jill didn't mind being in on it, then maybe it wasn't as big a deal as it seemed.

'You better not duck out on me in the middle of this,' Dustin told Jill. 'If you sign on, you have to stay.'

'I'll try it out for a week only, not because of the baby being a bother but because I understand my employer can be grumpy as all get out. If I stay on permanently, I expect combat pay in my Christmas stocking,' she told him without cracking a smile.

Sadie put on the apron the shop owner, Mrs Vickery, handed her. Sheer fortune had gotten her this job in a bakery. No one had to tell her that it was terribly hard to get hired at this time of year, particularly for a high-school graduate whose grades had been none too good. And, though no one in the town knew of her unplanned pregnancy, since she'd gone to another town to stay with her aunt during that time, it didn't help that she'd blindly believed her boyfriend, Curtis, when he'd told her how much he loved her. That he was going to marry her one day.

37

Sadie had thought that was wonderful. And she had enjoyed being close to him, like a man and a woman could be. The way he'd told her they should be. Loving each other like a husband with his wife.

She glanced out of the window, seeing the frosty flakes flying against the big front window, sticking there in miniature starbursts. Sadie started kneading bread dough, thinking that it would be a cold bike ride home. That almost didn't matter, because she knew Holly was safe and warm and loved this very instant, at the Reed Ranch.

Especially if the pretty woman had stayed with Mr Reed.

Her mother had been right, Sadie acknowledged. And if she couldn't have her baby with her, then at least she had a good home. Sadie was determined to be happy about that, and also about her new job. Extra income, no matter how small, might mean something other than greens or grits for Christmas dinner.

Her heart squeezing, Sadie said a prayer that baby Holly would have a wonderful Christmas, with all those people around to love her. The way she now knew it should be.

Different from the kind of love Curtis had actually given Sadie. Painful realization had sprung on her when she'd told Curtis there was going to be a baby. Because he'd told her what they were doing was right between a man and a woman who loved each other, she'd assumed that, now that there would be an infant, he would marry her.

38

Curtis's mocking laughter at her innocence still burned at the back of Sadie's eyes.

But that was all in the past. Sadie smiled wistfully as she thought about sweet Holly being held in loving arms at the Reed Ranch. She thought about her having enough food and a warm, crackling fire in the fireplace to someday watch with inquiring eyes. The bell over the shop door rang to announce a visitor, and Sadie regretfully put away the heart-warming picture she was imagining and turned to greet the customer.

She froze instantly, the half-smile on her face as crooked and awkward as a tree ornament hanging unevenly. 'What are you doing here?'

Curtis Lynch smiled and sauntered over to a counter. Picking up a fresh-baked loaf of bread, he pulled out a piece. 'I wanted to see you.'

Sadie's insides chilled. She was alone with a man whose cocky demeanor alarmed her, who had never meant any good by her when he'd had the chance. Not only that, but he was eating bread Sadie sensed he had no intention of paying for. The last thing she wanted was for kind-hearted Mrs Vickery to think Sadie couldn't be trusted not to invite her friends in for free food. Desperately hoping another customer would walk inside any second, Sadie said, 'I don't want to talk to you.'

'You're not still angry that I wouldn't marry you?' Curtis asked, his grin mean-spirited.

She couldn't speak. All those starry visions had passed some time ago – nine months ago. Bearing the mantle of pregnancy alone had caused Sadie to grow up and face facts. Now, she couldn't remember what she'd seen in Curtis in the first place.

Her silence seemed to annoy him. Curtis tucked the loaf of bread into his arm and glanced around. 'So, where's the brat?'

'The brat?' Sadie whispered.

'Yeah. I'm a proud papa, ain't I? You're not going to try to keep me from seeing my kid?'

Sadie felt sick. If she was certain of anything, it was that Curtis didn't have Holly's best interests at heart. 'The baby's not here.'

'It at your ma's?'

'No, it's not.' Sadie forced strength into her voice. 'I gave her up for adoption.'

'You did what?'

Curtis had stepped menacingly close to Sadie and now he shook her until she could feel her teeth rattle against each other. 'You stupid bitch! Don't you know how much money selling that brat would have got us?'

40

CHAPTER 3

Eunice showed Jill the room she would have during her stay at the ranch. It was light and cheery, with yellow-striped wallpaper on the walls and white eyelet curtains at every window. A window seat on the far wall, overlooking the front of the house, had a yellow, cabbage rose cushion in place.

'I love the room, Mrs Reed,' Jill said. 'I'll be very comfortable in here.'

'I hope you will, my dear,' Eunice replied pleasantly. 'What I think you'll like best is that the adjoining bathroom connects to the room Joey stays in. That way you don't have to go so far if he needs you at night.'

'I can't wait to meet him,' Jill said.

Eunice smiled. 'He'll be home from visiting his other grandparents shortly. Now, there's something I hope you'll do for me, Jill,' Eunice continued, stopping to pause in front of the vanity mirror hanging over an antique table. Her fingers lightly patted the silvery-white dross of her hair, twisted into a delicate chignon, which Jill thought suited her.

'I'll do whatever I can,' Jill replied honestly.

'I hope you'll call me Eunice from now on. I realize you're trying to show me respect, and it's plain to me that your parents raised you to be polite, but out here, we're rather informal. When late February comes and the wind is whistling down the chimneys and the ice keeps us from getting into town much, I'd like to think the two of us will have some good, old-fashioned friendship to keep out the chill. What do you say?'

Jill was pleased by the woman's overture, though technically she hadn't agreed to stay past the specified one week. It seemed Dustin's mother was already counting on her. 'All right, then, Eunice. Thank you for your kindness.'

'Nonsense. You're the one who's being kind. Dustin and I didn't dream we'd find another person to live with us before Christmas.' Eunice walked through the room, running a hand lightly over the walnut bureau and matching vanity. 'To be honest, I believe he worries about leaving me alone so much that he's neglected his cattle. And the ranch in general.'

Jill had noticed Dustin's concern for his mother's health. She merely nodded.

Eunice stopped in front of the window seat and peered outside before turning around to face Jill. 'You must be thinking that this employment sounds rather more like a baby-sitting job than anything.' Her smile was contagious and lifted her delicate eyebrows further on her broad forehead. 'I don't

42

want to scare you. Dustin may have told you that we Reeds are very independent.'

'He did mention that.'

'Good. Just so you'll know that you won't be tied to watching an old lady dodder away her life, I bought Dustin a cellular phone for his Christmas present. It's so small he can carry it in his jacket pocket when he's out riding.'

'That sounds like a good idea. Not that you appear to do much doddering, though.'

Eunice laughed, the sound tinkling and light. 'I certainly try not to. I don't know how Dustin will react to his mother being able to call him any time of day, though.'

'He'll probably think you're being very sensible. From what I can tell of your son so far, he's probably already thought of the idea and was too afraid to insult you by suggesting it.'

Eunice laughed again. 'You could be right. Dustin tries very hard not to make me feel like an invalid.'

'You don't appear to be very bothered by your arthritis,' Jill commented. Eunice appeared to have more energy in her than some teenage girls.

'I hope it hasn't slowed me down too much. I have good days and bad.' Eunice frowned suddenly. 'There's an awful lot to do on a ranch, and I wouldn't want Dustin to have to worry about me. Though I can't do as much as I could once, I still like to think I'm helping out some.'

'I'm sure you are,' Jill replied. To change the

subject, she walked slowly into the bathroom, admiring the spaciousness, and then into Joey's room. 'My, somebody had a lot of toys when he was a boy,' she said, instantly guessing the room had once been Dustin's.

Eunice had followed behind and now surveyed the wild-stallion printed curtains and denim bedspread in the room with some pride. 'Yes. Most of the toys were given away long ago, but some things – especially that wooden rocking horse – I couldn't bear to part with. Of course, that's Joey's favourite now, so I'm glad I kept what I did.'

Without warning, Eunice's eyes clouded up behind her spectacles. Jill was stricken. The pewter-framed pictures flashed through her mind instantly, and she thought about the little boy smiling out from them. There was obviously a problem in the Reed household. But since the Reeds hadn't mentioned the subject to her, Jill supposed it was closed. Quickly, she thought of something else to put the happiness back on Eunice's face. 'You know, I bet it's time to check on Holly. She might be stirring.'

'You're right.' Immediately, Eunice straightened her shoulders and turned herself to leave the room and go downstairs. 'It's going to be a whole new routine for me with an infant in the house. I'm so used to going my own way.'

Jill smiled, following. Dustin was used to going his own way, too. She thought about the cellular phone Mr Tough Cowboy was getting for Christmas. With baby Holly around, she had a feeling that phone would be keeping warm next to Dustin's ear.

Though it was still fairly dark when she awakened the next morning, Jill was relieved to see only a two-inch coating of snow on the ground, though she could tell by touching the window-pane that the temperature had dropped quite a bit since yesterday. Being further north would impact the temperature, too. She made a mental note to fetch her warmest clothes when she went to collect her things.

Baby Holly's basket was gone from Joey's room. Jill hurried downstairs, worried that she wasn't in time to get breakfast started. It wouldn't do to oversleep the first day on her job, though she was fortunate she'd awakened at all. That had been the most relaxed night of sleep she'd had since her life had undergone all these major changes.

To her dismay, Dustin and Eunice sat at the kitchen table already, drinking coffee. Baby Holly lay sleeping in a basket nearby. 'My! I thought getting up at six o'clock in the morning was sufficient!' Jill said in amazement.

To her relief, they both smiled. 'We really didn't expect you to get up so early on your first day as a guest in our home, Jill,' Eunice replied.

'I'm not a guest,' she said with some asperity, going to work on washing what few pans were in the sink. 'I'm your paid employee, and more grateful than you can know to have the job.'

Dustin got up, gently taking her by the shoulders

to steer her into taking a place next to his mother at the table. 'Don't be ornery, Jill,' he said, guiding her. 'My mother means that today you're a guest in our home. *Tomorrow* is much sooner than we'd hoped to have help. Now, what do you want to drink?'

'We have hot chocolate, coffee, and hot tea,' Eunice supplied.

Jill had sat down obediently, somewhat dazed by her good fortune. Of all things, it didn't seem quite right to be treated more like a member of the family than hired help. But she couldn't help thinking it was awfully nice of them to try to make her feel welcome, especially after her somewhat embarrassing appearance on the ranch yesterday.

'Hot chocolate sounds delicious,' she said slowly, meeting Dustin's eyes. His eyes were the colour of dark cocoa, she thought irrationally. That jet-black hair lay raffishly along the collar of a flannel shirt, and Jill blinked, thinking again how ruggedly, sinfully, handsome the man was. When she'd read the advertisement, the last thing she'd expected was that the man mentioned would turn out to be a Mel Gibson type.

Of course, that didn't erase the fact that his personality was a bit staid at times. Still, this man at least knew how to shoulder responsibilities, whether he was gruff about it or not. Unlike Carl, who had taken everything in life easy, including whether he had a stable job or if his checkbook was in the red.

'Jill?'

Somewhere in her fog of memories, Jill realized Dustin had said something to her. Snapping her gaze to meet his, she said, 'I'm sorry. I didn't hear you.'

He didn't smile or comment. He nodded, like her inattention had been obvious to him. 'If it's convenient, we can leave in an hour to go get whatever things you'll be needing.'

'Oh, that's not, I mean . . .' Jill looked at Eunice for understanding. 'That's so nice of you, but completely unnecessary. I wouldn't want you to leave your work because of me.'

Dustin shook his head. 'It isn't a problem.'

'No, I can drive back to Dallas myself. Honestly, you've got enough here, with Holly and all . . .'

'Aren't you coming back?'

His gaze was intense. 'Of course I'm coming back!' Jill exclaimed.

'I thought you said you could start immediately.'

'I can,' Jill said with emphasis. 'That's not the problem.'

'Then what is?' Dustin frowned, waiting for her answer.

'There really isn't a problem,' Jill said carefully, aware that her answers were locking her into a situation she wasn't prepared to deal with. An hour and better over to Dallas and back again, closed up in a vehicle with Dustin, was not her idea of a good time. They had very little to say to one another as it was. To be forced together would be excruciating.

'There's no need for you to have to shuttle me back and forth, though I certainly appreciate the offer,' she said, trying to sound like she did. 'But I can fend for myself.'

'Ah. She's as independent as we are.' Eunice nodded.

'I think I got that idea when she was making her way up the driveway yesterday,' Dustin said. 'Carefully, like any minute a shadow was going to jump out from behind one of those trees and get her. But still making her way despite the bogeys.'

'A shadow did get me,' Jill said tightly. Only the shadow had been a six-foot-four, devilishly handsome man.

Dustin laughed, the first time she had ever heard him do so. Though the sound was rich and full, it was also at her expense.

'Don't let Dustin bait you, dear,' Eunice said kindly. 'Being an only child made him lonely for siblings to tease, I'm afraid.' She shot her son a stern look. 'What he's not telling you is that there's a sheet of ice underneath the snow outside. It's best that he take you into Dallas in his truck. I'll feel much better knowing you're as safe as we can make you.'

'Oh.' Jill mulled that over for a minute. Eunice was right, in every way. Her little car wasn't made for driving on country roads made treacherous by the ice. Of course, leave it to Dustin not to say a word of that, but to just allow her to simmer in her own embarrassment. Glancing up, she realized he was still grinning at her. She made herself give him a slight smile, though it was forced.

But her smile hid her vow that the last laugh was

going to be on Dustin Reed. She would show him that she wasn't the ignorant city girl he seemed so certain he'd hired, on his mother's wishes.

Putting her cup in the sink, Jill said, 'I can be ready in half an hour, if you're anxious to get back to the ranch early.'

He nodded. 'You don't need much time to get ready?'

'Oh, I think you'll find that I'm a wash-and-wear kind of a girl,' Jill said as she sailed out of the kitchen.

'Honestly, Dustin,' Eunice protested after she was certain Jill was out of earshot. 'We didn't hire Jill to be your sparring partner. It's a tough life out here. She seems eager and ready to please, despite the drawbacks. Could you go a little gently on her? At least for a little while?'

Dustin looked at his mother in surprise. It was the first time, since his rambunctious college days, that a word of anything resembling criticism of him had left her mouth. 'Was I hard on Jill?'

'I thought so. Maybe I'm being sensitive, but the last two housekeepers did mention something about your moodiness worrying them a bit.'

He scratched his head. 'I was trying *not* to be moody. I think I was trying for levity.'

Eunice shook her head with a smile. 'You're trying too hard. I know Nina needed constant conversation and support, but I think if you relax a little, you may find Jill is more self-possessed than she appears. But don't tease her too much. Remember, she's got some emotional struggles right now, too.'

'You mean, I can keep the conversation to our orphan and what her responsibilities are with Joey, and two or three hours in the car won't seem like having a root canal?'

'That's exactly what I mean,' Eunice said. 'Holly and I are going to play while you're gone, and we may even have a hot dinner on when you get back.'

'Mother, don't,' Dustin said worriedly. 'You're doing enough by watching Holly. And the Copelands will probably bring Joey back while I'm in Dallas.'

'You see? That's just what I mean, son. You don't mean it, but you're being heavy-handed. A woman doesn't like to feel dependent, less capable. I think that's important to keep in mind when you're talking to Jill.' She smiled, to keep the sting out of her advice, but Dustin shook his head, at a loss.

'I'll try to remember,' he said, before kissing her on the cheek and leaving the room. Why did dealing with women seem to require a course in How Not To Be A Social Moron?

He had an uneasy feeling that Jill wasn't going to be an easy-A course, either. And that he might flunk, regardless of how hard he tried to get good marks.

'Ready?' Dustin asked.

'Ready,' Jill replied, allowing Dustin to help her up into the cab of his truck.

Starting the truck, he waved to his mother, who

stood watching from the parlor window. Naturally, the moment they were ready to leave, Holly had gone into a full-blown baby tantrum that couldn't be easily soothed. It had concerned him enough to suggest that perhaps he should call a friend over to sit with his mother while he and Jill were gone. Eunice had nearly snapped his head off with irritation.

'Dustin Reed, be on your way before I become upset with you. We'll be fine.'

He'd left, unable to ease the way he felt. Jill was waiting outside for him.

'Do you think she'll be all right?' he asked her.

'I think she'll be great. Apparently, your mother's arthritis has receded quite a bit today.'

'All right.' Dustin sighed in surrender. 'Women. I hope you both know what you're talking about.' But he couldn't help another anxious glance at the window.

Eunice was holding up an object in her arms, pointing down at it with a grin.

'Holly's gone to sleep again,' Jill said, smiling. 'You owe me an apology.'

'For what?' Dustin was outraged.

'For that snide comment about women. *I hope you both know what you're talking about*,' she repeated for his benefit. But she was still smiling.

Dustin backed the truck down the driveway. 'Sorry.'

He didn't sound that way at all.

'It's actually your mother you should apologize to,' Jill said lightly.

Dustin stopped the truck at the end of the driveway. 'Look. There's something we should get straight. I just apologized. It's something I don't do often. But if you keep harping on me, I'm going to say something you don't like again. Then you'll want me to apologize again, only I'll probably feel like I was justified in making whatever comment I did. I think we should go slowly on what I should say or not say.'

He paused. Jill's eyes were huge. 'Wow, that was a mouthful. Could you repeat that? I don't think I caught it all.'

Dustin stared at Jill, before he saw the twitching at the side of her mouth. The woman was *trying* not to laugh at him. Dustin shifted into gear and let the truck start picking up speed. 'I can tell it's going to be a long ride into Dallas,' he grumbled.

'It's always a shame to meet a man who can dish it out but who can't take it,' Jill said innocently.

'And that is supposed to mean what?'

'That you were plenty willing to use me as joke bait this morning. But now I've found something to get your goat over, and you don't like it.'

'I didn't say I didn't like it,' Dustin replied, his tone tense. 'I'm just not ready for it, is all.'

'What's there to be ready for?' Jill appeared honestly confused.

Dustin was, too. 'I think I'm not ready for such an attractive female to be living in my house,' he said honestly, glancing her way.

Jill's blue eyes went round with astonishment.

'Oh.' After a moment, she murmured, 'Thank you.' Then she didn't say another word until they reached the highway into Dallas.

Obviously, the lady hadn't been ready for an honest answer. At least, Dustin thought wryly, the truth had brought him a good stretch of time without having to make casual conversation with his new housekeeper.

Jill's parents, Lana and Bob McCall, weren't far off from what Dustin had expected. Lana was petite and blond and doted on Jill; Bob was easygoing, balding a bit, and doted on Jill. Their home was welcoming, though Dustin shied from looking at the stockings hung on the mantel. Bob, Lana, Jill, Andy, Darla, Tommy, they read. There was an extra nail where another stocking must have once hung, but had been removed for some reason. Dustin glanced at Jill, remembering that she'd recently broken off an engagement. He wondered if the empty nail was her ex-fiancé's. Poor fellow, Dustin commiserated.

Of course, he theorized, the guy could have always found another nail to hang his stocking on. If that were the case, maybe he wouldn't mind Dustin thinking alarmingly warm thoughts about Jill. He watched her give her mother and father exuberant hugs, then turn to look at him.

'Sit down, Dustin, please. I'll go get packed.'

Dustin sat, his posture stiff. Lana sat across from him and Bob squeezed in close beside his wife.

53

'So!' Lana said too brightly. 'Can I get you something to drink?'

'No, thank you, ma'am.' He tried to ease himself back into the pillows of the well-stuffed sofa, wanting to appear confident, but the truth was, the pillows hardly moved and he felt like he was a teenager waiting for his prom date, anyway.

'So!' Lana repeated. 'Jill's going to be living with you.'

It was a statement, but came out as a confused question. Dustin understood. 'Actually, no, ma'am. She'll live at my house, with my mother and an infant we're keeping for someone, and my son, Joey. It'll be quite a lot for her to do, being the housekeeper at the ranch. My mother and I sure appreciate her agreeing to try the job out for a while.'

He was careful to emphasize 'mother' as many times as possible. Lana looked a little less perturbed. Bob, he wasn't sure about.

'This is certainly unexpected. When Jill told me she was applying for a housekeeper's position, I wasn't thinking of . . .' She stopped uncomfortably. Dustin waited, ill at ease himself.

'Well, I don't think I – I mean we – didn't expect her to be living with a single male.' Red crept into Lana's cheeks. Bob cleared his throat.

'My wife died nearly a year ago, in a car accident,' Dustin said, careful to keep his voice neutral. 'But if I had a daughter, I'd worry about her as much as you're worrying about Jill, if she came home and told me these same plans.'

54

'I'm sorry about your wife,' Lana said, obviously meaning it. 'You understand that we're concerned, though we don't want you to think we're being . . .'

She paused. Bob cleared his throat. 'Parental,' he said helpfully.

'I understand parental perfectly,' Dustin said, relaxing a bit. 'I've developed a major dose of it since . . .' He'd started to say *since my wife died*, but stopped as he realized he didn't want to say that. It was much too personal. Rubbing his jaw as if he could massage out the sudden tightness, he said, 'You know, why don't you come out to the ranch for Sunday supper? My mother and I would be happy to have you. You might be interested in my cattle, Bob, and Lana, I think you'll find you have a lot in common with my mother.'

Lana's face lit with genuine excitement. 'Sunday supper would be wonderful. Don't you think so, Bob?'

'I don't think I've ever seen cattle close up,' he replied.

'Well, you wouldn't want to be too close, anyway.' Dustin grinned easily. 'I'll have my mother call you tomorrow. Please understand, we're not fancy at the ranch,' he warned.

'Tell your mother I'll be glad to bring whatever dishes will complement her menu, but I'm especially proud of my strawberry bread and ham rolls.'

Bob cleared his throat again, in what Dustin was beginning to recognize as a conversational prop. 'Jill, are you ready?'

'Yes.' She moved to the stack of belongings in the hallway. Dustin picked up most of it, and Bob got the rest. Jill said goodbye, with effusive hugs and kisses, before settling in the cab. Lana and Bob stood at the side, watching Dustin secure everything in the back.

'I'll tell Mother about your strawberry bread and ham rolls.' Dustin put his hand out for Bob to shake. 'We'll see you for Sunday supper at the ranch.'

Lana smiled, her eyes misting. 'Take care of her, Dustin.'

Bob muttered some appropriate comment. Dustin nodded. Then he walked to the cab and got in. Jill smiled as Dustin shut the truck door.

'That wasn't so bad, was it?' she asked.

Dustin shook his head, waving as they drove away. 'Do you need to go by your apartment to pick up anything else?'

She hesitated only a fraction of a second. 'Not right now. There was enough of my things at Mother's to last me for a week.' She was quiet for a moment before she turned to look at him. It wasn't that he'd turned to glance her way to know she was looking; it was that he could feel her gaze as surely as if light was beaming warmly on his face.

'Yes?' he asked, knowing his tone was brusque but unable to stop himself.

'Thank you for inviting my parents out. They've been so worried about my . . . engagement breaking off, and now I'm uprooting myself, which they totally didn't expect. I think they'd hoped I'd go home and stay with them for a while to lick my wounds. Coming out to see the ranch will make them feel much more at ease.'

'Forget it,' Dustin said roughly. 'It was a bribe.'

CHAPTER 4

Jill sat up straight in the seat. 'A bribe?'

'Yeah. I'm thinking if they know their daughter is safe and happy, then they won't want you to leave the ranch.'

'Oh. I hadn't thought of it that way,' Jill said softly.

They were silent the rest of the drive back, except for some tersely polite comments about the scenery. Dustin hadn't been deaf yesterday to Jill's intention to stay only one week if he didn't mind his p's and q's. Could she blame him for trying to ease things with her folks? Shoot, at the rate he was going, he was going to run out of housekeeper candidates by the New Year. Yet Dustin sensed he'd hurt her feelings with his blunt answer, and he really hadn't meant to. He was just telling it the way he saw it. Obviously, Jill was a tender-hearted little thing. He hoped his mother was right about her being perfect for the job. A tender heart wasn't likely to survive the harshness of life on a country ranch. The previous house-keepers hadn't possessed hearts, and they still hadn't been able to cut it.

Dustin was still mulling that over as he slowly drove up the long driveway to his house. The sheriff's cruiser was parked outside. Murmuring an apology to Jill, he shut off the car and got out, crossing the yard and taking the porch steps three at a time.

Inside, a miniature version of himself met him in the hallway. 'Joey!' he said. For a moment, he wondered if he should hug the child, but the serious expression on his son's face forestalled him.

'Hi, Daddy,' his son replied quietly. 'Grandma says you've . . . you've got a surprise for me.'

His mother must mean Jill. 'Yes. She's out by the truck.'

'My new mother?'

Dustin winced. 'No, son. A new housekeeper, to help around the house. And with the baby.'

'Oh. She's loud. And she . . . she smells funny.'

Dustin frowned as he looked down at the child. 'Jill does? Did Grandma tell you that?'

'No. I helped change her.'

'Oh.' Dustin was so relieved he didn't know what to think. There was so much on his mind it was like two trains colliding at once. 'Why don't you go outside and meet Jill while I check on Grandma? But be careful walking down the porch steps.'

'Okay.'

Dustin opened the door and called to Jill, who was eyeing the cattle which peered over the wood rails at her just as cautiously. 'Jill. I'd like you to meet my son, Joey.'

'Joey!' Instantly, Jill came forward to help the boy down from the porch. 'I've been wanting to meet you.'

'Why?'

She hesitated. 'Because . . . because I need a friend if I'm going to live here.'

Joey digested that. 'You won't stay long. You . . . you not be my best friend.'

'Well, I . . .'

Jill's eyes darted to Dustin's and he shrugged. Best she know now that Joey had suffered for his mother's passing. This job wasn't going to be a piece of cake.

'Hey, Joey, I bet you'd like to make snow angels,' Jill suggested.

'I'll get his coat.' Snatching up the winter things that Joey had apparently just taken off, since they were still lying by the door, Dustin handed them out to Jill. 'If you don't mind, I'm going to see what the sheriff wants.'

'Take your time.'

Jill's voice was as cool as the snow outside. Dustin watched while she competently buttoned and zipped his child into the jacket, then put the mittens and knitted snow cap on him.

'You . . . you want to make snow angels with us, Daddy?'

Dustin thought about rolling around in the snow and waving his arms to make wings with his house-keeper. 'No, son.'

'You'd make the biggest one of all,' Joey said, his voice awed.

Dustin made himself smile, all the while thinking that Jill's snow angel would have the best curves. Nodding to her, he turned and went inside.

The sheriff was in the kitchen. 'Marsh,' he said. 'I assume you would have met me at the door if something was wrong with Mother.'

'She's fine. Last I saw her, she was upstairs walking the baby around, showing her your old toys.'

Dustin relaxed a little. Marsh was sitting at the kitchen table, helping himself to a cup of hot coffee from the pot.

'What are you doing here, then? This a social call?'

'I'm not sure,' Marsh replied carefully.

Dustin wasn't really paying attention. He was watching Jill out of the kitchen window as first she helped his son lie down on the ground, then lay on her back beside him.

'I hope you'll take this in the spirit that it's meant, Dustin. But I've been thinking about your new housekeeper.'

'What about her?' Marsh had his attention now.

'Well, we don't know anything about Jill.'

'Little late to say that, isn't it?'

'I know, I know. It didn't occur to me until I was back at the office. But look, what if she's hunting for someone to take her ex-fiancé's place?'

'Meaning what?' Dustin's tone was curious.

'She said she'd come out to Lassiter to check out the job. Check you out, too, maybe?'

'I don't know,' Dustin said doubtfully. 'What's to check? I just met her family, and they're the typical family everyone wants to grow up in. Jill's the baby in a family of four kids. You name it, they're regular Ozzie and Harriet people.'

'Every family has its skeletons, Dustin.'

'I'm flattered, Marsh. I really am. But I think her family's still reeling over Jill canceling the wedding plans.' He sighed heavily. 'I wasn't planning on company this month, but I heard myself inviting her family out to supper Sunday, simply because I could tell they were worried about her living out here with me.'

'They saw immediately what a wolf in sheep's clothing you are.' Marsh laughed at his friend.

Dustin grinned, too. 'That's exactly what they were thinking. If they're so worked up about me, they haven't had a lot of men out to the house trying to sneak kisses from their daughter. I don't think she's looking for a replacement husband.' Actually, Jill was pretty stand-offish where he was concerned.

Marsh nodded. 'All right. It's my job to get the facts, not spread gloom and doom. I just wanted you to be careful, buddy.'

'When did you get to be such a suspicious person, anyway?'

The sheriff leaned back on the bench, crossing his arms. 'It's my nature to be suspicious. That's why I'm a law man. It's your nature to be stoic. That's why you're a rancher.'

'Oh, I see.' Dustin nodded. 'So, has your suspicious nature led you to check on Joey's grandparents and what they're up to recently?'

Marsh shook his head. 'I haven't been by the Copelands' house. But I did hear through the grapevine that poor old David's taken a bad turn.'

Dustin was instantly alert. 'David Copeland is ill?'

'Yeah. I'm not sure what they ran him up to the hospital for the other night, except everyone knows he's been having spells where he doesn't seem quite with us. This may have been a more pronounced episode of his forgetful state. My opinion, it's stress.'

'Brought on by Maxine, no doubt,' Dustin ground out between his teeth. 'I've never gotten the feeling that David was as keen to get Joey away from me as Maxine was.'

'Nope. Me neither. But then, I always suspected it was Maxine who engineered a lot of stuff in that family.'

Dustin forced himself to take a deep breath and relax. 'Let's change the subject before I say something completely out of the Christmas spirit about that old bat.'

They were quiet for a few moments. Marsh got up to stand beside him. After a swift peek at what had Dustin's attention, Marsh said, 'You believe in her, don't you, Dustin? In Jill, I mean. You really don't think she's man-hunting.'

Dustin looked out of the window again, seeing the wheat of Jill's hair shining in the sun. It was a few shades darker than Joey's, he thought irrationally. Walking away to put the kettle on to boil so she and Joey could have some cocoa when they came in, he said, 'Yeah, I believe she's on the up and up.

63

Mother's crazy about her, and Jill's great with the baby, besides. I have a funny feeling Joey is going to like her, too.'

He sighed, sitting down at the kitchen table and running a hand through his hair. 'I was more suspicious of Mother's motives in hiring Jill, to tell you the truth. We'd agreed on a woman more her own age, someone who could be a companion to her as well as a nanny to Joey. The thought did occur to me that maybe she was up to a little Christmas matchmaking. But I sure as heck ain't going to fall for a woman this soon, and Mother knows that. After I got past my doubts about her intentions, I realized she might be right about Jill. Some young blood around here might be good for Mother, and as you might have noticed, the last housekeepers didn't spend any time rolling around in the snow with my kid.'

'Nope.' Marsh shook his head, then glanced back out the window.

'And even if I'm wrong about Jill, what's it costing me to try this out a while?'

Marsh considered that a moment. 'Maybe it'll cost you nothing. But maybe it'll cost you your heart. And as I recall, friend, last time you spent your heart, you ended up pretty broke.'

Jill purposefully stayed outside long enough to allow Dustin to conclude his business with the sheriff. As much as the Reeds had tried to welcome her into their family, their private matters weren't her concern. But Joey was starting to get cold, so Jill headed inside.

'Hey, Jill,' the sheriff called as she and Joey came into the hallway to shake off their cold coats and mittens.

'Come join us for a cup of hot chocolate,' Dustin said. 'I've got the water warmed up.'

Jill came into the kitchen, helping Joey onto the plank bench beside the sheriff. 'Sit very still here, so you don't fall off, Joey.' She gave Marsh a warm smile. 'Hello, Sheriff.'

Marsh nodded. Jill turned away to fix the cups, only to find that Dustin had already done it for her. 'Thank you,' she said, meeting his gaze. Suddenly, she felt much warmer than she had a moment ago. Dustin's eyes crinkled at the corners in a silent response, as if he would have said 'You're welcome,' if he were more given to conversation. Jill sat down, scooting to the section closest to Joey.

'Now, be careful when you drink this, because it may be a little warm,' she cautioned.

Ignoring the chocolate, he quickly looked back to the sheriff. 'Can I see your star?' he asked.

Marsh undid the pin carefully, handing it to Joey for his inspection.

'It's shiny,' Joey said, sounding exactly like a little boy now. 'You . . . you like to be a sheriff?'

Marsh took the pin back as Joey held it out. A wry expression passed over the sheriff's face as he glanced first at Jill, then at Dustin. 'Sometimes, son. Sometimes I'm very happy to be the sheriff.'

65

He stood, nodding to Jill and ruffling Joey's hair, free now of the cap. 'I'll be seeing you, Dustin. Say goodbye to Eunice for me.'

'I will. Let me know if you talk to Holly's mother. I'm afraid there's not going to be any peaceful nights around the Reed household until she's safely returned.'

'Kept you up last night, did she?' Marsh asked as Dustin walked him to the door.

'Not me. Jill. I heard her go down to fix a bottle for the baby at about three o'clock in the morning.'

'Ah. Those three o'clock feedings. They're the greatest, aren't they?'

'Hell, no,' Dustin responded.

Marsh laughed. 'Hard to bond when you can't get the sleep out of your eyes.'

The sheriff was walking down the steps when Dustin said, 'Hey, Marsh, you ever eaten strawberry bread?'

'Nope. Not since my mother died. She was the only person I knew who fixed it. Why? Somebody give you some?'

'No. Mrs McCall, Jill's mother, is bringing some out Sunday. And some ham rolls.'

Marsh rubbed his hands together before getting into the cruiser. 'I'll be sure to stop by and check out the situation. Any woman who can make decent strawberry bread probably knew what she was doing when she raised her child.'

Dustin snorted. 'Just like your mother did.'

'Exactly. Set me a place at the table, buddy.' He grinned and drove away.

Jill was still sitting at the table when Dustin walked back inside. She'd heard most of the exchange between the two men, as the kitchen windows were close to the porch. Although innocent enough, the sheriff's comments made her wonder if their conversation had been about her rather than baby Holly.

'Did you have fun playing in the snow?' Dustin asked.

'We sure did!' Joey said enthusiastically.

'I think we did,' Jill said, running her fingers through the wet snarls in her hair. 'Did the sheriff give you any interesting information?'

Was it her imagination or did Dustin's eyes skitter away from her briefly? 'Not as much as I'd hoped for.'

'I see.' She couldn't pursue her instinct that the sheriff's visit had concerned her in front of Joey. 'Well, where do you want me to start?'

'Start?' Dustin seemed confused. 'Start what?'

'With my housekeeping duties. Joey and I will be fairly settled today, and I'm sure you want to get on with some of your business. Is there a list of things you'd like me to be in charge of, or shall I talk to Eunice about what's needed?'

Dustin got up from the table, seemingly relieved by the change of subject. 'You might ask Mother, because she's the one who really knows what needs attention around here. My only requirement is that dinner be served at six o'clock sharp.'

'I'll have it ready, sharp,' Jill replied.

Dustin nodded, walking from the kitchen. Jill had almost begun breathing easier until he popped his head back into the room.

'By the way, I enjoyed meeting your parents. They seem nice.'

Jill smiled at Dustin's attempt at social niceties. 'Thank you. They are.'

He nodded again, disappearing for good this time. A moment later, she heard the roar of the truck as it started up. Dustin had seemed anxious to avoid talking about the sheriff, she thought. But if there had been a problem, surely he would have mentioned it to her. Likely, she was borrowing trouble by worrying. Turning to the boy beside her, who was carefully sipping at his chocolate, she said, 'Well, Joey, we're on our own now.'

He shrugged. Jill might have been disheartened by his lack of response, except that she recognized the shrugs as one of Dustin's substitutes for conversation. Like father, like son. Neither one was going to be an easy convert.

Jill let her attention wander for a moment while Joey drank his cocoa. She still had to decide what to do about the apartment where she and Carl had planned on living. She was hanging onto it for another month, until she made certain this job worked out. They hadn't split up any of their belongings yet either, because Carl hadn't taken much with him when she'd told him she was breaking it off. Surely, he'd want to go back to retrieve his things. Either way, it was a loose end that needed tying up.

Holly's wail wafted down the stairs. Jill smiled at the tiny cry. 'That's my time clock punching in. Shall we go upstairs?'

'Okay,' Joey said, getting up from the table.

He sounded so old that Jill frowned. 'Don't you like having a baby in the house?' she asked.

Joey turned his gaze up to Jill. In his eyes, she saw neither excitement nor resentment.

'Who cares?' he said. 'She . . . she won't be here long, either.'

On the other side of Lassiter, Maxine Copeland fixed the private investigator she'd hired with unblinking eyes. 'What do you mean, you can't seem to find anything dirty to dig up on the Reeds?' she demanded coldly.

'Just that,' the little man returned. 'The two of them seem to be living their lives very quietly.'

'Their household wasn't so quiet the night my daughter died in a car accident,' she stated tersely. 'If Dustin Reed hadn't upset Nina so badly, my daughter wouldn't have driven out into that bad storm. Don't give me that innocent line. I assure you, if you dig hard enough, you'll discover that Eunice Reed was the reason for my husband's inattention for the last five years.' She gave a delicate sniff.

The investigator shook his head. 'David's records do reflect jewellery purchases, et cetera, but I can find no link between your husband and Eunice Reed.'

'I'm paying you plenty to find it,' she snapped.

'You hired me because I'm a damn good PI. I never agreed to make up lies. You'll have to find someone else to do your dirty work.'

'Fine. You're fired.'

The man nodded, getting up quickly and heading to the door. 'Best of luck finding a way to pin your suspicions on Eunice Reed. You'll need it. She's squeaky clean.'

Maxine slammed her palm against the table as he walked out. The evidence that David had been having an ongoing affair, covering a span of nearly five years, was driving her mad. She'd always known there had been women. But not a single, special woman who had claimed David's heart for that long.

To know that it had been Eunice Reed was enough to send her hatred boiling over into insanity. All Maxine's life, Eunice had had everything she, Maxine, had wanted. Homecoming queen. A marriage into a ranching empire. A son. Even Maxine's marriage into a wealthy family hadn't saved her from knowing that Eunice held a more respected position in Lassiter than she herself ever had.

If it took every penny she possessed, Maxine vowed that Eunice Reed was not going to get away without the town knowing of her illicit relationship with David. What a blow to Eunice's reputation if everyone should learn the truth. She was nothing more than a homewrecker.

Once the secret was spilled, casting its ugly shadows over the Reed Ranch, it would be a piece of cake to change public opinion about who should have custody of Joey.

Her grandson, Joey, was the one thing in life Eunice Reed wasn't going to get. Maxine was determined that, whatever it took, Joey would remain here with her.

Because it was all she had left of Nina. Eunice had won her daughter away in life, when Nina had married Dustin Reed.

At least Maxine could raise her daughter's child – and to hell with the Reeds.

71

CHAPTER 5

Dustin eased back in the saddle, enjoying the sound of the leather creaking as he stretched. He could finally tend to his work again, without worrying about difficult housekeepers quitting on him. Today he had ridden from one end of his acreage to the other, checking on livestock and seeing what damage the ice had done, just him and his horse occasionally blowing out steamy breaths in the frosty air. This was how it was meant to be.

Leaving matters concerning his house in Jill's capable hands was a major source of relief. How darn lucky for him that Jill had come to apply for the job. How very fortunate that his mother liked her. Eunice had certainly given the other two house-keepers a run for their sanity. Of course, *he* was a long way from relaxing around his new housekeeper, but Eunice had warmed to Jill like butter to hot ginger-bread – and since he really wanted a companion and watchful eye on his mother and his young son more than a sparkling clean home, this was all working out better than he could have hoped for.

'And the silence isn't bad either, is it, old boy?' Dustin said to his horse. He patted the gelding's neck, then turned toward the barn. Satisfied with the developing situation in his house, he could concentrate harder on the custody battle he faced in a few weeks.

He put the horse in the barn, slipping a blanket over it after rubbing it down. Making sure there was enough oats and water, Dustin gave the horse another solid pat on the neck. 'You never change, Rooster,' he said. 'You're a stalwart friend.'

Rooster gave Dustin a placid eyeing before turning his head to his water bucket. Dustin left the barn, rubbing his chapped hands together for warmth as he walked toward the house. Along the fence on the opposite side of the house several head of cattle wandered. With any luck, this year would produce a good calving. He needed that to happen, and not just for the money. Lots of calves would keep him busy, something he could expend restless energy on, which had consumed him since Nina's death.

Dustin opened the front door, his serene mood instantly exploding. Baby Holly was wailing, and from the sound of it, she was in the kitchen. Somewhere, he could hear Bugs Bunny besting Elmer Fudd, probably on the kitchen counter television. Over this din, he could hear a woman singing, with an occasional 'whee!' injected into the lyrics.

Baby Holly, apparently, did not care about 'whee!' when she was hungry. It was six o'clock and Dustin was starved, so he figured he and the baby were on the same track. It was an easy guess that if Dustin wanted his supper any time soon, he'd best get into the kitchen and nab the Christmas angel so Jill could fix his meal.

Striding into the room, Dustin quickly washed his hands. 'Hey, Joey,' he said over his shoulder. The child didn't say anything, but a quick glance at the screen showed Dustin that Elmer was losing the battle with Bugs. Joey giggled, satisfying Dustin that his son was amused for the moment. 'Here,' he said, taking Holly from her resting place against Jill's shoulder. Jill was in the process of warming a bottle and stirring something on the stove that smelled delicious.

Dustin grabbed up the bottle from the pan of water, testing it quickly on his arm before sitting down next to Joey.

'You don't have to do that,' Jill protested.

'It's either me or her,' Dustin said, nodding toward the big pot Jill was still stirring. 'I figure I don't get any of that until she gets hers.'

Jill met Dustin's eyes. 'She *is* louder than you are.'

Dustin grunted and popped the bottle into Holly's mouth, resulting in instant silence as the baby sucked hungrily. 'Was she good today?'

'She's a doll,' Jill confirmed. Leaning over to peer inside the oven at baking biscuits, she gave a satisfied nod. 'Just about done.'

Dustin wasn't sure if the wonderful smell of the bread or the wonderful shape of Jill's rear was more appealing to his senses. He turned his gaze to Holly, whose eyes were closed in rapt infant enjoyment of her feeding. 'Are you sure you don't mind?'

'Mind what?' Jill tossed a glance around her shoulder, but stayed leaning over, observing the biscuits.

Dustin frowned. 'Mind caring for a baby,' he clarified. 'You didn't know about her when you came to apply for the job.'

'No, I didn't. But she's very little trouble, really.' Jill walked over to the table to set out forks and knives. She met Dustin's gaze with an honest look in her eyes. 'Your son's been a dream, too. I think we're all adjusting to each other nicely.'

That was more balm to add to his improving mood. 'Speaking of adjusting, where's Mother?'

Jill folded blue checkered cloth napkins into halves, placing them beside the plates. 'Upstairs. She said she wanted to change her clothes before dinner.'

'Why?'

'Your mother spent most of the day on the floor with Holly. When she was awake, they played on the parlor carpet. When she was asleep, Eunice waited for her to wake up.' She shot Dustin a teasing grin. 'As I mentioned, Holly is very little trouble to me. Especially since Joey is becoming as fascinated by her as your mother is.'

'I hope it lasts,' Dustin said worriedly.

'Well, there's some novelty in knowing that we can only have Holly for a little while,' Jill admitted. 'It's hard to complain when you know she'll probably go home sooner than you'd like.'

Dustin gazed down at the infant now slowly working the last drops of formula from the bottle. She looked contentedly tuckered out. A good wail and a warm bottle obviously made for the kind of bone-deep relaxation that Dustin envied. 'Yeah, I guess you're right. I was so worried about you taking on all of us that I forgot to think about Holly probably not being here that long.'

'You never know.'

Dustin was silent for a moment. 'I guess I thought an investigation would take longer, since we're not sure if the baby's father is still a threat.'

'Did Marsh have any more information when he was out here yesterday?'

Jill's expression was questioning. He stared at her, as she waited for an answer. Those blue eyes looked so innocent, her face was so sweetly shaped and cute and – hell, he couldn't believe Jill would be husband-hunting. He couldn't believe anything about Jill was remotely crooked. Everything about her was round and feminine and adorable and motherly.

Or maybe, as Marsh seemed to have been suggesting, Dustin didn't want to see Jill in any light that wasn't favorable. For many reasons of his own.

Slowly, Dustin put the snoozing infant to his shoulder. Holly eased out a Texas-sized burp but was too satisfied with her meal to awaken. Jill reached to take her, but Dustin shook his head. He stood, carrying the infant from the kitchen and up the stairs. Down in the kitchen, he heard the sounds of Jill laying out supper. Dustin paused by the baby's basket, kneeling to gently lay her inside. With one hand, he drew the pink blanket over her. Holly paid no attention to his ministrations at all.

Dustin heard his mother carefully making her way down the stairwell. With one last look at Holly, he flipped on the baby monitor as he stood. His stomach rumbled, but he waited until he could hear the women talking and Joey's excited voice telling them about the cartoons he'd been watching. Only then did he go downstairs.

Maybe he'd lingered long enough with Holly that Jill would forget all about Marsh's visit yesterday. Lord knows, Dustin was trying to.

Cleaning up the kitchen was one of Jill's least favorite jobs. The trouble was, she liked to cook so many dishes from scratch that she ended up with plenty of pots and pans and ingredients to put away. But the bright spot was that Dustin and Eunice had seemed appreciative of her meal. There was a chocolate frosted cake sitting on the counter and Jill hadn't missed Dustin's frequent glances toward it. He hadn't exaggerated his enjoyment of a prompt supper time, either. The man had gone back for seconds, and then thirds.

Deciding that it was best to go ahead and start cleaning up the kitchen before Eunice could rise to help, Jill didn't linger over her meal. Both Jill and Dustin insisted Eunice stay seated at the table. He claimed he had matters concerning the ranch he needed to discuss with her, but since he immediately started to help remove dishes to the counter where Jill could rinse them, she knew Dustin was being protective toward his mother.

'Come on, Joey, let's go sit in the parlor since they won't let us help,' Eunice said. 'It's going to be so cold tonight, we may as well go ahead and light the fire now. It'll be nice and warm for us to have our tea in front of later.'

'Okay.'

Joey readily got up and followed Eunice. Jill was glad to see that he was careful to wait until Eunice made her slow way from the room before following closely behind.

'I'll call you in about ten minutes for cake,' Jill said as they left.

'That suits us fine, doesn't it, Joey?'

'Yeah!' he answered. 'Why . . . you . . . you like to drink tea so much, Grandma?'

Jill grinned at Joey's childish inquisitiveness. She heard the soft tone of Eunice's voice, but couldn't hear the answer. 'Joey seems to be accepting me,' Jill said, squirting dish soap into a sink full of hot water. 'Maybe not as quickly as your mother did, but I feel as though I'm making progress.'

'My mother is delighted to have people in the house. Christmas is tough enough without . . .'

Dustin paused, but Jill had an idea she knew what he was going to say. She made no attempt to cover the awkward moment with some pleasantry as she briskly scraped the plates clean. It was best to try to keep from saying something that might make Dustin feel worse about his wife not being here this Christmas.

'How much time are you going to want off for Christmas?'

Jill straightened. 'What do you mean?'

Dustin put down the glass he'd been drying and reached for another. 'You're going to need some time to celebrate the season with your family. If I have a general idea of how long you'll need off, then I can make plans around your schedule.'

'Hm.' Jill had been so glad to have a paying job that she hadn't thought about asking for holiday vacation time. 'Will you start cutting the cake and putting it on plates while I think about that?'

'Sure.'

After a moment, Jill noticed that he was concentrating on his task of cutting the cake, and at the same time she realized he was trying to be very careful not to let the moist cake crumble into pieces as he worked.

'Do you want me to do that, Dustin?'

'Aren't I doing it right?'

He looked concerned. Jill tried to smile reassuringly. 'You're doing fine.'

'Well, then, you keep working on your part, and I'll do mine.'

She turned to load silverware into the dishwasher, trying not to let Dustin's gruffness bother her. The Reeds had told her they were an independent lot, and she would have to do her best to figure out where the delicate line between her housekeeping duties and smothering the family was drawn.

It would be so much easier if she didn't want to care for them. Particularly Dustin. Unfortunately, she recognized another soul in pain when she saw one. Every instinct inside her wanted to do her best to make Dustin happy. It seemed that it took so little to make his gratitude come to the surface, as if he hadn't let anyone put him first in a long time. Certainly, he kept Eunice at arm's length, though perhaps that was because of her health.

For a moment, Jill wondered about Dustin's wife. Had she been a nurturing woman, filled with a desire to take care of her husband? Such small things seemed to please him. His gratitude made Jill enjoy doing things for him like baking a cake and yet she sensed his surprise in her actions. Almost as if he pulled back from allowing her to do more for him.

Maybe he didn't like being on the receiving end of their relationship. Maybe he didn't realize the good fortune this job represented to Jill. Perhaps if Dustin felt like he was giving back more he might ease up. It seemed to her that despite his stoic nature, Dustin had shown himself to be a giving man in many ways.

'Could I have all of Christmas Day to spend with my folks?' Jill suddenly asked. 'It's a lot to ask, because of Holly, I know . . .'

He stopped slicing the cake and licked some chocolate frosting from his finger. Her mouth went dry. A surprisingly sexual reaction shot through her and Jill turned away, amazed at the unexpected feeling.

'That's fine, Jill. Don't you want Christmas Eve to go to church with your family, too?'

There. Her theory was proven by his obvious concern. The man was still worried that he was asking her to take too much on with this job. Jill shook her head as she cleaned around the sink with the vegetable spray, telling herself she had imagined the sudden burst of sexual attraction she'd felt. 'I can go with you and Eunice, if that's all right.'

She thought she saw a flickering of that amazement in his eyes for just a second, but it was gone too quickly to be certain she wasn't imagining it.

'Fine with me,' he said. Quietly, he moved to put the plates on the table. 'If you're sure.'

'I'm sure.' In fact, she'd never been more certain in her life that what she was doing was the right thing. Spending Christmas Eve with the Reeds might give them a little something to be a bit happier about. Nobody wanted to be lonely at Christmas. No matter how much Dustin and his mother loved each other, Jill had an unsettling vision of the two of them sitting in a church pew during Christmas Eve service with nothing to look forward to. Nothing to brighten up their holidays with.

'There is something I've been wanting to ask you about, Dustin,' Jill began hesitantly. The lack of Christmas decorations in the Reed household had been an astonishing contrast to her parents' home, which had clearly revealed how Dustin felt about the holidays. It seemed that, for the most part, he preferred to ignore it. But for Joey's sake, Jill was hoping Dustin wouldn't mind a bit of a change.

'Go ahead. Ask,' he replied.

Jill drew a deep breath. 'What would you think about a Christmas tree in the parlor? Just a very small, table-top tree, that Joey could decorate with tiny ornaments?'

She had Dustin's full attention. 'Christmas tree?' he repeated. Obviously, the idea had not occurred to him.

'Well, yes.' Hesitating for a second, Jill plunged right back in. 'I could put it up and then on Christmas Eve there would be a place to put the presents to Joey from Santa. Christmas seems to be the only thing he's excited about, and a tree would . . .'

She paused, thinking about how pushy her words sounded. If Dustin didn't want decorations scattered around, it wasn't any of her business. She couldn't blame him for not wanting to celebrate a season that wouldn't include his wife. Her gaze fell and she wished she could take her words back.

Dustin stared at her. After a moment he laid down the cake knife, obviously deep in thought. Clearing his throat, he finally said, 'If you want to put up a Christmas tree, go ahead. I'm sure you'll understand that my enthusiasm is about nil for the holidays, but I'm not such a jerk that I can't see how excited Joey is about Christmas.'

Jill reached out to put a tentative hand on Dustin's

forearm. Once again, warmth spread through her, but she forced away the thought that she might be attracted to Dustin. She simply wasn't ready for it – nor for the possibility of rejection. 'You're sure you don't mind?'

They stood there like that for a minute, her hand on him and Dustin gazing into her eyes. He seemed to be thinking about something other than her question as he looked down at her.

Then he said, 'If I minded, I would have said so.'

The moment broken, Jill turned away, feeling a bit shaky. 'Great,' she murmured. He didn't reply, so Jill slowly turned her back and walked away from where he was standing to poke her head out into the hall. 'Eunice! Joey! Time for cake!'

Joey's whoop was audible in the kitchen. Jill turned back to the table, only to find Dustin standing still, staring at her intently. The child came speeding into the kitchen, launching himself into his place at the table and only barely remembering to wait until everyone could be seated before he dug into the dessert. Dustin's gaze roved from Jill to Joey, where it lingered just a moment, then he sat down next to the child.

Jill seated herself next to Eunice and picked up a fork to eat, wondering what she'd said to put that enigmatic expression on the handsome rancher's face. And did it bode bad or good for her?

Jill was pleased with the Christmas tree she'd purchased late last night. After she'd put Joey to bed and made certain Holly had her last bottle, she asked Eunice's permission to run into town to shop. Since it was the holiday season, the Wal-Mart was still open and Jill had been able to make her selections in plenty of time.

Joey had been thrilled to discover the tree, which Jill had placed on the coffee table in the parlor, just where his little hands could reach to place the tiny ornaments she'd bought. The tree itself was green and a bit shaggy with its plastic branches, but at about eighteen inches tall, just right for a child.

Now he was carefully pulling the cheap silver and gold plastic balls from their box, and laboriously placing hangers on them. Jill smiled, and realizing the boy would be busy for a while, decided to go upstairs and check on Holly.

The baby was just starting to stir. Jill picked her up, wrapping her pink blanket tightly around the infant as she held her to her breast for warmth. Holly smacked her tiny Cupid's-bow shaped lips and seemed to think about opening her eyes before apparently deciding that she was comfortable laying her head on Jill for the moment.

'Sweet baby,' Jill murmured. 'Are you going to give me enough time to warm your bottle before you start yelling this time? I'll feed you in the parlor and you can watch Joey decorate our tree. It's going to be beautiful, though you might not mention that to Mr Dustin, since he doesn't seem to think too highly of them right now.'

Holly stayed quiet as Jill walked down the stairs

84

with her. Quickly peeping in to see that Joey was still industriously inserting hangers in the ornaments, she went on to the kitchen and pulled a pan out to fill with water. Through the window, she could see Dustin, walking along the fence where the cattle were.

Dustin's tall physique moved with laconic grace as he walked toward the house, studying his cattle. It was cold outside, as Texas was having one of its coldest winters in recent times, but Dustin's only concession to the weather was a pair of leather work gloves and a tan coat with a lamb's wool collar. The ice had melted, but Jill couldn't help thinking she was much happier to be inside where it was warm.

Holly began squirming and Jill tore her gaze away from where Dustin had gone. 'Ready, now, are you?'

The baby opened her mouth for a pitiful yell. Jill chuckled and pulled the bottle out to test on her arm. Deciding it was fine, she stepped across the hall, talking to the baby as she walked into the parlor. 'Can't you do better than that? Mr Dustin makes more noise about his supper than you do.'

It was the truth, but Jill said it teasingly before she realized both Dustin and Eunice were standing outside of the parlor, staring at her.

'Oh, I'm sorry. I didn't know you'd come in,' Jill hurried to say. Holly let out an earnest shriek for her meal. Dustin's eyes were dark and deep as he looked at Jill without saying a word. Embarrassed, she quickly took a chair across from where Joey was working and put the bottle to the baby's lips. Holly quieted instantly, but Jill's insides were chaotic. Whatever had possessed her to say such a thing, innocent though it might have been?

'It's pretty, isn't it, Jill?' Joey asked, pointing to the tree.

'You're doing a great job,' she replied. Joey had carefully hung all the ornaments, though the silver balls were all together on one side and the gold were bunched together on the other side of the tree. Pride in his accomplishment glowed from Joey's face and Jill smiled at him, trying not to let her worry show. Her ears were trained in Dustin's direction, but he and Eunice were speaking so softly she couldn't tell if they were just exchanging good mornings or whether he was concerned about something. Jill could only hope her off-the-cuff comment to baby Holly wasn't going to stir up any discomfort between them. They'd only just gotten to the point where Jill was starting to think they might marginally relax around each other.

'Joey,' she said quietly, 'if you open that brown paper bag that's sitting beside the box the tree came in, you'll find a bunch of tiny candy canes. You can take them out of the wrapping and hang those next.'

'Oh, boy!' he said, scurrying to locate the bag.

Jill snuggled Holly more securely into her arms, telling herself not to worry. The baby seemed to like this adjustment, so Jill leaned back against the antique, curved-back sofa, forcing herself to quit trying to eavesdrop and pay attention to the bonding moment between her and Joey.

But she had no sooner allowed the tension to flow out than Dustin seated himself next to her. Instantly, she tried to sit up straight, but he shook his head.

'At ease.' His voice was gruff.

Jill lowered her lashes to stare at the floral-patterned carpet. The man wasn't so obtuse that he didn't notice how uncomfortable she was. A little warmth stole inside her stomach as she wondered what he was going to say to her.

But he seemed content to watch Joey slowly unwrap each candy cane, then situate it on a plastic tree bough. 'Are you having fun, Joey?' he asked.

'Yep,' the child answered, too engrossed in his work to pay attention to his father.

Dustin shot him a wry look, then glanced over at the baby. Holly still held the nipple in her mouth, but it was more of a lazy, relaxed pulling than a frantic suckling to fill her stomach. Jill looked up to find Dustin's gaze on her now, and a strange feeling shot through her.

'I hope you didn't mind my joke,' she said softly.

'Hm. I'm not sure if I did.'

Jill didn't know what to make of this. She couldn't decide if she was on the hot seat or not. 'I was just making conversation with the baby. I wasn't serious when I said . . .'

'That I make a lot of noise about my supper?'

She wished the sofa could fly and whisk her away from this awkward moment. 'I don't want you to think I mind fixing your meals, Dustin. It was just a comment to Holly that I thought a little more

87

enthusiasm was needed when demanding her supper.'

For a moment, she thought he might smile. But he didn't, and after a second, he stood. Jill swallowed as he stared down at her.

'I've got some things to finish up, but around three o'clock I'll be back to get Joey.'

Jill was so surprised she sat up, accidentally dislodging Holly from her bottle. Startled, this time the infant did let out an enraged cry.

'What are you two going to do?' Jill asked over the din.

Dustin glanced down at Joey, who was now looking up at him, his mouth open.

'It's time he and I had a man-to-man talk about women and their ways,' Dustin said.

CHAPTER 6

'**O**h, don't let Dustin annoy you,' Eunice said as she shuffled over to take the seat he'd vacated beside Jill. Having been standing in the doorway, she'd heard her son's parting shot to Jill. 'He's picking on you.'

Relief filled Jill. 'I'm glad you think so.'

'I know so.' Eunice frowned for a second, the porcelain skin on her forehead furrowing a bit. 'Although I've never seen him act this way around anyone before.'

'Lovely.'

Eunice looked at her. 'It is rather strange, isn't it? I mean, Dustin is a quiet person, but you seem to bring out a new side of him.'

She wouldn't know about a new side. It was hard enough to be comfortable with any of Dustin's sides. Yet she thought she understood what Eunice was trying to say: that in Dustin's own awkward way, he was trying to make her feel at home. Sort of like a sister, maybe.

The sudden thought occurred to her that perhaps that wasn't the way she wanted Dustin to view her at

89

all. He had said once that he found her attractive –
more attractive than he seemed comfortable with.
Was he *attracted* to her as well?

Or was that wishful thinking on her part? The man
was so clearly still mourning his wife that the idea
didn't seem likely.

Joey had finished with the candy canes and was
now searching the paper bag for more decorations.
He pulled out a tiny angel, his face joyous. 'Oh, I like
her.'

'She goes on the top,' Jill instructed.

Lifting Holly to her shoulder, Jill watched as the
boy put the angel on the top. Actually, the little tree
had a lot of life now that it was completely decorated.
She smiled at him, enjoying his delight with the
whole process. 'That's the prettiest tree I've ever
seen, Joey.'

He loved hearing that, Jill could tell. With one
finger, he gently caressed the angel's yellow-string
hair. 'Me, too.'

Holly let out a bubble of air, so Jill shifted her.

'Here. Let me have her now,' Eunice said, already
reaching for the infant.

Jill let her have the baby, then knelt to gingerly
pick up Joey's handiwork. Placing the tree on an
antique table sitting between two velvet-covered
chairs, she stood back to observe it for a moment.
'All we need now is a tree skirt.'

'Can we make one, Jill? Can we, can we?'

She smiled. 'Maybe.'

'I just happen to have a small piece of red felt we

90

could cut into a circle,' Eunice offered. 'There are also sequins upstairs in my sewing cupboard if that would help.'

'It would help us, wouldn't it, Joey?' Jill turned to give the elderly woman an appreciative smile.

'I can't help but think your parents are going to be proud of everything you're doing around here. I know we certainly appreciate all your hard work, Jill. You've lifted all our spirits.'

Jill had forgotten about her parents' impending visit. Now that she remembered about it, her little plastic Christmas tree seemed a bit forlorn to her. But she smiled for Eunice's benefit.

'Well, then, Holly,' Eunice said, 'how about you and I go up to peruse the cupboard? I promise you'll find more bits and pieces of things babies shouldn't put in their mouths, but just so you'll be in the holiday spirit, too, I think there's some nice green satin ribbon we could make into a headband for you.'

Eunice left the parlor, with Jill keeping a close eye on her. The arthritis didn't seem to be plaguing her, but the stairs always worried Jill. She wondered if it pained Eunice to walk up and down them. But since the day Jill had arrived, Eunice hadn't murmured a single complaint about her health.

Jill ruffled Joey's cornsilk hair, drawing a murmured complaint from him. She wondered what Dustin really had planned for Joey this afternoon. He'd been so quiet it was hard to tell.

Yet there was some comfort in knowing that the reserved man seemed to be starting to enjoy his son.

It had come as a surprise to her that the two of them seemed to lack a loving bond. Jill hated to see that their relationship was so stiff and formal. She knew not every man enjoyed having kids, but Joey was so much fun, when she could get him to loosen up. He'd loved making snow angels, and he'd loved decorating her substitute for a real Christmas tree. Perhaps Dustin was starting to realize what he was missing out on with his son.

Jill considered Eunice's words about Dustin's odd behavior. Maybe she *had* made some changes around the ranch – whether he was ready for it or not.

'How long will you be gone?'

Dustin shot Jill a mischievous grin. There was anxiety laced all through her question. 'I'll be home for dinner, six o'clock sharp,' he said, unable to resist the reference to 'the noise he made about his supper'.

Jill folded her arms. 'I assume you would tell me if Joey wasn't properly dressed for this excursion.'

'I would.'

She gave an irritated sigh, then bent down to rub Joey's hair and put a swift kiss on his cheek. Dustin thought about asking if he got one, too, realizing instantly his thoughts were going way out of bounds. He decided he should only bait the poor woman so much.

Jill stepped away, eyeing Dustin. 'I'll be expecting Joey back in the same clean condition and good health that he's in now.'

Dustin ran a finger along his hat in a mock salute. 'Yes, ma'am. Come on, Joey, we've got some important work to do.'

The child ran out to the truck, waiting for him to open the door. Dustin turned to make one last remark to Jill. 'Mother knows where we are, if you need anything,' he said before walking out the door.

'That's not playing fair, is it?'

'Life's tough,' he said with a shrug, before walking out onto the porch. He chuckled, plainly able to hear the heels of Jill's boots as she hurried up the stairs.

Thing was, Eunice wouldn't give Dustin's secret away for anything. Jill would just have to wait until Dustin was ready for her to know it.

He had a feeling she was going to like his surprise just as much as Joey.

Two hours later, Dustin walked into the house, waving Joey over to the parlor fireplace to wait. The child had pine needles sticking out of his hair and dirt smudges on his elfin face, beside the huge grin he was wearing. So much for the clean condition Jill had requested, but it couldn't be helped. Dustin pressed one finger against his lips for silence, and Joey nodded his understanding. The two of them had worked out a game plan.

Quietly, Dustin checked the kitchen, but Jill wasn't around. Hearing some soft singing coming from the direction of the laundry room, he walked in there. To his amazement, it looked like Jill was dusting the corners of the ceiling. She'd wrapped an old towel or something around a broom handle and was running the contraption along the tops of the walls. On top of the dryer, baby Holly lay in her basket watching Jill, comfortably soothed by the warm humming of the machine and Jill's singing.

Both the previous housekeepers – and his wife – had complained about the isolation of the ranch, and that there was little to do to relieve their boredom. Dustin folded his arms as he watched the woman carefully moving the padded stick along the wall edges. Jill seemed to have no trouble at all keeping herself entertained, even if it was dusting the walls.

More than that, she was keeping him entertained as well.

'H-h-hm,' Dustin said, clearing his throat loudly.

Jill jumped and let out a small squeal. 'You're back! Where's Joey?' she asked.

Dustin laughed and went over to offer Holly his finger to hold. 'I left him out in the woods. It's beneficial for a young boy to learn how to fend for himself.'

'You . . .' Jill paused at the serious expression on Dustin's face. 'No, you didn't. Where is he?'

'In the parlor, getting warm in front of the fireplace.'

'Oh.' Jill pulled off her rubber gloves, laying them next to the washroom sink. 'I want to hear all about his adventure.'

She reached to pick up Holly's basket, but Dustin wrapped his hand around the straw handle. 'I'll get her. You do whatever you need to with that giant cotton swab of yours.'

'Thanks.' Quickly, she pulled the towel off and tossed it into the washer, before setting the broom handle against the wall. 'Okay. I'm ready. I hope Joey enjoyed his outing,' she said, following Dustin as he walked.

'Seemed to,' Dustin replied.

Jill frowned, not realizing it. Dustin glanced over his shoulder as they walked through the kitchen. Jill felt his questioning gaze, but wondered why he wouldn't elaborate on the secret adventure. Then she saw Joey warming his hands in front of the fireplace. 'Are you frozen, Joey?'

Joey shook his head, though his bottom lip was quivering from cold. Jill drew back a little to stare at him, wondering at his attempt to be brave. She noticed Joey's gaze, which was directed at his tall, well-built father. Ah. There was the model of testosterone Joey was trying to imitate.

That was fine with her. 'How did the man-to-man talk go?'

'Fine. We have a souvenir from our outing that we'd like to present you with,' Dustin told her.

'Where is it?' Jill asked, starting to become suspicious at both their innocent expressions. She had a funny feeling she might be about to pay for her earlier comment about Dustin.

'It's outside. We want you to close your eyes, and no peeking,' Dustin commanded.

'All right.' Jill obediently closed her eyes, wondering

what the two of them had cooked up. They were acting very shady about the whole matter. 'Fortunately, I like mysteries.'

Startled, Jill felt Dustin take hold of her hand. It was warm, despite his being outdoors recently. He wrapped an arm around her shoulders as he led her toward the front door, and Jill couldn't help thinking that he smelled nice too. He felt big and strong and, well, just the way he looked like he might feel. Overwhelmingly masculine.

'Watch your step,' Dustin said, easing her down from the front porch.

Jill took baby steps, praying she wouldn't tumble to the bottom. Resisting the urge to peek, just a little, to get her bearings, she tried to make herself relax against the rancher.

'You can look now!' Joey shouted.

Jill opened her eyes to see that she was standing in front of Dustin's truck. Joey was hopping up and down like mad by the truck bed, so Jill realized that what she was supposed to see was back there. Walking around, she spied the reason for all the delighted excitement.

'A real Christmas tree! Oh, my! Did you cut this down yourself?' she asked Joey, instantly realizing that this was no store-bought tree.

Joey glanced at Dustin for confirmation, who merely nodded. 'Daddy showed me how.'

'I don't think I've ever seen such a nice, big tree,' Jill said for Joey's benefit, though she couldn't help noticing Dustin seemed appreciative of the flattery as well. He leaned against the truck bed, eyeing the tree proudly. 'It's beautiful.'

Dustin shrugged, trying not to look too pleased. 'Actually, it's not even a real fir, but I thought it resembled a Christmas tree.'

'It looks good to me.' Jill knew he'd done this for Joey, and for her, despite his own discomfort with the holidays. She'd have been touched if he'd appeared with a palm tree and decorated that with ornaments. 'Let's get it inside and see what we can do for decorations.'

Dustin let the truck gate down, reaching in to lift the tree upright where he could get a good grasp on it. 'Oh, I think you'll find Mother is going to fix Joey up just fine in that department. She's got more holiday junk than anyone in Lassiter.'

'Oh, good. Can I help you, Dustin?'

'Yeah. Hold the front door open, will you?'

Jill went on ahead, with Joey scooting through the door before Dustin carefully pointed the tree trunk into the entry way. 'See if I can get this in here without tearing off any branches,' he muttered to himself.

Jill propped open the door with her boot and tried to guide the tree from the top as he pulled from the other end. Suddenly it was lying in the entry hall, branches intact. 'Looks like a professional job to me, Santa,' she told Dustin.

'I've got good helpers.'

They looked at each other for a moment and Jill began to feel something inside her glow. Then Joey called, 'The tree stand is in here! Grandma's got everything ready for us!'

Eunice sat on the antique sofa, holding baby Holly up so she could watch the commotion of the tree being brought in and then painstakingly set down in the stand. From the kitchen, Jill brought in a pitcher of water and poured it into the stand.

'I see Holly is modeling a new headband,' she observed.

Eunice nodded, reaching up with one hand to push the evergreen-colored satin away from Holly's eyes. 'Isn't she adorable?' Without waiting for the only obvious answer, she instructed, 'The lights are in a box over there, Dustin.'

Jill reached for them, but Dustin closed his hand over hers. 'I'll do this, if you don't mind rustling up some hot chocolate and maybe a snack. I think Joey's hungry,' he said, cocking one eyebrow.

Joey had eyes only for the tree that nearly reached the ceiling. He was obviously not thinking about food. Jill raised her brows but didn't pull her hand away from Dustin's. 'I think it's his dad who is hungry.' Dustin merely grinned. 'I'll be right back with something to tide everyone over,' Jill said, walking from the parlor.

In five minutes she was back with hot chocolate and a tray of chocolate chip cookies. Joey and Dustin took a break to grab up the treats, so Jill sat down next to Eunice to admire the men's work.

'Do you want me to hold Holly for a while?' she asked.

'No.' Eunice smiled to take the brusqueness out of her answer. 'I want to enjoy this little bundle of joy as long as I can.'

Jill turned her gaze from the warm happiness shining from Eunice's watery-blue eyes. Holly was the recipient of all this extra love and attention because Nina was lost to the Reeds this Christmas. She sighed to herself, wishing that there was something she could do to help. Unfortunately, there wasn't anything she could do to make matters better. Glancing toward the mantel, Jill let her gaze run along the pewter-framed pictures of Joey.

She stole a look at Dustin. He was showing Joey how to dunk his cookie into the chocolate until he saw Jill watching him. Sheepishly, Dustin shoved the cookie into his mouth with a shrug.

'How about you help me start hanging the ornaments, Joey?' he asked.

Joey ran to join his father, which Jill was glad to see. Holly had just about fallen asleep, so Eunice placed her into the basket, setting it out of harm's way. The baby seemed mesmerized by the colorful, blinking Christmas lights that had been strung on the tree and seconds later, she closed her eyes.

'She seems pretty secure, doesn't she?' Eunice asked Jill. 'Considering everything?'

'I think she is. What's not to feel secure about, though, if you're part of the Reed household?'

Jill got up, taking the tray with her into the kitchen, realizing how true her words were. Certainly *she* was flourishing under the kindness the

Reeds had shown her. It was easy enough sometimes to imagine she was actually part of their family, and not just a woman who desperately wanted a fresh start in life. Of course, there was more to worry about with Holly, since her well-being had apparently been threatened, but perhaps Holly sensed her safety wasn't jeopardized here. She had Dustin protecting her.

Jill rinsed off the cookie plate, then meandered back to stand in the wide parlor doorway. Eunice was placing a festively patterned runner on top of the sideboard. Holly was still snoozing, and Joey was hanging ornaments in a tediously perfectionist manner. Dustin walked over to Jill and paused at her side.

'If you don't mind, I think I'll go upstairs to wash up. I feel a little gritty after cutting down that tree. Think I've got pine needles down the back of my shirt.'

Jill noticed the deep lines of weariness around Dustin's eyes. Of course, he'd worked outside in the cold all day, then come home early to take Joey on his first tree-finding mission, but . . . there was something more in the depths of his dark eyes that she couldn't quite fathom.

She thought she saw sadness, a wearying kind of sadness. 'You certainly deserve a break. Besides, I think you got everything started so well, Joey can finish decorating his first trophy tree by himself.'

'Yeah.'

Dawning pride beamed from his eyes as he glanced at his son, before he swung his gaze back to Jill. She started to say something, but Joey called out before she could speak.

'You . . . you under the mistoe, Daddy!'

Jill's gaze jumped upward. It was true. Eunice's hands had been busy, and she'd not missed putting a sprig of mistletoe in the doorway, cleverly twined with a bright red ribbon.

Joey asked, 'You . . . you hafta kiss her now?'

Jill's eyes widened. Dustin's gaze was pinned to hers. The weariness appeared to be gone, replaced by something else she wasn't sure about. He paused, perhaps considering Joey's words, maybe out of politeness. Surely he wasn't going to . . .

No. This was all wrong. Dustin was a grieving man. She was the housekeeper. Not knowing what to say, Jill turned and fled into the kitchen.

CHAPTER 7

Jill's quick escape had saved Dustin from making a stupid blunder. Kissing his housekeeper was not a good idea for all folks concerned. As much as he might have been tempted by the mistletoe, any fool knew that once he kissed Jill, nothing would ever be the same between them. In order for this relationship to work, it had to stay on an extremely formal, professional level. Otherwise, it was going to become even more awkward around the Regret Ranch.

Still feeling unsteady despite this assessment of the matter, Dustin turned to his mother. 'I'm going to shower. I have to go out tonight, and I don't want my potential clients run off by the sawdust and tree leaves I'm wearing in my hair.' He paused, thinking about the expression on Jill's face a moment ago. 'Would you mention to Jill that I won't be here for dinner after all? I've decided to treat the city boys to a real cowboy's meal.'

Eunice nodded. 'Go ahead, Dustin. I'll let Jill know the change in plans.'

'Thanks.' Dustin stomped up the stairs, thinking

that at least this way he could avoid Jill at the dinner table. Damn it, he had actually liked Joey's strange suggestion. He had to get a hold on himself, though perhaps in the morning the whole situation would have blown over to his satisfaction.

Eunice listened to her son walk upstairs before looking at Joey, who, completely unaware of the adult angst he'd stirred up, was engrossed in watching the tree lights sparkle. Actually, she thought Joey's idea about a kiss had been a good one, and quite opportune. The thought had occurred to her as she'd hung the mistletoe up in its customary place that perhaps something fortuitous might come of it.

The very way Dustin and Jill had reacted to the notion made Eunice smile. Electricity had sparked through the air as the two of them had stood stockstill, frozen with unconscious desire. It had been a rather unique moment to witness, those two people becoming aware of each other as they hadn't been before. Eunice pushed a tiny tendril of Holly's hair away from her temple. She liked Jill. She wouldn't mind at all if a little romance sprung up around the ranch, although neither Dustin nor Jill were exactly ready – or willing – for that to happen.

However, more than one romance had started during the season of giving, and even the most carefully sealed hearts had been known to unwrap.

After touring his big-city spenders around the ranch to show them the cattle and the way the operation was run, Dustin took them out to dinner. It was an experience he'd rather have foregone under normal circumstances, but with these two gentlemen ready to move the existing cattle stock they already had to his ranch, and perhaps buy a few of his steers to add to theirs, Dustin stood to add another layer of profit margin to the ranch account.

But it was tough to entertain when his mind was on Jill. He hadn't liked slipping out the front door without saying goodbye to her. Didn't seem right somehow. At the time, of course, it had felt like the best thing to do. Now, sitting in the dimly lit interior of The Cattle Drive restaurant, across from two city-slickers who thought they were hot stuff by wheeling and dealing in the commodity of beef, Dustin regretted his cowardice.

The woman deserved at least a goodbye called to her in the kitchen as he walked out the front door. It wouldn't have hurt anything. Dustin swallowed half his beer, then acknowledged that he'd been protecting his pride. A black-hearted monster inside him had whispered that Jill had looked mighty horrified that he might kiss her. That wasn't the usual reaction a woman had to getting close to him. Delighted, expectant, hopeful, he'd prefer to think though not to be bragging. But he'd never yet seen a woman with the look that Jill had been wearing.

It was a bit discouraging.

The dime-store cowboys seated at his table were enjoying nodding at the local women who had no more brains than to be flirting with men they didn't know. The fact that the men were with Dustin

104

probably gave the waitress and her friend the notion that the strangers were okay dudes. But Dustin couldn't help thinking that Jill wouldn't openly flirt with a man she didn't know.

Hell. She wouldn't even let her boots warm the floor under a mistletoe branch long enough to consider play-kissing a man she *did* know.

Half an hour later, Dustin had said goodbye to the men and waved them off onto the main road where they could head back to Houston. They'd been impressed with his outfit, as he'd expected. The Reed Ranch was a fine place to keep stock and Dustin was proud that they'd agreed on a good deal. All in all, it had been a very prosperous evening.

He paid his bill, then left the dinner table to sit at the bar. There was a television high up in the corner and a football game was on the screen. Just one more beer – five more minutes to give Jill time to be in bed so he wouldn't have to see her – and he'd head on home. He knew it was chicken-hearted, plain and simple.

'Hey, Dustin.'

The sheriff slid onto the barstool next him. Dustin was glad to see him.

'You off duty?'

'Yep.' Marsh whisked a hand over his checked shirt and grinned. 'Even the sheriff gets an occasional Saturday night off.'

'You got a date?'

'Naw. Looks like you're having a dry night as well.'

Dustin sipped his beer. 'I like it that way.'

'Shoot. That's not what we used to say when we were teenagers. If we didn't have a date on Saturday night, we cowered at home playing pool or watching TV.'

'I don't remember too many of those nights,' Dustin said with a shrug.

'Fortunately. Or we might have gone crazy with hormones.'

Leaning back on the barstool, his gaze glued to the television set, Dustin said, 'I like it better this way.'

'What? You like being without a woman on Saturday night?'

'Women have a tendency to drain the sanity out of your soul.' His tone was ironic.

'Hm.' Marsh thought about that for a minute, nodding his thanks to the woman who laid a beer down in front of him without noticing her I-can-get-off-early-tonight smile. 'Why do I get the funny idea you're not referring to Nina this time?'

He shook his head, not wanting to discuss what had happened. Or the discomfort it had worked up inside him. 'I'm not referring to anybody.'

Dustin could feel Marsh's stare on him. 'How come you won't look at me when you say that?'

'Because you're so damn ugly.'

Marsh laughed. 'Because you're lying. Something's got your underwear bunched.'

Dustin sighed, giving up the pretense that he was watching the TV when they both knew he wasn't. 'I got talked into putting up a Christmas tree today.'

'That seems pretty normal for this time of year.'

'Yeah.' Dustin snorted. 'Well, that meant decorations, and you know my mother has never skimped on the holiday doo-dads.'

'Always looks like Mrs Claus's house,' Marsh agreed cheerfully.

'You're a hell of a friend,' Dustin complained, eyeing Marsh with a help-me-out-here expression. 'Anyway, I found myself standing under the mistletoe with Jill.'

'Oh, I like that idea.' Marsh's eyes lit up.

'Don't like it too much,' Dustin growled. 'That's my mistletoe.'

'Yeah. But not your lady.'

Dustin didn't like the smug look on Marsh's face one bit. 'No, and she ain't looking, so don't be thinking,' he growled.

'How do you know she's not looking?'

He paused. For a man, this was a humiliating thing to have to admit, even to his best friend of many years. 'She didn't want me to kiss her while we were under the mistoe, as Joey called it.'

'That's supposed to mean she ain't looking? Sounds like she just ain't looking for *you*.' Marsh took a long swallow of beer before putting the mug down quickly. 'Hey, what made you think you should kiss her, anyway? You're not usually moving this fast, Dustin. I'm surprised at you.'

'It was Joey's idea,' Dustin said. 'He pointed out our location, asked if I had to kiss her, and damn my 'soul if the thought didn't appeal to me before I realized how stupid it was.'

'You were actually going to do it?' Marsh's eyes were round.

'Well, I'm not sure. But I was giving the idea some thorough consideration.'

'And while you were pondering this life-altering matter, the lady in question made good her escape.' Marsh hit the bar with his palm, laughing uproariously.

'I wish she'd thought it was so funny,' Dustin complained. 'Instead she looked like somebody'd given her a whack on the rear.'

'Uh-oh.' Marsh paused to wipe his eyes. 'And your pride took a meltdown.'

'Well, my mother was in the room, and – hell, yeah. It was awkward.'

'I wish I'd been there.' Marsh shot his friend a look filled with laughter. 'Don't take it so seriously, Dustin. It caught her off guard as much as it did you. And if she's trying to get over a fiancé, then she isn't going to be in the mood to be kissing anyone for a long time.'

'I thought you didn't trust her.'

'No. I didn't say that.' Marsh wrapped his hand around his empty mug, giving it a series of light thumps on the bar. He took the beer the waitress handed him, too deep in his thoughts again to see her smile, bigger this time. 'All I'm saying is that if she's really trying to forget a near-miss at the altar, then she doesn't even feel like kissing Santa Claus.'

'I thought your next warning about Jill would be

that she'd probably be out to steal the ranch out from under me. Considering her desperate situation.'

His friend scratched his head thoughtfully. 'Maybe Jill's not like other women we've tangled with. Once burned, twice shy. She might be looking for a secure roof over her head, but as for wanting to get hooked up again, maybe not. Maybe I let my mouth run away with me the other day.'

'It's probably dense of me, when you think how I got taken in by Nina, but Jill does strike me as being a pretty honest woman.'

'Just one who got caught in a bad situation.' Marsh ate some of the stale goldfish crackers that were sitting in a bowl on the bar. 'So, what are you going to do if her ex comes knocking?'

'Why would he?'

'I've been thinking . . .'

'Jeez. We just agreed that what you'd been thinking before about Jill wasn't worth two cents. That she wasn't a manhunter or a gold digger.'

'Yeah. But put yourself in the poor old ex's place. She shucked him. After he got over the shock and the blow to his pride, he might be thinking twice about letting such a woman get away from him.'

'You worry me, Marsh. If I didn't know better, I'd think you had the hots for my housekeeper.' Dustin couldn't help the astonishment in his voice.

Slowly, Marsh turned to look at him. 'Would it matter if I did?'

Dustin could feel his jaw slackening. 'I – what the hell's that supposed to mean?'

'Maybe just what it sounded like.' Marsh shrugged, but didn't remove his eyes from the tight lock on Dustin's. 'So would it matter?'

'I think it would,' Dustin said tightly.

'Well, then.' Marsh looked away, crossing his arms over his chest and hooking his boots around the barstool rung. 'Guess I know now why you've got such a hump in your back over Jill not letting you kiss her, then.'

Marsh had him, yet relief filled Dustin that his best friend wasn't interested in his housekeeper. Something had told him that was going to be a very bad thing for their friendship. All their lives, they'd dated very different women, and kept their friendship because there was no rivalry between them. One pretty smile had done just as well as another as far as both of them were concerned. Nothing worth losing blood over.

But now there was Jill, and for some darn reason Dustin couldn't fathom, his emotions were feeling very twisted.

'I don't know what my problem is,' Dustin grumbled, still amazed by the surge of territorial wrath that had flooded him. 'I've only had two and a half beers.'

'I think I know what your problem is, old friend,' Marsh said with a grin. 'That little lady's putting a rise in your Levi's.'

Around midnight, Holly decided she needed another bottle to tide her over until dawn. Jill got up and slipped on an old terrycloth robe and some house shoes before picking up the wailing infant. 'I think a change is in order, too,' Jill said soothingly. 'First, we'll get that formula warming.'

She snatched up a diaper from the bureau, which had swiftly become a makeshift baby accessory area and then hoping that Eunice wouldn't hear them and think she needed to come assist her, Jill hurried downstairs to the kitchen.

At the same time as she dropped the cold bottle into a cup of drawn hot water, the front door opened. Jill went to peer out into the hallway, carrying baby Holly in her arms. It was Dustin. And judging from the frown on his face, not too happy to see her.

'What are you doing up?' he demanded.

'I might ask you the same question,' she replied crisply. With a stern look at his mussed hair and western shirt that had come loose from his jeans, Jill said, 'It appears that I'm the only one with a good excuse for being awake at this hour.'

With that, she turned and marched into the kitchen. Testing the bottle for warmth, Jill dried it off. Dustin stood in the doorway watching, but she ignored him as she crossed into the parlor. Quickly, she plugged in the Christmas tree lights and then settled onto the antique sofa to feed Holly.

'Now what are you doing?' Dustin asked.

'Does anything about that question appear to be rather ridiculous to you?' Jill was a little cross herself from being awakened in the middle of deep sleep. She wanted Dustin to go upstairs, so that she and Holly could share a quiet moment watching the Christmas lights blink on and off in the darkness like so many tiny, colorful stars. The baby seemed delighted by the sight, and Jill had noticed that she fed better when she had something to concentrate on. Dustin hovering was not going to be good for Holly's concentration and relaxation. Nor Jill's.

Not to mention that she was extremely uncomfortable with what had happened this afternoon. Although Joey really couldn't be blamed for his innocent suggestion, it had later made her tense to be around her crusty employer. The man was probably thinking she was hunting for another wedding ring to salvage her life with, while nothing could be further from the truth.

Unfortunately, Dustin seated himself in one of the chairs next to the table-top Christmas tree. 'Jill,' he began.

She tightened her grip on the baby unconsciously, causing Holly to stop sucking and look up at her. Jill told herself to relax, but she had a feeling she wasn't going to like what she was about to hear.

'I've been thinking that with your folks coming tomorrow, maybe you ought to have the evening off. You could go back with them and have some time to do whatever.'

'I don't need any . . . why are you saying that?'

Dustin rubbed the back of his neck. She could tell he was tired.

112

'It was only a suggestion. I just thought maybe you could use a personal day all to yourself, without all this . . .'

Jill's hand suddenly felt trembly as she held the baby bottle. He was talking circles around it, but what Dustin was really thinking about was some space between them. It was painful for her to know he was embarrassed too.

'I need to work like anyone else does.'

Dustin watched Holly feeding for a second, then let his gaze travel up to Jill's eyes again. She wished she didn't feel so naked and exposed.

'Most people need a break sometimes, too.'

Jill didn't reply so Dustin tried a new tack. 'I know you said you'd try this job out for a week before you decided whether you'd stay on, but I'd like to know if you've made any plans along those lines since it's nearly been that.'

She was silent, wondering why he was asking all these questions and how they related. He certainly seemed to be giving her situation a lot of thought. Did he not want her to stay now?

'I know your folks coming out here tomorrow will probably impact your decision. It was pretty clear to me that they're concerned about you.'

'I make my own decisions,' Jill said tightly. 'About whether I stay here or anything else. My parents have nothing to do with it, except that they were overjoyed to have an invitation out to meet your mother and see where I was going to be living.'

'Easy, easy,' Dustin said soothingly. 'I wasn't

trying to imply that you needed their permission. I'm just trying to figure out what it will take to keep you happy here.'

'I think there's a good possibility that I might stay on,' Jill said, unable to help the formality in her tone.

Dustin said nothing, his eyes hooded while he listened. Jill thought about their near-kiss and decided that perhaps the rancher needed some convincing that she wasn't after his well-built body – or a promotion to Mrs Jill Reed.

'The three-thousand-dollar bonus at the end of the year is important to me.' He blinked, so Jill hurried on. 'I'm going to use the extra money to go to night school and finish my Master's. I only lack a few credits, and hopefully by then I will have found another job in my profession.'

There. If the man had any doubts about what she was after, she should have relieved him quite efficiently.

Holly finished drinking, lying across Jill's lap like a worn-out rag doll. 'If you'll excuse me, I'm going to carry Sleeping Beauty back to her basket. Unless you had something else you wanted to know?' she asked, not wanting to be rude, but not wanting to stay there with him any longer, either. In the peaceful beauty of the Christmas room, it was too easy to want to be comfortable with him.

But Dustin wasn't really paying attention, it appeared. His gaze was focused on a place above her soft pink slippers and the hem of her pink-and-white striped housecoat when she stood. Jill's calves were bare, because her nightgown was knee-length, but there was nothing interesting about what was exposed.

Unless she hadn't shaved her legs. Quickly, Jill counted back, realizing with a sigh of relief that she'd managed a quick swipe with a razor in the shower yesterday morning while Holly had snoozed.

'Goodnight,' she said, adjusting the baby on her shoulder.

'I'll turn off the tree lights,' Dustin replied. He turned his head to gaze at the tree and Jill couldn't help feeling a little sorry for him, all alone in the darkness. But it wasn't her worry, and the twinkling lights might cheer him.

She'd turned to go upstairs when his voice stopped her.

'Should I burn that trouble-making piece of greenery?'

A small smile hovered at her lips. 'Burning may be overkill. But I promise not to get caught under it again, if you promise, too.'

'It's a deal.' Dustin pulled his gaze around to meet hers, making prickles shoot through her. 'I don't think I realized until that moment what a caution having a small, bright child around was.'

'Oh, Joey's definitely a caution.' Jill chuckled. 'For a minute, I thought you were going to follow his suggestion, just to be polite.'

Dustin's eyes narrowed. 'No. I wasn't.'

Jill ignored the sudden emptiness in her heart.

What a mountain to make out of nothing. He'd never intended to kiss her at all. Why had she allowed herself to get so worked up about nothing?

Because suddenly you hoped he might kiss you, and that scared you to death.

But she wouldn't have wanted Dustin to kiss her just to be polite, either. She would prefer that he want to kiss her.

Unfortunately, the fact was, she couldn't risk caring deeply for another man. It would be so terribly stupid to allow herself to fall into an emotional trap, when she hadn't even gotten the deposits back on the church and wedding cakes let alone a firm grip on her heart.

Hadn't she learned anything from her mistakes?

'Goodnight,' Jill whispered softly, turning away from Dustin's watchful gaze. Baby Holly lay against her shoulder like a warm sack of flour, weighted with contentment and sweet dreams.

Jill walked up the stairs, wondering if she'd made the right decision to commit to a full year in the Reed household. There were a million reasons she might accidentally find herself caring for that strangely polite, but distant rancher.

Politeness was very different from passion, as she remembered all too well.

Dustin watched the tree lights blink on and off. He thought about Jill's smooth, bare skin exposed by her bathrobe and couldn't help thinking about her slipping into bed wearing one layer less.

The woman thought he might have kissed her to be polite. Didn't she know that polite kisses were reserved for aunts one hadn't seen in ten years? Not for a perky, gorgeous lady who was living in his house, running through his thoughts until he prayed for sleep so his mind would rest. No, she'd saved herself that afternoon with her quick and competent retreat.

Smart, unattainable Jill. It would take a noose and a Clydesdale to drag him back under that mistletoe.

Besides, he knew it wouldn't be fair to make her feel less secure in her position at the ranch by bringing something physical into their relationship. Dustin wanted Jill to view the Regret Ranch as her home for as long as she wanted to stay. Lord knows, he and his mother were benefiting far more from the arrangement than Jill was. He thought about her cleaning the walls with that oversized q-tip and wondered if she was happy here. If she felt safe, from him especially.

From now on, he would do everything in his power to make certain she felt secure, up to and including keeping his lips off hers.

However, once she was over her wedding-bell blues, if the lady ever hinted that she might want a kiss from him, he damn sure was not going to worry about polite behavior before he hauled her into his arms.

Marsh left the restaurant thirty minutes after Dustin did with a feeling of misgiving growing in his heart. He had a disturbing notion that his friend was contemplating his housekeeper having more than cook and bed-maker capabilities. Jill was certainly attractive, and any man would look twice, but she just felt too good to be true to Marsh. Why did she have to appear at this time in Dustin's life, when he was so vulnerable? The man was damn lonely and primed to make a mistake he might regret.

There was the big family supper tomorrow night. Marsh was attending, as he'd horned in on Reed family suppers many times before, anyway. It was easy being part of their family, when they had such big hearts and opened them to just about anybody. It wasn't until Dustin and Nina had started having problems that Dustin had become a bit quieter, perhaps a little surly. Marsh had understood that dealing with Maxine butting into their lives and screwing Nina up with her complexities had really been a drain on the marriage. For all its fortress-like position up on that hill, they hadn't been able to shut Maxine's discontent out of their home, which had writhed around Dustin and Nina's emotions like a demon.

Mama says you should buy me a better car. Mama says that if you really loved me, you'd spend more time at home with me. Mama wonders when we're going to have another baby.

Oh, Marsh had ached watching that marriage disintegrate into Maxine's bitter brew of unhappiness. He would have done anything to keep Dustin from being tortured that way, like a man being pulled apart on the rack.

It had escalated into the fiery winds of an angry, disastrous argument, with Nina leaving one night to go home to Maxine. Dustin could not – would not – stop her from going to the mother who it was clear now she would never be able to leave behind.

Marsh had been called to the scene of the accident. Never in his life would he forget the anguish of finding his best friend's wife trapped in the twisted car. He'd helped remove Nina's body before Dustin arrived. It was the one small thing he could do, to make certain that Dustin didn't witness the agony that Nina's desperation had wrought on her.

Then he'd gently removed Joey from his car seat. The child had been eerily quiet as he sat watching the colored lights of the emergency vehicles. Maybe he'd done all the wailing he could do and was played out. Marsh had held the boy until Dustin arrived to find himself a widower, thrust awkwardly into a single-father life. For the last eleven months, the Reed family had struggled to recover from the tragedy, without any encouraging sign that the curtain was about to come down so a new act could start.

Now Jill had come into Dustin's life, bringing spark and her saucy tongue and a new life-blood pumping through a family that so needed a transfusion.

Unfortunately, Jill McCall had wounds of her own to recover from. How much of the Reed family misfortune was she willing to help see them through? Worse, what if Dustin *was* subconsciously falling for this woman – how hurt would he be if she exited in the middle of the act?

Marsh shook his head, worried that he saw flashing caution lights ahead in his friend's future.

CHAPTER 8

'Is there anything I can do, Jill?'

She turned around at Eunice's soft question. Eunice had come into the kitchen, probably anticipating Jill's desire that everything be just right for her folks and Jill appreciated her thoughtfulness.

'I think we're in excellent shape. Since you baked up those pies yesterday, and I'd frozen some casseroles, there really wasn't much left to do except set the table.'

Which she'd done yesterday, knowing that her parents would arrive about an hour and a half after church today. She knew she'd feel more relaxed if everything was pretty much ready, so putting Holly's basket in the formal dining room and enlisting Joey's assistance with laying out the tableware, Jill had been busy. All that was left to do was warm the casseroles as the chicken had been roasting since early this morning.

'You've done a marvelous job.'

Jill smiled at Eunice's compliment. 'I like to cook, especially for my parents. I really haven't had much chance to.'

Peace with her past had stolen over her yesterday as she'd laid out the holly-printed napkins, pulling them through silver napkin rings. It was kind of Eunice to allow her to have her folks out for supper, and considerate of Dustin to suggest it. Her parents were going to fall in love with Eunice, and the ranch. Nobody knew better than Jill how disappointed they'd been that her engagement had fallen apart. She'd almost been able to feel their hearts breaking for her.

Their visit here today should relieve them, though. Jill smiled, feeling very serene and happy about the whole thing. It was going to do her a world of good. She let her eyes rove over the kitchen counter one last time, to make certain that all the food was ready and waiting to be ladled into attractive crockery. Though she was still dressed for church, Jill wanted to take five minutes to refresh her make-up and brush her hair. Then she wanted to slick Joey's soft, fly-away hair down with some water, even if any headway she made would be gone in a second. Of course, baby Holly needed the satin headband Eunice had made her, and Jill hadn't been able to resist a green velvet dress with a white collar she'd seen at the discount store where she'd picked up the ornaments the other night. Holly would look so sweet in her new outfit.

The doorbell rang, startling Jill out of her thoughts. 'I'll get it, Eunice,' she said, wiping her hands on her apron. As an afterthought, she untied the apron and tossed it onto the plank kitchen table before crossing into the hallway.

It was too soon to be her parents, Jill knew, but perhaps they'd skipped church in their anxiety to visit. She smiled and opened the door.

The man she'd most wanted to forget stood on the porch. 'Carl,' Jill said weakly, her bubble of happiness instantly bursting inside her. 'What are you doing here?'

Her ex-fiancé seemed supremely uncomfortable, not happy to be paying this call. Sheepishly, he replied, 'I have to talk to you, Jill.'

'I think we said everything that needed to be said.'

'Aw, Jill. Can't we discuss this?'

'Carl.' Jill's voice was stern. 'I don't think we should discuss anything more than when you're going to get your things out of the apartment. How did you find me, anyway?'

'Your mother told me. She doesn't want us to break up, Jill. I'm sorry about everything . . .'

'Sorry about using the secretarial pool as a dating service, Carl? After declaring your love to me?'

She started to shut the door. He put his hand out quickly to stop it from closing. 'Okay, okay, Jill. Wow. You don't have to be such a bi – you don't have to be so bitter,' he amended.

'I'm having company in a while, Carl. Please say your piece and then make yourself scarce.'

'Can't I come in?'

Behind her, Eunice cleared her throat. 'Jill, I'm going to take Holly and Joey upstairs while I'm getting ready. You're welcome to use the parlor, of course.'

'Thank you, Eunice,' Jill said, turning to give the older lady a grateful smile. 'Would you like an introduction?'

'I shouldn't think so, dear.'

She couldn't help feeling that Eunice was very much in her corner. 'This won't take long,' she assured her, before turning around with a sigh. 'Come in, Carl, but wipe your shoes and please, don't make yourself too comfortable.' She pointed to the parlor area.

'Man, you've really got yourself a cozy place here, don't you?'

'None of this is mine.'

'I've got to hand it to you, Jill. It looks like you've managed to land on your feet.'

Jill gave an unladylike snort. Apparently Carl had thought she couldn't survive without him. After she'd discovered he had roving eyes, however, she had known that in the long run, she'd be much better off without him. 'I'm surprised you didn't know me well enough to know that I can take care of myself.'

He looked at her thoughtfully. 'Ah, yeah. You sure are looking pretty, Jilly. You always were a helluva looker.'

Jill watched without enthusiasm as Carl made himself comfortable on the antique sofa. That was *her* place, she thought angrily, a place that had come to mean welcome sanctuary during the times she fed baby Holly. Together, they enjoyed the quiet and the twinkling Christmas lights, which thankfully weren't turned on right now, or she'd really have felt encroached upon. As it was, she deeply resented Carl's intrusion into her life.

'I look the same as I always did,' she snapped.

'You can be such a pain, Jill. Here I am trying, and you're not making this easy on me at all.'

'So sorry. I wouldn't want to cause you any distress, Carl.' She sighed, realizing that any further conversation between them was totally pointless. 'I have people arriving any moment for dinner. You've come at a bad time.'

Carl stood and started to walk toward her. At that moment, Dustin entered the room. Jill had never been so glad to see anyone.

The change in Carl was immediate. He puffed up like a rooster, standing up as straight as he could, though he'd need an extra few inches in his shoes to measure Dustin's height.

'Heard there was company, Jill. Name's Dustin Reed,' the rancher said easily, holding out his hand to Carl.

'I'm Jill's fiancé, Carl Douglas,' Carl replied quickly.

Jill winced. That was not how she would have introduced him. 'Not exactly,' she murmured, ignoring Carl's frown.

'It's a mighty long way for you to come out, but . . .'

'Oh, it was that,' Carl agreed. 'Of course, I'd drive to the end of the world to be with Jilly.'

Dustin crossed his arms, staring all the while at Carl. Jill's ex looked visibly cowed.

'We're a bit busy with company coming out, as Jill mentioned.'

'Yeah, yeah right.' Carl started scooting toward the doorway. 'Well, I guess I'll hit the road. It was nice meeting you,' he said to Dustin.

'I'd like to say the same,' Dustin said.

Carl looked uncertain as to how to reply to that. Swinging his gaze around, he said, 'Jilly, walk me to my car?'

'Come on.' Reluctantly walking in front to lead the way, Jill noticed that Dustin stayed behind in the parlor.

They'd only made it to the porch when Carl's anger exploded. 'Who the hell does that guy think he is?'

Jill made no reply as she gauged the distance to the sports car. She couldn't get there fast enough.

'I mean, his attitude stinks! That guy thinks he's the Marlboro man or something. He acts like he owns you.'

'Nobody owns me,' Jill said in a tense voice.

He was quiet as he reached the car. 'But the Marlboro man likes you, doesn't he?'

'Hardly.' She wasn't lying. Dustin and she had a long way to go before they stopped acting like polar magnets.

'I think he wants to get in your pants. Or has he already?'

'Oh, for heaven's sake!' Jill's patience ran out like sand in an hourglass, except it had only taken about fifteen minutes. 'Must you be so crude?'

126

'Well, it's obvious by the way he looks at you, like you're a piece of juicy steak he can't wait to sink his teeth into.'

'Only you would compare a woman to a piece of meat, Carl. Please have your things moved out by Friday. I really must turn in the notice.'

Carl paused, staring at her. 'You're really going through with this, aren't you? You're calling it quits between us?'

Jill was surprised. Had he forgotten who'd required a stable of secretaries and temporary typists to satisfy him, though he'd sworn they hadn't meant a thing to him once she'd found out? 'Yes, I'm going through with this.'

Slowly, he said, 'I guess I didn't think you would.'

'I don't understand. You thought I'd wait for you forever, like some virginal heroine waiting on her hero, until you'd had your fill of the spice of life?'

Carl's expression was considering, as if he was seeing her for the first time. 'I thought, once you lost your job, that you'd realize how much you needed me.'

'I'm afraid I don't get the – wait a minute. You're not saying you had anything to do with me being laid off?' Jill was horrified.

'Well, after you broke off our engagement, it occurred to me that if you were out of work, you'd think about us more seriously. I was hoping, anyway. So, I mentioned it to Lyle and the company had been looking for some jobs to eliminate . . .'

She fought off the desire to slap him. Lyle was the

personnel manager and obviously, Carl hadn't wasted any time bending the ear of the person he knew could help him. 'You are a snake. I don't know what I ever saw in you. Go away before I kick holes in your car.'

He didn't like the threat to his fancy sports car, because he instantly opened the door. 'Think about it, Jilly. I wouldn't have done it if I hadn't loved you.'

Disgusted, Jill turned and began walking away. If that was love, it was sick and twisted.

'You'll always be the only woman for me,' Carl called. The sports car roared as he started it.

She told herself he wasn't going to be the only man for her. Shaking, she walked inside the house.

In the parlor, Dustin and Joey were talking about something on the tree. She needed about five minutes to compose herself before her parents arrived. Carl's unexpected appearance had left her feeling weak and bitterly upset, so she tried to slip past the doorway.

'Are you all right, Jill?' Dustin called.

'I'm fine.' Jill wouldn't have said anything else. She simply was too embarrassed to discuss it. 'Thank you for trying to protect me.'

'I wasn't, I swear.' Dustin's face was completely innocent.

She shot him a jaundiced glance. 'Please. I've just listened to all the baloney I can take in one lifetime.'

Dustin shrugged. 'Sorry. Maybe I was in a white knight mode, somewhat. Mother was waving the

128

emergency towel at me, and I probably got carried away.'

'The emergency towel?' Jill asked. Joey stared up at his father, listening.

'Yeah.' Dustin's expression seemed purposefully nonchalant. 'Because I'm out on the east side of the property so much, she can't reach me, especially in weather like this when her hips act up. We devised a system of hanging a dish towel out the window for certain times. Yellow for a phone call. Green for lunch. Red for an emergency.'

Jill felt surprise flow through her. 'The towel was red.'

'Yes. It's only been red once before, and that was when my father had his heart attack.'

'Oh, my,' Jill whispered. Suddenly, it dawned on her just how much a part of this family she was starting to feel like. Eunice's and Dustin's concern for her was heartwarming. Still, this situation wasn't forever. 'I don't know what to say. I think I'm still feeling slightly overwhelmed by Carl showing up.'

Actually, she was more disturbed by the emotions Dustin was stirring up inside her. He nodded at her comment.

'Mother wasn't certain you'd want any interference. But she said you didn't seem too happy to see the guy. I hope you don't mind my butting in.'

'No,' Jill said softly. 'Actually, you do a very nice white knight impression.' She stared at him for a moment, realizing how very different Dustin and Carl were. Carl lived for pleasure of the moment.

Dustin seemed a lot more solid. She took a deep breath, unwilling to think about how secure he made her feel. Yet, the very fact that the man she'd thought she loved had purposely cost her a livelihood that was important to her was deeply scary. She'd gotten extremely close to walking down the aisle, all the while thinking she'd known her fiancé, when she hadn't. Dustin was given to silent moods and keeping to himself. How could she ever really be sure she knew him any better than she had Carl?

As far as she could tell, Dustin found attachments difficult, even to his own son. It would be unwise to find herself in the same position twice. Carl's traitorous behavior had stunned her, and even now, she found it difficult to believe what she'd heard with her own ears.

'If you don't mind, I'm going upstairs to freshen up,' she said, tearing her gaze from Dustin's. 'Joey, why don't you come with me? I'd like to slick that hair down.'

'Go on.' Dustin waved her away. 'You need a moment to regroup. Joey will live without his hair being slicked. Besides, it wouldn't last more than five seconds.'

He ran his hand carelessly over Joey's hair, instantly making the fine blond strands go awry. Jill didn't think he even realized he'd mussed his son's hair in a fatherly and affectionate gesture. She forced a smile to her lips, thinking that Dustin was right. Joey would be fine, and she wanted to go upstairs and take a moment to indulge in some deep breaths.

Nodding, she turned to go upstairs. The doorbell rang, and Jill halted, knowing her parents had arrived. She didn't want them to see her like this, anxious and no doubt having some runaway mascara around her eyes. Not for anything did she want them to think she was unhappy at the ranch.

'Go on,' Dustin said, his voice rough. 'I'll stall 'em.'

'Thanks.' Jill didn't take a second more to express her gratitude. She flew up the stairs, feeling immensely guilty for dumping her duties on Dustin, but badly needing to force herself back into the pleasant mood Carl had stolen from her.

Dustin flung open the door, Joey at his heels. 'Marsh. You old buzzard. I should have known you'd get here first.'

The sheriff walked past him after wiping his boots on the mat outside. 'Yep. Hated to think you might not have anyone to help you set out the *hors d'oeuvres*.'

He pronounced it hors-doovers. Dustin had to grin. 'Eat them, you mean. Anything you're supposed to set out would never make it to the table.'

'Exactly. That's what I said.'

'Well, you came too late, then. Jill's had everything ready for hours.'

'She's an organized little thing, isn't she?' Marsh dumped his Stetson on Joey's head, much to the child's delight, as he walked into the parlor. 'So, there's the ornery twig that caused so much trouble.'

Dustin ignored his friend's glee. 'Don't start, my

friend. We've had plenty of excitement here today without you kicking up some dirt, too.'

'What'd I miss out on?'

'Just the ex showing up. Nothing more interesting than that.'

'Hm.' Marsh looked around the room at the big Christmas tree and the smaller version. 'Don't guess the mistletoe got him any better luck than it did you.'

'I don't think so.' Dustin left the Christmas room, knowing Marsh would follow him into the kitchen. 'Jill was more upset to see him than I thought she might be.'

'Really? Still harboring feelings, is she?'

Dustin sat down at the table in a leisurely manner that betrayed the fact that the same thing had crossed his mind. 'Seemed to have her hand planted pretty square in the middle of his back, pushing him out the door.'

'Well, you never know with women. They don't know what they want.' Marsh grabbed a soda from the fridge and sat down across from Dustin. The sound of the can being opened was loud in the sudden stillness.

Dustin considered his friend's words. Women *didn't* always know what they wanted; men didn't, either. Jill had been upset, but not pining upset for that city boy. He briefly wondered what she'd seen in her ex-fiancé, then asked himself what she might see in him, any better than that city boy.

He wouldn't let himself think about it. 'The guy had some coconut-smelling stuff in his hair. I could smell it five feet away. Oh, hell, that reminds me. Joey, come here!'

His son ran into the room. 'What?'

'I forgot Jill wants your hair slicked down.' He ran his hand under the faucet to get it wet and mashed it across the cowlick. 'There. That ought to do.'

Joey instantly ran his hand through it, undoing Dustin's handiwork before running up the stairs. Marsh laughed.

'She's changing you already, friend.'

'What's that supposed to mean?' Dustin glowered across the kitchen.

'I never saw you do that before. Heck, you've never acted like Joey was much more than your shadow. Jill must be working on you.'

'You're fixing to uninvite yourself from Sunday dinner, Marsh,' Dustin growled. 'I may have been a little slow in the fathering department, but I don't see you being too eager for a bunch of rug rats, either.'

'Nope. Can't see it myself,' Marsh said cheerfully. 'I do see Jill being hellaciously beautiful with a big nine-month belly, though.'

'Yeah?' Dustin sat down again, unwilling to be drawn into what he knew was Marsh's attempt to rile him. 'Don't reckon she's going to get pregnant, so I guess you'll have to miss out on the show.'

The doorbell rang, interrupting what Marsh's next jibe would have been. Dustin crossed into the hallway and opened the door.

'Howdy, everybody. Come on in,' he said, taking Mrs McCall's items from her hands. Beside him, his mother appeared. 'Mother, this is Lana and Bob McCall, Jill's folks. Bob, Lana, this is my mother, Eunice Reed. Jill's finishing dressing, but she'll be right down,' Dustin said, taking the things into the kitchen. He could hear the greetings his mother was issuing and Joey's little feet thundering down the stairs to greet the newcomers. In the hall Marsh stood waiting to be introduced.

'This is our local sheriff, Marsh,' Dustin said, giving him a slight shove into the hallway. 'My best friend since way back.'

The McCalls shook Marsh's hand and he beamed at them. 'The Reeds have been looking forward to your visit. I think you'll find your daughter is in the best of hands,' Marsh said.

Lana looked a little startled, Dustin noticed. He shot a frown Marsh's way. 'Have a seat in the parlor, please. I think Jill's set out some snacks for us.'

'Your home is beautiful,' Lana told Eunice.

'Thank you. You'll be interested to know that your daughter is responsible for the festive atmosphere in this room.' Eunice pointed to the various holiday decorations. 'We so appreciate you letting us have her for a while. She's brought so much happiness to our home.'

'Oh, I'm so glad.' The delight on Lana and Bob's face was easy to see. They were crazy about their youngest child. If they knew that Jill's ex had been by just moments ago and how badly he'd upset their daughter, they'd have a fit.

Dustin cleared his throat. 'I'll go check on Jill and see if she needs any help with Holly,' he said.

The truth was, Jill was taking longer than he'd expected. With the additional ringing of the doorbell, he was certain she'd have hotfooted it downstairs. Maybe she needed a good, strong shoulder to lean on more than he'd realized.

Dustin went upstairs, hesitating outside her bedroom door. He knocked lightly. She didn't answer, so Dustin walked to Joey's room. There was no Jill, no baby Holly being readied in a last-minute frenzy in there.

The sound of retching in the connecting bathroom startled Dustin. After a second, he realized Jill was in there, obviously very sick to her stomach. He wasn't sure she'd eaten breakfast, having been busy with the preparations, so she likely hadn't eaten something that disagreed with her. Dustin moved to the door, uncertain as to what to do. He'd known City Boy had upset her, but enough to make her that sick?

I do see Jill being hellaciously beautiful with a big nine-month belly. Marsh's words came back to hit him with the force of a storm gale. Dustin bowed his head, wondering if they were all going to have the opportunity to find out.

He felt a little ill himself, just thinking on it.

CHAPTER 9

Silently, Dustin walked away from the door. Of course, he should make certain she didn't need any assistance. But knowing Jill, she'd be plenty furious if she knew that her private moment of suffering had been witnessed.

Dustin went down the stairs, promising himself that if she wasn't down in five minutes, he was going to make Jill let him in. Or at least, reassure him that she was going to be okay.

Exactly four minutes forty-five seconds later, according to Dustin's watch, Jill came down the stairs. She walked into the parlor with a smile on her face and Holly propped up on her shoulder, looking like a madonna to Dustin's worried eyes. Jill didn't look like a woman who'd just been heaving her insides. He shot a critical eye over her body, but all he could see was shiny blond hair waving gently at her chin, emphasizing her sparkling smile. Her skin perhaps was a trifle paler than normal, but her blue eyes were as large and luminous as ever. But still, after she finished kissing her folks in welcome, she turned, her eyes meeting his and lightning fast, her gaze skittered away.

What the hell was going on? Dustin wondered. Had he said something to make her want to avoid him?

His mother got up, taking the baby from Jill's arms. 'Eunice says you've done all this decorating yourself, Jill,' Lana said. 'Everything looks wonderful.'

Jill shook her head, sitting down on a chair near Joey. She pointed to his son. 'This little fellow here is responsible for the beauty of that tree –' she pointed to the table-top tree whose branches still sported the lopsided effect of silver ornaments bunched on one side and gold on the other – 'as well as that tree, which he and his father not only cut down but decorated as well. I can't take credit for any of it.'

'Your daughter's very modest,' Eunice said. 'We don't know what we would have done without her this Christmas season. Jill, are you ready for us to adjourn to the table?'

'Yeah! Let's . . . let's eat,' Joey shouted.

'It sounds like we have some hearty appetites here. I'd better get a move on.'

Jill stood, her smile even, but Dustin wondered if perhaps it seemed a bit forced.

In five minutes, Jill, Lana, and Eunice – after handing the baby over to Dustin – had all the hot dishes set on the sideboard. 'We're going to be informal today and let everyone serve themselves,'

Jill announced. 'There's tea, water, or wine, which I'll pour, if everyone will tell me what they want.'

Drink requests were turned in, and Jill went to the kitchen to fill them. Dustin handed the baby off to Marsh, who accepted her as gracefully as if Dustin had handed him a moldy head of lettuce. 'You've got to work, too, if you're going to mooch,' Dustin told him before hurrying after Jill.

Jill was in the kitchen putting ice cubes in glasses, her back to him as he approached. 'Jill,' he said softly.

'Oh, my!' Turning startled eyes on him, she said, 'My mind was obviously elsewhere.'

'I . . .' Oh, to hell with it. Why beat around the bush? 'Jill, are you okay?' he asked.

'Yes. Don't I look all right?'

'You look . . .' He started to say beautiful, then realized that probably would go over like a lead balloon, no matter how true it was. 'You look fine. A little pale, maybe.'

'Oh.' She shook her head, returning her attention to pouring the drinks. 'Maybe I didn't put on enough blusher. Would you mind carrying these out to the kitchen?'

Dustin took the glasses, casting one last look over his housekeeper. Lack of make-up wasn't the problem, but she was obviously going to stick to that story. There was no way he could tell her what he'd heard. What little he knew about Jill told him she wasn't receptive to broadcasting her personal life around. And she would never, for crying out loud, tell him she was pregnant, if that were the case.

Because plainly she wasn't going to tell anyone.

Lunch was an ordeal Dustin got through only by keeping his mind on a million other things. The McCalls were a wonderful family, but it did put him a bit on edge feeling like he was eating with the all-American family. He walked outside to the fence line after inviting Bob to go with him. Bob had declined, instead choosing to dry dishes while his daughter and wife washed. Obviously, there was going to be a family pow-wow in the kitchen. Dustin could only hope that Jill's parents weren't going to try to get her to return with them permanently. Then he'd have to advertise for another housekeeper, and that was getting to be a drag. Especially when he finally had one that fit their family better than he'd ever expected.

Outside, the sky was grey and lined with white, stringy clouds, confirming the cool, crisp feeling of winter in Dustin's bones. No matter how warm the house, no matter how cheery the company, he still felt cold. A big-eyed steer moved its heavy girth toward him, less fearful than the other cattle. Dustin stared the steer down, but it came closer anyway.

Kind of like Jill, always edging closer to that empty space in his soul.

'Didn't you get enough to eat?' Marsh asked, coming to rest his arms on the fence beside

Dustin. He pointed at the steer. 'That's a big piece of meat, even for a tall guy like you.'

'I ate enough. I didn't think you were going to fill up that cavern you call a gut though.'

Marsh grinned. 'Why go hungry when there's all that good food for a man to eat?'

'You ought to get married.' Dustin's voice was sandpaper-rough. 'Then you might not have to mooch off my table so much.'

'Nope. What I need is a cook, which I can't afford on a sheriff's salary.'

Dustin snorted. 'Don't poor-mouth to me. We've made plenty of money selling steers the last couple of years. You've got no woman to erode your profits, so don't tell me your bottom line isn't healthy these days.'

He felt Marsh's gaze narrow on him. 'Your head more sore than usual today? Got indigestion?'

'No.' Dustin knew he was being a bear, but he also knew Marsh was tough enough – and friend enough – to take it.

'No wonder Jill isn't smiling much, if you've been so lovely to be around.'

Dustin stared at his friend, ignoring the jab. 'You noticed? You noticed she doesn't seem very happy, like she's not quite herself?'

'Would you notice if the sun didn't come up tomorrow?' Marsh sounded surprised.

'Are you sure you don't have a thing for my housekeeper?' The thought tore at Dustin again, as it had the other night in the bar.

'As much as being in-laws to the McCalls might appeal, the answer is no, I most certainly do not have a thing for your housekeeper. I happen to have my eye on China Shea.'

'China? The red-haired China we went to school with? The one that never acknowledged your presence after you said with legs like hers she'd either be a Las Vegas showgirl or a hooker?'

Marsh looked embarrassed. 'I wish I hadn't said that.'

Dustin crooked a brow. 'I know you do. She flat-handed you into the next county. You looking for another slap?'

His friend crossed his arms with a stubborn expression. 'I'm just trying to ease your concern about whether my eye is following Jill around. It may be, but not because I'm attracted to her. Now. Get back to Jill and the ex.'

Dustin threw one last undecided glance Marsh's way, before sighing. 'There really isn't anything else to the story. Jill wasn't too happy to see him, but other than that, it was sort of a non-event.'

'Hm. The lady lays tracks when she's done.'

'Meaning?'

Marsh picked up a piece of dead winter grass from the ground, absently sticking it in his mouth. 'Girl is through with boy, girl packs bag and heads north to start over. Appears to be cut and dried, for girl. We won't be calling her Second-Thoughts Jilly.'

'That's what he called her.'

'Second-thoughts Jilly?' Marsh looked amazed.

'No. Jilly. Boy called her Jilly.'

'So? Who cares what he does? He's history.'

Dustin shook his head. 'She does not look like a Jilly to me. That is not a nickname kind of woman.'

Marsh mulled that over. 'You're right. I mean, you might call her babe or honey if you had her in the sa – '

'Shut up,' Dustin growled, completely aware of what Marsh was about to say. 'You get my drift.'

'Yes, I do,' Marsh said cheerfully. 'Jill is not a Jilly-girl. But I still don't get what's eating you. Unless City Boy managed to get some of that mistletoe action going that you were deprived of. And you're not telling me.'

'Hell, no. I'm not jealous, so don't start with that crap. Jill was in the bathroom throwing up, and it's got me worried.'

'Oh.' Marsh raised his eyebrows. 'The plot thickens.'

'Hellfire,' Dustin said, rubbing his neck with an impatient hand. 'Why did I think you'd be any help?'

'So she ate a bad egg for breakfast. Why the alarm bells for that?' Marsh said, ignoring Dustin's comment.

'She didn't eat breakfast.'

'Well, then . . . she's got appendicitis. Or the flu. Hell, I don't know. Why do you care, anyway?'

Dustin was too embarrassed to mention what insidious thought had been roving around in his head. 'Forget it,' he said roughly.

Marsh punched him in the arm. 'I told you she was too good to be true. Your housekeeper throws up after she sees her ex-fiancé's ugly mug. Jill's just too damn normal for you, that's the problem.'

Dustin perked up. 'You think that could be it? She doesn't strike me as the nervous type.'

'Well, it's possible. I mean, women throw up when they're sick, nervous, and pregnant.' Marsh paused for several moments, before fixing him with a stern stare. 'I don't suppose you're moody as all hell because you're worried your housekeeper might be pregnant?'

He pursed his lips before biting out a reply. 'Maybe.'

'Ah.' Marsh rolled his neck, before looking up at the sky. 'Shades of Nina.'

'I'm just saying you didn't have to give Carl my address, Mother. I'm not angry with you. I just didn't want to see him.'

Lana looked distressed. Bob looked even more so. 'We thought we were doing the right thing, dear. We had no idea he'd show up without phoning. But he seems so heartbroken . . .'

Jill shook her head. 'Carl is many things, but he is not heartbroken. I know you meant well, but please, don't do anything like that again. Let's all make a solemn vow to remember that Jill is a smart woman, a woman with a degree and who once held a nice paying job, not just the baby in the family whom everyone needs to take care of. I canceled my wedding because I realized my fiancé was a poor choice. I call that a smart decision.'

'Yes, dear.' Lana fluttered her dish towel toward her eyes, before remembering that it wasn't for drying her tears. She snatched up a tissue instead. 'We're sorry we caused you any distress. We just worry so.'

'You would have worried a lot more if I'd married him, believe me,' Jill muttered. 'Carl was only interested in the fact that I was a successful business woman. I made him look good. It would have been much too beneath him to be seen with someone from the secretarial pool.' Of course, it hadn't been beneath him to sleep with them.

'Oh, I'm sure that couldn't be . . .' At Jill's quelling look, Lana hesitated. 'Well, I suppose it doesn't matter now. What matters is that you're happy. Are you, dear?'

'I think so.' Jill ran more water into the sink, pausing only when she thought she'd heard baby Holly cry out. But Eunice was watching her, so she was in good hands. Eunice would call if she needed Jill.

'We're just a little concerned, honey, that you'd choose to do this . . . this maid's work when, as you mentioned, you were a successful business woman. You didn't study all those years to wind up being a housekeeper.'

Jill sighed. 'Look. I love both of you. I know you're thinking of my well-being. But I really needed a break. I know it sounds crazy, but I wanted a change of pace. These people *need* me, which is flattering. Does that make sense?'

Her parents exchanged glances.

'This *is* a nice place,' Bob began.

'But, of course, we really don't know these people,' Lana finished his thought. 'I mean, they seem nice enough, especially Eunice, but one never knows. Your father and I are so worried that you just picked up and left, then went to live with strangers. Frankly, we're a little hurt you didn't come home.'

Jill sighed. 'Would your feelings be hurt a little less if I told you I don't want to be the baby anymore? That I need to do things on my own, without everyone in the family doing for me?'

Her father cleared his throat as her parents shared an uncertain look. 'Dear, we haven't wanted to mention this,' Lana said softly, edging closer to Jill, 'but we're a little worried about you living out here with that . . . um, Dustin.'

'Why?' Jill shot her mother a questioning glance.

'Well, he, ah . . . he's not what we're used to, maybe. I mean, here's our soft-hearted little daughter, going out to the boonies to live with this man. You have to admit he's awfully overwhelming. So tall, and dark, and well, he doesn't smile much, does he?'

Jill frowned. No, Dustin didn't smile much. But it was the first Christmas since his wife had died, and that alone gave him a reason not to feel like ringing in the holiday season. She thought he'd made a giant effort on everyone's behalf –

especially hers – to ignore his own pain. He had a new baby living in his home that cried sometimes and which he knew absolutely nothing about, except that she might be in danger. Nothing to smile about there. And though he hadn't said it to her, his whole demeanor turned much gruffer when Joey's other grandparents were mentioned. Especially when it was time for Joey to visit them, as it was tonight. Sunday evenings, Dustin had explained, as well as Wednesday evenings, were the Copelands' time with Joey. No, she supposed the man didn't smile a lot.

'Dustin is a quiet man,' Jill said. 'He works his cattle so much of the time that I only see him at meals. Eunice and Joey, and baby Holly while she's here, are really the biggest part of my job.'

'Oh, we're so relieved,' Lana said, speaking for Bob as well. Her father bobbed his head in agreement. 'We were so worried you might rebound too quickly. Dustin's quite the opposite of Carl in appearance, and . . . well, you know . . . personality.'

Oh, yeah. That hadn't been too much of a leap for even her sweet-minded mother. Jill had gotten a chance to observe the difference between the two men just this morning, more than she'd ever wanted. Carl had seemed skinny and rather pasty next to Dustin's outdoors, healthy-all-over physique. Just thinking about it shot a lightning strike of desire through her. But being turned on by a man wasn't a reason to fall for him.

'I'm not on the rebound, Mother. The last thing I want is to give my heart to another man, only to find I'd made a mistake.'

'Oh, you are being so sensible, Jill. We were alarmed that you might fall for that dark air of mystery Dustin has.'

'Oh, please! There's nothing mysterious about the man, except that he works hard and is trying to get over his wife's death. I'm not going to fall for him any more than he'd fall for me.'

'You see why we'd worry, though. He might be looking for a new mother for his son . . .'

'Mother, please!'

'Well, subconsciously anyway, Jill. I mean, one has to wonder, and it's so odd that they're keeping a baby they know nothing about. And here you are, knocking yourself out to be a nursemaid, but that might be appealing to a man who . . .'

'Mother, he *hired* me to take care of this family, which pretty much means he wouldn't have to marry me to get what he wanted, which was help. Don't you think?'

'A wife would be much cheaper,' Bob inserted. 'No payroll.'

'Daddy!' Jill was astonished.

'Your father has a point,' Lana said primly. 'Though he's more generous to me than he sounds, the truth is, his concern is valid. We want you to think about things before you leap from the fire into the frying pan.'

'There is nothing to think about,' Jill said tightly.

'I'm staying here for a year, as I agreed to do. Then, I'm getting my bonus, and I'm leaving.'

'How's everything coming along in here?' Eunice asked, walking slowly into the kitchen with baby Holly in her arms.

'Here. Let me take her,' Jill said, going to take the infant. She shot an assessing glance Eunice's way, wondering if she had overheard any of the conversation brewing in the kitchen.

Eunice's face was unconcerned as she picked up an empty cup to put away. 'Lana, your strawberry bread was wonderful.'

Lana's face relaxed into a genuine smile. It was obvious that her parents' problem wasn't with Eunice, but with the grim-eyed rancher who'd sat and stared at Jill for most of the meal. She walked into the parlor to gaze out the window at the two men leaning against the fence rail. She'd been able to feel Dustin's stare on her on several occasions, and could only wonder about it. Not once had he smiled at her, though he wasn't prone to doing that, anyway. Still, he'd seemed very remote, a fact her parents had obviously picked up on.

She sighed, patting Holly's back in a soothing motion. Touching this baby was a wonderful experience. All the soft skin and fat-padded appendages soothed Jill whenever she held her. Joey sat in front of the tree coloring in a cartoon book, and Jill smiled. He was a good boy, another source of contentment for her. Plainly, Dustin was discovering that his son was a joy to be around, although he didn't completely have the knack of it. Something still seemed to be holding him back from any show of pure affection when it came to his son.

So the man was a trifle grumpy, not just with her but with everyone, except his mother. Even Marsh suffered his share of Dustin's grouchiness. Yet the sheriff seemed willing to bear the burden, as evidenced by his continued presence.

Maybe Dustin hadn't always been this way. Maybe once he'd been a more easygoing man, just as she'd been a more trusting woman. The reason their set-up was operating well was that they both understood that anything more than a working relationship was absolutely out of the question.

No matter how much help they needed from each other.

After Joey's nap that afternoon, Jill packed his clothes into a small suitcase. Folding a few small shirts and pants made her feel something she couldn't remember feeling before. Oh, Holly brought her a rush of warmth whenever she held her, but as she'd tucked Joey's miniature versions of Dustin's clothing away, a strange day-dream had overtaken her. She'd actually found herself thinking about how it would feel to always be there for Joey, to always clean and fold his clothes, and put them away.

Startled, she'd closed the suitcase with a snap, realizing the disastrous turn her thoughts had taken. The child was starting to mean a lot to her, and uncomfortably, Jill knew she had actually dreamed for a moment about becoming his new mother.

She couldn't do that without involving Dustin, however, so whatever fantasies she had about loving Joey and watching him grow into a man would simply have to stay locked inside her head.

'Are Joey's things ready?'

Jill jumped at the sound of Dustin's deep voice interrupting her thoughts. She nodded, telling her heart to stop racing from the abrupt appearance of her employer. 'Yes. Here's his suitcase, and here's his favorite bear.'

Dustin reached out to take the things from her. Without saying a word, he walked from the room and went down the stairs.

She knew Joey was already there, waiting and dressed in the clean outfit Jill had put on him after his nap. The child had been tuckered out after all the excitement of having company in the house for Sunday supper, and he'd looked a bit rumpled. After changing him, she'd slicked his hair – to no avail – but with every intention of making Dustin proud of his son.

Even as he had to tell Joey goodbye.

The doorbell rang, and Jill halted at the landing. She hovered there, feeling out of place during this odd and uncomfortable family moment. She heard a woman's shrill voice greet Joey, then a few sentences of muffled conversation from Dustin. A moment later, the front door closed. An eerie silence descended upon the house.

Dustin's heavy tread at the bottom of the stairs threw Jill into action. Hurrying into her room, she closed the door, knowing that he wouldn't want to attempt to make conversation with her right now. Eunice was in her bedroom with Holly. Jill had heard Eunice tell Dustin that she didn't want Maxine to see the baby. Dustin would probably head straight to his mother's room to tell her what had been said between himself and Maxine.

'Jill.'

Dustin's voice outside her door surprised her. She opened it, immediately checking his expression for his mood. His face was impassive.

'Yes, Dustin?'

'Thanks.'

Jill was puzzled. 'For what?'

'For packing Joey's things for me.'

'I . . . um, you're welcome. It's part of my job.'

It was also part of her pleasure, but she couldn't say that.

'Would you like the evening off?'

'Well . . .' She hesitated, realizing that with Joey gone, her hands would be a little emptier. She wasn't any happier about the thought than Dustin was. Somehow, all the holiday excitement had gone right out of the house with Joey's departure. 'Maybe I'll take Holly into town for a stroll.'

'Mother and I can watch her tonight. You worked hard on the meal today. Why don't you just take some time off?'

Jill shook her head. There was no reason for her to

151

do that. If anyone needed some time to themselves, it was Eunice and Dustin. 'No, thank you, although I appreciate the offer. I'd really enjoy myself a lot more if I took Holly with me. We'll go for a stroll around the town square and see what decorations are out.'

Dustin shrugged. 'Suit yourself. Let me know if you change your mind.'

He walked down the hall into Eunice's room. Their voice tones carried to Jill, though she couldn't hear the words. She could hear, however, their unhappiness. With Joey gone, there would be no laughter in the house tonight.

Changing into a pair of jeans and a bright blue knit sweater, Jill fluffed her hair and put on some clear lipstick to keep her lips from chapping in the cold. Then she went to retrieve Holly.

At her knock, Eunice called, 'Come in.'

Jill went in, a trifle amazed to see Dustin sitting on the vanity chair, holding a drooling Holly. Eunice sat in a stuffed chair nearby and she smiled when she saw Jill.

'You look very nice, my dear. Rather wasted on baby Holly, I should think. Why don't you let us keep her tonight? Or better yet, why don't you let Dustin take you to a movie?'

Jill's and Dustin's gazes met in a collision of shock. Watch a movie, in complete darkness, with a man whose son she was starting to love too much? With his father, whose fine physique and handsome face she struggled not to notice?

Dustin was too polite to utter the shocked denial

she was sure he'd like to issue. Jill shook her head, reaching to take the baby from him. 'No, thank you, although it's nice of you to offer. I'm going to change Holly into a nice outfit, and then we two wild women are going out on the town to show off our duds. Aren't we, Miss Lady?' she murmured. Turning at the door, Jill said, 'We'll see you later, though.'

Dustin and his mother murmured a goodbye and Jill hurried off down the hall. No, being alone with Dustin would not have been a good thing for either of them. He was miserable without his son, and she was miserable knowing it. They neither one would have a good time, especially trying to act like they were comfortable around each other.

Jill put the satin headband on Holly that Eunice had made her, then changed the infant's diaper before slipping a nice, warm wool dress over her head. White tights and booties completed the look. 'Now, we're ready to see the town,' Jill told the baby.

Carefully strapping Holly into the car seat and making certain the umbrella stroller was in the trunk, Jill started off down the road. She happened to glance into her rearview mirror, and though she wasn't completely certain, it looked like Dustin's large form was standing in the doorway, watching them leave.

For a moment she felt guilty, leaving the two of them alone in that big house. It was going to be awfully quiet. Probably unbearably quiet. But surely they'd spent many an evening like that, with each other for company. Eunice and Dustin would probably treasure one night without children underfoot, as well as minus the housekeeper.

Jill drove slowly into town, enjoying the beauty of the winter countryside. Holly's eyes followed everything that went past her vision. Obviously, she was pleased to be out of the house as much as Jill was.

The truth was, she *had* needed to get away. Carl showing up this morning had upset her so badly she just needed to find some space and think. How could a man she thought loved her betray her in such a manner? How had she missed his controlling nature? Oh, certainly, some warning bells had begun sounding a few months ago, when it was clear that her feelings had begun to change. But never, never had she imagined he would sabotage her career as well as her pride. At the ripe old age of twenty-six, it occurred to Jill that she might never find that man she could trust with all her soul.

'Prince Charming was really a hallucination of some wishful writer,' she told Holly wryly. 'Although –' she shot a look at the baby who was now looking in the direction of Jill's voice – 'if I didn't know better, I'd think you had managed to entice Mr Reed with those cute dimples and fat wrinkled arms and legs of yours.'

Holly sneezed, and Jill laughed. 'Okay. It's your mind he's fallen for.'

Maneuvering the car into one of the angled parking spaces situated around the town square, Jill got out of the car. Retrieving the stroller from the trunk, she unstrapped Holly and placed her in it carefully.

154

Locking the car, Jill wrapped Holly's pink blanket around her, leaving only her little face peeking out.

'There. We are a pair of wild and crazy women,' she told her cheerfully.

After thirty minutes she'd made it around the square. Holly was intrigued by the twinkling Christmas lights, and the foil wreaths and bells adorning the street lights. But Jill worried she might start getting cold, so seeing the bakery shop at the end of their journey, she pushed the stroller inside.

A blast of warmth and the inviting aroma of baked bread made Jill sigh with contentment. 'Oh, this was the right choice, Holly. We'll have us a little snack, and take home a loaf of bread for dinner tomorrow night,' she said, slipping the blanket away from Holly's head so she wouldn't be too hot inside the store.

From the corner of the store, a shop assistant approached shyly, her gaze riveted on the baby in the stroller. Jill was proud of her charge, all dressed up and looking so pretty as she lay in the stroller. Obviously, the assistant thought so, too, as she came closer to take a look.

The girl was probably high-school age. Not old enough to want to cuddle the infant as a grandmother might. Still, she smiled at the smitten expression on the girl's face.

'This is Holly,' Jill said to make conversation, 'and she's come to buy a loaf of bread from you.' She started to request some of the delicious-looking rolls sitting behind the glass as well, but the way the girl had crept close to the stroller made Jill pause. In all her life, she'd never seen anyone look so . . . fascinated. Holly was beautiful, but the way the girl reached out with a trembling finger to stroke the baby's cheek melted Jill's heart.

'Isn't she lovely?' she said.

Briefly, the girl glanced up before immediately gazing back down raptly into the stroller. 'Oh, I think she is.' Lightly, her fingers traced over the pink blanket, feeling the baby's warm, fat tummy. 'Could I . . . could I hold her?'

Jill hesitated, but couldn't think of any reason to deny this request. Besides, it would be good for Holly to be out of the stroller for a while. 'If you'll be extra careful,' she said, lifting the baby gently from the stroller. Handing the baby to the girl, Jill smiled at the pure happiness on her face. Holly did seem to make everyone feel that way. She herself experienced that same feeling of wonder whenever she held her.

The girl snuggled Holly against her neck, closing her eyes for just a moment. Jill stared, thinking that she'd never seen anyone so starved for love. Maybe the girl was an only child, lacking siblings to lessen childhood loneliness.

Dustin had grown up as an only child. Eunice had pointed out he'd been lonely for brothers and sisters to tease. And to love.

'Thank you ever so much,' the girl said, shyly handing Holly back to Jill.

'You're welcome. She feels good, doesn't she?'

156

'Like heaven.'

The girl's voice was almost a sigh. Jill tucked Holly back in, after checking to make certain her diaper was still dry. 'I want to pick up a loaf of that French bread, and maybe some of those rolls,' she said, after settling Holly.

Anxious to please, the girl scurried back behind the counter. She put the bread and rolls into a white paper bag, taking Jill's money and putting it into the register.

'Thank you very much,' she said politely. Her gaze dropped to the baby again. 'For everything.'

'Thank you for the bread,' Jill said. 'Goodbye.' Turning the stroller, she opened the door and pushed it out into the slowly darkening night.

Without realizing it, she nearly pushed the stroller into a bystander. 'Oh, excuse me,' Jill said, horrified that she had nearly hit the man. He stared at her without saying a word, then his gaze fastened on the baby. His perusal held just as much hungry interest as the girl's had possessed, but there was no innocence in his eyes.

His head was shaved and he wore a gold loop earring in one ear. When he looked back up at her, Jill was shocked by the flat coldness in his gaze. Backing the stroller up, her vision deflected from the man to the bakery store window. The shop girl was staring out at them, her mouth frozen in a shocked O.

Alarmed, Jill realized she might have put baby Holly in grave danger. Without another thought, she

157

jammed the stroller forward, skidding around the black-jacketed man whose wide-legged, aggressive stance took up the better part of the concrete walk. Her blood on fire with fear, Jill hurried toward her car.

CHAPTER 10

Her movements stiff and panicked, Jill snatched her keys from her shoulderbag as she tried to walk as normally as possible toward her worn-out car. There had to be a way to get Holly into her car seat without giving that sinister looking man a chance to grab her. The stroller could be abandoned if need be.

Telling herself to be calm and not to overreact, Jill shuffled the bag of bread and her purse down to her wrist as she unlocked the car door. Too frightened to look up to see if she'd been followed, she tossed her things to the car floor. Swiftly, she picked Holly up and fastened her into the car seat, all the while acting as though she weren't petrified out of her wits. Risking a quick peek, she saw that the man had gone into the bakery and was locked in confrontation with the shop girl. Jill could see her head moving back and forth in an emphatically negative response to whatever the man was asking her. He glanced toward Jill's car, pointing purposefully. Jill grabbed the stroller and collapsed it, throwing it to the floor of the car to land on the sack of bread and her purse.

Jumping into the front seat, she frantically checked to make certain all four doors were locked. She jammed the key into the ignition and hit the pedal, causing the car engine to roar to life. The man had come out onto the pavement and was heading toward her car. Jill gasped, threw the car into reverse as she backed out of the parking space. Praying there was no innocent pedestrian in front or behind her, she threw the gear into drive. Crushing the gas pedal, Jill sped away, peripherally aware of the man's running form beside her car. He slapped once at the window – hard.

'Oh, Lord!' she cried. Holly set up a wail from the back seat. Not about to slow down, Jill ignored the just-turned yellow signal at the crossing, hurtling away from what she was certain was Holly's nightmare. The child had been entrusted to her safekeeping; not for anything would she let Eunice and Dustin down – nor Holly. Her gaze kept bouncing to the rearview mirror, even though it appeared she hadn't been followed.

Driving at a faster pace than she normally would have, Jill held her breath until she knew she was getting close to home. Despite the early darkness of winter twilight, she could see the white, crushed rock trail leading up to Dustin's ranch like a ghostly pointing finger. Jill's breath finally eased from where it had lodged in her throat as she drove under the metal sign from which the R and E swung haphazardly in the night wind.

The fear gradually lessened, though her blood still pounded in her throat. Even as she stopped the car and got out, snatching Holly from her car seat to hurry toward the porch steps, Jill was aware of the feeling of security that washed through her mind. She'd made it to the ranch, and Dustin wouldn't let anything happen to Holly.

Tearing through the front door with the baby clutched in her arms, Jill hurried through the entry, halting when she saw Dustin and his mother in the parlor.

'Jill, honey, what's wrong?' Eunice asked.

'I . . .' She glanced down at pretty little Holly in her arms, her headband now askew on the wailing face. With gentle fingers, she pulled it off the baby. 'I think I stumbled across Holly's parents,' she said.

'What?'

Dustin was instantly concerned. Eunice walked over and took the baby from Jill, cooing to her as she left the parlor. The sounds of her getting a bottle ready wafted from the kitchen.

'Sit down and tell me what happened.'

It was an order her stiff legs couldn't obey. 'I'm not sure. I went to buy some bread, and I let the girl hold Holly for a minute. Maybe I wasn't thinking very clearly, but she was so hungry, Dustin, she was so hungry . . .'

Jill was mortified to feel tears starting to slip down her cheeks, but she couldn't stop them.

'The baby was hungry so you were going to get her a loaf of bread?' he asked.

She shook her head, realizing she was muddling the story with her rapid-fire speech. Trying to take a

161

deep breath so she could slow down and make sense, Jill felt more tears squeezing from her eyes. The shock of what had happened was sending queasy shivers through her legs.

'Here, it's all right,' he said, coming to close her into big, strong arms. 'Don't cry, babe. What does this girl have to do with the baby being hungry?'

Against Dustin's wide, flannel-covered chest, Jill let everything pour out, every detail. 'Holly wasn't hungry. The girl, she had such longing in her eyes that I . . . well, I don't suppose I acted wisely, but I could actually feel her yearning to touch the baby. I was so proud of Holly and she is quite adorable . . . it never occurred to me that the girl might be Holly's mother. I let her hold the baby.'

She turned tear-soaked eyes on Dustin. He felt the impact clear to his knees. He'd never seen cool, rational Jill, the lady who had brought a sense of calm to the ranch, act like this. Distraught, irrational, emotional were words that came to mind at this moment. But the Jill he knew wasn't an irrational person. This had upset her greatly. He glanced down and saw her bottom lip tremble slightly, and resisted the urge to make her feel better by kissing her.

'Slow down a little. You haven't done anything wrong. I don't see how you could have run into her mother. Are you sure something else didn't happen that upset you this way?'

Jill's fingers clenched on his biceps. He felt the tension in her.

'No, Dustin. I think it was her. There was a man

162

outside when we were leaving. I nearly ran into him with the stroller. A second later he was having an argument with the girl in the bakery, but then he came out and ran after my car. Oh, Dustin, I have never been so terrified in my entire life.'

She laid her head against his chest. He gritted his teeth against the trembling he could feel her trying to control. Jill was scared to death.

Eunice came into the room, carrying a tray. 'Well, Holly took her bottle and went to sleep, obviously unaware of her predicament. There's something to be said for you keeping such a cool head, Jill, that you got her and yourself home safely.'

'It was too close.' Jill tensed in Dustin's arms. 'When I saw him running beside my car, I thought my heart would stop.'

Dustin felt a violent trembling go all the way through her.

'Here's some hot chocolate, Jill, although if you want something stronger, we still have wine left over from lunch. There's some whiskey in the bar that goes nicely in hot tea. I'm certain we could all use a bit of fortification right now.'

Jill shook her head, detaching herself from Dustin's arms to take one of the cups and go to sit on the sofa. 'Thank you. I think this is just what I need, plus a few minutes in front of the fire.'

'Did you happen to get the girl's name, Jill?' Eunice asked curiously.

Dustin saw Jill's brows crease into a frown. 'I don't even think she was wearing a name-tag. I'm

163

so sorry, Eunice, I wasn't being as careful as I should have been.'

'Nonsense. If anything, perhaps Dustin and I shouldn't have let you go into town alone. I certainly never dreamed you'd run into anyone connected to Holly, but still you shouldn't be a prisoner in this house.'

'Mother's right,' Dustin agreed. 'We'll just have to think of another way to get Holly out and about. Right now, I'm going to call Marsh, though.'

Dustin left Jill in his mother's capable hands, satisfied that his housekeeper was starting to calm down. Dialing the sheriff's car phone, he spoke only one sentence. 'Jill found herself some trouble in town, Marsh.'

'I'll be right over.'

Dustin hung up. He left the kitchen, confident that Marsh would be on the case. With Jill's quick action, she had avoided a situation that could have jeopardized Holly – if the man had managed to wrest the baby away from her. The woman was truly impressive. Her job should not require her to endanger herself or perform heroic acts, and he felt guilty about that. Maybe he *would* slip a little combat pay in her stocking, just as she'd once teased. Turning out the light in the kitchen, Dustin went back to the parlor, seating himself less than one foot away from Jill on the divan. Until he was certain she was fine, he was going to be her shadow.

At the bottom of the drive, a black-jacketed motor-cycle rider watched the kitchen light go off. The

164

porch light was still on, as if the Reeds were expecting company. Well, they weren't expecting *him*, but the warm beam of light would give out enough illumination for a check of the dilapidated car parked next to the house. Creeping forward on silent feet, the stranger confirmed the car was the blond-haired beauty's.

When he spied the infant car seat in the back, he laughed, a low, evil sound of triumph.

'It was horrible, Mama! He ran after her car, and I thought he was going to catch her! I thought I would die watching! I wanted to call the police, but I didn't know if I should, and . . .'

'Here, now. Calm down, gal. That lady knew what she was doing,' Vera Benchley told her daughter as she patted her on the back in soothing circles. 'They're home safe now, and I assure you, Eunice and Dustin aren't going to let anything happen to our sweet baby.'

Sadie tried to control her shaking but she couldn't. The tremors went through her like swift electrical currents. 'How do I know, Mama? How do *you* know? I can't bear this anymore! Holly felt like a misty angel in my arms, so fat and sweet. She smelled like powder and love and . . . I can't stand knowing that Curtis might get her, Mama! I'd never see her again.'

Vera shook her daughter, once, and pushed her down into a chair. 'Pull yourself together, gal. We'll figure out what to do.'

Sadie twisted her fingers in her lap. She couldn't stop thinking about Curtis running after her baby. 'How do you know, Mama, that Miss Eunice will still want to help after what happened tonight? She may not like her housekeeper being frightened like that.'

Vera sat next to her daughter and pulled her daughter close. 'Miss Eunice doesn't lack for courage, Sadie. She's a strong lady.'

'How do you know her so well? Have you even spoken to her recently?'

Her mother shook her head. 'No. But with some friends, the connection is always there. It isn't a matter of how often you talk, or where either of you live. It's something in the heart, that you just know the friendship will always be there. And it will be there until we die, honey, between me and Eunice.'

Sadie didn't understand how one of the town's richest girls and her poor mother could have much in common, least of all a deep, lasting friendship. 'How? How could you have ever known her? Or become a friend?'

Her mother smiled softly as she pulled a gentle hand through Sadie's hair. 'I might not have, we might never have been more than class-mates, if she hadn't borrowed my shoes one night.'

Sadie glanced down at the worn low-heeled shoes her mother was wearing, suitable for walking into town since they didn't own a car. It was impossible to imagine tall, elegant Mrs Reed wearing a pair of Vera Benchley's working shoes. Vera and Eunice might be approximately the same height and possibly near the same shoe size, but they were nowhere near the same station in life.

'Why would she need to borrow your shoes?' Sadie asked, trying not to sound as incredulous as she was. The last thing she wanted to do was hurt her mother's feelings.

Vera chuckled, the sound low and amused. 'Because on Homecoming night, the night beautiful Eunice Sinclair was going to be crowned Queen – everyone knew it – somebody cut the heels off Eunice's shoes and then sprayed them orange. They were ruined beyond hope, and needless to say, didn't match Eunice's stunning navy and white satin gown at all.'

'Oh, Mama!' Sadie couldn't imagine anyone doing such a thing. 'Who would have done that to her?'

The smile completely erased from her mother's face. 'Maxine Copeland, of course. Any day of her life, any breath she's ever breathed, Maxine Copeland would have given her soul to trade with Eunice Sinclair Reed.'

'So, what did you do?'

Vera shrugged. 'I happened to pass by the room that Eunice was dressing in. She'd just discovered the shoes and was telling her mother in a loud, strong voice that she'd walk barefoot onto the field. Peeking in, I saw Eunice patting her tiny mother's shoulder, assuring her that everything was going to be fine.'

Vera paused, and when she spoke again, her voice was quiet and dreamy. 'Listening to Eunice comfort

167

her mother in her own moment of misfortune, I thought she was the most amazing person I'd ever seen. Completely unselfish. And, oh, Sadie, she looked like a queen standing there, with her hair swept up into an elegant chignon and a smile for her mother's sake. It was as if a hand pushed into my back and forced me into their private moment.'

Vera shook her head. 'I walked into the room, uncertain as to what to say. Eunice looked at me with that gentle smile of hers, which I never saw on any of the other rich girl's faces. Somehow I stuttered out that she could borrow my shoes.'

'Were they pretty, Mama?' Sadie whispered.

Her mother laughed softly. 'No, child. They weren't pretty at all. But they were shoes, and they were the right size. Eunice slipped them on and declared them perfect. She said she wouldn't lift the skirt of her gown too much as she walked and no one would ever know. Fortunately, my shoes were dark navy, and low-heeled enough to stay hidden.'

'What did you do, Mama?'

'Mrs Sinclair walked me to her car, knowing that I would never dare to go back without shoes to the stadium. The car was parked on enough of a hill though that I could see the girls standing on the football field. I could see the sparkle of the crown in the stadium lights. There I sat until Homecoming was over, and Eunice came to the car wearing the crown only she deserved. Then they drove me home. But before I got out of the car, Eunice pulled me close and told me I had saved her special night.'

Vera snorted. 'The only thing I saved for her was her nylons she would have torn going onto the field barefoot.'

Sadie could see the admiration for Eunice in her mother's eyes even after all these years. 'Were you friends after that?'

'Did we see each other socially? No, gal. We did move in different circles, and I would have been dreadfully uncomfortable had she tried to fit me in. Eunice was graceful enough to understand that. But that night she told me she would never forget what I had done, and if there was ever, ever any way she could help me, I was to ask. I need help now, and I've asked.'

'So many years later, will she remember her promise?' Sadie worried that still they were asking too much. A pair of shoes was one thing; her child's well-being was another.

'I know two things, Sadie. One, is that Eunice is the only person I would trust with Holly. Second is that she is the kind of person who never forgets what she says, and never goes back on her word.'

Vera paused for another moment. 'I would even trust Eunice with knowing that Holly is your baby, except that when we realized she was in danger, I acted quickly and didn't think through the details. I sent her enough of a clue, I think, that she'll know that the baby is my flesh and blood. But in case Curtis comes back, honey, it's best if we aren't seen around the Reed Ranch. We don't want to make him suspicious.'

'He already is, although I denied that the child was mine. Maybe we should tell the police what's happening.'

'We could tell the police, but they might not believe the threat is real. They might make us take her back. How could I ever protect her? Both of you?'

Sadie winced at the sadness in her mother's voice. Desperation was a curse they'd had to deal with. There hadn't seemed to be another way, outside of moving away permanently. Though they'd never spoken it aloud, Sadie knew her mother and she shared the same hope: that one day Curtis would go away, or get put in jail, so they could live in peace. It didn't seem fair to give up their home, shack that it was, and be forced away from what little livelihood they had, just because she'd had the misfortune to fall for the wrong man. 'I know we've done the right – '

Loud banging erupted on the bedroom window, hard enough to shatter the glass. Sadie screamed, barely aware that her mother had thrown her arms around her.

CHAPTER 11

'What was that?' Sadie gasped.

Her mother didn't reply. She stared at the window. 'Did you lock the front door when you came in, Sadie?'

'I don't know. I was so upset I might not have.' She couldn't bear not knowing what was outside her window. 'You go check the door, Mama.'

'Okay.' Vera ran from Sadie's room. She stood, slowly going to the window. Cautiously, she pulled back the second-hand curtain her mother had bought at a garage sale.

Curtis jumped up from his hiding place under the ledge. Sadie bit back a scream, knowing he was deliberately trying to frighten her.

'What do you want?'

'You, babe.' His laughter came through the thin window pane, mean and calculated to hurt.

'Mama's calling the police. You get out of here and don't come around anymore.'

He held his hands up to his heart, faking fear. 'I can only stay a minute, babe. Just wanted to let you know I found our little girl, safe and snug as a bug in a rug up at the Reed Ranch. You really didn't think I'd let that skinny-assed woman have my flesh and blood, did you?'

'You leave her alone, Curtis! That's not my baby and you're going to get yourself in big trouble if you're not careful.'

'Yeah, sure. Hey, how about me and you make another one of those darlin' angels?'

Sadie could hear his sick laughter as she flung the curtain closed. Her mother stood in the bedroom doorway, her expression determined. She held a gun in trembling hands.

'Mama! What are you doing with that shotgun?' Sadie could hardly believe her eyes.

'Fixing to end my nightmare. Has he gone?'

'Yes.' Sadie glanced at the curtained window again, then ran to fling her arms around her mother's neck. 'You'll go to jail if you kill him, Mama. We have to think of another way out of this.'

'I can't stand the way he talks to you.' Vera's eyes were haunted. 'I'm afraid he's going to . . . try to hurt you again.'

'Oh, Mama.' Sadie's eyes welled up. 'Put the gun away. We've got to think about Holly right now. I think Curtis is actually crazy enough to try to kidnap her.'

'Not while I can do something about it,' her mother replied.

'Do you feel like you could sleep now?' Dustin didn't miss the flash of panic in Jill's eyes.

'I don't think so yet. But you don't have to sit up with me. I'll just sit here in front of the fire a little longer.'

They were both feeling restless since Marsh's visit. He'd been unable to allay their fears. Though he praised Jill's quick action, he also warned that there were to be no more outings with baby Holly. Tomorrow, he'd go by and talk to the girl and try to figure out some more pieces of the puzzle.

'We just don't know what we're dealing with here. We may be overplaying it, but I think caution is called for until we know what his next move might be. Though I don't think he can trace you here, Jill, since you said you didn't think you were followed.'

After Marsh left Eunice had gone upstairs, carrying baby Holly in the basket to sleep by her bed. Jill protested, but Eunice insisted Jill needed one night of rest without being awakened for early morning feedings. Dustin agreed wholeheartedly with his mother, but knew it went against Jill's grain not to be taking care of what she perceived was her responsibility.

'Well, here, then.' He went to the hall linen closet and pulled out a few old blankets. If Jill wasn't going to be able to sleep, he wasn't going to leave her down here to shake in her boots by herself. After all, the reason for her distress was a situation thrust on her by the Reed family.

Tossing the blankets down in front of the fire, Dustin pointed to them. 'One for you, one for me. You'll be more comfortable there than sitting on that antique sofa.'

'Dustin, you don't have to sit up with me,' Jill said, melting to the floor to sit on the nearest blanket. She yawned, appearing surprised. 'Goodness, I just might fall asleep in front of the fireplace.'

He settled next to her, a careful twelve-inch distance between them. Resting his head on his forearms, he said, 'A good sleep wouldn't hurt you any.'

Jill leaned back, stretching her feet toward the fire. 'I don't suppose it would. But I can't hear Holly if I'm down here.'

Dustin shook his head. 'After what you've been through, we owe you one night of sleep without Holly waking you for her grub. Mother and I can switch off.'

He watched as her eyelids drifted closed for a second. 'When does Joey return?'

'Tomorrow.' Dustin didn't mean to sound gruff, but Maxine's constant plaguing of him was something he didn't want to think about right now.

'Oh, good,' Jill said. She stretched out on her back, looking like a contented cat. 'I found a gingerbread man recipe in one of your mother's cookbooks that will do nicely for our baking project tomorrow.'

She never ceased to amaze him. Joey was going to flip when he found out what was in store for him. Dustin eyed the long-legged woman, all laid out on the blanket with an extra bunching of material at the top to serve as a pillow. She'd opened her eyes again, to stare into the crackling fire. He thought about what she was risking for his family and realized that, no matter how much it went against his nature to talk about his personal situation, he owed her an explanation about some things.

'Jill, there's something you need to know.'

She rolled her head to glance his way. With the firelight playing on her skin and the contented expression on her face, Dustin felt himself beginning to heat.

'What is it?'

He took a deep breath. 'I have a custody hearing in one week that will decide who gets Joey. Me, or the Copelands.'

Her eyes widened, the lashes fanning nearly to her eyebrows. 'No wonder you don't like them very much. Why are they trying to get custody of your son?'

Dustin turned his head to stare into the fire, wishing with all his heart he didn't have to tell her. But it was the only fair, right thing to do. After all, she needed to know that matters might get even more out of line at the ranch – none of which she'd counted on when she was looking for a place to heal her wounds and start over.

But he couldn't skirt the issue forever. Taking a deep breath he said, 'The Copeland's daughter, Nina, was my wife. We didn't have the best of marriages, although I will admit that I was crazy enough about her in the beginning. Even when she told me she was pregnant, I thought marriage between the two of us would be a good thing.' He dropped his head to his hands, hating the sound of his own failure. 'It wasn't.'

'Every marriage has its ups and downs.'

Jill didn't sound condemning at all. He glanced up, almost surprised at her quick defense of what he'd just told her. Her face, sweetly rounded in the flickering light, held an encouraging expression.

'Yeah. Well, maybe ours had more than most. We both made mistakes. But it wasn't destined to work.' He wasn't about to say that Nina's allure had quickly worn off with her constant demands for *more, more*. More of anything than he could provide. The dairy farm that had been in existence since his grandparents' day was doing poorly; milk prices had bottomed out. When he'd taken over, he'd sold off the stock and carefully purchased high-quality beef stock. With a couple of good calving years, and taking on some select customers whose cattle he allowed to graze on his ranch, he'd begun to turn the ranch around.

Apparently though, Nina had married him believing that money was no object once she married into the Reed family. They had plenty, of course, but he hadn't wanted to foot huge shopping forays into Dallas while he was trying to trim costs at the ranch. One month Nina's credit card bill had been the same as his feed bill for the cattle.

To make matters worse for his new bride, all that working to salvage his family's livelihood meant he hadn't been home a lot. Nina was certain he'd been having an affair. Dustin snorted, knowing who had

176

most likely planted that insidious seed into his wife's brain. Once there, it had taken root, growing like the wildest Johnson grass.

'The night Nina died, we'd had an argument,' he said quietly, staring into the fire as if any answers to what had gone wrong might be contained in the hot-burning coals. 'We had the worst argument we'd ever had in our whole marriage. For the first time, I . . .'

He cut off his words, unhappy to have to release his deepest, darkest demon. Risking a glance at Jill, he saw that she continued to give him her undivided, seemingly non-judgemental attention. 'Well, for the first time, I major-league lost my temper. As much as I hate to say this, I'm amazed my nearest neighbor didn't call the police. I didn't know I could yell so loud.' He shook his head. 'The only shouting I'd ever done before was at the cattle.'

'You strike me as a fairly even-tempered person.'

Jill's eyes were warm, glowing with an under-standing Dustin knew he didn't deserve. He'd had no business letting his temper get away from him that night. It was no excuse to say that all the little things he'd tried to shrug off had festered and suddenly blown up – the infidelity accusation had rubbed him rawer than anything. All he knew was that he spent his life working his butt off so Nina could have a roof over her head and some nice clothes and a trip into Dallas every once in a while. To find that he'd been tried and damned in the court of infidelity had shook him to the core. He'd known Nina needed lots of attention; as the only child in Maxine and David's family this meant she'd spent her life being catered to. But hell, she'd known what kind of man he was when she started cozying up to him. He'd never had a reputation for being a woman-chaser. He worked hard to succeed, to keep the ranch together that had provided housing and food for three generations of Reeds.

Nina had admitted once that marrying him was a dream come true for her. She liked the sound of Nina Reed, Mrs Dustin Reed. She'd liked having accounts all over town where she could purchase whatever her heart desired with only a signature on the bottom line. He got the bills.

But none of this needed to be said in his defense. The cold hard fact was that he was as much to blame in the marriage as Nina was. And he had lost his temper in a frightening way that night. It was as if she'd pushed all the right buttons and suddenly there was an atomic explosion.

Damn it. Dustin closed his eyes, remembering Nina's limp, lifeless body. The price had been much too high.

'Dustin?'

He glanced toward Jill, shaking his head. 'I like to think I keep a cool head. Unfortunately, I upset my wife so badly she left in a killing thunderstorm. I basically signed away her life.'

'Oh.' Jill was looking at him with those bottomless blue eyes of hers. Dustin felt shame wash over him. But at least it was out. Now she knew the truth, knew what she was up against.

'Yeah. Oh,' he repeated her words softly. 'That's why the Copelands want Joey. They feel I murdered their daughter.'

Jill had been lying on her back, but now she rolled to her side and propped her chin on her hand. She didn't say anything, but he knew she was listening. As if she knew it didn't matter what she said; nothing could be changed. But at least she listened.

'So.' He sighed deeply. 'Because of that, and the fact that I've pretty much ignored Joey since Nina died, they filed for custody. On the grounds that I'm an unfit father.' He snorted. 'An unfit human being.'

'You've made great strides,' Jill said. 'It was only a matter of time, and you've been getting the hang of it. Not every man becomes a great father just because a wet, sticky, yelling infant has been handed to him. It takes practice, for men and a lot of women, too.'

He was warmed by her quick support on this issue. Actually, the charge that had hurt him the most was that he wasn't a fit parent. As if Joey were neglected, unloved. He would take part of the blame for Nina's death – he *had* lost his temper that night. As much as he would have liked to stop her from going out into the storm, she'd wanted to go home to her mother. She'd insisted on taking Joey. What could he have done – except what he hadn't been able to, with his pride caught tightly inside him. He should have apologized. Should have said something.

But he'd thought letting her go was the best thing to do. It had been a treacherous mistake.

He did love his son. Unfortunately, with the suit

filed before he'd gotten over the shock of his wife dying, Dustin had been stricken, unable to cope with the thought that now Joey was being torn from him. He hadn't known what to do. Maxine was relentless in telling people in the town what a lousy father he was, what a dirty rotten husband he'd been.

It had all taken a toll on him. He'd lain awake nights thinking about how he was going to explain all this to his son one day. *Son, I love you, I honestly do, no matter what the court records say. But they said the Copelands were more fit to raise you . . .*

'You've helped me,' he finally said. 'You've helped me unbend. I've been too afraid of letting go with Joey.'

'He loves you,' she said softly. 'He idolizes you. I've never seen a child love his daddy so much. What big boots he tries to fill.'

Dustin felt tears stinging his eyes. 'The whole thing just pisses me off so much. Have you ever listened to my boy stutter?'

Jill nodded.

'He didn't until Nina died. I think sitting in that car, not knowing what the hell had happened, had an effect on something inside him. I don't know what, and I haven't taken him to a doctor because it's just a crazy hunch I have. I keep thinking, he's been through a trauma, he'll outgrow the stuttering. But I can't comfort him; I can't take the time to say "slow down, son, I'm listening to every word you say," because I know he could be taken away from me soon. So I try not to think about it.'

'Oh, Dustin. You don't have to tell me any of this. It doesn't affect the way I feel about my employment.'

He stared at her, unable to believe her words. 'I have to tell you, because you were trying to escape a hell of your own. And you ran right into mine. It wasn't fair of me not to tell you that things were going to be difficult here at the ranch.'

'I knew the job wasn't going to be easy when I met my employer.'

Jill's sassy grin took the edge off her words. Dustin tried to tell himself she meant what she was saying. But still he wanted to make sure she understood.

'Your employer is probably just going to get grouchier, right up until the day of the hearing. I might improve afterward. But if I lose Joey . . .'

'If you lose Joey, you'll file an appeal,' Jill interrupted.

'Yeah.' Dustin rubbed his chin. 'Why didn't I think of that?'

'Because you don't want to lose him at all. And you shouldn't. But if by any quirk of the justice system you do, it won't be forever. You're a deserving father.'

'You think so?'

'I think you deserve a little more time. Parenting is not something one learns like math. And Joey's stutter is no different than the one I had as a child.'

'Really?' Dustin couldn't imagine beautiful, confident Jill stuttering.

She laughed, the sound as heartwarming as the

Christmas tree with its blinking lights glowing in the corner. 'Yes, Dustin. I was the youngest child. It was difficult getting a word in edgewise. When you're competing with three older siblings, you might want to talk fast, but your mouth will only go its own speed. At least that's what the speech therapist told my parents.' She gave him a playful slap on the arm. 'It's normal, Dustin. He'll probably grow out of it, particularly once you're not under so much stress. And if he was traumatized, the two of you can go for some family counseling. My take-whatever-it's-worth opinion is that you might try to relax and enjoy your son. He's pretty cool.'

Dustin grinned. 'Yeah. It's kind of weird having my miniature around.'

'Well, Joey at least lets his hair down every once in a while,' she teased.

'Hey, I'm letting my hair down now, aren't I?'

'I think you've been trying to scare me off. Except for what happened today, you should know I don't scare too easy.'

The smile slipped from Dustin's face. 'Speaking of that, Jill . . .'

Swiftly, she sat up, laying a finger against his lips. 'Let's not talk about it. Let's not talk about anything serious anymore. You should just zone out in front of the fire.'

He caught her finger, and then her hand in his. 'Who can loosen up around here? All we need now is a resident ghost to stir up trouble.'

'I think you have all the trouble you can handle.'

Jill pulled at her hand, but he wouldn't let her get

away. With a start, he'd just realized how near this woman was. How very near this gorgeous, deeply understanding woman had become to his heart. Dustin tugged her, and incredibly, she moved closer without resistance.

'I might be in the mood for a little more trouble,' he told her.

'You'll find it with me,' Jill said softly. 'It's a mistake to make a pass at your employee.'

'I'll allow you to file a complaint.' He knew he might regret it later, but for now, the thought of kissing Jill was pushing his common sense from his mind. Ever so gently, he pressed his lips to hers.

Her mouth moved under his, seeking a deeper fusing, and Dustin felt sparks ignite inside him. 'Jill,' he whispered against her mouth hoarsely.

'I haven't filed my complaint yet. Keep going,' she said, easing up against him.

At that moment, Dustin knew that the comfort Jill was offering he wanted, desperately. He wanted to give and take and forget about everything that had happened today. Carefully, he pressed his body against hers, nudging her onto her back without ever taking his lips from hers. He sought her warmth, feeling fire leap through him as he felt her daintier body underneath his. There was power in the feeling of Jill bonded to him.

His jeans rasped against hers. Jill moaned, reaching up to tangle her hands in his hair. Pressing small kisses down her neck, Dustin breathed in the wonderful fragrance that was Jill, all soft and delicate.

The swell of her breasts was womanly and enticing; Dustin pressed a kiss against each swell before returning to Jill's lips.

Her eyes were closed, but her hands had moved slowly down his back to his buttocks. She slipped her hands inside his jeans to rub the skin. Dustin thought he might die from desire. Somewhere a faint shred of decency called to him, urging him to remember that this woman deserved his protection.

'Jill.'

Her eyes snapped open. 'I haven't cried "uncle."'

But she knew by the look in his eyes that he'd remembered. Dustin had remembered who she was and why she was in his home. The fact that she had prayed the most delirious kiss she'd ever experienced would never end didn't matter. Even as she'd moved closer to him, she'd known that kissing Dustin was a thing of the moment. Later, they would no doubt tell themselves it had happened on a strange and tragic day when events had whirled out of control; they had both merely reached out to find an anchor in the storm. And they had found each other.

But Jill was realistic enough to know that the moment was all they would share. Still, she hated that it had ended. She had never felt anything like this before. The way Dustin had kissed her had fulfilled some basic needs and one private fantasy.

He pulled away though she could see the fire still simmering in his dark eyes. Jill sighed, knowing it was for the best, and told herself to be happy for the magic she had experienced. This wonderous man wanted her. She'd always wondered if he was attracted to her. After learning that Carl – who'd insisted they should 'wait' until they got married – was sleeping with anything that had permed blond hair and three-inch red fingernails, Jill wondered why he hadn't been attracted to her. Something inside her worried that she lacked the necessary sexual allure to make a man want to kill to jump into her bed.

Dustin Reed had blown that worry clean away. With the length of his body pressing against her, she'd been able to feel his desire. *She turned him on.* Something very female inside her was pleased that it was the handsome, thoroughly masculine cowboy who still had one leg twined inside hers who thought she was sexy.

It was best to let Dustin off the hook. Before he felt responsible for kissing her, she needed to let him know she understood what had happened.

So she smiled. 'Thank you.'

'For what?'

Completely feigning her nonchalance, Jill untangled herself from Dustin and leaned back on her elbows the way she had been previously. 'For comforting me. For making me feel better. I think I can actually go upstairs and sleep now.'

Lie. It was killing her to leave him on the blanket. He was staring at her like she was nuts. Jill forced herself to her feet.

He caught at her jeans. 'Jill, don't just thank me and walk away. I don't want us to feel bad about what happened.'

'Of course not. It's perfectly natural for two human beings to reach out in a crisis. I'm glad we could be there for each other.'

His brows furrowed at her words. 'You're not upset? You won't worry that it will happen again?'

Jill's heart sank a little. 'No. I won't worry that it will happen again.' She had known in the beginning it was a dream that might only come true once. 'Goodnight, Dustin.'

He sat up and turned to look into the fire. 'Goodnight, Jill.'

It didn't feel right, leaving him sitting there alone. His back looked broad and strong outlined by the yellow light of the fire. He might be strong, but he was still alone.

Jill forced herself to turn away. Reluctantly, she went upstairs, knowing she was doing the right thing.

CHAPTER 12

Dustin awakened to the sound of pounding on the front door. He'd spent an uncomfortable night in front of the fireplace, which was now letting in drafts of cold air. Cursing to himself, he got up to open the door.

'I should have known it'd be you. You're going to have to get your own eggs and sausage out of the kitchen. I'm not cooking, and nobody else is awake,' Dustin grumbled at Marsh.

'Breakfast sounds good, but actually I need to talk to you. You look like hell. Didn't you sleep last night?'

Dustin scrubbed a hand over the prickly growth on his chin. Lord, he needed a shave and a shower. 'No. Orange juice?'

Marsh glanced into the parlor as he walked by it. Dustin knew he hadn't missed the blankets on the floor. He went into the kitchen, mentally bracing himself for Marsh's question.

'Heat go out upstairs or something?'

'No,' Dustin growled. 'I spent the night in front of the fire because I thought it was a cool thing to do.'

'Hm.' He looked at Dustin closely. 'Why do you have pink lipstick on your mouth?'

'Because my lips were chapped.' Frowning at Marsh, he reached up in the general area he thought the lipstick might be and rubbed hard. Trouble was, he'd kissed Jill pretty thoroughly. The lipstick could be anywhere.

'You're not really wearing lip prints this morning,' Marsh said jovially.

Dustin cursed.

'It was just a hunch I had. I suspected your sour mood might have less to do with sleeping in front of the fire than having a rock in your underwear all night.'

Dustin slammed a palm on the counter. 'Are you finished?'

Marsh sat down at the table, propping his boots up. 'Nah. Cook, while I talk.'

'I'm not your wife,' he grumbled. But he tossed the orange juice container at Marsh and started hunting in the refrigerator for eggs.

'I hope to hell not. My wife's gotta be pretty.' Marsh poured himself some juice, then got up to set another glass out, which he placed at Dustin's seat. 'Okay. I went to check out the girl at the bakery early this morning, figuring a bakery opens extremely early or who's gonna feed folks? So she might be fixing biscuits or something.'

'That's why you're on my porch before my rooster's had a chance to crow? You couldn't get breakfast anywhere else.'

'Foul, foul,' Marsh said, shaking his head. 'Mrs Vickery says the girl isn't coming back. There was a message on her machine this morning.'

'I assume you're going to her house.'

'I would, if Mrs Vickery had known where she lived. Unfortunately, she was paying the girl under the table.' Marsh clicked his tongue. 'Good, upstanding Mrs Vickery. It's always the quiet ones, isn't it?'

Dustin cracked an egg into the pan, feeling his temper sizzling along with the egg white. 'Now what, damn it?'

'We'll see. We'll have to keep a close eye on things. Meantime, I'll check out some other folks who might know where this girl lives.'

'Mother knows everybody and the dogs they own in the county. She ought to be able to tell you.'

Marsh nodded. 'Yep. Say, how did Jill do last night?'

Dustin's hand jumped. He yelped as he burned himself on the skillet. 'Do what?' he demanded.

Marsh paused. 'Run that under cold water. Was she all right?'

'She's fine, damn it.' He ignored the advice about cold water. He could have done that last night, too, but who wanted a cold shower in December?

'Hey, buddy, I'm asking you if that poor woman who ran for an orphan's life she barely knows was able to calm down enough to sleep last night. I'm not inquiring as to whether she meets your Playboy bunny measurements – hey, wait a minute. You didn't . . .'

189

'Marsh!'

'Holy smokes, Dustin, you've been worrying if she's pregnant! Even you wouldn't make the same mistake twice.'

'I kissed her! That's all.' He glared at Marsh. 'It was a simple, thanks-for-everything-you-did kiss. Nothing more.'

'Uh, yeah, buddy. And China Shea spent the night with me last night.'

Dustin snorted. He slapped a plate with two eggs, yolks burst, in front of Marsh. 'At least then you'd be waking *her* up at such an ungodly hour instead of me.'

'Nah. Some habits are hard to break. I'll bring her with me when it's breakfast time at the Reed Ranch.' He stared down at the eggs, before looking up to stare at him. 'Listen, Dustin, I think you're taking your housekeeper a bit serious.'

Toast flew up out of the toaster, a bit crisper than was edible. He hadn't been able to concentrate on the biscuit directions for thinking about Jill, so he'd taken the easy way out.

Reaching for the two dark pieces, he tossed one onto Marsh's plate. 'Rest easy. Nothing serious is going on. I shouldn't have kissed her, but no mountains moved, so what the hell.'

'You're lying like a rug.'

Dustin shrugged.

'Only a friend would say this, Dustin. I hope you'll remember that before you punch my lights out. But you fell for Nina under similar circumstances. If you think about that, maybe history won't repeat itself.'

His hand stopped in mid-air, leaving the toast unbitten. 'That was a major leap, even for you, Marsh.'

'No.' Marsh shook his head. 'You fell for Nina right after your father died. The shock factor had set in and the first hot pair of panties that came your way felt like southern comfort.'

Dustin tossed the toast to the plate. Marsh held up a hand.

'Don't deny that you blame yourself for your father's heart attack. You had an argument about the ranch. He died, and you got left holding a bag of guilt.' Marsh stared him down. 'If you hadn't been hurting so bad, you might have been able to see that Nina was after you for your money. For your name. She was a social climbing woman, and you know it. Pregnancy bought her that ring. But, Dustin, at least she was pregnant with *your* child. If Jill's pregnant, you're going to have to overlook the fact that you're falling for a woman who's having another man's baby. Even if she's not pregnant, you're at a bad spot in your life, especially with the custody battle coming up. You might accidentally make another poor choice.'

'You're full of crap.' Dustin wanted to reach across and sock Marsh a good one. Problem was, the man was speaking out of concern. He was right about one thing. Dustin *had* reacted to Nina out of pain. Her potency would have been lessened greatly had he not been searching for something.

191

It's perfectly natural for two human beings to reach out in a crisis. I'm glad we could be there for each other.

Jill's words haunted him. Had she known? Felt that same way? Had their kiss been simply a momentary connection, nothing more?

He knew it was best if that was the case. Yet, his heart was telling him he wanted the kiss to have meant something to her. Meeting Marsh's eyes, he shrugged. 'Thanks for the therapy. What's that gonna run me?'

'Not a damn thing, as long as you listened. Remember, she's the housekeeper, not a bedwarmer. Hey, I gotta get back. I've got to check on . . . Good morning, Eunice. How are you doing?'

Dustin turned to see his mother holding baby Holly, and a freshly showered Jill. Damn, but she looked good.

'Any news, Marsh?' Eunice asked.

'No. The shop girl's gone, quit her job.'

Jill gasped. Dustin pushed away the unappealing breakfast, getting up to put his plate in the sink. Since the household was all up now and completely aware that he'd slept in his clothes, he might as well go feed the cattle.

'Who was she?' Eunice inquired as Jill went to fix a bottle.

'Sadie Lauren. Know her?'

Eunice sat down at the table. Dustin eyed his mother. He could tell she knew by the expression on her face.

'I thought as much,' she sighed. 'The reason you

don't recognize the name is because Sadie is Vera Benchley's daughter. Her father's name was Lauren, but Vera remarried.'

'You knew Holly belonged to them?' Marsh asked.

'I suspected.' She adjusted Holly and pulled out the end of the blanket. 'This crown is newly stitched on the blanket. Vera did me a favor once in high school, for which I have always been grateful. I'm sure she was aware I'd help her in a flash, whatever the favor. Vera's a good woman. I had a hunch about this stitchery, because Vera's an excellent seamstress – people around here hire her to do fancy sewing – but I didn't want to mention anything until I was certain.'

'I'll go by and check the house. Once I explain that we'll protect Holly and keep this a private matter between us, maybe they'll help me put the squeeze on the father.' Marsh got up, nodding to the ladies. 'Thanks, Eunice. 'Bye, Jill. Weather's supposed to get bad today. If you're going to stroll Holly around the property, you'd better do it early.'

'I will,' she murmured.

Dustin noticed she didn't glance his way. 'Let us know what you find out,' he said, walking with Marsh to the door.

'I will. Meantime, remember lightning can strike twice.'

'Shut up,' Dustin told him sourly. 'I told you, it wasn't worth making a mountain out of a molehill over.'

'I'm taking your word on it. The man who keeps

his jeans on doesn't wind up wearing a wedding ring.'

Dustin slammed the door. Unfortunately, Marsh was right. However, he was completely in control of the situation.

Silently, Joey put his toys away. Grandmother Copeland had told him it was time to go home. He was glad. He missed his father and Grandma Eunice. Most of all, he needed to get home to see if Jill was still there. He just knew she'd left while he'd been gone.

Grandmother came into the room. 'Time to go, Joey.'

He followed her downstairs and out the door. A man, who they called a driver or something, was holding the car door open. He got in, and Grandmother settled onto the leather seat next to him. The car rolled forward as the driver started it.

'What do you want Santa to bring you for Christmas, Joey?' she asked.

He didn't have to think about that. 'Jill.'

'Who's Jill?'

'The new lady at our house. She . . . she's boo-ti-ful.'

'Oh?' His grandmother's eyebrows raised. Joey thought that was good. She was interested in his story. 'What does she do?'

'She takes care of us. She . . . she takes care of Daddy.'

'I see.' Grandmother Copeland stared at him. 'So you want her to stay?'

194

'Yes.' Joey nodded his head. That would be wonderful. He wondered if Santa could manage that for him. 'Maybe . . . maybe she be my mother.'

His grandmother turned to look out the window. She was no longer thinking about his Christmas presents. Joey zipped and unzipped the zipper on his down coat, trying to make a game until he got home. The drive always seemed to take forever until he was back with his daddy and grandma again.

Jill paused at the top of the stairwell. The shrill voice she'd heard before was speaking, only this time it was louder, more strident. Joey came flying up the stairs, throwing his arms around her the second he saw her.

She patted his back as she hung there, listening though she was struck by the sudden perception that she wasn't going to like what was being said.

'You can't believe I'm going to let you get away with this, Dustin Reed. If you thought I was making your life miserable before, this certainly doesn't make me want to change my mind.'

'I didn't expect you to change your mind, Maxine.'

'So you went and hired some sweet young thing to take Nina's place! Even as dense as you are, you had to have known how I'd feel about that. I guess you did, since you've kept her well out of sight.'

'We're hardly on social terms, Maxine. Why would I introduce my housekeeper to you?'

'Don't you think I'd be interested in the person who's caring for Joey?'

'I didn't think who changed the beds around here was a matter for public concern.'

'Well, let me tell you something, Dustin. When Joey tells me he wants this woman to be his mother, I know he's thinking that for a reason. Something's happened to make him hope for that possibility. And I'm warning you, that is something I won't stand for. I won't have you replacing Nina with some woman, and getting custody of Joey, so that all the pieces can just be wrapped up nicely in your life, with me standing out in the cold and Nina forgotten. Oh, no. I will never let that happen.'

She could hear Dustin's deep sigh. 'Exactly what will make you happy, Maxine?'

'I want you to get rid of her.'

'Get rid of Jill? She's the only housekeeper we've been able to keep.'

Joey moved away from her legs to rush into his room. Jill knew she should go to him, but the distress in Dustin's voice kept her rooted in place.

'The other two were older, suitable females. Somehow you ran off good help. I'm starting to wonder if good help was truly what you were looking for.'

'I'm not sure what you're getting at.'

Jill knew, and she was certain Dustin did, too. The way her scalp was tightening made her realize her position at the Reed Ranch was suddenly very tenuous. Maxine Copeland was a determined woman.

'Let's not mince words, Dustin. Either this woman or you have done something, said something, to make Joey think there's a long-term relationship in the offing. Far from running away from this position, this girl appears to be getting close with Joey.'

'What's wrong with that?'

'It's not her place. I can't help whether or not you're sleeping with her. But I can make certain she doesn't insinuate herself into Joey's affection, where she can manipulate herself into becoming a part of this family. I'm very angry that you've so casually discarded the memory of my daughter, less than a year after she died. I'm not going to have you replacing her like this. This Jill isn't going to become Joey's stepmother, not if I have anything to say about it.'

'I think you're all worked up about nothing, Maxine. What Joey said was a harmless enough wish for a boy his age. Of course he wishes his mother hadn't died. But since she did, it's natural for him to want someone else to love him.'

'You understand that very well, don't you, Dustin?' Maxine's voice was mocking. 'But you won't even mention my daughter's name. You say "she" and "her" but you don't say "Nina". Because you've already moved past her. You're not going to admit it, but I can tell.'

'Maxine . . .'

'No, don't "Maxine" me. It is a very bad time for you to upset me with this decision of yours, but I might have known your glands would be talking louder than your brain.'

There was a pause. Jill's heart was beating so loud she felt like the floor was trembling.

'I was hoping this wouldn't turn nasty, Dustin. I hoped you would come to your senses and realize that this was no place for Joey, that he'd be better off with someone who can be with him full-time and help him get over his grief. It never occurred to me that you'd hire someone to take Nina's place, to become a mother to him. However, you should know that I intend to win this custody suit. Stand warned that I will use every card in my hand to do so. My chances are excellent, especially once the fact that your mother had a long-term affair with my husband is revealed.' She paused to let that sink in. 'Loose morals appear to run in the family, which is an unfortunate thing when one is trying to prove their fitness to raise a child. Good day.'

Jill's hand flew to cover her mouth. The front door slammed. Dustin cursed, loud enough for the words to carry up the stairs. Before she could get caught eavesdropping, she hurried to her room and closed the door. Leaning up against it, she pressed her eyes together, feeling sick. Without realizing it, she had developed into a problem for Dustin. Marsh had called her a bedwarmer. She'd been willing to overlook that, knowing that Dustin would straighten him out about their relationship. In time, she would have her own chance to give him hell about his comment. But Maxine apparently thought she was sleeping with her employer and was convinced enough about it to want her fired.

She might not be sleeping with Dustin, but she

definitely hadn't pulled away from his kiss last night. In fact, she'd wanted much, much more.

Jill hung her head. Her being at the ranch was causing a horrible amount of trouble for Dustin. The best thing she could do would be to resign her position and return to Dallas.

Crossing into Joey's room, she found it empty. He must have run into Eunice's room to hide from the terrible words being flung around downstairs. Poor Joey. Whatever innocent thing he'd said to his grandmother had stirred up a devastating tornado. Her heart squeezed tightly as she thought about his Christmas wish. Well, she couldn't be his mother, but even if she had to leave the ranch, Joey, with his flyaway cornsilk hair, would always live in her heart.

She heard Dustin's boots thundering against the floorboards as he strode down the hall. Cringing inwardly, she waited for him to pound on her door. Whatever happened, she would go – and go gracefully.

'Mother!' she heard him shout.

A door opened. 'Yes, Dustin?'

The door closed again. Jill slowly opened the door to Joey's bedroom, peering out into the hall. It was empty, but she could hear Dustin in his mother's room. She hesitated, thinking that Eunice and her son needed this time to talk without Joey having to be a part of it. The least she could do was offer to take him outside to play.

She went to Eunice's door, her hand raised to knock.

'Maxine seems to think she's holding a trump card,' she heard Dustin say. 'For whatever reason, she's got it in her twisted mind that you and David had an affair.'

There was a long pause. Jill realized that there was no way she could disturb their conversation now. She started to move away from the door.

'As much as I hate to say so, I can see why Maxine might think that,' Eunice's unhappy voice admitted.

CHAPTER 13

Dustin couldn't believe what he was hearing. His mother was well-recognized in Lassiter as an upstanding pillar of society, a model for other women to follow. Why would anyone suspect her of having an affair?

A soft knock kept him from unleashing the harsh-edged question whirling in his brain. He flung open the door.

'What is it?' he demanded. Jill jumped, obviously alarmed by his tone.

'Um, would you like me to take Joey downstairs?' She peered around the door. 'And Holly, too?'

The baby was sleeping, totally unaware of Dustin's fury. He glanced at his son, who had nestled up against Eunice, in either a protective or looking-for-protection stance. Sighing, Dustin held the door open further. 'If you wouldn't mind. Holly can stay in here, though.'

Jill's gaze flew to Joey. She gestured to him, and he went to her without hesitation. Quietly, the door closed. Dustin could hear footsteps hurrying down the stairs. His temper had definitely made an impression on his housekeeper. His mouth thinning, he leaned against the wall. 'I find this very hard to believe, Mother.'

'Well, it's an unfortunate time for this to come out, Dustin. I'm truly sorry it has. I'm more sorry that Maxine believes it. The truth is, David used to spend quite a bit of time over here after your father died. It was harmless, of course, but you know how Maxine's mind works.'

'Where was I?' Dustin could hear the growl in his voice.

'Oh, out courting Nina. Running around with Marsh. Most of the time, you were trying to get the ranch up and running again.' She hesitated, before meeting his eyes. 'I would venture to say that you were doing what I was doing, trying to get over your father's death.'

'You must have spent a good bit of time together for her to think there was an affair.'

Eunice chuckled, but it was a sad sound. 'Well, I'm not completely sure what David's reasons were for coming around. At the time, I suspected he needed a reprieve from Maxine. He never said so, naturally. But about twice a week he'd come by around five o'clock and we'd have a whiskey and soda. We'd talk. Mostly, we shared a love of bird-watching. The pecan trees attract many birds, and from the porch we could sit and watch them fly in. To be honest, I don't know what I would have done without David during that time,' she said, her voice softening.

Dustin understood that feeling. He'd felt the same way, only he'd turned to Nina. It had seemed so right and natural at the time. But, blinded by grief, he'd allowed the relationship to deepen to a point it should never have gone.

'I don't know what I'm going to do,' he said, running a hand through his hair. Grasping the chair at her vanity, he turned it around and straddled it. 'This is just more poison for her to spew. If she didn't know about your friendship before, how did she manage to find out now?'

His mother shook her head. 'She hired a private investigator.'

'How do you know that?'

'He told me.'

'David did?'

'No. The investigator.'

Dustin narrowed his eyes. 'He was doing a job for her and he told you?'

Eunice shrugged. 'She fired him. He was an old acquaintance of mine. It wasn't unethical, Dustin. There was nothing to uncover, but she wanted dirt. He felt like I was going to be backed into a bad position and was kind enough to warn me. I don't think he liked the possibility of his reputation being slandered, either.'

Dustin couldn't believe what he was hearing. 'You didn't tell me this before?'

'I'm sorry, Dustin. I would have remembered sooner or later. With the scare over baby Holly and what-not, it flew right out of my head. It didn't even strike me as being that important, since I'd expected Maxine not to pull her punches. I knew she would be watching our every move. It is, after all, a custody battle. She has to prove something about us that will assure the judge we're unfit to have Joey.'

'I guess.' Dustin rubbed his forehead tiredly. 'Why didn't I think of that?'

His mother laid a comforting hand on his arm. 'Because that's the way Maxine's mind works, not yours, honey. You don't have so much experience with her deviousness.' She leaned back, massaging her lower back with one hand. 'I've known Maxine Copeland all my life. I *know* what she's capable of. Frankly, I think she's losing her edge.'

'You don't mean that.'

She nodded her head assertively. 'I do. If all she can come up with is smoke and mirrors, I don't think the judge is going to be impressed.'

'He's in her pocket.'

'But David's not.'

Dustin stared at his mother, then shook his head. 'David isn't with us much anymore. Even if he was coherent the day of the trial, I wouldn't dare to hope he'd go against Maxine in any way, whether it was denying that you two had an affair or any other nefarious charge she manufactures.'

'Well, all I know to do right now is keep the faith. Joey is going to be here for Christmas, and I don't believe anything else.'

He let out a deep breath before shooting a quick

look her way. She had ceased rubbing her back, but was now sitting up straight to find a more comfortable position. If she was suffering lower back pain, that might indicate her arthritis was going to flare up again. Optimistically, it could be from the strain of picking Holly up and holding her constantly. Though he hoped it was the latter, he hated to think of his mother sitting in a hard wooden courtroom seat for hours if she wasn't feeling well. The case was going to be difficult enough to sit through as it was.

'I hope you'll pay no mind to Maxine's bitterness about Jill.'

Dustin raised his brows. 'You heard.'

'Honey, the whole county heard. Including Jill, I imagine.'

He nodded wearily. 'I don't know what to do about it.'

'I should think I pass as a decent witness to your good behaviour, Dustin. Maxine is just consumed with sadness over Nina's death.' She rolled her shoulders and sat up straighter. 'Actually, she's eaten up with guilt, because she knows her own role she played in her daughter's death. It's so much easier to blame you, though.'

'I don't think she'd agree with you about that.'

'Of course not. Maxine needs to hate us so she won't have to take responsibility for her meddling. If she'd left the two of you alone, your marriage might have had a prayer.'

Dustin shook his head. 'I couldn't give Nina what she wanted.'

'No, and David couldn't give Maxine what she wanted. It's a vicious cycle.'

He frowned, considering her words. It was a well-known fact that the Copelands didn't have the happiest of marriages. Maxine ran the show, while it appeared that, over the years, David had learned to stay out of his wife's way. There were rumors of shady business deals and flaunting of their upscale, in-town life, but never was David's name mentioned. While people tended to try to avoid Maxine, her husband was a well-liked member of the country club golf set, his personality and generosity winning him many friends. In fact, he'd been one of the first people to call when Dustin's father had died.

But David hadn't satisfied Maxine, apparently, not by the amount of money he made nor with the social standing he was able to achieve. In the end, he'd faded away rather than continue trying to meet his wife's endless yardstick for success.

'Try not to think about it anymore, Dustin. I think what needs to be done now is to decide about Jill and let her know. I would venture to say she's pretty worried about her position right now.'

'Yeah.' Dustin pounded his fist lightly on the vanity top. 'Truth is, Maxine worried me with that little speech. It wouldn't be good for Jill's name to get dragged through the mud. She doesn't deserve to get wrapped up in our concerns.'

'Dustin.' His mother tapped him on the arm meaningfully. 'Let Jill decide what is a concern to her. She hasn't indicated that she'd like to desert us yet, so why should you push her out the door?'

'It isn't fair to her, Mother. You and I both know she'll stay.'

'So don't let Maxine get her way on this.'

'I have to consider that it's one more thing for her to muddy up the water with.'

'Our water is clean enough to filter out some dirt, Dustin. I expect you not to allow Maxine to cow you. She's brought this trouble on herself, and while I am deeply sorry for her loss, I don't see why we should have to give up any more than we have just because she's a spiteful old woman.'

Dustin thought about that for a moment. 'Jill may decide this has all been too much for her, anyway.'

Eunice shook her head. 'She has plenty of starch in her, Dustin. I don't think she'll be giving you her resignation.'

'She did say she needed the bonus pretty badly.'

'Bah! If you think that, go ahead and give her the three thousand dollars. When she stays anyway, then what excuse are you going to come up with for her staying?'

'Hell, I don't know why she would.'

'I do. Jill fits in here as naturally as calving does to springtime. She loves Joey. She likes me very well, I'm pleased to say. And though you can be a pain, Jill seems to be able to sail on through a day without tacking for your mood shifts. We're a good family, Dustin, though we're on a hard stretch of road right now. Jill sees that. But if you want to let Maxine have her way, go ahead and tell Jill to go.'

'Jeez.' Dustin waved off his mother's pitiful expression. 'I have to think about what's right for us, not about our housekeeper's employment status.'

'Fine. You talk to Jill about it. The two of you can surely decide what the best route is to take. But don't keep her hanging too long, Dustin.'

'All right.' He got up slowly, feeling like he'd pulled an all-nighter. Jill deserved to have a say in the matter, but he didn't want to talk to her about it. Not after last night's kiss. There was too much swirling through his mind in a kaleidoscope of chaos. Who was right? Marsh? Maxine? Was he doing the wrong thing by keeping Jill on, when he knew he was sexually attracted to her?

To complicate it all, he knew there was so much more than attraction racing through his veins. He liked looking at the woman, and knowing he was going to find her calm disposition warming his home at the end of a brutally cold work day was like a beer when he was tired, dusty, and thirsty. There wasn't a moment when he worried about his son anymore, either. He knew Joey was in kind, caring hands – and those hands had been soft and welcoming last night to Joey's father.

As much as he wanted to take his mother's advice, deep in his heart Dustin knew he couldn't avoid the truth. There was more going on between he and Jill McCall than dishwater and clean-swept floors.

Jill forced herself to focus on the precise cutting of the gingerbread dough. It seemed no sooner than she got one laid out than Joey had him dressed with colorful sprinkles and red hots. She might actually be enjoying the process if her mind would stop mulling over what Dustin was going to say to her after he talked to his mother. If she was smart, she'd start packing her bags during Joey's nap-time. It was going to be humiliating to linger a moment longer than she had to if Dustin told her she had to leave.

Which he had every right to do, in light of the custody problem. Maxine certainly planned to make everything as difficult as possible on him, and Jill's presence had sparked a fuse. Jill figured she should offer to resign, but then she'd have to admit to eavesdropping. Not only that, but she just wasn't a quitter. If Dustin wanted her to go, she would. It would be mortifying, but she would thank him for her employment and make a graceful exit.

It would be devastating, though – because of the kiss. She should never have done it.

Now he might feel obligated to keep her when he shouldn't. Perhaps he would think she expected more because of what had happened. She sighed and pressed out another cookie.

'Look, Jill. I . . . I make him happy.'

Joey pointed to the crooked curve of sprinkles where the gingerbread man's mouth was. Jill nodded and managed a smile.

'You . . . you happy now, too?'

'Oh, Joey.' Jill put down the cutter and gave him a hug. 'I'm very happy. I like doing this with you. I thought about it a lot yesterday while you were gone.' She brushed some flour off his face. 'I used to love making gingerbread men when I was a little girl. It's even more fun showing you how to do them.'

'You . . . not smiling. You making brows.'

She hadn't been smiling while she'd been thinking about what Dustin might say to her. There probably had been a frown line etched on her face. The concern on Joey's upturned face, serious and yet hopeful all at once, touched her.

'Well, I won't make brows anymore. I've been thinking too hard, but now I'm not going to think about anything but you and these spicy little guys, okay?'

'Okay.'

Joey went back to carefully placing red hots for buttons on a gingerbread man. Jill kept her lips pressed into a smile, glancing the child's way occasionally.

'Jill?'

'Yes?'

'You . . . you gonna stay for Christmas and . . . and watch me open my presents?'

She hesitated, trying to think of an answer that would satisfy Joey, yet be truthful as well. Dustin strode into the kitchen, poured himself a cup of coffee, nodded briefly in her direction, and left. The front door slammed.

Her heart sank. She looked back at Joey. 'I'd like to,' she said simply.

He went back to his work, but Jill's concentration

was shot. Dustin's demeanor had resembled a thundercloud and he'd barely looked at her.

Whatever minor easing of tension they'd managed to achieve had reverted to friction again. She couldn't help thinking that the Reed Ranch might not be her home much longer.

It was a very painful thought.

Dustin was letting Rooster pick his way along a stream when he heard Marsh's loud whistle. He returned the signal, then waited for his friend to appear. Moments later he did, astride one of Dustin's geldings.

'You must have news or you wouldn't have ridden out here to find me,' he said.

'Yep. And I'm a damn good friend to do it, too.'

He pulled his hat a little further down over his eyes to shield them from the light. Marsh had managed to park himself in the path of west-riding sun. 'Give me the bad news.'

'They're gone, Dustin. Sadie and her mother have left town. They've had their mail routed to a post office box and canceled their newspaper.'

'Where did they go?'

Marsh shrugged. 'No one seems to know. Or else they're not telling. Would your mother have an idea of where any of Vera Benchley's family might live?'

Dustin pushed his boots into the stirrups to shift his position while he thought about it. 'She might. But how do you know they'd hunt out family?'

'I don't. I'm grasping at straws.'

'Yeah.' They all were. 'Why would they leave, if Holly is theirs? Why would they leave her behind instead of taking her with them? Wouldn't she be safer out of town?'

'I don't know. Dustin, I hate to say this, but I'm beginning to think this picture isn't hanging on the wall straight.'

'What the hell is that supposed to mean?'

Marsh looked away briefly. 'All I know is this. Jill McCall shows up on your property at the same time a stray baby does. She claims she has a scare in town, but we don't have any eye-witness to that. It was a helluva good story. Your mother definitely buys it, right down to imagining that a stitched crown on a blanket is a message. What I don't get is, why isn't there any record of birth in any of the hospitals, and why the Benchleys wouldn't alert us to their problem, if, in fact, there was one? Why dump the baby on your land if she was in so much danger? And where is this guy with the shaved head that Jill supposedly saw?'

Dustin tried to throttle his temper. He reminded himself that this was his friend, his *best* friend of many years, who was only trying to look at the situation from a cop's perspective. Stranger things had happened than what Marsh was suggesting Jill might have done. Still, it was all he could do not to give his horse a swift kick and leave Marsh alone by the stream.

'Maybe there is no record of birth because the baby was born at home. If Vera's such a damn good seamstress, maybe she's good at other things, too,' he said, careful to keep his tone neutral. 'I don't know why they didn't go to the police, unless they were simply scared out of their skin to do it. For all I know, the guy might have threatened them if they did say anything. As for the guy in question, I don't know where he is. You're the one who keeps his ear to the ground with the local youth. Do your damn job and ask around.'

'I am, damn it, Dustin. And you know I am. But I wanted to run this past your thick skull and see if we could thresh out any alternative story line than what we're getting from your housekeeper. You wouldn't be so damned touchy about the thing if you weren't . . .'

Dustin's eyes narrowed. 'If I wasn't what?' he asked, his voice dangerously soft.

'Well, hell! If you weren't blinded by that bright smile and that daisy-fresh appeal of Jill's. I mean, damn, friend. Every time you walk into the room, Jill looks like she's seeing the dawn of a new day. She lights up like a star on a Christmas tree.'

He kicked the horse into motion, intent on getting away from Marsh and everything he was saying. He didn't want to hear it, and he wasn't going to hear it. What he was saying about Jill was ridiculous – both about the baby and about her.

Marsh galloped up alongside him, throwing out an arm to drag him off the horse. They went tumbling to the ground, rolling down into a ravine, punching at each other and swearing like devils.

213

'You sorry ass son-of-a-gun,' Dustin shouted, pinning Marsh to the ground. 'You could have killed me! Or you, not that it would have been any great loss!'

'I'd like to kill you, 'cause I think that's what it's gonna take to get you to listen. You mule-headed son-of-a-bitch, you're thinking with your crotch and not your head!' With a roar, he threw Dustin off of him, leaping to his feet in a boxing stance.

'I'm not buying the crap you're peddling, *friend*. You can't solve the case, so you'd rather lynch Jill than keep working it.'

Marsh circled warily. 'I'm the best damn lawman around. I never leave a case until it's solved. If you don't think Jill's cooked up this scam, then you tell me where the bald-headed boyfriend is.'

'I hope he's in hell. That's where you're going when I get through with you,' Dustin said, lunging to pack a punch at Marsh's jaw. It connected solidly, but the sheriff got one off too, before Dustin backed up, eyeing his opponent cautiously.

'I don't think he exists, except in the mind of your housekeeper. She's bought herself a pretty secure position, with everybody worrying about the baby getting snatched.'

'Not too damn secure after the visit Maxine paid me today,' Dustin growled.

Marsh relaxed his arms slightly. 'What the hell are you mouthing off about now?'

He relaxed his stance a little too, though he didn't completely release the fisted position of his hands.

Marsh was known to get a thrill out of a sucker punch every once in a while. Not that he'd ever pulled it on Dustin, but he would never have bet Marsh would drag him off a galloping horse just to chit-chat, either.

'Maxine learned I had a new housekeeper, courtesy of Joey. He was a bit too enthusiastic about her, and Maxine automatically leaped to the same conclusion you have. That Jill is a bedwarmer and on her way to becoming a permanent one.'

Marsh had the grace to look sheepish. 'I've been wondering if Jill heard me say that.'

'She's heard plenty today I'm sure she'd rather she hadn't.' He tried to release the tension in his chest but couldn't. There was a spring of fury inside him, all coiled up and ready to burst any second. Punching Marsh had taken a little of the tightness out of him, but it wasn't all gone yet. 'Maxine wants me to fire Jill. I didn't take her seriously, until she leveled an accusation against my mother. That she had an affair with David Copeland.'

'Oh, yeah, right. And Santa isn't a fairy-tale fat boy.'

Dustin completely relaxed his arms, knowing that Marsh and he could finish their conversation now without their fists. 'Well, that's how determined she is to win this thing. She made no bones that she's going to make everything much more difficult if Jill remains at the ranch, replacing Nina in the family, to her mind.'

Marsh whistled at his horse, which came to graze at his side. 'The old bat's crazy.'

'Yeah. But you can see that Jill isn't exactly the most popular person in Lassiter. No one, except my mother and me, seems to think her being here is a good thing.'

'I just want you to think, buddy. There's something niggling at me about that woman that I just can't put my finger on. All that sweetness and light bothers me. Maybe it's Nina, remembering that's the way she acted when she was trying to hook you. I don't know. All I do know is that I feel like I'm reading a book, but the last page has been thrown away. How can there be so many pieces to this story missing? Jill's the one answer that ties everything together.'

Dustin shook his head. 'She was too frightened that day. And she doesn't say anything, but I've noticed she doesn't stray far from the house with the baby anymore. Used to be you couldn't keep her indoors. Now she's like a hearth cat.'

'I saw two blankets in front of that hearth. Maybe she likes the company.'

'Shut up. I told you, we kissed, no mountains moved, it was no big deal. The woman was scared and I took advantage of it. Not that it's any of your business, but it's been a helluva long time for me.'

'Me, too,' Marsh agreed. 'Still, there just aren't any other suspects. Why wouldn't the Benchleys at least come to me?'

'Because they were afraid? Because Sadie might have been ashamed? Because they hadn't taken the threat seriously, and once the boyfriend caught up with the baby, they took off without thinking about asking for help?' Dustin snapped his fingers. 'Because Sadie was at risk, too.'

'Okay, I can go with that. But how hard can a guy with no hair be to track down? I've spent a couple mornings hanging around the square and asking questions, but I can get no satisfaction.'

Dustin walked over and grasped his horse's reins. 'I don't know, but something's got to give. I think Mother's arthritis is flaring up again, and that's going to be another problem. Jill's so afraid for the baby she won't go to the grocery with her anymore, which is right, but Mother won't be able to watch the baby if her hips act up.'

'You may have to stick her in the saddle with you.'

'Nah. I don't think Jill rides.'

Marsh laughed loudly as he got on his horse. 'Man, you are out of control. I meant the baby, bozo.'

He snorted and got on his horse, too. 'You'd best watch your mouth, because I'm not sure you're still my friend after today. As I recall, the only way you eat is at my table.'

'Yeah, well, you just count yourself lucky I don't haul your ass into jail for assaulting an officer of the law.'

Marsh turned his horse toward the house, letting the beast have his head, but Dustin followed more slowly. Whether he liked it or not, the fact that his friend didn't believe in Jill the way he did wasn't a good sign. Always before they'd been inseparable, like two sides of a coin. Now they were on different sides, and it was hard to tell which side was right.

Jill waited nervously for Marsh and Dustin to return. Whatever the lawman had wanted to speak to Dustin about, it wouldn't wait for him to return. Usually, the sheriff made himself comfortable in the kitchen with a snack. Today, he'd thanked Jill politely enough and gone to saddle himself a horse. He hadn't even nabbed a gingerbread man.

It was a bad sign when Marsh's stomach couldn't waylay whatever was on his mind. Now she was jittery.

She'd put Joey down for his nap and checked on Eunice and baby Holly. Both were fine and Eunice insisted she didn't want any help with the baby. The two of them looked cozy, so Jill went into her room and thought about packing her suitcase. She even went so far as to drag it out of the closet, knowing that there really wasn't anything Dustin could do about the situation except ask her to leave. She'd seen the look in his eyes as he stormed through the kitchen.

Then she put the suitcase back, telling herself she was being fatalistic. Her feelings were going to get hurt, and she'd have no one to blame but herself, of course. But she might as well look on the bright side and hope that there was the slimmest chance she could stay.

She sat in the kitchen, staring at a cookbook and not registering anything it said about the roast she needed to put in the oven. When the front door opened and shut with a resonating boom, her heart leapt into her throat.

The two men entered the kitchen, filling it with their big-shouldered height. She swallowed, looking from one to the other.

'I see you found him,' she said lamely.

'That I did.'

Marsh sat down across from her. Dustin leaned against the kitchen counter, before pouring out a tumbler of tea.

'If you want one, you'll have to get it yourself,' he told Marsh.

'Naw. Thanks.' Marsh pinned her with a look. 'The Benchleys left town, Jill. There's no sign of when they left, or when they're coming back.'

'Oh, no.' Her mouth dried out. 'How do you know they left town?'

'They stopped their mail and newspaper.'

'Oh, dear. I suppose this means they were really frightened. That doesn't make me feel any better.'

'No?'

She couldn't fathom the look in Marsh's eyes. Dustin watched from his corner, but didn't make an effort to join the conversation.

'Maybe they'll be back soon,' she said lamely. What did he want her to say? Suddenly, she realized she was on edge, and it was because of the sheriff. He was watching her too closely. 'Maybe the baby wasn't theirs,' she offered. 'Maybe it was someone else's.'

'Maybe it was.'

'But I saw the look in that girl's eyes, Marsh. She

was dying to touch Holly, but then she looked terrified when that boy came. I would swear with my last breath that she was the mother.'

'I haven't been able to locate the boyfriend.'

'He shouldn't be too hard to spot in a crowd,' she said thoughtfully. 'I would recognize him immediately.'

'Would you?'

Her temper flared. 'Yes, I would! That was the most frightening moment of my life! I have nightmares about that nasty look on his face, and the meanness in his eyes.'

'Dustin's been a strong shoulder for you to lean on.'

'Yes, he has. He – wait a minute.' Jill stopped, leveling a stern eye on the sheriff. 'I don't like the tone of your voice, Sheriff.'

'Easy, Jill. There are a lot of questions that haven't been answered. I'm trying to find out if you remember anything else that you haven't mentioned.'

She got to her feet. 'No, you're not. You're suggesting that I've got a thing for my employer. You also don't believe me about the hood who was hanging outside of the bakery. I'm beginning to think you're a sad excuse for Lassiter's law.'

Angrily, she turned her back to him, and started putting the cookies on a flat tray. She waited to hear Dustin come to her rescue, but he didn't. Wrath built inside her.

'I knew there had to be something hidden behind that sweet exterior of yours, Jill. You've got a feisty mouth on you.'

I've got a real feisty mouth on me when I know that a baby's in danger and the sheriff's too lazy to look farther than his best friend's kitchen to find the guilty party.'

'Whoa, you two are going at this the wrong way. Marsh, damn it, ask the questions you want answers to, and . . .'

Jill whirled on Dustin. 'I'll answer nothing else. That is not my baby. I did not steal her, I did not have her, I am not a woman with a ticking biological clock.'

'Are you pregnant?'

Staring at Dustin, Jill could feel her mouth hang open. 'Pregnant? What makes you ask that?'

He shrugged, infuriating her.

'Because my ex showed up one day? You really are frightened some woman's going to rope you in again, aren't you?' She knew that Nina's pregnancy had been the reason he'd gotten married because he had told her himself. She had basically thrown herself at him the other night. No doubt his very manly boots were shaking that he might find himself the recipient of another trip to the altar.

'You're the last man on earth I'd set my sights on, Dustin Reed,' she told him. 'You're mean. You're moody. You haven't got anything going for you except a nice family. You aren't anything like the man I'd want for myself.'

Suddenly, to her extreme mortification, she burst into tears. The last few hours spent worrying about her future had taken their toll. To find out that she apparently was on everybody's suspect list was demoralizing.

'Aw, Jill, don't do that,' he said.

'Why not? Because it's a true expression of emotion? Because you're too macho to have a good cry as much as you'd like to? Because it's embarrassing?'

Over his shoulder, Marsh handed her a tissue, which she accepted, jerking it from his hand. Dustin hadn't bothered to answer her question. Backing away, she tore her gaze away from Dustin, before hurrying up the stairs.

'What a couple of jackasses we are,' Dustin said.

'That got way out of hand,' Marsh agreed.

'It didn't get us anywhere, either, except on Jill's bad side.' He looked sorrowfully at the defrosting roast. 'I'd better take the family out to dinner tonight, if I know what's good for me.'

'Damn it,' Marsh said, getting to his feet. 'She's telling the truth.'

'I told you.'

'But she didn't answer your question about being pregnant.'

'No, and she shouldn't. It isn't any of my damn business. It's just that if she's pregnant, she couldn't possibly have recently given birth. I want badly to know the answer, so I didn't ask it right. Truth is, it doesn't matter whether she is or isn't.'

'You going to tell her she has to go?'

'No. I'm going to hell with the devil on this one. Maxine can drag all the accusations into court she

222

likes. Jill stays, if I haven't made her so mad she can't stand to see my face.'

'You better watch that temper of hers. I think you're going to be in big trouble with Jill for a while.' He picked up a gingerbread man, but didn't bite into it. 'I wish that guy would surface so I could nail him.'

'Could be he's gone into hiding, too.'

Marsh straightened. 'Or he followed the Benchleys. Knew where they were going.'

Dustin sighed. 'Get to work, buddy. So far, all you've managed to do is piss off my housekeeper – and me.'

'Well.' Marsh sighed heavily. 'Guess it's time for me to go, then. The weather report said the roads were going to start freezing again around twilight.'

'Watch the porch when you leave; there's still some slick spots from the last freeze. I don't want to take your sorry butt to the hospital when you slip off the steps.'

'I'll let you know if I find anything else out.'

Marsh walked outside, as Dustin watched from the door. He was steamed with his friend, though he wasn't going to talk about it. Their friendship had taken a major hit with his attitude toward Jill. Of course, Dustin knew he had no one to blame for his own asinine behavior.

A second later, the cruiser pulled down the lane. A piece of paper flew off the car and onto the ground, where it blew toward the porch in the wintry wind. Dustin turned to go inside, before halting. He thought for several seconds, his skin tightening from the cold.

Not from the cold. Some strange sensation pulled him back outside. Reaching down to pick up the piece of paper, Dustin told himself it was good to retrieve it so it wouldn't blow into the area where some of his stock might get it. He'd cut open far too many a good steer that had died without seeming cause, only to find a bottle cap or six-ring plastic some idiot had thrown out a car window and that had then wound up inside his cattle.

He told himself he was being cautious, even as he unfolded the small piece of blue-lined, white paper. The kind any school kid might use for class work. The writing was round and uncertain, as though written by a teenager who hadn't quite crossed the threshold into adulthood.

Dear Mr Reed, Pleas protreckt Holly. Curtis Lynch is going to steal her.

CHAPTER 14

Dustin stared at the piece of paper. 'Curtis Lynch?' he muttered to himself. The wind picked up, blasting chilly breezes against him, but he didn't move. It wasn't a family name he knew. Dissatisfied, he thrust the paper into his jacket pocket and went inside to leave a message for Marsh to call him.

After calling the police station, Dustin hung up the phone, knowing he could no longer avoid talking to Jill. He walked up the stairs and knocked on her door. There was no answer. He tapped softly again, but when she didn't open the door, he got worried. Slowly, he turned the knob.

Only Jill's nicely rounded, denim-covered rear end was visible from the doorway as she knelt inside the closet. Though that sight definitely got his attention, he was more interested in what the rest of her was doing, engaging in a task that looked suspiciously like packing.

'What are you doing?' he demanded.

She shrieked and whirled to glare at him. 'What are *you* doing in my room?'

He took a deep breath and reminded himself that he'd come to get himself off the hot seat and that she had every right to be mad at him. 'I came to apologize for what happened downstairs.'

'I should think so! Do you think everything your friend thinks, particularly that I'm a baby-napper of some kind, and a liar – or do you just imagine I'm after you?'

'Neither. I didn't butt in when Marsh was talking to you because I knew you could handle him. I thought it would be more convincing if I let you do your own talking. Apparently, you didn't need me to intervene, because Marsh believes you wholeheartedly.'

'Great.' She smiled sarcastically. 'Now if only I could convince you that you're not quite the catch you seem to think you are.' Angrily, she tossed a pair of shoes into the case.

He held his hands up in surrender. 'Jill, I heard you throwing up the day your folks came out. It worried me.'

'But you kissed me anyway, even thinking I might be pregnant?' Her expression was questioning.

He wasn't going to admit that he was attracted her, enough so that it didn't matter whether she'd be buying booties in a few months or not. 'Well, kissing wasn't going to get you pregnant, if you weren't already.'

'No, it's not.' She lowered her gaze. 'I'm not pregnant.'

He couldn't explain the enormous relief that filled

him, so he reverted to the attitude he knew best. 'Good. Then I won't have to pay you for maternity leave.'

Her head snapped up. There were fireworks in her eyes. 'Dustin Reed, you're somewhat of an ass.'

A chuckle escaped him. He did like this lady's spunk. 'Yeah, well. Would you care to be seen in public with an ass? I figured Marsh and I have about thrown you out of the mood to cook, and I have a suspicion Mother's not feeling too well, so we might as well eat out tonight.'

'That sounds like an appealing peace offering, although I'm not ready to let you off the hook completely,' she said. 'But what about Holly?'

'What about her?'

'Well, should she be out? Where anybody can see her?'

Dustin thought about the note in his pocket. After a moment, he handed it to Jill. She read it, her eyes widening.

'When did you find this?'

'A few minutes ago. It was stuck under the windshield wiper on Marsh's cruiser.'

'Sadie's been here, then! Not too long ago.'

He shook his head. 'There are rain splatters on the paper, so it's been there for a while. I don't think Marsh saw it when he drove out here. They might have seen him checking out their house and put it on his car in a hurry before he left.'

'So Sadie and her mother are too frightened to visit the police station.'

'That would be my guess.'

'And this Curtis knows the baby is here.' The expression on Jill's face was heartbroken. 'I was so careful not to be followed. I must not be as good at high-speed getaways as I thought I was.'

Dustin crossed his arms. It wasn't necessary for Jill to take the blame for some punk's determined pursuit of Holly. 'He could have found out she was here any other number of ways.'

She sank back on her heels. 'No, he couldn't have. No one knows I'm working here. Sadie wouldn't have told, even if he tried to beat it out of her. I should never have gone into town. Now I've put that sweet baby in danger.'

'Of course I don't agree with you, but I will say that them leaving town isn't a good sign.'

'It does seem very desperate. Obviously something's scared them. I think Holly and I should just stay in tonight.'

Dustin nodded, although he hated what his problems were doing to Jill's life. Basically, she was a prisoner in his house. He didn't like that idea at all. Meeting her eyes, he tried another tack. 'I feel like you deserve a night out though. It's the least I can do for you.'

Sudden electricity hummed to life between them. Jill's soft lips parted as she considered his suggestion. Then she shook her head, pulling her gaze from his.

'I don't think that's a good idea. Thank you, anyway.'

He felt relieved by her polite turn-down. The

minute he uttered the words, he'd known he was making a mistake. They couldn't afford any time alone together, not when they had so many strikes against them.

'How about a bucket of fried chicken, then?' he asked, trying to sound as nonchalant as possible. 'With some mashed potatoes and salad?'

'That gets my vote. Ask your mother if chicken suits her, although I have a feeling she'll be just as glad not to have a mess in the kitchen tonight.'

'You noticed she doesn't seem quite herself?' Dustin wondered if Jill's worry for his mother went past the housekeeper-employer relationship. They did seem to get along very well. That in itself was a comfort to him, because he knew Jill would take care of Eunice in the event she fell or became ill. With Nina, there had always been a stiff distance between her and his mother. Two opposite sides, battle lines drawn sometime when he hadn't even realized it.

'I'm not sure if she isn't herself, or if it's something else,' Jill said thoughtfully. 'I'm not sure if any of us is quite ourself right now. I know I've been ready to jump out of my skin ever since I saw that awful hood.'

'It doesn't help that we have another winter storm rolling in,' Dustin told her. 'Are you sure you don't want to get out before the roads get icy?'

Jill stood and crossed to the window. Looking at the landscape, she said, 'I'm just as happy to stay indoors where it's warm.'

And safe. It was unspoken, but Jill was right. None

of them had been able to relax, Maxine's unfortunate visit having added to the air of tension. He cleared his throat.

'Jill, I'm sure you heard some of what was said between Maxine Copeland and me this morning.'

'Mostly Maxine,' she murmured, not looking at him.

'I don't want you to worry about anything where she's concerned. She is a very confused and unhappy person who wants everyone around her to be miserable, too.'

She met his gaze. 'You're not letting me go?'

'I'm too much of an ass for that, remember? Way too selfish,' he assured her. 'You're the only housekeeper who will stay on with us, anyway.'

Although she smiled slightly, he could tell Maxine's words had found their mark. He wanted to reassure Jill, but if he said what he really wanted to, he risked stirring up the uneasiness between them. She had to have heard Marsh call her a bedwarmer. The last thing he wanted her to think was that he hoped she would become that.

'I'm going to speak to Mother, then I'll be off to get the chicken,' he said gruffly. 'Let me know if there's anything you want from the grocery store since we're looking for bad weather.'

'All right.' Their gazes touched, and as crystal-blue eyes met dark ones, a flash of wary communication passed between them. She'd ceased packing her suitcase for the moment, but he sensed she hadn't enjoyed the day's events. For Jill to cry, her feelings had to have been pretty hurt. Reluctantly, he turned in the doorway, uncertain as to what to say.

Then he swivelled around. 'Jill, you can leave the ranch any time the job gets to be too much for you. Your bonus is assured whether or not you stay the entire year. You can call it combat pay or whatever you like, but you damn well deserve it. You have nerves of steel and a determined stubbornness that I've never seen in a woman other than my mother. You fit in this family, and we'd miss you like hell if you left.'

Those lips had parted again, those eyes had widened as far as they could go, all having an unnerving effect on him. Dustin turned and slammed the door behind him, figuring he'd probably made a huge jackass out of himself for sure this time.

But if saying his piece would keep the lady in his home, then he'd gladly accept the label of jackass.

Astonishment flowed through Jill at Dustin's words. His support was warming. The fact he was standing behind her despite Marsh's and Maxine's misgivings was wonderful. But the best part was that now she knew Dustin at least respected her.

Of course, men respected some women, and then other women they wanted. She sighed and emptied the suitcase before pushing it back into the closet. The fact that she fell into the former category was a good sign, she supposed. It meant she wouldn't have to hunt for another job right before Christmas. That would be so disheartening.

Carl obviously had not respected her or he wouldn't have punched such serious holes in their relationship. A little respect between her and Dustin was probably the best she could have hoped for anyway.

It was better than him seeing her as a convenient bedwarmer.

Or was it? She had been too mortified to tell him that she and Carl had never once shared a bed. His opinion on lovemaking was that a couple only entered the marriage bed once they had paid their dues at the altar. She let out her breath in a disdainful pff! of air. Oh, she wasn't pregnant – and fortunate that was, because it would have been such a disaster.

The truth was, this time, she definitely might consider becoming the object of a man's desire. If that man was Dustin.

However, as with Carl, that seemed unlikely. Dustin had too much on his mind, had too many winds from the past buffeting him for him to be recklessly nursing a passion for his housekeeper.

She sighed, knowing in her heart it was for the best, but wishing things could be different all the same.

Dustin returned with the fried chicken and trimmings and set it on the kitchen counter. No one had come downstairs, so he shrugged out of his jacket and hung it in the hall closet. Maybe confession made a man hungry, because since he'd told Jill how he felt, he had been starving. If the rest of the crew didn't get downstairs soon to get their dinner, he'd eat the entire bucket.

He went to the stairway to shout that dinner was ready. Jill was halfway down, and the hesitant look in her eyes made him swallow his shout. 'Dinner's ready,' he said gruffly.

'I'll set out some paper plates and napkins.'

She followed him into the kitchen, but as he turned to ask her if any of the food should be put on the table, he found her back turned to him. Studiously not looking at him, she said, 'I don't think I'll put out paper plates and napkins, after all. It will feel more festive if we use the checkered napkins and dinner plates.'

The woman was avoiding him. He didn't like it, but maybe once they both sat down to eat, matters would get better. Dustin decided it would be best if he acted helpful by putting out tea glasses and the pitcher.

'Is Mother coming down?' he asked.

'I'll check on her again in a little while. When I heard your truck pull in, I looked in her room and she and Holly were both napping. Joey's washing his hands so he'll be down in a second.'

She fixed a plate for her and one with smaller portions for Joey. The thought of eating with his taciturn housekeeper was starting to kill Dustin's appetite. It bothered him greatly that the tension between them had increased over the last few hours. Although he knew that kiss in front of the fireplace could never be repeated, he was hoping for some kind of happy medium.

Still, they had some time now. Perhaps it would stay quiet for a few days around the ranch and give them a chance to let the harsh words and hurt feelings subside a bit. He sat across from the place Jill had taken. She smiled at him, although it wasn't her typical bright, dazzling smile.

He missed that smile.

'Jill . . .' he began, but the ringing of the phone cut him off. Getting up, he snatched the phone receiver from off the wall. 'Yeah?'

'Dustin, I got your message. What's up?'

Since it was only he and Jill in the room, Dustin swiftly relayed the contents of the note. There was a long pause at the other end of the line before Marsh spoke again.

'That little scrap of paper on my car said all that? Hell, I must be losing it. I hate to think I might have missed that warning. Sadie was obviously worried enough to risk leaving that note. Makes me think Lynch could be much closer than I thought he was.'

'Me too.' Dustin could hardly bear to think about it.

'Look, I'm going to send an extra cruiser by tonight, just to be cautious. You're all staying in tonight, right?'

'Yeah. With the roads turning bad and then that fun little message, we opted to stay in and eat fried chicken.'

'Excellent idea. Dustin, I'm sorry as hell about this.'

'Don't be. I had started to go inside before some

234

sixth sense told me I should go back and pick up the paper.'

'Yeah, but it kinda scares me that my sixth sense isn't working.'

'Just find that Lynch guy and we'll forgive you for not being perfect.'

Marsh sighed. 'Hell, I wish I could. No one in the town claims to have seen him. Jill's description doesn't seem to match anyone they know. He didn't go to high school here, either, because I checked the school records office.'

'All we need is some outside gang of punks moving in to cause trouble in Lassiter,' Dustin said in a surly tone. 'I'm going to have my shotgun loaded for bear, though, just in case.'

'Check the window and door locks. And Dustin, if you get the slightest bit worried, or Jill does, have the dispatcher contact me immediately. I'll be out there on the double.'

'I know you will. Thanks, Marsh.'

Hanging up the phone, it was all Dustin could do to meet Jill's gaze. Joey skidded into the kitchen, stopping when he saw his father.

'Hi, Daddy.'

Dustin blinked, wondering if the child had always been so reserved with him or if he was just now noticing it. He wasn't an overly affectionate man, but right now, he felt like pulling his son up to him and hugging him tightly. Jill was watching him with a curious look in her eyes. He reached down slowly and ruffled the hair on his son's head.

'Hi, son,' he said.

Joey jumped onto the plank bench and dug into a dinner roll. Dustin sat next to his son, glancing up to find Jill smiling at him, that big gorgeous smile of hers that he loved.

'I'm learning,' he told her.

'Yes, you are.'

He didn't want to think about how good her praise felt. Instead, he said, 'Well, what should we do this evening, since we're basically housebound?'

Jill's delicate brows arched inquiringly.

'If not for Holly's sake, then the weather would have us shut in.' Dustin tucked into a big helping of mashed potatoes.

'Was Marsh concerned?' Jill asked with a protective look Joey's way.

He knew she was trying not to voice too much in case of upsetting his son. Dustin slid a careful look at Joey before nodding. 'He's going to have extra patrols tonight.' He cleared his throat, wishing he could say more to soothe her but Joey's presence made it difficult. 'We should just be on our guard.'

Joey glanced up, looking back and forth between the two of them. 'So,' Jill said, her voice too bright, 'perhaps tonight is the night we string popcorn then, and have hot chocolate in front of the fireplace. We could even practice our Christmas carols.'

She was determined to keep herself and the rest of the household busy, Dustin realized. He had accounts he could review; in fact, time spent in his office would be beneficial. But he always had put the

236

ranch first. Tonight, when his mind was so tangled with worry, and his family – Jill, too – would try to hide their fear, maybe he'd be better off making popcorn balls. Or whatever it was Jill had suggested to keep their mind off the cold winter storm outside already sending its cold, drafty fingers into the house.

'Sounds like a plan to me,' he said.

'Yeah!' Joey agreed. 'You . . . you help me, Daddy?'

Dustin paused, his fork halfway to his mouth. Slowly, he put the utensil down, turning to Joey. 'Yes, son. We'll do everything together tonight.'

'Oh, boy!'

The light in his son's eyes caused Dustin's heart to squeeze tight. How could he have missed doing the things with him that made happiness beam from his face like radiant starlight? How had he allowed his own frozen soul to ignore his child's needs?

His gaze traveled to his housekeeper, who sat watching him with neither praise nor condemnation in her eyes. If not for Jill's steady, patient encouragement, he might not have realized what he was doing to Joey – what he was doing to both of them by allowing his fear of losing him to take over.

He had more to be grateful for this Christmas season than he'd realized.

Picking his fork up again, Dustin trained his gaze on his plate. He told himself that he was getting sentimental on a night when he needed to be clearly alert to danger. There was no time for him to get all mushy when there might be someone out there waiting for his attention to wander. As it did whenever Jill was around.

He was about to put a bite of chicken into his mouth when Holly's sudden piercing wail, markedly different from her usual call for dinner, bolted him from his seat and up the stairs.

Curtis Lynch stared into the old, peeling mirror in the gas station restroom. Pulling off the cowboy hat he was wearing, he inspected his image. Without his black jacket and gold earring, and sporting this ridiculous flannel shirt and felt hat, he passed for any other shit-kicker in town. He looked like a good ol' boy, just like that big, dumb rancher who was hiding Holly. Thought he was hiding Holly. As if anyone stupid enough to spend his life cleaning up after cows and horses could outsmart Curtis Lynch.

Oh, he didn't have a college education. But he'd spent his life growing up on the streets, and learned a hell of a lot more there than he ever did in some wise-ass classroom. Hadn't he told Sadie that? A hollow laugh rolled out of him. Guess he'd taught her more about life than she'd ever have learned without him. He'd scared her so badly she wouldn't cause him any trouble now. Her mama and her had hotfooted it out of town, and right smart of them that had been. It would have been a shame to have to slap that old woman around – though he couldn't deny he would have enjoyed it. But it had all worked out for the best, as usual. Their absence gave him a plenty nice place to hole up in until he'd accomplished his mission.

Night was falling, the air becoming thick with snowflakes. That would be bad for visibility, which was very good for him. Putting the cowboy hat back on, Curtis lit a cigarette, craving the nicotine in his system. Leaving the gas station, he headed across the street. The only western shop in town was still open, despite the threatening weather. Another hit of luck for him, because he needed one last piece to his costume. One of those heavy winter coats the farmers were always wearing would keep him warm until the right moment to snatch the brat.

Glancing in the shop window, Curtis eyed the lady with big hair and sloppy clothes working the counter. Some dumb cow-chaser's even dumber wife. He could steal a coat and be gone without her ever knowing he'd been in the store.

'Eunice!' Jill cried, hurrying into the room behind Dustin. 'Are you all right?'

The elderly woman sat up in her bed, rubbing at her eyes as if she was trying hard to awaken. Holly had quieted momentarily when Jill and Dustin had raced into the bedroom, but now she set up another wrenching series of wails.

'My goodness!' Eunice said, moving her legs off the bed. 'Did I miss Holly's wake-up call?'

Jill carefully picked up the baby, patting her on the back soothingly. 'Maybe she never gave her usual warning cry.' She shot a worried look at Dustin. Was his mother all right, or did he see the same lines of tiredness around Eunice's eyes that Jill saw?

'The baby might have been napping so hard she didn't realize how hungry she was until she woke up. It sounded like she went from zero to sixty in about three seconds,' Dustin said, his tone crisp yet comforting. As if nothing worrisome had happened. Jill realized that both she and Dustin were on edge or they wouldn't have done those Olympic-style sprints up the stairs.

'She certainly did.' Eunice rubbed her forehead with a blue-lined hand. 'Or I was sleeping extra-hard myself.'

'I don't doubt you needed a rest,' Jill told her. 'But I agree with Dustin. I'm going to take her downstairs for a bottle. Eunice, if you're hungry, Dustin brought fried chicken for supper. I can bring some up if you like.'

Eunice shook her head. 'I'll be down soon. Thank you, Jill.'

Jill nodded, hurrying down the stairs. The baby was throwing every fiber of her little body into her wailing, and tense as Jill had already been, the crying was tearing at her nerves. Swiftly, she fixed the bottle and sat down on the plank seat, popping the bottle into Holly's mouth.

'Ah. Much better.' Looking up with a sigh, Jill straightened stick-stiff when she realized Joey was no longer sitting at the table.

'Joey? Joey?' she called. She stood with the baby in her arms when she didn't receive an answer. Telling

240

herself she was worrying too much, she went to the parlor, thinking he might have gone to see the Christmas tree since he knew they were going to string popcorn tonight.

He wasn't in there either. Jill hurried to the staircase. 'Dustin, is Joey up there?'

Instantly, the rancher poked his head out into the hall. 'No. You mean he's not down there?'

'I can't find him.' Even though she didn't think Joey was at risk, the bizarre note and easygoing Marsh's sudden warning to stay in the house had made her jumpy. 'I thought maybe he slipped into Eunice's room.'

Dustin crossed the hall and pushed Joey's bedroom door open. 'Son, what are you doing?' Jill heard him say.

Her knees felt weak with relief. Clutching Holly tight, she went into the parlor and sat down. She heard boots on the stairs but didn't look up, assuming father and son would go into the kitchen.

Instead they entered the parlor. 'Joey thought Holly might like to hold his favorite bear since she was crying so hard,' Dustin said. Joey held out the stuffed animal, which Jill took with a shaky smile.

'Thank you, Joey. See, Holly? You have a bear to keep you company now, too.'

'She . . . she need him,' Joey said, pointing to the bear. 'He be her friend.'

'That's very sweet of you, Joey.'

'Come on, son. Let's go finish dinner.' Dustin took his son by the arm, gently, and steered him into the

241

kitchen. Jill tucked the bear into Holly's basket and followed, settling herself back in her original place.

Dustin sat, pulling open a roll to butter it.

'Did you tell her about the note, yet?'

Dustin shook his head. 'She's so worn out and worried that I hate to say anything that will make her feel worse. I think Maxine's accusation is really leveling her. Now that she's given us a peek at the kind of cards she intends to play, Mother is trying not to get too worked up about it.'

'And probably worrying about it more, instead.'

'I think so.' Dustin sighed. 'What a Christmas.'

'Well, we'll manage somehow.' Jill got to her feet. 'I'm going to get Holly's basket so I can keep her down here while I clean up the dinner dishes.'

She headed up the stairs. Peeking into Eunice's room, she saw her resting comfortably again. Slipping in, she moved Holly to her shoulder and snagged the basket with her free hand. Quietly, she closed the door and went back down the stairs and into the parlor, wanting to light the fire so the room would get warm in time for popcorn stringing.

Gently, she snuggled Holly into her basket, then knelt in front of the fireplace to light the fire. Easing back on her heels to watch the wood slowly kindling to life, Jill reveled in the quiet beauty of the room and the sense of peace the decorated tree and sparkling lights brought her. Eunice had placed Santas with flat, weighted bottoms on the mantel, so that their feet hung merrily above her head. The tiny tree on the table adorned by the skirt Joey had helped make

242

brought a smile to her face. There were a lot of good things in this Christmas season, too, though Dustin had too many worries on his mind to appreciate them.

A sudden sound outside the big-paned window drew Jill's startled gaze. When there was no other noise, she commanded herself to relax. 'Just the wind in the pecan trees,' she told herself. Humming a Christmas tune to herself, she went to the window, forcing herself to look out and face her fear.

Down on the road passing in front of the ranch, she could just make out a police cruiser going by. Marsh had promised extra vigilance by his people, and obviously they intended to make sure the ranch was secure. Jill sighed with relief and went to move some of the ornaments on the tiny tree, giving herself time to calm down before she went back to the kitchen.

'Oh, a diaper change,' she told Holly. 'We need a diaper after that nice nap and bottle you had. Why didn't you say something?'

Picking the basket up, she walked into the hall. A quick glance into the kitchen showed her that Dustin and his son were putting away the dinner dishes for her. 'Forks there, spoons there,' Dustin guided Joey as the silverware was placed into the dishwasher.

Jill hurried upstairs, wanting to get Holly changed and be back down before the kitchen was all cleaned up without her help. There was no point in Dustin thinking he had to coddle her just because they'd had a small difficulty between them this morning. He

243

appeared eager to let matters smooth out between them; she wanted the same thing.

Deftly, she changed Holly and hurried back to the kitchen. Unfortunately, the work was finished.

'You men work fast.'

Dustin threw a dishtowel over his shoulder. 'It was only a couple of dishes. Not too hard for us.'

'Well, then. Let me get the popcorn popping and see how good you are at that.' She laid the baby's basket on the table, noticing that Dustin didn't seem to be in a big hurry to leave the kitchen. Joey flipped on the television and settled down in front of a Charlie Brown Christmas show.

Small snowflakes crackled as they hit the window. 'Look, Joey,' she said, walking closer, 'we're going to have all kinds of snow tonight.'

'We . . . we can make snow angels to . . . tomorrow.'

He looked all ready for that. 'Yes, we can,' she said with a smile.

A sudden red burst outside the window grabbed her attention. Her heart rate picked up as she peered hard through the darkness. There was little she could make out except that the red light was on top of a car parked at the end of the lane.

'Dustin,' she said quietly, 'something other than the storm may have just become a problem.'

CHATPER 15

'What is it?' Dustin leaped to his feet, feeling his heart hammer against his chest as he looked out the window. The whirling red light drew a blazing warning signal in the frosty night. 'I'll go check it out.'

'Be careful.' Jill met Dustin's gaze. A high-voltage current jumped between them, stronger than anything she'd ever felt before. She couldn't bear to think of him getting hurt. Or worse.

'I'll be fine.' He turned and went into the entry hall to shrug into his jacket. Her heart clenched when he picked up his shotgun. Pulling open the door, he disappeared into the frigid darkness. Cold draughts hit her in the face, making her gasp, so when his truck roared to life, she closed the door and hurried back into the kitchen.

'Joey, why don't we go upstairs?' For some reason, she felt like she needed to be up there keeping an eye on Holly. With all of them forming a protective shield of sorts, they'd have the best chance of keeping her safe.

'Are we . . . we going to make popcorn?'

'Oh.' She was so rattled she'd forgotten. 'That's a great idea. We can carry it upstairs and let your grandmother help us string it if she wants to. It will be like a party.' She smiled reassuringly at the child. 'As a matter of fact, let me go ask Eunice if she's ready for her dinner tray.'

'Daddy going to . . . to come to the party?'

Joey's hopeful eyes turned to her. Automatically, Jill glanced out the window. The flashing red light had been turned off. No movement of any kind cut through the darkness. Her heart beat a little more normally. 'I'll bet that just as soon as the popcorn is ready, your dad will be able to join our party.'

'Okay.'

Jill smiled, hugging Joey before she went up the stairs. As she pushed Eunice's door open a crack, she saw Holly's eyes were open and looking around. Eunice snored lightly, her breathing deep and regular. Obviously she was worn out.

She lifted Holly's basket, edging toward the doorway. As she walked downstairs, Jill tucked the blanket closer around the infant. 'Goodness, it's gotten a little drafty down here,' she said. 'But I'll fix that in no time. You'll like hearing popcorn pop, Holly.' She skidded to a stop in the kitchen.

'Joey?' She walked back into the hall to check the parlor. 'Oh, no,' she breathed.

The front door was slightly ajar, about three inches, but that was enough to let her know where

246

Joey had gone. Flying to the door, she rushed outside to stand on the porch. 'Joey!' she cried. 'Honey, come to Jill! It's too cold out here!'

No answer. Her heart pounded crazily in her chest. Joey had been determined for his dad to join their 'party'. Dreadful intuition told her that the natural anxiety of a child had led him to seek out his father and make certain of his presence.

'Joey!' she called out again. There was no help for it. She stepped off the porch, the Moses basket clutched tightly in her hands. Moving quickly through the darkness, an awful feeling clawed at Jill's stomach. Dustin was going to be furious with her for not keeping a closer watch on Joey. If anything happened to Dustin's son, he would never forgive her.

'Joey!' she cried desperately. Suddenly, in a channel of bitter night air, she could hear sobbing. The lane seemed like it would never end before she made it to Joey. Draining relief almost knocked her to her knees when she saw the forlorn child standing in the middle of the driveway, tears gleaming on his face.

'Oh, honey.' She set Holly's basket on the ground and hugged Joey tightly to her. 'Why did you leave without telling me?'

'I want . . . want my Daddy. He . . . he said he help me.'

'Oh, Lord. Sweetheart, he'll be back soon.' She said it confidently and hoped she was right. Joey was shivering with cold. Jill pressed him against her leg as she stood. Placing the basket over one arm, she kept

Joey as close to her as possible to keep him warm and walked back to the house.

From his camouflaged hiding place among the pecan trees, Curtis Lynch watched the touching moment with a grin. People could be so stupid. Anybody could see this group was dumber than most. The woman wasn't wearing a coat in the freezing weather and she'd brought the thing he wanted out into the cold with her. The cops were still busy with the speeder they'd stopped – now all that stood between him and success was one lone, coatless woman, hampered by an additional child.

He could snatch the baby and zoom away on his motorcycle before anyone ever heard her scream.

Striding from the darkness, his gaze never wavering from the woman with the basket, Curtis flexed his hands for the easiest theft luck could have provided him.

Jill heard the crackling of leaves, perceiving in that split-second that she might be in danger. Gasping, she started to run, but a hand came out of nowhere and grabbed her arm, yanking her to a stop. Reflexively an ear-piercing scream left her throat, but as she twisted to get away from her attacker, she turned and saw the terrible determination in his eyes.

'Dustin!' she screamed. Struggling to keep the basket handle in her grasp, she and the man whose face she'd never been able to forget engaged in a tug of war. Joey was crying and beating the hood with his fists. Holly's wail mixed in with Jill's scream. 'Marsh! Dustin!'

The man reached out, slapping her hard against the face. Jill reeled, but her hands stayed tight around the handle. The straw made tearing noises and for an awful moment, she feared it would simply pull apart, dumping Holly to the ground.

'Help!' she screamed, placing a decisive kick to the attacker's leg. He cursed and slapped her again, harder. Jill's ears rang and tears burst into her eyes. Automatically, she reached out and jabbed him in the eye.

Red fury exploded inside Curtis at the sudden pain in his eye. The bitch! He was going to kill her before he made his get-away. She was stronger than he'd counted on and putting up a helluva fight – she was going to get him caught if he didn't put her down now.

Drawing back with his fist, he slammed it into her face, hard enough to take a man to the ground. She slipped on the slightly frozen gravel, going to her knees. The child was still beating on him with his fists, like irritating rainwater falling on his back. Curtis dealt him a small slap and watched the child fly like a rag in the opposite direction. Now, fortune was within his grasp. He'd be over the border before tomorrow's light.

The woman had risen to her feet, blood running from her nose as she hurried to the little boy. The sudden sound of tires grinding and horn blaring told him it was time to retreat. Carrying the basket under an arm like a package, he hurried to his hiding place, vaulted his motorcycle and jammed it to life. The baby was thrashing, not liking being crunched up as he held the basket between his knees for balance. Tough. He didn't have time to make the princess more comfortable.

Motorcycle roaring, he sped through the stand of pecan trees on a path that went at an angle to the main road.

Dustin's heart nearly stopped at the sight of Joey lying on the ground. Jill bent over his son, but when she raised her head, he saw the cost of his family's need to her.

'Oh, Jill.' He crouched to take his son in his arms, nearly crying at the helpless feel of his own child weeping against him. Joey had needed him and he hadn't been there for him. The look on Jill's face was more than enough to tell him that Holly was gone.

Eunice met them at the door. 'My heavens! Jill, are you all right?'

'I'm fine.' She nodded, reaching to take Joey from Dustin's arms. Tears shone in her eyes. 'We'll be okay, now, Dustin. Please go get Holly back.'

Jill was right. There wasn't time for him to stay and care for them the way he wanted. Even now, he could hear the burst of sirens wailing down the main road, alerted no doubt by his furious pounding on the truck's horn. He'd certainly done his best to sound the alarm.

'I'll get her,' he promised, determination filling him like red-hot lava inside a volcano. And when he found Curtis Lynch, the hood was going to have to smoke cigarettes through a gap in his teeth for the rest of his life. 'Don't worry,' he said to Jill, before turning to run to his truck.

At the bottom of the hill, any sign of police presence was long gone. From the distant sirens, he could tell Curtis had headed away from town. Traveling toward Oklahoma, no doubt. The baby-napper had made his exit from an obscure path in the pecan trees. Dustin knew a farm road where he could meet up with the motorcycle. Jill's puffy face, swollen from what looked to have been a pretty mean punch, jumped into his memory, taunting him. She'd put up the struggle of a lifetime to have earned that blue-bruise mark of distinction. Oh, he was going to meet up with that motorcycle.

He promised himself that there would be hell to pay when he did.

Speeding his truck around the curve of the farm road, Dustin didn't take his foot from the pedal when he saw the police blockade up ahead. He honked, cruising on through, knowing that Curtis would have been too smart to take the obvious path. Taking another turn in the road, he came out on a road used mainly by tractors and other slow-moving machinery. It was a dangerous road because it wasn't well-paved, and the meandering curves met the busy main road all at once in a dizzying array of traffic.

Pushing the truck to its limit, yet watchful of any headlights he might see so he could slow down in time, Dustin knew he had to be close to Lynch. Still, the tightness inside him wouldn't relax until he knew for certain that monster wasn't going to elude him.

Suddenly, he realized there was another vehicle on the road ahead. It had pulled to the side, its oblong shape only a darker shadow in the night. He slowed, a strange sort of premonition in his mind.

It was Marsh. Dustin pulled alongside, backing his truck into place along the cruiser.

'What the hell took you so long?' Marsh demanded.

Dustin ignored him. 'He hasn't been by?'

'Nope. Turn your lights off. We don't want him getting suspicious and turning back. Last radio transmission said he never made it to the police barricade.'

Dustin nodded. Of course Lynch was too smart for that. 'Good.'

'Yep. Now we just wait and watch.'

'How are you planning on stopping him?'

'Nothing says I have to. I can tuck in for a nice long drive into Oklahoma if necessary. The gas is going to run out of his tank eventually.' He patted the seat beside him. 'Got me some root beer in here for emergencies.'

'I'm going too.'

'Nah.' Marsh shook his head. 'You don't like root beer and you'd disturb my concentration. You can follow in your truck if you like, though. Better yet, why don't you park it about twenty-five feet up the way, sort of angle it a bit so you can follow when we whiz past you?'

'Why don't I put out some flares?' The idea hit Dustin out of nowhere. 'You have any flares, Marsh? Maybe he doesn't know this road as well as we do. Maybe he doesn't realize it dead-ends if you don't stay on the farm road.'

'Hey, you're thinking like a cop now.' Marsh went to his trunk, opening it to retrieve some flares. He lifted his head. 'But you better hurry. I think I hear something, and it doesn't sound like a pedestrian.'

Dustin heard it too. Running up the road, he lit the flares and tossed them to the ground in a misleading direction. Then he waited off the shoulder, prepared to run out to re-route any unfortunate driver who might slow down for the signals.

But it was a motorcycle heading their way. The whining roar of the motor was unmistakable. 'Come on, Lynch,' Dustin muttered to himself. 'Have I got a surprise for you.'

As he'd expected, the rider slowed, then came to a complete halt. The road was difficult to see in the darkness, the curve making matters worse. Dustin could hear cursing, then a baby's wail. White-hot anger ripped through him, nearly as blinding as the motorcycle's headlight. From the other direction, he saw Marsh snaking forward. Curtis got off the bike, walking the road, obviously confused. Dustin stayed still, seeing Marsh halt in the shadows. A second later, he was creeping toward the bike.

Lynch whirled, aware he had company. He hurried toward the motorcycle, but not before Dustin landed on him in a tackle.

'Shit!' the man lying underneath him screamed. Lynch bucked, freeing himself for a moment. The two of them rolled over and over on the hard-packed dirt, each vying for control. Though Dustin was taller, he immediately sensed his opponent was no wimp. Mean strength was an advantage as Lynch pummeled him with blows. Dustin knew those same fists had hit Jill and his son, and uncontrollable rage burst in his veins. Working himself into a sitting position above the hood, he sent a knock-out blow to his chin. Lynch was suddenly still beneath him.

Marsh walked forward with the basket. 'Good work.'

'Yeah.' Dustin rubbed his sore chin. 'Thanks for staying out of it.'

'You didn't need my help.' Marsh laughed, the sound carrying in the sudden stillness. 'He's flatter than a rug.'

Dustin stood, not proud at all of his handiwork. The baby's wail was reassuring in a way, but it was also an up-front reminder that he had a family scared-stiff and injured at home.

'I guess I should help you haul his ass to your cruiser,' he said reluctantly. 'Get your cuffs. I need to get back.' He peeked into the basket, seeing tiny fists beat the air. 'I don't think she suffered any damage.'

'No. She's just pissed to be out for a breezy night ride when she could be at the Reed Ranch basking in front of the fire,' Marsh said, laying the basket down and striding forward to handcuff Lynch.

The sight of Lynch rising to his knees caught Dustin off guard. Marsh cursed and moved swiftly, but not before the hood pulled a small gun from inside his jacket. Dustin launched himself forward to protect his friend, but his motions seemed delayed as a fire-burst rent the stillness. Marsh hit the ground with a groan.

Roaring, Dustin threw himself on the punk. Marsh might be dead, all because of this creep. If he didn't wrest the gun away, Dustin knew he was going to end up in the same condition as Marsh. Dead on the side of the road. The hood aimed a purposeful knee at his groin, but Dustin arched, taking it painfully on the thigh. Enraged, he delivered a crushing chop to Lynch's temple.

'Don't kill him,' Marsh's voice came weakly.

'Why the hell not?' Dustin demanded. The man lay still underneath him and Dustin grabbed the gun away, checking for any other weapons. 'It would be a pleasure.'

'I know.' Marsh struggled to sit up while Dustin handcuffed the hood's hands behind his back, leaving him lying facedown on the frozen road. 'He's not worth it, Dustin, believe me.'

'Yeah. Okay.' Reluctantly, he moved away. Marsh was right. He wasn't going to feel good about killing that son-of-a-bitch when the raw anger finally dissipated later. 'Are you going to bleed to death?' he asked Marsh, suddenly concerned by his friend's lack of conversation. The sheriff was usually like a Hallmark card with a witty remark for every occasion. 'Marsh?'

But there was no reply. Gnawing fear shot through Dustin. Checking his friend over, he saw that the hood had made target-practice of Marsh's leg. Cursing and praying, Dustin pulled off his jacket and his flannel shirt. Carefully, he wrapped the shirt around Marsh's leg, though he wasn't certain it would do any good. Shrugging his jacket back on over his T-shirt, Dustin lifted Marsh to his feet, dragging him to the truck. Jerking down the gate, he let Marsh slump over so that he could push him inside. Tossing some horse blankets over him, he slammed the gate, praying that the sheriff wouldn't awaken until he got him to the hospital.

And praying that, once there, he *would* awaken.

Putting baby Holly's basket securely in a seat belt on the truck seat, Dustin threw an uncertain glance Lynch's way. He'd come to eventually. But there wasn't a lot of time for him to waste sympathy on the punk. Picking up the body like a bag of heavy manure, Dustin snatched the cruiser keys from the ignition, opened the trunk, and stuffed Lynch inside. Closing it, he strode to the front and grabbed the radio inside.

'This is Dustin Reed. I'm on the farm road outside of Lassiter, just at the fork. You'll see flares. Suspect is in trunk. Marsh was hit, so I'd appreciate nobody stopping me for a ticket as I come into town.'

He threw the radio down and ran to the truck. The truck bed was still; Marsh hadn't moved. Dustin jammed the truck into gear and sped into town.

CHAPTER 16

'Jill, dear, are you going to be okay?'

Eunice's worried face hovered behind Jill in the mirror. Her face was bruised, swollen definitely, but nothing was broken. The punch had landed under her eye and across from her nose on the cheek-bone, so although it had felt like her face had been shattered at the time, Jill knew she was fortunate not to be undergoing cosmetic surgery tonight.

'I'm fine, Eunice,' she said, applying another cold compress to her face. 'I'm starting to get a little sore in my arms and legs, but that will pass, too.' She sighed deeply, looking down into the washbasin as she rinsed the cloth out. 'I just wish somebody would call and tell us that Holly is safe.'

Eunice patted her shoulder. 'The Christmas season means believing, Jill. I believe that Holly will be back here soon, snug in her little basket. I can't imagine anything else.'

It *was* the season to believe, and if ever they could use a miracle, now was definitely the time. 'I just keep hearing her cry . . .' Jill broke off, too distraught to continue. The phone rang, and after another soothing pat on the back, Eunice left to answer it. Joey, at least for the moment, had come through the situation pretty well. Jill had assured him the mean man was never coming back, and that Dustin would bring Holly home safely. Though he was anxious for his father to return, he was equally anxious to get on with the popcorn stringing. She smiled, letting the child's one-track joy in the season lift her spirits.

'Jill! Dustin wants you on the phone!'

She dropped the washcloth and hurried down the stairs. Eunice's ashen face told her the news wasn't good.

'Yes?' she said into the receiver.

'Can you come down to the hospital and get Holly?'

The relief she felt at hearing his voice weakened her knees. All at once, she realized Dustin wanted her to come retrieve the baby. An obviously recovered, doing-just-fine, baby.

'Of course I can! I'll be there as soon as I get directions from Eunice.'

'I'm in the emergency room right now. They're treating Marsh for a gunshot wound, but he's going to be fine. I don't know when they'll move him to another room. Check here first, I guess, then ask at the desk. I'll be with him.'

'I'll be right there.'

She hung up and ran to the hall to get her coat. 'Did Dustin fill you in, Eunice?'

'Yes. Bad as it is, it could have been much worse, I suppose. Did he say if Marsh's wound is life-threatening?'

Jill shook her head as she pulled on gloves. 'Dustin didn't say, but I assumed it wasn't since he mentioned they might move him to another room.'

'Oh, good.' She gave Jill rapid directions to the hospital.

'Okay. I should be back soon.' Hurrying into the kitchen, she snagged a few gingerbread men off the tray. She could sneak them to the sheriff. If anything would make him feel better, it would be food.

Jill found the two men easily, not from the desk nurse's directions, but by the bellowing she could hear clear at the end of the hall.

'For heaven's sake,' she said, entering the room, 'it sounds like a brawl in here. Is there a boxing match on TV?'

Dustin's eyes collided with hers in a frozen, suspended moment. She wanted to run to him, to ask him if he felt as bad as he looked. His raffish jet hair was in wild patterns of disarray. The square jaw she admired was sporting a bruise and there was a split in the lips that had claimed hers so firmly. She dropped her gaze, distressed to think that Dustin might have ended up like Marsh with a bullet hole in him.

'You're one to be talking about boxing matches,' Dustin grumbled. 'You look like you've been in one.'

She smiled, though it hurt. It was much easier to

make light of what they'd all been through than to agonize over it. Laughter felt much better than crying, so for once she was falling in with Dustin's and Marsh's manner of dealing with discomfort.

'So. The lawman's laid up.' She walked over and stared down at him. 'You know that this is what you get for doubting me.' To counteract her words, she dumped the cellophane-wrapped gingerbread men on the blanket covering his chest. 'I don't suppose getting shot is going to interfere with your appetite.'

'Nope.' He waved a swiftly-unwrapped cookie at her. 'Thanks.'

A red-haired woman walked into the room at that moment. Marsh grinned when he saw her. 'China! If I'd known you were the kind of woman who couldn't resist an injured man, I'd have taken a bullet much sooner.'

Jill glanced at Dustin, who merely shrugged. His mouth was turned up a bit at the sides though, so she knew this visitor was a welcome, if unexpected, one.

The statuesque woman froze him with a glare. 'I see the rumors of your demise were much exaggerated, Tommy, to borrow a famous quote.'

'You only came to see if I was still alive?' He managed to inject hurt feelings into his tone.

China obviously wasn't impressed. 'I came to see if a man with a mouth as fast as yours could actually be shut up by anything. Apparently not, because you're still talking.' Her eyes softened for the slightest moment. 'I have horses to feed, and I only pay one sick visit per jerk, so I'm going to be on my way. Ordering a plant for your funeral obviously won't be necessary.'

The sheriff had sat up and run a hand through his hair, in an attempt, Jill guessed, to make himself more presentable to his guest. By the uncertain averting of the visitor's eyes, Jill thought he was already held in admiration – however grudging.

'China, this is Jill McCall. She's been living at the ranch with Dustin.' He hesitated under Jill's frown. 'Um, she's the latest in Dustin's string of house-keepers. Jill, this is China Shea.'

Stepping forward to shake China's hand, she understood why the sheriff might be so buffaloed by the woman. Her eyes were a deep green, honest and welcoming with their brightness. Though she was tall, her genuine smile made Jill feel comfortable immediately. 'It's nice to meet you,' she told China, meaning it.

'Same to you. Dustin, did you finally have all you wanted of Tommy's crude mouth?' She indicated the bandaged leg.

Jill had been surprised by China's use of Marsh's name. Now she was even more amazed by Marsh's sheepish grin. It was obvious that China could have told him to jump over the moon and he would have given it his best attempt – just to win her heart.

'I didn't shoot him, though I've been tempted many times,' Dustin said with a shake of his head. 'He could use some tender, loving care though.'

China shot a wry look Jill's way. 'Thank God for nursing staff, then. He can get all the TLC he needs

262

from people who are trained to pamper him. Well,' she said brightly, turning to Marsh once more, 'I suppose you'll stay out of trouble in here. Don't get mouthy with the nurses, Tommy, they're in charge of the needles. Jill, it was nice to meet you. Dustin, say hello to Eunice for me.' She started to sail out the door before pausing in the doorway. 'I'll be rooting for you next week, Dustin.'

Without another glance at the patient, China exited. Jill met Dustin's eyes in a moment of shared conspiracy. There wasn't a more perfect woman for Marsh in the world. He could do all the macho blustering he wanted to with China, but Jill suspected the earthily beautiful redhead had Marsh over a barrel.

'That woman wants me,' the sheriff said cheerfully.

'Yeah. Like she wants to be abducted by space aliens,' Dustin said.

'One day I'm going to let her have her way with me.' Marsh settled himself back against the pillows.

Dustin rubbed his chin thoughtfully, making Jill ache to inspect that bruise. 'Maybe China will fall down a flight of stairs and hit her head. If she doesn't remember who you are, you might have a better chance with her.'

Marsh ignored him. 'I can just feel those long, slender legs right now, locked around me in . . .'

'Perhaps a neurologist should examine him,' Jill interrupted. 'He appears to be suffering from delusions.'

Dustin laughed. Their eyes met again, and she smiled tentatively.

'Come on,' he told her. 'Let's leave this rascal to his fantasizing. I'll take you to the nursery to see Holly.'

'Bye, Marsh.' Jill allowed Dustin to propel her from the room. Once they left, the feeling between them changed from cordial to tight awareness. With his hand on her arm, Holly felt the strength in his fingers and a strange connection to her soul. Without even denouncing the thought in her mind, Jill suddenly knew that she cared far more for this rancher than she'd ever allowed herself to imagine.

Marsh wasn't the only one fantasizing, apparently.

'How's Joey?'

'Fine,' Jill said, a little breathlessly. They were heading toward the nursery at a good pace. Trying to keep up with Dustin's longer legs was exercise her pained body was protesting. 'Can we slow down a little?'

'Sorry.' Dustin halted immediately. He stared down at her, making shivers fly along her skin. 'How are *you*, Jill?'

'Much better than I look,' she said softly. His gaze on hers was searching and intense. The bruise on her cheek-bone received the most fierce scrutiny.

Before she realized what was happening, his lips met hers in a kiss that wasn't at all apologetic. His arms wrapped around her and tears sprung to Jill's eyes. If Dustin's gratitude was the reward for what she'd been through, then the price had been well

264

worth it. Of course, his gratitude wasn't what she really wanted. But it was a start.

Though the feel of being molded together was sheer heaven, after a moment she reluctantly pulled away. There were plenty of people witnessing their kiss and she didn't want more gossip circulating about their relationship than necessary. Dustin may have been overwhelmed into forgetting Maxine's threat for the moment, but Jill didn't want to be a source of any more anxiety than necessary.

'Sorry,' he murmured.

'Don't be,' she was quick to return. 'I'm not.'

He reached out and caressed her jawline. 'You scared the hell out of me tonight. I don't think I realized that such a sweet city girl could be such a tough lady.'

'I didn't know myself. I'm sure extra adrenalin had a lot to do with it.' She tried to smile, but the fight with Curtis had cost her. They both knew it.

'It was a pisser, wasn't it?' His face was grim, his cocoa-colored eyes deep with regret.

'Yes, but it's over. We came through it fine and now all I want to do is see Holly. She's had a very frightening introduction to the world.'

Dustin nodded. They turned a corner and stopped in front of a large glass window. Babies inside bassinets were engaged in either crying or sleeping. She saw Holly at once.

'Look at all the pink bows they've hung on her bassinet,' she whispered.

'Yeah. Her hard luck story got around pretty

quickly. Arriving in a torn straw basket generated a lot of sympathy.' He chuckled. 'She's a regular celebrity now.'

'I guess so,' Jill murmured. 'We did okay, didn't we? Sadie and Holly can start over now. Like a real mother and daughter deserve to.'

He slid his hand up to rub her back soothingly. 'Last time I saw Lynch he was occupying trunk space. I suspect he'll be spending enough time in a Lassiter jail that Sadie and Holly can get on with their bonding.'

Jill slid him a teasing glance as he stared through the window. 'Do I need more than one guess as to who chose a trunk for Lynch's temporary residence?'

He shook his head without saying anything. Jill smiled and stared back through the hospital window. Eunice had been right after all. It was the season for believing. Gesturing to one of the nurses, she pointed to Holly, indicating that she should bring her out.

'I'm ready to go home,' she said, more to herself than Dustin, but he gave her hand a squeeze.

'Thanks for coming down here to get her. I'll help you sign her out, but I'm going to stay here a while longer and make sure Marsh stays out of trouble.'

'You mean Tommy.'

'Yeah, Tommy.' He grinned at her. 'He deserves everything he gets from China, trust me.'

'She seems plenty capable of handling him.' She gasped as a nurse laid Holly in her arms. 'Hey, angel! What excitement you've had!' Nuzzling the baby to her cheek, Jill sent a silent prayer of thanks that the baby was safe. Catching Dustin's gaze on her, she automatically retreated to the banter she was learning to use. 'No more staying out so late, missy. We have curfew for young ladies like you.'

Dustin chuckled and led her to the desk. She signed a few papers, then took a deep breath. There was so much she would like to be able to say to him but their location and their situation prevented it. 'See you later,' she said as nonchalantly as possible.

'Okay.'

She turned and left the hospital. Their goodbye wasn't adequate, but it was about all either one of them was comfortable with. The events of last night had accelerated their relationship into a tense awareness of how close they were becoming – whether they'd ever wanted it or not.

Strapping the baby into the car seat in her beat-up old car, Jill said, 'It's well after midnight, Holly. Way past time for you to have a bottle and snuggle into your bed.' She glanced at the forlorn basket. 'And tomorrow we'll hunt a new baby carrier for you.' She sighed as she pulled out of the parking lot. The baby glanced around at the bright lights as they left, seeming to dismiss it all with a wave of her fist.

'That's kind of the way I feel,' Jill agreed. 'Hopefully, tonight was as bad as it's going to get. I'm not sure I have the strength for much more excitement.' The truth was, she reflected, she'd come to the ranch to inject some much-needed change into her life. After being fired, and Carl's painful betrayal, Jill had wanted a change of scenery. A new life, a fresh start.

'Well, I certainly got that,' she told Holly dryly. Dustin's grateful kiss in the hallway flashed through her mind, making her skin tingle. Despite everything that had happened, she felt her life held more importance, more meaning, than it ever had.

Deep in her heart, she knew that feeling had a lot to do with Dustin.

Jill checked on Eunice, who was still resting. She smiled to see that Joey was tucked into bed with his grandmother. Apparently, Eunice wasn't taking any chances in case Joey had a nightmare. It was entirely possible he could. The memory of the child beating Holly's abductor with small, determined fists, then flying a foot through the air when Curtis slapped him sent a chill coursing through Jill. She dropped a kiss on his forehead and checked his cheek for a bruise. There was none, but she was glad Eunice had thought to put him in her bed for the night. It would be a miracle if they all didn't suffer from night sweats tonight.

Carefully securing all the doors and taking a last turn through the house to check the windows – though she knew Curtis was safe in jail now – Jill fed Holly a last bottle, changed her into a nightie and tucked her into the basket. Placing it beside her own bed, she then changed into a long cotton nightgown and readied herself for bed. She'd just turned out the lights when she thought she heard Dustin's truck pull into the drive.

Seconds later, the sound of the front door closing

confirmed her guess. Jill held her breath as Dustin's heavy tread went past her door. Slowly she relaxed, realizing that a tiny hope had blossomed inside her that he might call goodnight through the door. Of course, with her lights out, he wouldn't want to disturb her. Feeling strangely dissatisfied, Jill got under the covers.

Her eyes had just about closed when she thought she heard a light tapping against the door that connected to Joey's room through the bathroom. That door opened and a faint knock came on her door.

'Jill?'

'Yes?' she whispered back.

Dustin opened the door and walked into the room. Jill's breath caught. He looked big and broad-shouldered as he hovered in the doorway. His gaze swept the bed.

'I was looking for Joey. Is he in with Mother?'

Pulling the covers up for modesty, Jill sat up. 'Yes. She must have been worried about him having nightmares.'

'Did he seem okay?'

'He was sleeping fine. I didn't want to say this earlier, but he took a bit of a blow tonight, too. I wouldn't be surprised if he doesn't sleep the whole night.' Jill felt the fear she'd been repressing with easy teasing finally cracking. 'I'm so sorry, Dustin,' she said. Her voice broke and she could feel tears pressing against the back of her eyes. 'It's all my fault Joey got hurt. I'd gone upstairs. I left him at the kitchen table. He went outside to find you and . . .'

Dustin perched on the edge of the bed, reaching to draw her into his arms. 'Jill, don't cry. If it had been me, I wouldn't have done anything any differently.' He took a deep breath. 'Besides, it's just as much my fault.'

'Don't try to make me feel better by blaming this on yourself.'

He nestled her closer and pulled both of them to lean against the headboard. 'Joey wouldn't have been so intent on finding me if he was sure I'd be around, Jill. He's at the age where he needs a father who places him first. I haven't done that. I'm going to now.'

She sniffled. 'But you're not the one who planted the idea of a popcorn stringing party in his head.'

Ruffling her hair so that he could place his hand at the base of her neck, Dustin said, 'We are damn sure stringing all the popcorn he wants to tomorrow.'

'I agree. A peaceful afternoon around the fireplace is what we all need.'

Dustin nodded, but he was no longer thinking about fireplaces and peaceful afternoons. The terror and adrenalin he'd built up in his body had flowed out in waves when he'd walked inside Jill's room and sat down to comfort her. His son was safe, Holly was safe, and now his mind was free and thinking about Jill's body underneath that cotton.

He thought about how soft she'd be. He needed some softness now. He thought about how warm her body was. Warmth sounded mighty appealing to him. He thought about how Jill had kissed him back tonight. He remembered the swell of her breasts as he kissed them the other night. There was a shifting, a tightening, in his groin. Dustin groaned. 'Are you all right?' Jill asked anxiously. 'You're not sore any place?'

Actually, he was sore all over. But suddenly all the pain he'd endured this evening seemed centered between his legs. 'I'm fine,' he said, trying not to think about it.

'You don't sound fine.'

Jill's sweetly concerned voice poured more heat on an already burning fire. 'I am.'

Unfortunately, she turned her head up to look at him, causing her breast to brush against his arm. Dustin couldn't take any more punishment, as innocent as it was.

'Jill,' he said on a husky whisper, matching his lips to hers. They fit, again and again, meeting and moving in a sensual rhythm. He had no business doing this; if he was a gentleman he would leave. But Jill's hand crept tentatively to his T-shirt and then underneath. Any protest he might have been able to work up died instantly.

'If we're going to stop, now is the time,' he warned her.

'Let's not.' Her hand drifted to his mid-section.

Lord knows he didn't want to try too hard to change her mind. Dustin pressed kisses along her nose, then along her chin before realizing he had a slight problem. 'I don't have any protection,' he told her, cursing the fact even as he knew this was because he'd never planned to make love to her, had studiously avoided making her feel like she'd been hired to perform that chore as well as everything else she did at the ranch.

'I'm on the pill,' she said, her tone hesitant with the admission. 'Um, since I was engaged, I thought it would be a good idea to . . . um, be prepared.'

The last thing he wanted to think about was that rather weak excuse for a fiancé of hers. He could almost smell the coconut mousse the guy had been wearing. Jealousy ripped through him with a thousand knife-edges of pain, but like a balm to the emotion torturing him, Jill's voice came to him in the semi-darkness.

'Um, I was more prepared, actually, than I needed to be, but I haven't stopped taking them. They seemed to help with my cycle, and . . .' Jill trailed off.

He felt her tense beside him. 'More prepared than you needed to be?'

Her hesitation was clear. 'He didn't um, want me . . . that way. So, I would very much appreciate it if you don't stop now.'

He was confused. 'Are you saying you never made love with your fiancé?'

'I'm saying that.'

'Because you think he didn't want you?'

'Actually, it was a matter of fairly public knowledge that he preferred different pastures to mine.'

Dustin rolled over, pinning her gently underneath

272

him. 'I knew there was something wrong with that guy from the moment I laid eyes on him.' Reaching, he pushed her nightgown up, allowing his hand to slide along one long, silky leg.

She wasn't wearing any underwear.

'*I* want you,' he said fiercely, his discovery launching him past any easy and gentle lovemaking he might have managed for her sake. Capturing a breast in one hand, he said, 'I want you so bad I feel like I'm going to explode.'

'I hoped you'd want to make love to me,' she told him. 'I've been wondering if that backside of yours is as wonderful naked as it looks in jeans.'

'You've been looking at my butt?' Dustin raised his head.

'Mm. It doesn't scowl at me.'

He felt a small hand glide boldly along his buttocks. She was intent on conducting an exploration of her own. Still, he couldn't let her remark pass.

'I thought you women liked silent, mysterious men.'

Jill pinched his rear. 'The problem with you is you're silent out of bed and talk too much in it. We need some reversal here.'

'Are you telling me to get on with the action?'

'Yes.'

He bent his head to fasten his lips around a nipple he'd freed. His thumb gently stroked the other breast, peaking it. Her moan let him know he was doing all the right stuff. He let a hand move up to stroke a smooth hip, then made a lingering exploration of the shape of her thigh. She was soft-skinned and delicately built, yet firm and muscled. No longer able to deny himself knowing her, Dustin slid his hand up her leg, finding the curls harboring her womanhood.

'Oh, Dustin,' she whispered. If this was heaven, she was glad she'd found it. The man was making her feel like the sexiest woman alive. He wanted her, though she sensed he was trying to go slowly with her. All that talking had served to let her know he didn't want to rush her. Kneading his back to revel in the feel of his muscles and strength, she arched against him. 'Don't make me wait any longer,' she pleaded on a sigh.

That was all it took to break through his hesitation. He moved over her, and Jill gasped as they became one. It was wonderful, it was earth-shattering, and as she felt herself sharing the man-woman rhythm with him, Jill knew that Dustin was claiming a part of her soul that had never been touched before.

Jill awakened the next morning, feeling for the clock beside her bed. The spot beside her where Dustin had lain was cold, so he'd been gone a while. Squinting, she saw that it was six-thirty, well past the time he would leave to check the cattle.

A vague, misty memory of her lips being kissed as she slept passed through her mind. Smiling, Jill hopped out of bed. Holly was starting to shift in the basket, a sure sign that she would soon want her breakfast. If she hurried, she still had time to grab a fast shower, which would give her the right set for the day.

Unable to resist a glance outside, Jill saw that snow blanketed the earth in a peaceful conclusion to the night's events. The sight made her pulse slow. Maybe it was all over. Maybe this beautiful snowfall was a sign that the worst had passed, and from here on out, a bright new day was in store for them. The memory of Dustin's hungry desire put a wistful smile on her face, and Jill closed her eyes for a second. Their loving might not have been the right thing to do, and they would both have to deal with the consequences later, but it had been the most wonderfully satisfying night of her life.

Yet surely it could never happen again. That went without saying. There was too much possibility of Joey discovering them if he wandered into Jill's room at night. It would be disrespectful to Eunice for them to indulge in a continuing sexual relationship. Most of all, sneaking around to engage in illicit loving would cause a little of the glow she felt now to dissipate. What had happened last night was dizzyingly wonderful beyond belief, but it could never be repeated. It had been too perfect the way it was – but more than that, the cost could be too high for Dustin and his family, and she couldn't allow that to happen.

Out of the corner of her eye, Jill caught sudden movement among the pecan trees. Startled, she peered harder, suddenly frightened again although she knew Curtis Lynch had to be in jail. Surely he couldn't have gotten bailed out?

Then a soft smile bloomed on her face. Dustin was lying on his back in the snow with Joey, the two of them waving their arms up and down, their legs back and forth, as fast as they could. Jumping up, they examined their handiwork. A very small snow angel was left in the snow next to a rather impressively sized angel. Joey clapped his hands. Jill could see the smile on Dustin's face clearly from her vantage point.

Maybe there had been a silver lining to the thunderous clouds that had hovered over them after all. A Christmas-blessed, gold and silver lining.

Dustin Reed had discovered his son.

Holly didn't want to wait until Jill showered, apparently. The baby's wail turned Jill from watching the loving moments between father and son. 'Okay, okay. You first, then me,' she said good-naturedly. What could spoil such a wonderful day?

Throwing on her housecoat and hurrying downstairs with the baby, she swiftly warmed up a bottle, and was sitting feeding Holly when the front door blew open. The stamping of feet and, 'Brr-it's cold!' traveled to her ears. A second later, Dustin stood in the kitchen, holding his son and staring down at her as she fed the baby.

Suddenly Jill felt shy. Her eyelashes lowered as she looked at Holly instead. Dustin loomed large and powerfully attractive over her; memories of last night's wonderful touching swept her. She couldn't think of the right thing to say.

'We . . . we been making snow angels, Jill.'

Joey's sweet voice broke the discomfort and gave her something to focus on besides his sexy father. 'I saw you, Joey. You made some beauties.' She forced her gaze to Dustin. 'I feel guilty that I overslept.'

Dustin shook his head before looking at Joey. 'You needed the rest. I was up and I heard Joey moving around in Mother's room, so I went in and got him. He wanted to make snow angels, and after our ordeal last night, it sounded like a great idea.'

He had put off chores to take some time with his son. Clearly, Holly's unexpected presence at the ranch had caused a ripple effect of good changes for both her and Dustin. 'I would have been glad to come out and help you.'

'Thanks, but we needed to be on our own.' Joey and his father's gazes met with smiles on both sides. 'There's just some things we men have to do together.'

'Yeah,' Joey agreed. 'Can . . . can we have some hot chocolate now?'

Jill laughed, getting up to put on the kettle. Dustin seated Joey at the table.

'I'm going upstairs to change, then I need to get to work,' he told Jill. His gaze made a fast sweep of her, from her ankles to her face. Heat prickled her cheeks.

'That's fine,' she said quickly. 'I can take over from here.'

He nodded, but didn't say anything. Her heart pounded as hard as his boots on the stairs as he went up. For just a moment, she thought she'd seen desire burning in his gaze.

Quickly she brushed the thought away, though it warmed her faster than any hot chocolate could. Putting a cup down in front of Joey that was only partially filled, she said, 'Give it one more minute to cool before you try to drink it, Joey. I don't think it's that hot, but be careful, just in case.'

'Jill, can I see you for a moment?'

Dustin's deep voice, couched in a command, made her jump. In her attention to Joey's cocoa, she hadn't heard him come back down. She went into the hallway, noticing at once that he looked suddenly haggard. The relaxed happiness was gone from his face.

'Yes, Dustin?'

'I went in to check on Mother since she's usually up by now and I figured we made enough noise when we came in to wake anybody. She doesn't look good. She must have taken a bad turn in the night. I'm going to run her down to the emergency room.'

'What do you think is wrong?' The rosy glow from last night evaporated swiftly as she saw the worry etched on Dustin's face.

'I don't know. I knew she hadn't been feeling well, but I thought it was her arthritis. It took me a while to wake her, and then when she tried to get out of bed, she couldn't.'

'Oh, no!' Sheer anxiety clenched her stomach. 'All the drama last night must have taken its toll.'

'I don't know, but I do think a doctor should see her, pronto. Can you hold down the fort?'

'Of course! Go *on,*' she told him. 'We'll be fine.'

278

He turned and went upstairs. Jill waited in the doorway until he reappeared, lifting his mother and carrying her down the stairs. Independent Eunice didn't even offer a slight protest. Jill's insides chilled as she hurried to open the front door. The woman she'd always thought of as so strong had a distinctly pale color to her skin. She watched as Dustin carefully put his mother into the truck and tucked a blanket around her. He drove away and Jill went inside, closing the front door with a sinking feeling in her heart.

Christmas is for believing, Eunice had told her. Jill went into the kitchen to fill a bowl with cereal for Joey, repeating the mantra to herself. If there was ever a time to believe in the miracle of the season, it was now.

279

CHAPTER 17

Jill took Joey's wet clothes off in the laundry room. Some pajamas she'd folded were lying on the dryer and Jill snatched them up, deciding it wouldn't hurt if he ate breakfast in his Bugs Bunny jammies just this once. Not taking him upstairs to dress now would mean she could sit at the table with him and finish feeding Holly while he ate. That way she could be with both of them at the same time.

Joey seemed to have forgotten last night's troubles as she swiftly dressed him, then led him back to the table.

'Can . . . can we watch cartoons?'

'I don't see why not.' Jill flipped on the TV and settled on the plank seat with Holly. Joey dug into his cereal, completely unconcerned. She sighed with relief. Truthfully, she'd worried how he would act when he found his father had left. But he didn't say a word, and she realized that Dustin was usually gone by daybreak so the routine was simply familiar to Joey. He didn't ask what was wrong with his grand-mother, either. Jill thought that since she'd been

280

hovering in the doorway, she'd blocked his view of his father practically carrying Eunice out the door. Jill thought the best thing to do about that was wait until Joey did have questions. With any luck, Dustin and his mother might return before Joey even noticed her absence. After all, whatever was plaguing her could be something relatively simple.

Jill commanded herself to hang onto that hope.

After about thirty minutes had passed, she felt Holly's body go slack against her. 'Uh-oh,' Jill said. 'Don't you go to sleep just yet.'

Joey had finished eating and since there had been no way for him to get a bath last night, she decided this was the best time to get everyone bathed. She was about to move from the table when an imperious knock sounded at the front door.

'Who could that be?' she murmured. Wishing that she'd had a chance to at least comb her hair before seeing anyone, Jill cradled Holly in her arms and went to open the door.

The woman on the porch was a stranger to her, but her stiff posture told Jill immediately that this wasn't a friendly social call.

'Where's Dustin?' she demanded.

'I'm sorry.' Jill fixed the woman with a frosty eye. 'I'm afraid I didn't get your name.' She hoped that would be enough to remind the woman of her manners.

'My name! Don't take that tone with me. I don't need some city twit giving me any lip. Now, where's Dustin?'

Obviously, she wasn't getting through to her. After last night, she wasn't letting anybody in she didn't know at least by name.

'If you'll pardon me,' Jill began closing the door, 'we're not receiving callers this morning.'

The woman's hand shot out and pushed the door open. 'Just because you're sleeping with Dustin doesn't mean you've come up in the world, honey. You're still only a maid. Now, you'd better let me see my grandson before I call my lawyer.'

Jill could feel herself blanch as she suddenly recognized the shrill voice. Not only had she just been royally insulted, but this nasty woman was Joey's grandmother. No wonder Dustin didn't like her.

And obviously Mrs Copeland didn't like *her*. Belatedly, she remembered that Maxine had been incensed by Joey's hope that Santa would give Jill to him as a Christmas present. Feeling herself blush a little with embarrassment, she moved from the doorway. At the same time, she glanced over Maxine's shoulder and saw a car with a driver waiting.

'I apologize,' Jill said. 'I wasn't aware of who you were. We had a strange incident here last night – '

'You did?' Maxine's black eyes pierced her. Jill realized that in trying to save herself she might be giving the woman ammunition to use against Dustin.

'Well, it was nothing really. But since I don't know many folks in town, I'm very cautious about who I open the door to.' She hoped her tone was soothing.

'What's that?' Maxine stared at her belligerently.

'What's what?'

'That baby you're holding. Is it yours?'

'Oh, no, it's not.' Swiftly, she remembered that Marsh had wanted her to be the cover story for the baby's appearance. And Maxine wouldn't be thrilled to hear that they were in charge of protecting this child. She sensed the first accusation out of her mouth when Maxine got inside the courtroom was that Dustin had placed his own son in jeopardy. 'I mean, actually it is.'

Maxine stared at her. 'Is it, or not?'

'Yes, ma'am. I misunderstood your question,' she fabricated.

'Humph. Where's Joey?'

'In the kitchen eating breakfast.'

'At this late hour? Don't you have him packed and ready to go yet?'

'Packed?' Jill echoed. 'Ready to go where?'

Maxine snapped her fingers. 'You're about the most useless help I've ever seen. You've been here plenty long enough to know that today is one of our visitation days.' She looked around the hall, hunting for something. 'Where's Dustin? I'm going to give him a piece of my mind.'

'He's not here.' Jill shifted Holly to her shoulder. Briefly she wondered if offering Joey's grandmother a cup of hot tea would calm her long enough for Jill to get him packed. Why hadn't Dustin warned her that today was a visitation day?

Because he'd had far too much on his mind, she knew. Discarding the idea of allowing Maxine any further than the hallway – she couldn't remember the woman doing anything more than screeching from the porch before – Jill arranged a competent smile on her face. 'If you'll give me just a moment, I'll get Joey's things.'

'Well, if Dustin's not here, where's Eunice? I can't imagine her leaving my grandchild alone with *you*.'

Instant dislike poured into Jill's spine like cement. She straightened to look down upon the made-up and mean face. 'I am more than capable of doing my job, Mrs Copeland. Dustin and Eunice place their absolute trust in me.'

'Dustin, is it? I might have known Eunice wouldn't have taught her help her place.'

'Mrs Copeland, I'm sure you're not aware that I have a college degree. Far from being trained "help", I used to do the training in my position as marketing manager.'

'Of course.' Her tone was scornful. 'That's why you're chasing dust bunnies for Dustin. You're so highly qualified.'

Jill blinked. In all her life, she had never encountered such undisguised venom. 'Just because you have a visitation that I wasn't quite prepared for is no reason to insult me. Dustin took Eunice to the hospital this morning. She wasn't feeling well. It never occurred to me that I should have Joey ready.'

'What do you mean, Eunice wasn't feeling well?'

Maxine's eyes narrowed to slits. Jill instinctively took a step back, not knowing what the woman was homing in on. Surely the fact that Eunice was ill wasn't an ace for Maxine to play, was it?

'It may be her arthritis acting up. I'm not certain,' Jill hurried to cover her tracks. 'I'm sure she'll be home soon.'

'Nobody goes to the emergency room for arthritis, you twit. Don't try to fob me off. I've heard a lot of stories in my time, so don't insult my intelligence.'

Jill drew a deep breath. 'I don't know what's wrong with her. I'm trying to be optimistic.' She stopped herself from saying *you pathetic old woman*.

'Go get Joey and his things,' Maxine told her tersely. 'I'll be waiting in the car.'

She turned around, her heels thumping decisively on the wooden steps. Immediately, she looked back at Jill. 'I didn't get your last name. I suppose you can at least remember that?'

'My name is Jill McCall.'

Maxine nodded, then got into the car. Jill's eyes widened. 'What a witch,' she whispered against Holly's downy head. Taking her time as she went into the kitchen, she said, 'Joey, your grandmother is here.'

'I know.' He looked at her funny.

'No, I mean Grandmother Copeland.'

'Oh, no.' His expression was distressed. 'Do . . . do I hafta go?'

'I'm afraid so, honey. Let's get you dressed.'

'Please, Jill?'

His forlorn gaze tugged at her heart. 'I didn't think about what day it is, Joey, but you have to go to your

285

grandmother's.' She skipped saying that going against custody arrangements might get Dustin in a bunch of trouble. That was the last thing she wanted.

'We . . . we didn't string popcorn.'

She hugged him tight. 'You'll be back tomorrow, and we will then, okay?'

'Okay.' His sigh was heavy.

Jill shepherded him upstairs to dress, wishing she was in a position to send that ornery old crone home alone. Fact was, she didn't think Joey needed the stress right now. After last night, he could use some hugs and kisses.

He wasn't likely to get them today.

'I can't believe Eunice would allow such a slut in her home.' Maxine tapped a fingernail impatiently on the desk, then got up to stare out the window at Joey. 'She must be slipping.'

Her husband made an open-handed gesture. Maxine shook her head. 'I think you would have thought it was a big deal if you'd seen the housekeeper, David. There was a bruise the size of my fist on her cheek, like she'd been in a bar-room brawl of some kind. She hadn't made any attempt at dressing for the day, nor was her hair the slightest bit combed. It's plain that farm hours don't agree with her, but by eight o'clock in the morning, one ought to be able to get their teeth brushed, at least. And Lord only knows who the father of her poor innocent child is.'

Outside, Joey was trying to catch winter snowflakes with his tongue. There wasn't more than an inch of snow on the ground, but the weather reports were calling for accumulation in the night. Maxine blew out a breath. 'I nearly flipped when I realized that Joey wasn't dressed or ready. You know very well the child rises by six and not a minute later. Why he hadn't been fed by that late hour is beyond my contemplation.'

Again, her fingernail beat out a tattoo on the desk. She looked to her husband. He shook his head slightly. 'I know. It breaks my heart for Joey's sake.' Narrowing her eyes, she sent a thoughtful look David's way. He didn't seem as distressed as she was over the matter, but of course, a man didn't have the fierce instinct in him necessary to protect children. Joey was all she had. Oh, there was David, but now that she knew of his infidelity, she knew he'd never really been hers.

Or he might not be that concerned because of Eunice. No matter what she'd been able to say or do about the woman over the years, David still believed Eunice Reed walked on water. There was no human being who possessed his respect the way she did.

It irritated Maxine beyond belief. Right now, David's lack of worry over this morning's incident was like a slap to her face. He should support her. This once, he should see that Eunice wasn't the goddess he imagined she was. She had put a bleached slut in charge of caring for their only grandchild. But he seemed more upset that Eunice was in the hospital. No doubt if that wheelchair had wings, David would be with her right now.

He was looking out the window now, watching Joey with a wistful expression on his face and completely oblivious to Maxine's angst. After a moment, he maneuvered the wheelchair from the room. She heard him trying to wrench the door open, but she didn't move to help him. It was obvious he was trying to get outside where he could watch Joey from the porch, but he didn't need to be pampered. He hadn't been there for her; why should she be there for him in his hour of need?

Maxine crossed to the phone, dialing a number from memory. It was answered on the first ring.

'Sal Moriari here.'

'It's Maxine, Sal. I have something new I want you to check out.'

'I'm taking notes. Shoot.'

'Dustin has a new housekeeper. All I know is that her name is Jill McCall. I want to know where she came from and what she's doing at his ranch.'

'Cleaning house?'

By Sal's tone, Maxine knew he wasn't trying to blow her off. He wanted to know what had alerted her suspicion. 'I got the distinct impression her talents didn't lie in polishing brass, Sal. One thing she mentioned is that her last position was as a marketing manager.'

'Ah. You think her move from corporate executive to chief cook and bottle washer may be something we can use against them?'

Maxine carried the cordless phone as she went to sit in a damask-covered chair. 'I know something isn't right in that house. The fact that they hired this woman without any thought to Joey's well-being incenses me. She appears to lack qualifications and yet she has managed to put the notion into Joey's head that she could become his mother.'

'Hm. Ambitious little thing, isn't she?'

'To say the least.' Her voice was deliberately curt. To her mind, there was nothing to recommend the woman; certainly, in comparison to her own beautiful and cultured daughter, Nina, the housekeeper failed miserably in comparison. But she had heard that a man got used to the convenience of sex once he was married. If something happened to the wife, often the man remarried in about a year's time – presumably to recover all the comforts a wife could provide him.

Fate would be so cruel to replace Nina with a bleached-blonde, unrefined social climber who used her body to blind Dustin into marriage. Where would that leave Joey? Out in the cold, of course. 'I want to file a motion for custody until the trial date, Sal.'

'The trial is in four days. I'm not sure the paperwork can be processed that fast no matter who I lean on.'

She thought about the swollen state of Jill's face. The purple and black bruise had been a terrible thing to see; she had hardly been able to look the woman in the eye.

In her heart, she knew Dustin wasn't capable of such extraordinary violence. Nor did the woman appear to have lacked such spine that she would stand for abusive treatment. She snapped her fingers. Of course. Maybe in Dustin's absence, while he was taking his mother to the hospital, the housekeeper had taken advantage of the opportunity to consort with unsavory types. It was an unfortunate situation. Maxine wondered where Joey had been during this time. *Could he have witnessed any of this violence?* The thought was painful. She could ask him about it, but to do so would be hearsay. The word of a child. And the truth was, if Joey had been exposed to any rough meeting between the housekeeper and some riffraff, she didn't want to remind him of it. *Poor little thing*, she thought, closing her eyes. *He's already been through so much.*

'Never mind the motion, Sal,' she said, suddenly aware of the awesome responsibility she faced. 'With Eunice being ill and that odd woman alone in the house with Joey, I wouldn't dream of taking him home tomorrow. Talk to the judge and see what we can swing, certainly. But now that I've got more evidence that Joey is not living in a safe environment, he stays with me until everything is said and done. And in light of these new events, I don't think Joey will ever have to leave me again.'

'Tell you what,' Sal said thoughtfully, 'I'll just drop by the Reed Ranch and tell them we're going to file papers if they raise any ruckus between now and then. It's either our way or no way, and as I see it,

Dustin isn't going to be too anxious to do anything that might make him appear unstable.' He was quiet for another moment. 'As a matter of fact, knowing Dustin, this may be just what we need to get a reaction out of him we can use in court.'

'Sal.' Maxine smiled. 'There isn't another lawyer like you on the face of the earth. What would I do without you?'

'You'd find a way to win, Maxine. But I wouldn't worry anymore. I think we've got the Reeds on the run now.'

CHAPTER 18

The house seemed still and too quiet without Joey. Eunice's comforting presence was missing; the anticipation that flashed through Jill when Dustin might stride in at any moment was gone. It was just her and Holly now, and Holly was taking a nap.

Jill took a shower and tidied her room, with one ear listening for the phone all the while. The fact that Dustin had not called worried her. She knew he was aware of her concern for his mother, so he would want to reassure Jill as soon as he could. Telling herself not to panic over the silent phone, Jill reasoned he hadn't called because he didn't know anything about Eunice's condition yet. Though she couldn't bear to think of it, Eunice might be worse off than they could have known. Jill's stomach tightened at the thought. *Eunice is in fine health*, she told herself, even as a shadow crossed her mind, ugly and ill-conceived. *What if she's dying?*

Jill sighed, vehemently wishing that thought had not popped into her conscious. Losing Eunice would be like losing a best friend. She'd learned about patience and courage from Eunice, and graciousness, and probably a multitude of other things she didn't yet realize.

The doorbell pealed downstairs, softly but enough to interrupt her distressing worry. Jill wiped away a tear that had slipped down her cheek. It was too early for Joey to come home. Nobody else she knew would ring the doorbell.

Walking quietly down the stairs, Jill cautiously peered out the peephole. She was taking no chances after Maxine's disastrous visit. Though she'd handled the unpleasant scene as best she could, doubtless Dustin was going to be displeased that she'd upset Maxine.

Jill could see that the caller was a young girl, no older than her late teens. The girl shifted from foot to foot in the cold, apparently alone. Jill didn't see a car – or driver for that matter – from her tiny viewing space. The girl knocked on the door, obviously unwilling to leave until someone opened it. She glanced up and with a start, Jill remembered her from the bakery.

'Sadie!' she exclaimed, jerking the door open. 'Sadie! What are you doing here?'

The girl jumped, looking a bit scared.

'How do you know my name?'

'Because . . . oh, never mind. We can't talk with you shivering in the cold. Come in.'

Sadie glanced nervously around her as she came into the foyer. 'Are you sure?'

'It's fine. Come in the kitchen and I'll get you something hot to drink.'

Sadie followed obediently. Jill pointed to the kitchen table and she sat, all the while stiff and uncomfortable.

'Where's my baby?' she blurted.

'Taking a nap,' Jill answered. She wasn't the least bit surprised that Sadie's first concern was for Holly.

'Is she all right?'

Jill glanced Sadie's way as she put a cup of hot tea she'd warmed in the microwave in front of her. 'She's just fine.'

An audible sigh of relief gusted from Sadie. 'I've been so frightened.'

She could well imagine. 'I bet you have. Obviously you know Curtis is in jail or you wouldn't be here. How did you find out?'

'Sheriff Marsh asked Eunice where Mama's family was from. I guess he called the sheriff there to ask if he knew us. We got the message through him at my aunt's house.' Sadie looked up at Jill with worried eyes.

'Is that where you stayed while you were pregnant?'

She glanced away. 'Yes. So Curtis couldn't find me.'

Jill seated herself across from Sadie. 'I expect Holly to wake up in about ten minutes.' She glanced out the window, seeing no car. 'How did you get here?'

'On my bike. Mama got a ride from somebody in

town so she could go see Miss Eunice at the hospital, but . . . I couldn't wait to see my baby.'

'Hm.' Jill ran several thoughts through her mind. 'Are you planning to ride back with Holly on your bike?'

'That's how I got her here.'

She recognized defensiveness in the girl's tone. Yet, in all good conscience, she couldn't allow Sadie to pedal Holly back home in the cold. Not while Jill's perfectly good car was sitting in the driveway. From the jutting of Sadie's chin, it was clear that her independent nature was asserting itself now that she was in control of her own life. Without Curtis robbing her of that important asset.

'Well, Sadie, there is a slight problem.' Jill stared at her nails, trying to appear deep in thought. 'Holly's basket is a bit torn. I was going into town to get her another one today, but as it is, I don't think it's safe to travel with her the way her basket is.'

Sadie's face fell. 'Oh.'

'As I say, I was on my way into town and . . . well, perhaps when Holly awakens, I could just run the two of you home. That way she'll be safer.'

And in a car seat, Jill thought to herself.

'Would you mind?' Sadie asked shyly.

'Not a bit. We'll just toss your bike into my trunk and then I can drop you off on my way.' Jill forced herself to sound cheerful. Not that she wasn't delighted for Sadie and Holly's sake, but it was going to be mighty quiet around the ranch with both of her charges gone. She almost felt like her job description was dwindling to nothing. 'Would you excuse me for just a moment?'

Sadie nodded. Trying not to appear worried, Jill walked out of the kitchen and went up the stairs. She had seen an old-fashioned black desk phone by Dustin's bed once, when she had gone into his room to grab the sheets for washing. He was by nature very tidy, and had explained to her that his room didn't require her attention. He preferred she concentrate her energies on the children in the household and his mother, being more caretaker than maid service, he'd told her. But this was the only phone in the house besides the one in the kitchen, and she couldn't make this call with Sadie in the room with her.

A nearly overwhelming sense of masculinity assailed her as she entered the darkened room. The furniture was dark wood, and the window hangings were heavy and opaque. It was antique and old-fashioned, similar to the parlor furniture, although that room had been recently painted and carpeted. It was almost as if the decor in this room hadn't been changed since the Reeds had first lived in the house. As she reached out to take the phone from the cradle, Jill realized this was the room Dustin's parents must have occupied when his father was alive. Apparently, Dustin had kept everything the same as it had always been, right down to this out-of-date rotary phone.

Not wanting to waste time with Sadie downstairs, Jill dialed information and asked for the hospital phone number. When she had gotten that, she dialed the number and asked for the sheriff's room. He answered on the first ring.

'Sheriff Marsh here.'

'This is Jill McCall. You sound like you're at work instead of in a hospital.'

'I'm not letting some peashooter slow me down. So, is this a social call to check on my health, Miss McCall?'

She grimaced at his sarcastic tone. If she hadn't spent days listening to Marsh and Dustin badger each other, she would think the man purely didn't like her. It certainly felt personal.

'I can tell you're fine, Sheriff,' she said dryly. 'Sadie is downstairs, saying you let her know she could pick up Holly. After the morning I've had, I decided I'd better double-check with you first.'

'Bad day, huh? Dustin hasn't even left the hospital yet.'

'He hasn't? Is . . . Eunice all right?'

'I haven't been able to pry that information out of any of the nurses. The doctor is having additional tests run on her.'

'Oh. It sounds serious.' Jill's heart sank.

'I think the old gal has seen spryer days, that's for certain,' Marsh said. 'Do you want me to have Dustin call you when he lights?'

'No.' Jill couldn't hold back her worry. 'I want you to tell me if it's all right for Sadie to take Holly.'

'I've cleared it with CPS. The Christmas angel is free to go home.'

She let out a sigh that was both relieved and despondent. 'Thank you.'

'So, what's the problem?'

'I don't have one.' Jill wrinkled her forehead. 'At least, I hope I didn't create one this morning.'

'If you need to talk, I'll let you bend my ear.'

It could be a way to get the word to Dustin that Maxine was upset, Jill thought. Hesitantly, she said, 'Maxine came by this morning to pick up Joey. I didn't have him ready, which seemed to offend her.'

'Everything offends Maxine. She's just looking for something to complain about.'

'She wasn't very nice.'

'No kidding.'

'No.' Jill remembered how Maxine had seemed so disgusted with her. 'It was more than that. She was . . . angry.'

'Blow her off, Jill. Maxine Copeland has toys in her attic. They've been rattling around up there all her life.'

'I wish I could forget about it that easily. But I'm terribly worried.' She tried to take a breath that would reach into her ribcage but couldn't relax that much. That woman had been listening too closely to Jill's answers, waiting for any mistake, anything she could use against Dustin. She had felt it. 'Thanks for trying to ease my mind, Marsh. I'd better get back downstairs to Sadie. She's probably about to die from waiting to hold her baby.'

He chuckled. 'I'm glad it's all worked out for her. Are you taking them home?'

'Yes.'

'I'll let Dustin know where you've gone. He should be in here soon.'

'I'd appreciate that, Sheriff.'

She hung up and went down the hall into her bedroom to gather together Holly's clothes and diapers and other items. She packed them into her own suitcase, which Sadie could return to her when she was settled again. It was hard putting together the little pieces of the child's life who had come to mean so much to her, though she knew this was the happy ending they had all hoped for. Once everything was packed, she took the holiday dress from the closet. Helplessly, she held the dress to her, smelling Holly's sweet scent, before laying it in the case. The tiny tights she'd bought for the baby were placed on top of the dress, and the evergreen satin headband Eunice had made followed. For just an instant before she closed the case, tears pricked at her eyes. She was happy for Holly, very happy. But it was so hard to see her leave. Telling herself not to cry, Jill picked up Holly's basket. The baby slept on, oblivious to the change in her fate.

'You're going to be so surprised, Holly. You get to go back home to your mother, and your grandmother. Isn't that a nice Christmas present?' she murmured soothingly, all the while wondering who she was trying to comfort.

Sadie jumped to her feet when Jill walked in. 'Oh, baby!' she whispered, her voice a hoarse cry. Her fingers reached out to take the basket carefully. 'Oh,

Lord. I was beginning to think I'd never see you again!' Without heeding the infant's sleep, Sadie set the basket on the table and snatched her out, holding the child close to her chest. Sadie's eyes were closed as she reveled in the moment. Jill's mind spiraled back to that other time Sadie had held her baby in the bakery and so much had gone wrong after that.

Yet it had all turned out for the best. She smiled and went to get her purse and car keys. 'Are you ready to go home?' she asked.

'We sure are,' Sadie said. 'We sure are.'

The drive to Sadie's house went too fast. Jill was surprised to note how short the distance seemed between her home and the Reed Ranch. She wouldn't want to travel the distance on a bicycle the way Sadie had, but looking at the small frame house where Sadie lived, Jill couldn't help thinking she knew how the girl had made it all the way there.

Determination must have pushed Sadie's feet. Jill looked at the worn little house and for a moment worried about Holly's and Sadie's safety. That was ridiculous, of course. Curtis couldn't bother them anymore. She told herself that Holly would be so loved by her family that she would grow up rich by that measure, if by no other.

'Well, Sadie,' she said, turning off the car. 'May I help you take these things inside?' She was half afraid the girl would refuse.

But Sadie smiled. 'You're awfully nice to offer.' She opened the door and got out, removing Holly

300

from the car seat. Sadie held Holly's basket close to her as she walked to the front porch. Trying to ignore the sadness inside her, Jill took the bike from the trunk, then got the car seat out and carried it to the porch. Taking the suitcase from the car, Jill followed Sadie into the dark interior of the house. A light snapped on and Jill breathed a sigh of relief. They might be poor, but the Benchleys kept their home nice and neat.

Sadie placed the basket where she could keep an eye on Holly before turning. 'I forgot to ask you your name,' she said softly.

'Oh, how silly of me. I suppose I thought – never mind.' Jill was embarrassed. 'My name is Jill McCall.'

Sadie smiled at her softly. 'I always thought of you as my angel.'

'Oh, that's nice of you,' Jill said uncomfortably. 'But I'm far from that, I assure you.'

'I can't help thinking it. I saw you pick my baby up when you found her, and I knew then everything was going to be okay. Well, maybe not okay, but better.' She twisted her fingers together. 'Leaving her was the hardest thing I've ever done.'

'I'm sure it was.' Having tasted Curtis's violent nature first-hand, Jill thought Sadie was very brave.

'He did that to you, didn't he?' Sadie pointed to Jill's face hesitantly.

She had forgotten in the shock of seeing Sadie. Gingerly, she touched her bruised face before nodding. 'Yes.'

'You see? You are my angel. It should have been me.' Sadie's eyes filled with unshed tears.

'No. It should have been no one.' Jill knew she was stronger than Sadie, less vulnerable to Curtis in any way. It had been an awful night. She had endured some tough treatment. But in the end she had survived. Sadie might not have survived Curtis's rough handling.

'The Reeds saved my baby. I'll never forget that.'

'They're good people.' Jill thought for a second. 'Sheriff Marsh probably wouldn't mind some baked goods when you've got a chance to take some by the hospital.'

'Is he sick?' Sadie's eyes went wide.

She shrugged. 'Not if you listen to him talk. But Curtis got off one shot that just happened to hit the sheriff.'

'Oh, no! He didn't tell me.'

'I imagine not,' Jill said dryly. 'But he's not pleased about it. That boy's going to spend a lot of time in jail for assaulting an officer of the law, and likely attempted murder, too.'

Sadie sat as if her feet could no longer support her. 'He's bad. Curtis is bad all the way through.' She stared up at Jill. 'How could I have loved him? How could I have fallen for someone with so much badness in him?'

Jill shook her head. She walked over to the window to look out as she considered Sadie's words. A moment later, she swiveled to face her. 'You're not the only woman on earth to fall for the wrong guy, Sadie. As unfair as it seems, it happens to the best of us.'

'You didn't . . . did you?'

She shrugged. The two of them had more in common than anyone might have guessed. 'Maybe not with the pure evil Curtis had. But I thought I loved someone who supposedly returned my love. He didn't love me at all. I think he really wanted to own me. And when he couldn't, he tried to hurt me in other ways.' She stood straight as a thought occurred to her. 'Actually, he did hurt me for a while. But I don't hurt anymore.' *Not since I came to the Reed Ranch. I have as much to be thankful for as Sadie.* The realization that she, too, had been healed by the Reeds amazed her. She had gotten the Christmas present of peace that she had hoped for when she came to Lassiter, despite everything.

'I was so ashamed to leave my baby.' Sadie held Jill's gaze shyly. 'I didn't think anyone would understand why I had. Somehow I feel like you understand me.'

Jill went to hug her. 'I do.'

Sadie returned her hug. 'Thank you for protecting my baby.'

'Thank you for letting me. She's a doll.'

She heard a sniffle. 'Maybe you'll have one of your own someday,' Sadie said.

A surprising pang shot through Jill's heart. She stood, barely able to smile. 'I'll just pop by every once in a while to play with Holly, if you don't mind.

Eunice is going to fret to get her hands on that baby occasionally.'

'I hope she's going to get better.'

Another pang hit her, harder. 'So do I. Listen, is there anything I can get you? You probably haven't had time to get to the store. Anything you need?'

'No. Mother will be home soon, and to tell you the truth, I'm looking forward to just sitting and holding my baby.'

Jill nodded. She understood and appreciated that need. As soon as Joey got back from that battle-ax's house – no, his maternal grandmother's house, she reminded herself sternly – she was going to hold him and kiss him, and help those little fingers string that popcorn he'd been itching to string.

'Well, goodbye, Sadie,' she said softly. 'Goodbye, Holly.' She said these words even though the baby wasn't awake to hear. Jill shot one last look at Sadie, trying to tell her heart to stop beating so nervously. It felt strange to go off and leave behind the infant she'd fought for last night. 'Call me if you need anything,' she told Sadie, before walking out and closing the door behind her. Some fine foster parent she'd be, she told herself, boo-hooing over leaving a ward she'd known was temporary. She couldn't help it, though. It was a perfect happy ending, and she'd feel better later, but right now, Jill wanted to get home and indulge herself in a moment of sadness. Lord, she wouldn't know what to do now that she could sleep through a whole night without warming a bottle.

Occupying herself with morose thoughts like that,

Jill drove her little car up the ranch drive. Dustin's truck was in its usual spot. Quickly, she parked the car and hurried to the house. She couldn't wait to hear about Eunice's condition.

She couldn't wait to see Dustin.

Hurrying inside, she nearly collided with him in the hall. He took her into his arms to steady her. Jill stared up at him, quickly checking his face for signs of serious news. He appeared relaxed – until his gaze went from her eyes to her cheek.

'Whew. That looks worse than it did last night,' he said, tracing the outline of the bruise with his finger. 'I left so fast with Mother I don't think I noticed it this morning. You should see a doctor, Jill.'

'No. I'm fine.'

He pulled her back to look at her closely. 'I'm surprised your cheek-bone didn't break.'

'Didn't hit me hard enough,' Jill said lightly.

He swore, calling Curtis a few choice names.

'I'm more worried about Joey. I hope he didn't bruise.' She stiffened, remembering Maxine's dreadful visit. 'Did you remember today was Joey's day to go to – '

'Damn.' Dustin's eye riveted back to her face. 'I'm sorry. I don't suppose Maxine was nice to you?'

'Um . . .' Jill thought about how upset she'd been that Joey had been in his pajamas. 'I . . . maybe you'd better call to check with her. She seemed pretty upset with me, and . . . I don't think I handled it very well.' That was putting an optimistic light on it, Jill thought.

'I do want to talk to Joey.' Dustin went into the kitchen, saying over his shoulder, 'I'm sure Maxine wasn't any more or less herself than usual.'

He picked up the phone and began dialing. A shudder went through Jill. With heavy steps, she went up the stairs and into her room. The likelihood that Maxine had decided not to ring Dustin's ears with complaints about her was remote. She sat on the bed despondently. As Dustin's voice rose with so much irritation that she could hear it through the floor, Jill closed her eyes in dismay.

Maxine was keeping her word.

CHAPTER 19

Joey sat in Grandmother Copeland's kitchen, hearing her voice carry angry tones all the way down the hall. The cookie in front of him lost its appeal. Whoever Grandma was mad at was in big trouble. He sighed and looked around the big kitchen. His stomach hurt, and he wished his father would come and get him. Grandmother's cookies didn't taste like Jill's, and though he loved his grandfather, Joey was sad. Everybody in the house was making brows. If he could just go home, he thought everything would be much better.

Swinging his legs, Joey wondered what baby Holly was doing. Sleeping, probably. All that baby did was sleep. He understood she was going to go home one day, but he sure did like having her around. She made a lot of noise sometimes, and one time when she burped and he'd been sitting too close to her, he thought she smelled like a sandwich. That had made him laugh.

She was soft, too. He liked touching her head because it reminded him of the velvet on Rooster's nose. One day, maybe Holly could ride Rooster with him. Suddenly, he wondered if Santa would bring Holly's presents to his house for her. Joey sat up straight. What if he had to stay at Grandmother Copeland's for Christmas? Santa Claus wouldn't know where to find him. Santa would go to his house and see the little tree Joey had decorated with Jill and the big tree his daddy had chopped with him and leave the presents there.

Grandmother Copeland yelled louder. Joey started to cry.

Eunice opened her eyes slowly, waking up instantly when she realized who was sitting beside her in the hospital room. 'How are you, my friend?' she asked.

Vera smiled and patted Eunice's arm lightly. 'Better than you, I think.'

'Oh, I'm fine.' Eunice shook her head, knowing it was true. She was simply tired, perhaps, and getting old. Her mind didn't feel old, but the body was obviously running down. 'I'm not the spring chicken I used to be, of course. But I'll be up and going in a few days.'

'Did we do this to you?' Vera asked.

Her deep-brown, worried eyes passed over Eunice's body. Eunice couldn't help a smile. 'No. Your grandbaby kept me young and made me feel alive again. And I slept through all the excitement, anyway.'

'I suppose you wouldn't tell me any differently.'

'Well, I will tell you that I always wanted a little

girl of my own.' She rolled her head on the pillow to look at Vera. 'Oh, don't mistake me. Dustin was enough child to keep me busy, and he's grown into a fine man we were always proud of. But there was a time when . . .' She hesitated for a moment, her eyes downcast. 'I was pregnant one more time,' she said softly. 'I thought maybe I was going to finally get that little baby girl I so badly wanted.' She smiled to herself. 'I miscarried two months into my pregnancy. It just wasn't meant to be, I guess, because there never was another baby. So getting to hold yours was a blessing to me that I cherished.'

Eunice's voice was deep with sadness, perhaps even with regret. Vera knew that was something Maxine would never understand about Eunice: she hadn't gotten everything in life she had wanted. Vera looked at the woman who still resembled the girl she'd known, very much a Homecoming queen despite her age. Frailer now, maybe, but with the same spirit. 'I can still hear you comforting your mother about your shoes, Eunice. Nobody in the world would have guessed how hurt you were.' She sighed, remembering. 'You're comforting me, now.'

Eunice covered Vera's hand with her own. 'No. You're comforting me. And that's what friends are for.'

Vera leaned back in the chair. Together they sat there, and though Eunice's eyes closed once again, Vera didn't move, except to take her hand from under her friend's. This time, she covered Eunice's hand with her own.

★ ★ ★

Dustin walked right into the room that was Jill's. 'You read the situation correctly,' he told her. 'Maxine's ticked.'

She was always ticked. Even he had been able to tell that this time she was losing it. Dustin shook his head. The very thought or mention of Jill was gas on a fire to Maxine. Like it or not, he needed Jill. His mother would hopefully come home soon, but since she'd suffered a minor stroke, she was going to need some care. Joey needed someone to look after him. Dustin preferred for all of his family to have a caretaker who loved them. It was clear Jill had become very close to his mother and son. He was in a fortunate position to have hired someone who was so special to his family.

Dustin sat on the bed next to Jill, though he was hardly aware he'd done it. 'I wish I understood Maxine's concerns.' He paused, trying to sort through everything he'd just heard. Maxine had called Jill a slut, which had not surprised him. But it was her vehement accusation that Jill wasn't fit to care for Joey that bothered him. 'I'm trying to, I really am, but for the life of me, I don't know what she wants me to do. Well, besides build a shrine to Nina.'

He snorted, wishing he hadn't said that. It sounded so mean. Jill laid a comforting hand on his arm.

'You have to understand,' he said, shaking his head. 'Nina and I were not a perfect couple. But we did know each other very well in some ways. As

310

parents, we were learning, and enjoying the process. Even if we didn't see eye-to-eye on how the money got spent, or how much of her mother's interference I would put up with, when it came to the baby, we both wanted to do things right. I can't build a shrine to Nina; she wasn't perfect. If she was alive, she damn sure wouldn't build a shrine to me, because I made enough mistakes in our marriage to test the patience of a saint. But damn it, I tried. And I believe in my heart Nina is not smiling about her mother's actions.'

'I think Maxine feels like she's going to be left out, Dustin,' Jill offered quietly. 'I think that's what's rubbing her the wrong way about me.'

'Left out of what?'

Jill took a deep breath. 'Let's go along with what she appears to be imagining. As difficult as it is to pull this one up, let's envision us sending out wedding announcements.'

'Oh, boy.' Dustin's eyebrows shot up.

'Yes.' Jill nodded. 'Pretty scary. But work hard at this, Dustin. We're getting married, which we already know is going to bother Maxine, because she desperately misses her daughter. Life is now going on without Maxine . . .'

'Praise God. I don't think your mother likes me all that much, but at least she doesn't appear to be quite as devious.'

Jill stared at him for a moment. 'We'll get back to that later. Life, as Maxine views it, is leaving her out as we stand at the altar. Marsh is the best man, and Joey is the ring bearer.'

For the first time, Dustin brightened. 'He'd look kinda cute in little tux tails and boots.'

That stopped Jill for a second, Dustin noticed. He wondered what he'd said.

'Never mind.' She took a deep breath. 'What I'm getting at is, the first thing on Maxine's mind is if she should even attend our wedding.'

'Did we invite her?' Dustin didn't think he had. Why set himself up for trouble?

'Well, I don't know. We'd have to read Emily Post or something. If you leave her out, in such a small town, you risk offense and gossip. If you include her, you risk Maxine sitting in a pew pricking a voodoo doll that looks like you while you're saying your vows.'

'I'm starting to see.' For the first time, and probably because he was hearing it from a woman's point of view, Dustin really was beginning to understand.

'Okay. Now you've got three grandmothers in the picture, all of whom want to spend Christmas with Joey in the holidays. You know they're not all going to break bread at the same table, so you're going to have to do some shuffling. Naturally, Maxine does not want to be left out on Christmas Day, but in her heart, she's scared to death she will be.'

'If I had my choice between her and Lana, it would be Lana, hands down.' Dustin shot a grin at Jill when she tried to look insulted.

'Do I detect some cynicism where my folks are concerned, Dustin Reed?'

312

'Nope.' He shook his head. 'But I could tell they didn't cotton to me. I've got to tell you, most parents have been glad to welcome me into their home.'

'It wasn't really you they were concerned about,' Jill said, not looking directly at him anymore. 'I told you, they've been very concerned about my wedding breaking off.'

'I thought we just got married, pin pricks and all.'

'I . . .' Jill looked adorably confused. 'What are you talking about?'

'Well, we went through the whole scenario. It felt pretty real to me.'

'It did not! I was just trying to tell you how Maxine might feel, not that I'm in the perfect mood to empathize with her right now.'

Dustin tried to act outraged as he leaned Jill back to kiss her. 'That's just like a woman, to lead a man on. Here I thought we had something serious going . . .'

The ringing of the doorbell quieted the waves of desire pounding in his blood. Dustin sat up, tucking his shirt back in. 'That's Joey, I guess. Maxine hedged when I asked her when she'd be bringing him home, but maybe she decided to come on.'

Jill didn't follow him, which he thought was probably smart. The less Maxine saw of Jill, maybe the less upset she'd get. Now that he had a clearer vision of what might be upsetting her, he intended to let her know that, despite their differences, he wanted her to always have a special relationship with Joey.

313

He opened the door, prepared to greet Maxine quickly and stop any spiteful words from leaving her mouth. His own snapped shut when he saw who was standing on his porch. 'Evening, Mr Reed,' the man told him.

He recognized Maxine's lawyer at once. With foreboding, he automatically nodded.

'The Copelands are going to keep Joey until the custody hearing,' the lawyer said without preamble. 'Maxine is terribly concerned that her grandson is in an environment at this time that is inappropriate for him.'

'She's always claimed that,' Dustin snapped. 'What's changed?'

'Specifically, your choice of household help. The woman appears to be poor quality for overseeing the care of your son.'

'You tell Maxine – '

The lawyer held up a hand. 'Please, Mr Reed. I've been instructed to file papers with the court, which I can do tomorrow, if you press my client on this issue. She is in no mood to heat this battle to a more emotional point; however, she will do that if necessary. Considering the situation, I recommend we leave it as it is.'

'You're not my damn lawyer,' Dustin growled. 'Don't give me advice.'

The man backed off the porch. 'Mr Reed, any further conversation between us is probably not prudent. Considering the lateness of the hour and the nature of the situation, I chanced stopping by instead of merely calling you with Maxine's instructions. I hope I won't find that I erred in this matter.'

Dustin advanced on him. 'I suppose you want my gratitude.' He bit off saying, 'I'll show you my gratitude with my boot if you don't get out of here,' realizing that threatening Maxine's lawyer was foolhardy, and this visit could very well have been engineered to get a violent reaction from him. It would certainly be the killing blow for his hope of retaining custody of his son. Despite the red fog of anger and fear crowding his brain, Dustin forced himself to turn around and put one foot in front of the other until he'd reached the sanctuary of his foyer. He closed the door, and then his eyes.

Joey wasn't coming home tonight. Or even tomorrow night. Only the judge could decide now whether Joey would ever come back to Dustin at all.

'Maxine.'

'Yes. Let me go into my office.' Instantly recognizing the private investigator's voice, Maxine switched the cordless phone for one in her office that allowed her more privacy. 'What have you found out?'

'It wasn't too difficult to discover who Dustin's housekeeper is. She used to work for a firm in Dallas, but she was fired recently.'

'Fired?' This was an interesting piece of news. 'How do you know?'

'It wasn't too difficult to run some inquiries. She had worked at the same company for a long time, so it was listed as her source of income on certain applications that were in her credit files.'

'But how do you know she was fired?'

'I called the Personnel Department. As you know, all they will verify is that she worked there for a certain length of time. However, I did indicate that speaking to someone who had known her closely would be helpful as I was trying to determine whether she was an appropriate choice for a loan to cover college expenses. I said that she's interested in getting an MBA degree.'

'That was a good story.'

'Good enough to get me through to a very helpful man named Carl Douglas, who said he was a long-time associate and close friend of Jill's. According to Mr Douglas, Jill was fired because her work wasn't up to the company's required standards, though he personally felt they should have given her another chance.'

'So, all she's fit for is washing Dustin's clothes. Interesting.'

'Yes. I'm not sure we can totally rely on this guy's word, though. He didn't know anything about a baby, which seemed strange to me if they're such close friends.'

'All I needed to know was that this housekeeper isn't on the up and up. In fact, this scenario is becoming more and more clear to me. The reason the stories don't jive is because Jill McCall is neither housekeeper nor family member. She's some little trollop Dustin managed to get pregnant, and they're worried to death I'll find out about it. Obviously, she isn't a high-quality individual, or she wouldn't look like so many miles of bad road.'

'Is there anything else you want me to find out?'

'Not right now,' Maxine said thoughtfully. 'I've sent notice over to the ranch that should keep Dustin and Eunice on their toes for a while. As I see it, everything is just the way I want it right now.'

'Let me know.'

'You can be sure I will.' Maxine hung up the phone, lost in thought for a moment until she heard crying. Instantly, she rose, hurrying into the kitchen.

Joey sat in his grandfather's lap. David was trying his best to comfort the boy, with his stiff fingers and nearly useless arms.

'What's wrong, Joey? Did you fall?'

'I . . . I wa – want to . . . to go home!' Joey cried. Tears poured down his cheeks and his eyes were huge with unhappiness.

Maxine felt a stab of anxiety in her heart. 'Joey, maybe we can play – '

'I . . . I want my daddy!' he shrieked. 'Daddy! Daddy!'

David's hands frantically worked to rub circles on Joey's shuddering back. Maxine grimaced. 'Here, let me do that.'

She reached to take Joey but he drew back from her touch.

'No! I . . . want to . . . to go home!'

'Well, it's not time, Joey. You need to stay here a little while longer. You just need a little nap.'

317

Joey hopped off of David's lap. He ran from the room. Knowing what she was going to see there, Maxine forced herself to meet David's gaze.

'David, I . . .' She stopped herself. The condemnation was clear in her husband's eyes. 'David, you don't understand. You didn't see her. That woman is a mess, and strange things are going on over there. I truly don't believe it's the best place for Joey to be.'

He pursed his lips. Then he shook his head. With one finger, he pointed to the doorway Joey had rushed through, then pointed to his own eye.

'Damn it, David, he's a child. Of course, he's going to cry. A little homesickness is no reason for us to give up now.'

Shaking his head again, he slowly turned his wheelchair and went to the kitchen window to look out. His back stayed turned to her.

His lack of support infuriated her. 'Damn you! Don't you turn your back to me! After you spent our best years chasing after other women, I deserve your attention now! And don't think that I don't know that it's the love you've harbored all these years for Eunice Reed that's keeping you from seeing the truth of the matter.'

He did turn around then. Maxine kept her vision trained on her husband. That accusation had definitely gotten a reaction from her carefully remote husband.

But he was waving his hand in a negative manner. Maxine frowned. 'Don't try to dig your way out of it now, David. We're too far gone in this custody battle to stop now.'

Rolling his wheelchair to a kitchen drawer, he forced his hand to open the drawer and take out a pen and pad. Maxine watched impassively. There was no need for David to write anything down. She understood him clearly. She also expected him to rise staunchly to any defense of Eunice.

Painstakingly, he wrote a few block letters, which looked more like a kindergartner's writing than his own. 'No affair,' Maxine murmured. 'That's not true, David. The private investigator says you made several jewelry purchases. I never received any of those particular items. They went to someone.'

Again, he touched his pen to the paper. It rolled into his lap, but David managed to rescue it and tried again. 'Vault,' Maxine read. 'Why would you buy jewelry and put it in a vault? Everyone knows it's not a secure investment in most cases.'

David shrugged.

'They weren't enormously valuable purchases?'

He shook his head.

'Then why? Why couldn't you just tell me?'

He tightened his lips as if he were trying to decide if he could trust her. *Private*, he wrote.

'You expect me to believe this story?' Maxine was incredulous.

Her husband shrugged but didn't remove his eyes from hers. For some reason, she had the uncanny feeling he was telling the truth. On the paper he penned *Needed money* with excruciating care.

'Oh, David. You didn't buy jewelry from women who needed money, did you?'

He shook his head. Once more, his hand went to the paper. *Loan*.

'Oh, for crying out loud, David. Do you mean to tell me you've been running a pawn shop out of the house all these years?' Though she tried to sound stern, inside Maxine was unspeakably relieved to discover David hadn't been buying jewelry for other women. 'Has anyone ever bought back their things?'

She sighed when he shook his head again. 'So we have a vault full of fairly worthless jewelry?'

Want them some day, he carefully wrote.

'Oh, David.' Wasn't that just like her soft-hearted husband to loan out money to people for things of no value, then fully expect that several years later those folks would turn up to pay him for their junk? 'What about Eunice?' she asked, hating to have to know the answer, but craving to know the truth just the same. His frequent visits to the Reed Ranch could have had nothing to do with business, she knew. Eunice didn't need money, and David admired her far too much for their relationship to have been platonic. It squeezed her heart just to think of the two of them together.

With one finger, David reached out and touched her wrist for just a moment. Maxine stared silently. He touched his finger to his heart, and then slowly, he again touched her wrist.

It was as if all the breath she had in her suddenly expelled, leaving her limp and unable to speak.

Maxine sank to her knees in front of David and put her head in his lap. She felt him touch her hair hesitantly; when she stayed still, he caressed the tight curls more boldly.

For the first time in years, Maxine Copeland cried.

CHAPTER 20

Jill heard Dustin's boots on the stairs. He didn't stop at her room as she'd expected. Instead, he went down the hall to his own room. For a moment it was quiet, then she heard him talking loudly to someone.

She knew she should get up and close her bedroom door. She should go downstairs and get something ready for him to eat. By the tone of his voice, she could tell the call was personal and one he probably wouldn't appreciate her hearing.

Getting up to make her way down the stairs, the sudden mention of her name caught her ears. Jill paused, knowing in her heart that what she was doing was going to hurt her. People who listened to conversations about themselves invariably got their feelings hurt.

'Jill is not the problem, for chrissakes. I'm not sure what Maxine's whole problem is, Roger. All I know is, I was informed that the Copelands have decided Joey is in danger. Until Thursday, I don't get a chance to tell my side of the story.'

He was silent for a few moments. 'Jill has done a

superior job of taking care of our family. I can't imagine what Maxine thinks Jill has done wrong. I do know she's been upset since she learned Jill was here.'

Jill went down the stairs, her heart torn. On the one hand, she was warmed by Dustin's support. On the other, she had cost Dustin his child. She should have known better than to stay on at the ranch, knowing Maxine's vehement dislike of her. Oh, dislike was a weak word for the truth. Maxine had been determined to make certain Jill wasn't going to stay a part of Joey's life. She had warned them, and Jill had been a fool to ignore it. Dustin was a good man. He would never have asked her to leave. His temperament wouldn't allow him to bend on an issue he believed in, and he honestly felt Jill was good for Eunice and Joey.

Unfortunately, she hadn't turned out to be good for the family in the long run.

She set about making a light supper of sandwiches and soup for Dustin to eat. A moment later he ran down the stairs, slamming the front door behind him. As if it was an afterthought, the door flew back open.

'I need to go out for a while, Jill,' he called into the house.

'Okay!' she called back, her heart sinking.

Hearing the door shut again, Jill went into the hall and opened the door to walk onto the porch. She waved to Dustin, and as he backed the truck up, he waved to her, too. The wind blew cold and bitter as she watched him leave. In her heart, Jill knew what she had to do. She had waited too long.

Back inside the house, she rubbed her arms for a moment, thinking. Covering the sandwich with plastic wrap and putting the soup away for him to warm later, Jill made sure the kitchen was tidy. Then she got a few trash sacks. It wasn't an efficient way to carry her few things, but she'd packed baby Holly's things in her own suitcase, knowing Sadie would get around to returning it eventually.

The suitcase being the least of her problems, trash sacks would have to do. Jill put her possessions in the bags, throwing her cosmetics in her night case. After she finished, she carried her things out to the car and stowed them in the trunk. Tears started to prick at her eyes, but Jill wouldn't let them come. Not yet.

Going back into the house for the last time, Jill took a piece of paper and a pen from a drawer. She wrote a few lines, the hardest words she'd ever had to write.

Dear Dustin,
I find it necessary to resign my position as house-keeper. After the happiness I have known in your home, with you and your family, it is hard for me to leave. However, it is time for me to get on with my life, and to stop hiding from my problems. I hope you can understand.
Jill

It didn't sound right. Nothing about her letter felt good. In fact, Jill felt sick and the tears she was holding back felt like they were going to spill any

324

second. Living with the Reeds had healed her in many ways, made her happier than she'd ever been in her life. Her relationship with Dustin was a thing born of unwilling respect and attraction, all the more surprising because it had happened when she had never dreamed it would. Dustin had taught her that she was a desirable woman. That had been the most wonderful thing that had ever happened to her.

But she couldn't allow herself to take advantage of the healing the Reeds brought her. Not when she was costing them the child they loved. Jill touched the paper she'd written on to her lips, then crossed into the parlor to lay it underneath the tabletop Christmas tree she had so enjoyed watching Joey decorate. She laid her house key on top of it. No longer able to hold back the tears, Jill closed the front door behind her, making certain the doorknob stayed locked. Then she ran to her car, telling herself she couldn't leave town without saying goodbye to the woman who had believed in her from the start.

Eunice opened her eyes, at first thinking her room was empty of visitors. Vera had not left her side, though Eunice figured it was probably killing her not to get to see her grandbaby. No matter how many times she'd tried to convince her to leave, Vera had only smiled and patted her hand. Eunice knew Vera and that they had that strong, stubborn streak in common. She sighed, knowing the truth was that she appreciated Vera's devotion.

A voice immediately said, 'Is there anything I can get you?'

'Jill.' Eunice managed a tired smile. 'How nice of you to come.'

'I shooed Vera off. I hope you won't mind a substitute.'

'Lord, no. The woman needed a break.'

'Well, she said she'd be back as soon as she showered and got something to eat.'

'She will be, too.' Eunice smiled, casting an eye over the beautiful young girl who had come to sit at her side. Life could be so strange sometimes. Here was this lovely person with a huge bruise on her face, and somehow Eunice thought she had never looked lovelier. Maybe it was because Jill was such a strong woman herself, someone Eunice identified with. She'd never heard her complain, never heard her offer anything but a kind word to everyone. She'd earned the Reed gratitude forever with her kindness to Joey and baby Holly.

She'd earned Eunice's gratitude for the slow, giving comfort she had shown Dustin. She patted Jill's hand without speaking, aware that Jill had been patient with her son. Oh, every mother hoped for a woman that would care for and adore a son the way she did; a woman who could overlook most of the man's flaws and see the best in him. Jill seemed to be built that way. Not that Dustin was a hero by any stretch; Eunice would admit that in a second. But he was a man with heart, a good man who needed a good woman.

Jill fit the picture, but even Eunice knew there were an awful lot of odds for Dustin and Jill to surmount.

'Are you feeling better?'

'I think so.' Eunice smiled self-deprecatingly. 'I can't really tell.'

'Have the doctors given you a diagnosis?'

Jill's concern was touching to Eunice. 'Apparently, I had a minor stroke, a not very unusual incident among folks my age. They can come and pass, sometimes without the person noticing.'

'Will you be able to go home soon?'

Eunice nodded. 'They're running a few more tests, but I should be free soon. I can't wait to see Joey.'

'Um . . .' An expression of extreme discomfort crossed Jill's face. 'I don't think he's going to be home.'

Eunice was instantly alert. 'What do you mean?'

'I'm not sure . . . Dustin didn't tell me exactly. And I wasn't exactly eavesdropping either, but I heard.' Jill seemed stricken. 'A man came to see Dustin this afternoon. I don't know what they said, exactly, but I did hear him talking to someone on the phone in his room. He was angry. I know he was talking about Maxine on the phone, and how she didn't like me. Then he left.'

Jill's voice dropped to a whisper. Eunice pushed herself up on the pillows.

'What possible reason could she have for pulling this now? The court date is Thursday.'

'Maxine came to pick Joey up and I didn't have

him ready.' Jill's gaze dropped, ashamed. 'I was in a bathrobe myself. She said with you in the hospital and Dustin gone so much, she was surprised you would leave Joey in my care.'

'It isn't any of her business.'

'Dustin hasn't discussed any of this with me. But I don't think I misunderstood Maxine's unhappiness. And he was very upset when he left today.'

'Oh, for heaven's sake.' Eunice she shook her head, wishing she had her strength back. 'This time Maxine's gone too far.' She thought for a minute, looking at the woman with the shiny blonde hair curling gently at her chin. 'Don't let this worry you. Dustin will take care of everything.'

Jill raised unhappy eyes. 'I have to worry about it, Eunice. I've cost Dustin the person he loves the most. It's terribly unfair, when he and Joey are just now coming to know how much they care for each other. I can't do that to him.'

'He didn't tell you what happened because he knew this was the way you'd feel. He knew you'd feel you had to leave.'

'I do.'

Eunice pursed her lips, staring hard at Jill. 'Dustin wouldn't want you to let Maxine run you off. He's not that way. Once he's given you his loyalty, he'll protect you.'

How different from Carl, thought Jill. She let her gaze drop, unable to let Eunice look inside her soul to see how much she was hurting. 'That's why I have to leave. I can't let Dustin's loyalty to me affect his custody situation with his son. It would be a pretty poor way to say thank you.'

Eunice clicked her tongue. Her hands worried the blanket for a minute. 'I don't know. I see your point, but I also know how Dustin is going to feel. I don't think he's going to be happy about this at all.'

Jill knew that too. He wouldn't back down; it wasn't in his nature. She was going to have to do it for him. It was the right thing to do. After all, she'd wished many times there was something she could do to help Dustin get his son back. There was only one thing she could do – say goodbye to the Reeds.

Slowly she rose, taking Eunice's hands in hers. 'Thank you for everything you've done for me, Eunice. I got the best Christmas present in the world when I came to your home. I have my self-respect back, and for that, I can never thank you enough.'

Enice's eyes welled with tears. 'You gave us an awful lot, too, Jill.'

She shook her head. 'No. You gave me your strength, when I didn't have any left of my own. Now you need it yourself, for you and for your family. I won't forget you, not ever. I know why Ms Benchley trusted you with her grandchild. It's plain to see why Dustin treats you like his best friend. You are a person with rare honesty and goodness, and if I ever become half the woman you are, it will be more than I ever would have been before I met you.'

'Oh, Jill. Everyone has weak spots in their life. We needed you more than you needed us, honey. You're a survivor. Believe me, Jill, you are everything you want to be, and it isn't because of anything we did for you. In fact, it's just the opposite. Why, your mother's going to flip when she sees your face. She'll never want you to come back to Lassiter again.'

Jill placed Eunice's hand back on the bed with a sad smile. 'I'll be fine. Don't worry about me. Goodbye, Eunice,' she whispered, before turning and hurrying from the room. It wouldn't matter what her mother or anyone else wanted her to do; Jill could never go back to the house on Setting Sun Road anyway, not without jeopardizing Dustin and Joey's chance for happiness.

Eunice closed her eyes after Jill left. She had never felt so tired. This latest development didn't feel right; she couldn't help thinking the situation was going to be worse now that Jill was gone. *Darn Maxine, anyway. All my life she has been determined to get what is mine.*

There was so much more at stake now than a pair of pumps to wear to Homecoming. Their battle had become personal and hurtful. Maxine was never going to forgive Eunice for Nina's death. Oh, she hadn't been the reason for Nina's car accident, but as far as Maxine was concerned, Eunice might as well have driven her off that cliff herself. She claimed her anger was directed at Dustin, but Eunice knew Maxine was really trying to get to her. After all these years, Maxine still hated her. Believing that

David and she had conducted an affair had been tinder on an already burning fire. Eunice pressed her eyes together tightly. She had to think. There was something she could do, but her mind wouldn't give her the answer. She was just achingly tired, but maybe if she rested, the answer would come to her.

Dustin read the note Jill had left, disbelief making it difficult to comprehend what the delicately scrolled handwriting revealed. Reading it through another time trying to counteract the astonished anger flowing through him, Dustin crumpled the paper into a ball, hurling it into the fireplace.

'Damn it! Of all times for her to run out on us.'

Without Joey, without Eunice being in the house, it was pretty clear Jill had run out on *him*. As if nothing had existed between them, she'd resigned her position as housekeeper.

Like hell! A frown settled on his face. Had their lovemaking meant nothing to her? Had his light-hearted chit-chat about getting married not clearly signaled his strong feelings for her? No, he hadn't told her he loved her, but it should have been obvious. He had been in no position to talk of love or a lasting commitment with him in the heat of a custody battle. He had know that there was little he could offer her.

Of course, he had even less to offer her now. Strangely, and perhaps perversely, he felt that was why Jill should have stuck around. He needed her support. With his mother ill, and the possibility of

Joey being taken from him a very real specter, he needed Jill's warmth to keep him from running into the pecan trees and shrieking like the madman inside him wanted to do. Jill kept him sane.

He was feeling very close to the edge.

His gaze focused on the ragged tiny tree she had bought for Joey, decorated with cheap, forlorn ornaments. Joey had been so proud of his handi-work. Dustin avoided looking at it, his gaze snagging instead on the big tree he had chopped down for Joey. Hell, that was partially a lie. He had brought that tree home for Jill, because he could tell she was homesick, that she missed the Christmas spirit so generously displayed in the McCall household. In-stantly, his gaze bounced to the antique, curved-back sofa where Jill had spent so many nights enjoying the tree lights as she fed baby Holly. He could see Jill so clearly, with her precious holiday decorations that he had not wanted.

He needed her so badly.

Jill had made her decision. It was something he would have to live with, whether he liked it or not. The anger he felt at her desertion would pass, but he didn't think the hurt would dissipate so soon. It was worse than he had thought it would be, most likely because her departure was as sudden as everyone else's he'd cared about had been. His father, Nina, and even Joey, though it wasn't his fault; all those surprise partings had taken an emotional chunk out of Dustin's soul. Jill's choice to leave sliced like a razor, neat and clean, yet unique in its pain.

Dustin made himself take deep breaths of air. His lawyer had told him to play it cool for now. He could not storm the Copeland house like a renegade father and kidnap his own son, as much as he desperately wanted to do it. Maxine's trump card was, unfortunately, very potent and full of potential to Dustin if he acted on the anger that filled him. Four days, though they seemed like an eternity, were not the end of the world, the lawyer advised.

Fancy that piece of crap from a man who had no children. Dustin slammed his fist into his palm. If Marsh was here, he'd have some stupid wisecrack to take the bite out of what Dustin was feeling. If his mother was around, she'd say something about believing in the spirit of Christmas and that everything would be all right. If Joey were here, the two of them could go throw birdseed out for the birds and watch them fly in.

But none of his family was around, and now Jill was gone. For the first time in his life, Dustin felt the agony of being completely alone.

CHAPTER 21

Wearing jeans and a T-shirt fit for loading boxes she had never unpacked at her parents' house, Jill looked around the contemporary apartment where she and Carl had once planned to spend their newly married life. Sheets, towels, and other items necessary for starting a home filled the boxes. There was no reason to take them out now.

She was surprised to see that Carl hadn't moved out very many of his things. She had told him she was turning in the notice, which she had done the day after he'd paid his surprise visit to the ranch. In some ways, Carl was a strangely motivated person, but getting his possessions out of her hair apparently wasn't something that motivated him greatly.

She tried not to think about how depressing it was to have to look at all of his stuff. One phone message at Carl's office was all she was leaving to warn him that if he didn't get over here at a pre-arranged time and move out, everything he had parked in the apartment was going to the charity drop-off.

After that, she could get on with packing up and removing her things. It was bad enough that she'd had to leave Dustin's house with her belongings in sacks; it was past time to find a place she could afford and settle into. She couldn't go on living like a bag-lady forever, she told herself sternly.

Casting a critical eye around the apartment, Jill wondered about leasing a new place this close to Christmas. Hopefully, something would be available. Of course, she could move the sofa and furniture that wouldn't fit into her folks' garage into storage and lodge with them until Christmas was past, but that option seemed worse than unpacking boxes by herself on Christmas Eve.

Wandering into the kitchen, Jill sat down at the table. Her parents would want her to come home. For the second time in two months, her life had drastically altered, but it would feel so much like she was running home to escape her problems and she was too old to do that now.

The real problem lay with her heart, though. Jill put her chin on her hand, realizing the only place she wanted to be for Christmas was at the Reed Ranch with Dustin. And Joey, and Eunice. It wasn't going to be Christmas without them.

Suddenly, she saw the newspaper lying on the table. It was the same one she'd circled ads in just after Thanksgiving, leaving it behind as she'd gone to Lassiter. Reading the ad over again made her heart clench.

WANTED: HOUSEKEEPER FOR RANCH HOUSE. *Cleaning and meals for a man, young boy, and an elderly woman.*

335

Memories washed over her in a flood. She had been so worried, so afraid of what those strangers might be like. Now there were faces to go with the description. The Reeds had been so much more than just a man, a boy, and an elderly woman.

They had become her family. Their home had felt like hers. For just a little while, she had belonged.

She would give anything to be in Dustin's arms right now.

'When can I spring you out of here?' Dustin asked, automatically sending a glance toward Marsh's injured leg. Though the gun the thug had shot Marsh with had been small caliber, enough blood had been lost that the hospital had kept him overnight for observation. Dustin was itching to get his friend out of the hospital – and his mother, too. Jeez, it was bad enough that Maxine had pulled a fast one on him, leaving him without his son. Having his mother and best friend in the hospital at the same time was too cruel. Shoot, he might as well check out a room for himself, Dustin thought sourly.

With Jill doing a vanishing act on him, he had no reason to get home. Hell, if he didn't get everybody he loved out of this disinfectant-stinking hospital, he might find himself hanging candy canes from their bed rails.

Marsh chuckled. 'Didn't say anything about letting you spring me.'

'I am, though. As soon as I get the nod from the doctor.' It was his responsibility to take his friend home. Marsh had been wounded on his behalf – and Dustin knew his carelessness had been the reason Lynch had managed to get a shot off. He should have made certain the hood wasn't packing hardware before he'd let go of him.

'Nope.' Marsh shook his head. 'Can't let you do it. But I'm already okayed to go home.'

Dustin jumped to his feet. 'Well, hell, man! Why didn't you say so? Let's get out of here.' He grabbed Marsh's boots from the corner they were occupying.

'Dustin, China's going to be here to take me home.'

He stopped in the act of stuffing Marsh's boots into a bag. 'China?'

'Yeah.' The grin on Marsh's face was telling. 'But I appreciate the thought, dude.'

'Ah, yeah. Okay.' Dustin put Marsh's things down as if they were hot. For some reason he felt let-down, maybe even left out. He'd been so wrapped up in his own misery that he hadn't considered Marsh might have someone in his life. Dustin didn't have anyone right now; perhaps he'd assumed Marsh didn't, either. They could share their down times together, the same way they always had. Maybe not playing pool and hiding out in his parents' rumpus room the way they'd done as teenagers, but sharing a beer and that wordless understanding that men were good at. Lord, he needed that.

Now Marsh seemed to be moving toward a relationship he'd been wanting for a long time. Dustin dredged up some happiness for his friend. 'Jeez,

Marsh, I didn't think China was ever going to let you within a foot of her.'

'Me neither.' His smile was huge. 'She must have changed her mind when she realized I was the only decent single guy left in Lassiter.'

Dustin sat down heavily in the hard chair beside Marsh's bed. 'Ah, no. Actually, now there's me, too.'

'Jittery, are you? Cooling things off?'

He only wished it was that simple. 'I think Jill got the jitters. She's gone.'

'Just like that?'

'Just like that.' Dustin nodded. Even now it hurt.

'Ungrateful wench. After everything we did to her, too. Letting a punk beat up on her, not to mention Maxine . . .' Marsh broke off, his banter falling flat. 'I'm sorry, buddy. No explanation, no nothing?'

'Jill left a note. It was your basic Dear John, I've-got-to-get-on-with-my-life letter.'

Marsh rubbed the bristles on his face thoughtfully. 'Man, I thought she was in it for the long haul.'

Dustin certainly hadn't seen Jill's departure coming. 'What can I say? Maybe in the beginning I worried that the situation was overwhelming. But Jill was pretty cool about everything. Level-headed, you know what I mean?'

'Yeah. I do.' Marsh nodded his agreement.

'Hell, I don't know.' He couldn't talk about Jill anymore, not even with his best friend. It was just too damn hard. 'Guess I'll go see Mother, if you think China's going to be here soon.'

'Yep. Say hi to Eunice for me.'

Nodding, Dustin left Marsh's room. It was only a couple of floors to his mother's room, but once he got there, he fell into the chair by her bed, feeling winded. Like the breath had been knocked out of him.

Eunice opened her eyes and smiled at him. 'You don't look like you've been eating right.'

Who could eat? There was nobody in his house. He was used to a baby wailing and Bugs Bunny cartoons blaring and Jill humming and his mother's encouraging words while he ate. It was too damn quiet.

'I'll pick something up on the way home.' Glancing over his mother's finely-lined skin, he thought she seemed much better. 'You look like you're on the mend, though.'

'I am.' Eunice smiled.

'Great. Get the hell out of the bed and I'll get in it.'

She laughed. 'Dustin, in a few days, you're going to be a new man.'

'Yeah? How's that?' It sounded good, but he couldn't feel that type of instant rejuvenation coming on.

'Joey will come home on Thursday.'

That would do it. 'Barring the judge siding with Maxine.'

'I've been thinking about this. Nothing Maxine thinks she can testify to is sufficient in the eyes of the court to warrant taking a child away from his only surviving parent. Who also happens to have a parent of his own to help rear the child.' She was quiet for a moment. 'I don't even think anything she can bring up about Jill is enough to convince the court that she shouldn't be allowed to be a care-giver.'

'Jill isn't here, so I guess that's one less worry.'

'Is it?' Eunice slanted him a questioning look.

'Well, as far as the custody situation goes.'

'I didn't think you were that worried about Jill's impact on the custody problem.'

He shrugged. 'I never was.'

'Then go get her back.' His mother pinned him with a no-nonsense look. 'She left because she was afraid Maxine was going to use her against you in court. Jill felt certain her presence was causing such a problem with Maxine that in the end she would wind up costing you Joey.'

'No.' Dustin shook his head.

'No, what?'

'In my mind, Jill is just like you. So, no, she couldn't have cost me my son.' He glanced up to meet his mother's gaze. 'Maxine doesn't see it that way, I suppose.'

Eunice snorted. 'It wouldn't make it better if she did. Maxine has been after me like a tiger since we were girls.' She sighed deeply. 'I think you're right. I don't think Jill would have cost you your son. But I know she felt like you might have to choose: either you had her, or you had Joey. Maxine is a convincing person, and if additional complaints were brought up, Jill knew you would be in trouble because of her.'

'I didn't tell her about Maxine's threats.'

'I know. Jill heard you on the phone in your room.

She didn't hear much, but she got enough to upset her.'

Dustin stared down at his hands. His fingers were woven together hard enough to make the skin whiten. 'I love her.'

Eunice laid a gentle hand over his. 'I know you do. I do, too. So does Joey. You have to go bring her home.'

'I can't.' Dustin halted for a moment, trying to sort out of his feelings. 'I'm too angry with her for leaving. Everything you've told me makes it a little better, but it's the cold hard fact that she walked out on me. She walked out on Joey. I keep thinking how much it's going to hurt him that she just disappeared.'

'Try to see it her way, Dustin.'

'No.' His voice was curt. It was something he couldn't explain to his mother. Nina had always been wanting to leave, wanting to go home. He wouldn't have forced her to stay. No matter what their problems had been, he had wanted their family to stay together. But he couldn't make her want him.

Jill had left. It had been her own choice to leave without discussing the matter with him. After all, it was his own personal business, involving his family, his son. She had acted without consulting him; she had wanted to go. He would not try to change her mind.

This time, even his mother's advice couldn't sway him. A woman walking out on a man was a woman who had her mind made up.

He stood, jamming his Stetson on his head. 'Did the doc give you a release date?'

'Tomorrow morning,' she said softly, her eyes too bright. Lord, he didn't think he could bear it if his mother suddenly sprouted tears. He wasn't trying to be obstinate. Some things were just the way they were.

'I'll be here to get you then.' He leaned over, giving her a kiss on the cheek. She patted his cheek in return.

'I'll be ready.' Her smile was brave.

He stared at her for a moment, realizing she probably felt the same way he did about going home. Like it wasn't truly going home. It was just going to be the two of them.

Damn it. Rage flooded Dustin as the unfairness of it smote him. *Damn it to hell. I've had all I can take.*

'I'm going to get Joey,' he ground out between his teeth. 'If I have to open the bedroom window and pull him out, I'm going to get my son.'

His mother hesitated for only a moment. 'I know I'm supposed to say something wise at this moment, something about trying to stay out of jail at Christmas and what-have-you. However, you have a lawyer for that.' Eunice folded her hands. 'I will enjoy eating supper tomorrow with my grandson.'

Dustin nodded. Without another word, he left.

China let Marsh lean on him as he pulled up from the hospital bed. The woman felt heavenly. He'd never

342

really thought he would ever get this close to her. She smelled sweet, and that fiery hair of hers tickled his face so nicely. The curves of her body pressed against his sent enough lust pouring into his body to make him consider trying to talk her into rumpling the hospital bed sheets with him.

'Are you all right?' she asked.

The concern in her eyes sent pure electric voltage shooting through him. 'Never been better.'

'Where's Dustin?' She didn't pull away from him, so Marsh settled himself against her as they man-euvered toward the wheelchair that would take him to the exit.

'Checking on his mother.' Marsh thought about that for a second. Dustin sure had seemed down about Jill. About everything, in fact. He should probably stop by and check on the old lady – and Dustin – before he left. 'Would you mind wheeling me past her room on the way out?'

'Okay.' She leaned over as he half-fell, half-sat in the wheelchair. He took in the view of her cleavage like a starving man.

'Doing all right?'

'Doing fine,' Marsh said happily.

He was content until they reached Eunice's room. 'Hi, Eunice. You look like you're feeling better.'

'Hello, Marsh. China.' She nodded graciously. 'I am ready to go home, thank you. I have spent enough time in this dreary place. I'm ready to get on with a merry Christmas.'

'I bet you are.' There was an odd light shining in

Eunice's eyes that tweaked Marsh's sixth sense. 'Where's Dustin?'

'He's gone to get Joey,' she said calmly.

A rush of shock hit him. 'I thought Maxine had . . .'

'It doesn't matter what Maxine does. It's time we start calling the shots. She's run over us long enough.'

If his friend was pulling such a stunt, he was ready to go to the nut house. Eunice belonged in there with him. 'I know you've been pretty upset by everything, but this isn't the time to go jumping off the deep end.'

'On the contrary. The Reed family is not going to be held hostage any longer by a woman who has had it in for me for longer than you've been alive.'

'Oh, great.' Marsh had a sickening picture of Dustin and Eunice eating mashed potatoes and Spam in jail on Christmas. 'Who the hell do you think gets to drag your son's ass into jail for bothering a helpless old man and woman? Or for trespassing on their damn property, or any other charge Maxine dreams up?'

Eunice crossed her arms. 'Marsh, watch your mouth. I don't have to listen to that language, even from the sheriff.'

'Oh, for crying out loud.' He cast a helpless glance back at China, who had been standing silently behind his wheelchair. 'Are you hearing this crap?'

China nodded. 'Yes, I did. I think she just asked you to mind your manners.'

'No, China, did you hear where Dustin's . . .' He stopped, frowning at her. 'Don't tell me you agree with what they're doing?'

'Marsh, put away your badge for a minute. Dustin isn't going to do anything crazy.'

'He is! Do either one of you realize how much I am *not* going to enjoy arresting my best friend?' Marsh glared at China, then sent one Eunice's way for good measure.

'I think Dustin is at the end of his rope, and frankly, I think it's about time. We haven't done anything wrong, for heaven's sake. We're being treated like we have. The law has certainly not been on our side, pardon me for saying so, Marsh.'

Marsh shook his head, dragging in a deep breath. 'Okay. I see that the voice of reason is not going to be heard in this room today. Eunice, as the mother of my best friend, I must say that I do not agree with what you are doing. I will not like hearing what happens to your son when Maxine calls the law in. However, I am trying to remember my manners enough to ask you if there's anything I can do for you.'

He folded his arms across his chest. The Reeds were an independent bunch. Dustin had not asked for help from him. His mother wouldn't either. But still, at least he could stay polite, even if he had to throw her son in jail.

'Yes, there is, as a matter of fact. You can go to Dallas and explain to Jill that she is very much needed here.'

'Oh, wait . . .' Marsh hesitated, astounded. 'You're not serious. Dustin's kidnapping his own son, and you want me to go haul his housekeeper back to Lassiter. Are we all going to eat meatloaf in prison this holiday? Shall I order tap water to complement the menu?'

Eunice fixed him with an unwavering stare. 'I will consider this favor sufficient return for having practically raised you.'

He couldn't believe the old woman's spunk. 'Even if I did go – and I'm not saying I will – what makes you think Jill will listen to me any more than you do? She's a sassy lady.' It occurred to him that Jill wasn't any sassier than the two women looking at him right now. Marsh was starting to feel outmaneuvered.

'I don't know if she will listen to you. She never did much of that,' Eunice admitted. 'However, Dustin won't go, and he's busy at this moment, anyway.'

'He's going to be busy mopping floors at the jail,' Marsh said morosely.

Eunice ignored him. 'Jill misunderstood her place in this tangle, and it's up to you to explain it.'

'Come on, Marsh. Quit being such a wet blanket.'

Marsh swiveled at China's words. 'Oh, thanks for the support. I'm being a professional, a cop, which I can't stop being.'

'Maybe you could if I drove you into Dallas.'

She smiled at him. Marsh felt his gut turn over. 'I can't help what I am,' he said quietly.

'Neither can Dustin. He's a father, Marsh. Would

346

you do any differently if you were in his shoes?' she asked softly. 'It's Christmas.'

It was the softness that undid him. The woman could make him see the sense of standing out naked in a snowstorm with her compassionate eyes and sympathetic voice.

'I don't like this,' he growled. 'Jill has never taken a shine to me.'

'You were always suspecting her,' Eunice pointed out helpfully.

'Not always,' he defended himself. Actually, he had been. First of dumping a baby, then being out to win herself a wedding ring. 'Can I at least go home and take a shower? Change into some fresh clothes? I gotta have a shave.'

Eunice nodded. 'Thank you, Marsh. You've made this old lady very happy.'

'I'm not saying this will work,' he warned her sternly. 'The woman's got the disposition of a mule.'

'I'm going to be eating supper with my grandson and Jill tomorrow,' Eunice said quietly. 'I don't believe anything else.'

CHAPTER 22

Dustin pulled his truck into the Copelands' drive. He stared out the windshield, wondering what Joey was doing right now. It was nearly lunchtime on a cold and blustery December day. Taking a deep breath, he told himself to remain calm no matter what Maxine said to him.

Ringing the doorbell, Dustin ignored the chill seeping through his jeans as he waited for someone to answer. To his surprise, Maxine herself answered the door.

By the look on her face, she was just as shocked to see him.

'Morning, Maxine.'

'What are you doing here?' Her voice was as brisk and frozen as the weather.

'I think it's time you and I talked,' he replied. Though his tone was mild, his jaw was clenched with the effort of playing it cool.

'You'll excuse me if I don't invite you in?'

Maxine glanced over her shoulder. Dustin surmised she was keeping his visit secret from either

Joey or David. It really didn't matter. He could have his say just as easily out here on the porch.

'I want you to get your lawyer off my back, Maxine. You have no right taking shots at me that you know full well aren't true.'

'Oh?' Her eyebrows raised. 'You can honestly tell me Joey is in good hands at your house?'

'I'll admit that with Mother being in the hospital, matters are a bit difficult. My suggestion is that it would have been more courteous of you to call and offer to keep Joey while Mother was ill.'

Maxine pursed her lips. 'You wouldn't have let me take care of him. Not with that housekeeper hanging around.'

'I probably wouldn't have thought of it, but you could at least have offered. Jill could've used a break.'

'Really. Looked to me like she'd had one.'

'What's that supposed to mean?'

'Oh, come on, Dustin. If you're going to drive out here to try to back me into a corner, I may as well be very frank with you. This housekeeper-family relation story is a bit thin. Jill didn't fall from some long-forgotten family tree branch, and she's not your housekeeper, either. Obviously, you feel responsible for her, the reason why I can only guess. Could that bundle of joy Jill was hauling around be yours, by any stretch of the imagination?'

Dustin's jaw dropped. 'That baby wasn't mine. Nor was it Jill's, Maxine. She was caring for it until the mother could.'

'I see.' That stopped her for only a second. 'Do

you think caring for every stray misfit in the county is healthy for Joey? I know your mother and father had a pack of foster brats running through their house over the years, but do you think continuing that situation is best for your son?'

He could feel his teeth gritting with the effort not to curse. 'Any community work my parents did will probably continue with me some day.'

'Are you planning on marrying that girl? I've got to tell you, Dustin, I've seen women not as sleazy as her walking the streets in Dallas.'

His blood began to simmer. 'Jill is a fine woman. There is nothing sleazy about her.'

'Did you miss the enormous bruise on her face?' Maxine crossed her arms belligerently. 'Somehow I don't think she got that from dusting doorknobs.'

'No. She didn't,' he said tightly. He couldn't tell her about Sadie and the danger Holly had been in without Maxine accusing him of endangering Joey. That would be her next line of defense, he knew. 'But Jill is gone now. So other than assuring you that she was a wonderful person, this conversation is pointless.'

'Gone?' Maxine seemed startled by that. 'Didn't have what it took for ranch life, I imagine. She looked like she lacked staying power.'

Jill had possessed plenty of everything required to stick out the difficulties of living in the country. However, he didn't need to argue about Jill. 'Maxine, this battle between you and me is not what's best for Joey. If his well-being is what you're really concerned about, then let me take him home.'

'No.'

A little body flying into his arms halted whatever words Dustin would have said. 'Daddy!'

He nestled his face into his son's hair. 'Joey! How are you doing, big guy?'

'Okay. Are . . . are we going home?'

David wheeled next to Maxine, his eyes fastened on Joey.

'Hello, David,' Dustin said. Obviously, what Marsh had mentioned about David's health was true. The old man was failing. Dustin hated to see it. David Copeland was a good-hearted soul. He deserved a star on his gravestone, if only for putting up with Maxine's venom all these years.

David nodded at him. 'Are . . . we going now, Daddy?' Joey asked.

'Yes. We're going now, son. Say goodbye to your grandparents.' Dustin picked his son up, holding him so that he could wave goodbye. Maxine started forward, but Dustin held up a warning hand. 'Don't do this, Maxine. You're only going to regret it one day.'

'But . . . you can't do this!' Maxine's tone was astonished. 'You just can't . . . I'll file more papers with the court! David, he's . . .'

Her husband's gaze was expressionless as he watched them leave the porch and get into the truck. 'David,' Maxine protested.

He shook his head: No.

'We can't let him . . .'

Again he shook his head. No. His eyes were sad as the truck drove away, but he turned his wheelchair and went inside.

Maxine followed. 'We can't give up like this. We nearly have Joey for our own. For always.' She went to stand beside him. He reached out and took her hand in his.

'David, I can't stand losing him. I can't bear this. Joey should be ours. They can't possibly take care of him the way we can.'

David looked at her. 'Love . . . you,' he said haltingly. 'Be . . . happy.'

His eyes were huge as he pleaded with her to give in. She sank to the floor, resting her head in his lap to cry hot, furious tears. Nina was lost to them, and now Joey. Giving up the battle meant recognizing those harsh facts. They could have won; they had set the board up with all the pieces in the right places.

Inside herself, Maxine knew David was right. Bitterness poured out of her as she realized this. In the most peculiar way, it felt good to give up. Though she desperately wished some of Eunice's good fortune had just once come her way, Maxine knew they had done the right thing.

David twined his hand into her hair, gently massaging her neck. She gave in to his comforting, telling herself that when she felt better, she was going to start helping him with the physical therapy he needed.

It was just the two of them from now on.

★　★　★

'Is Holly . . . Holly still at our house, Dad?'

Joey's inquisitive face was turned his way. Dustin dreaded the answer – and the following questions he knew had to come.

'No, son. She got to go home with her mother. But we'll get to see them often, I feel sure. Mrs Benchley has been visiting your grandmother quite a bit, and she'll bring Holly when she comes out to the ranch.'

'Oh.' Joey was very quiet as he thought about this. 'Jill is . . . is at our house?'

The wide-eyed hope in his son's eyes made Dustin ache. He thought over his reply carefully. 'She went home too, Joey.'

'Why?'

'She just had to.'

'Will I get to see her again?'

'I . . . I don't think so.' Dustin put an arm out to wrap around his son's shoulder. 'Jill was helping us out for a while, but she had her own home to go to.'

'I knew it. I knew she . . . she not stay. She not my best friend.'

Well, she hadn't turned out to be Dustin's, either. He squeezed Joey, not sure what to say. The child was too young to understand that adult relationships didn't always work out. Joey had become attached to Jill, just like Maxine had warned. Dustin liked to think they had all benefited by Jill's presence, but now that he was trying to explain her leaving to Joey, he wondered if another important female being displaced from Joey's life would leave an emotional scar.

353

'She didn't want to go,' he heard himself saying. 'She just . . . needed to be with her own family.'

It was such a lie, and look who was doing the stuttering now. Dustin pursed his lips, finding himself on the horns of a dilemma. Joey didn't say another word as they pulled into the drive. Dustin stopped the truck, and Joey got out, dragging his little tennis shoes on the way to the house.

Dustin hurried to catch up.

'We didn't string popcorn, Dad. She . . . she promised.'

'I tell you what, Joey,' he said, scooping his son up to his chest. 'Your grandmother will be home tomorrow. Why don't we plan on doing something special then?'

Joey wriggled down out of his arms. 'It won't be so fun.'

No, it wouldn't. But they had to go on. 'Joey, I'm not really in the know about stringing anything, and I don't know that your grandmother will feel up to it. But I'd be happy to take you out for a ride on Rooster. Maybe we could even roast marshmallows in the fireplace tomorrow night. What do you say?'

Joey smiled wanly at him. 'Okay.' He headed into the house and up the stairs.

'Where are you going, buddy?' Dustin called.

'Get my bear.' Joey went into his room and looked around. Holly's basket wasn't there. He went into the bathroom that connected to Jill's room, slowly pushing the door open. The bed was neatly made; the room looked kind of empty. Jill wasn't here anymore, just like his father had told him.

Joey went back into his room and sat on the bed, swinging his legs. Even his grandmother wasn't here. It was just him and his dad now. He was glad to be home, and he was glad his dad was with him, but it sure didn't feel the same.

With a sigh, Joey decided he must not have been a good enough boy for Santa to grant his Christmas wish. He wasn't going to get Jill for his new mother.

'Jill, honey, is everything okay?'

Lana's voice resonated with concern. 'Everything is fine, Mother. How did you know I was here?'

For a second, Jill fervently hoped that perhaps Dustin had called her parents' house inquiring as to her whereabouts.

'That sheriff from Lassiter called here. He said you'd left the ranch and gone home. Hon, are you sure you're okay?'

'I'm fine, Mom.' Jill held in an impatient sigh. All she needed was her loving folks digging into her personal life. They would want to talk about everything in minutiae, which would be very painful.

'Your father and I are a little surprised, Jill. I'm sorry it didn't work out in Lassiter, but is there any reason you didn't come home? It's hard to be there for you if we don't know you need us.'

'I had to pack up the apartment. I couldn't avoid it any longer. It's not that I didn't want to see you and

Dad, it's just that I really have a lot of loose ends to tie up.'

'Oh.' Lana's word was a sigh. 'I don't suppose you need any help.'

Jill closed her eyes against the hurt she heard in her mother's tone. 'Thanks, Mom. But this is really something I have to do on my own.' There was too much pain occupying her heart right now. She needed silence to think, to plan her future. She needed silence to decide what she was going to do without Dustin in her life.

'Okay.' Lana sounded resigned, though unhappy about it. 'Call us if we can do anything, Jill.'

'I will, Mother. Did Marsh happen to say what he wanted?'

'Um, to know if you were here, I guess. You didn't leave without giving notice, did you?'

To say the least. However, she couldn't tell her mother the reason behind her swift departure. 'I believe the Reed family and I were in agreement that I come back to Dallas.'

'Oh, dear. None of this sounds very good. You're not in any trouble of any kind, are you?'

'Mother!' Jill gritted her teeth. 'It just didn't work out, all right?'

There was a sigh of tried patience from the other end. 'Fine, dear. Anyway, I simply told Mr Marsh that you weren't at our house, which was true. And that was the end of the conversation, except he did mention that my strawberry bread was as good as his mother's.'

Lana sounded pleased about Marsh's compliment. Jill grimaced. That sneaky lawman knew all the right buttons to push with her mother. 'Thanks for letting me know, Mother. I've really got to get back to packing up these boxes though. I'll call you later,' she said, trying not to make Lana feel rushed. She didn't want to hurt her mother's delicate feelings, but she had to get some serious moving done.

'Well, all right, then. Your father and I may swing by later and see how you're doing.'

'Okay. Bye.' Jill shook her head as she hung up. No doubt her parents would be on her porch step soon. Taking a rubber band from the kitchen drawer, Jill pulled her hair into an untidy, but serviceable, ponytail. The first chore to start with was finding a rental truck to load the boxes into.

Sitting down at the kitchen table, Jill leafed through the phone book for the closest place that might have a truck. She read through several ads, finally deciding on one. Picking up the phone, she had started to dial the number, when the doorbell rang. Frowning, Jill hung up. All she needed today to really give her the crazies was for Carl to show up. For a second, she contemplated not opening the door. Of course, Carl had his own key, so he probably wouldn't stand out in the hall and ring. She did need him to get his stuff out, though. Resigned to dealing with an unpleasant situation, Jill went to the door and peeked out the peephole.

Her jaw dropped. If she didn't know better, she would think Marsh was standing outside her door.

The cowboy hat looked familiar, as did the square-faced, determined profile. Keeping the chain on the door, she cautiously opened it. 'Marsh?'

'Hi, Jill.'

'What are you doing here?' she asked, her stomach somersaulting.

'Uh, me and China were in the neighborhood and we thought we'd stop by.'

She could see someone standing behind Marsh. Jill held back a groan. 'I'm not really in a position to have company,' she said, trying desperately to think of a way to keep the sheriff out of her apartment. She had a funny feeling he was here on business, courtesy of Dustin.

'Come on, Jill. At least let me say my piece. The old lady'll be disappointed if I come home without talking to you.'

At the mention of Eunice, Jill slid the chain off the door and opened it. Marsh made his way in, limping a bit. China offered her a sympathetic smile as she followed.

'How is Eunice doing?'

'Much better, I think. Ready for her life to get back to normal, anyway.'

'I suppose my mother told you where I lived.' Jill closed the front door and pointed toward the kitchen. It was the only place with chairs and no boxes.

'Nope. Lana told me you weren't there, and since I knew she wouldn't lie to me, 'cause she thinks I'm such a nice guy, I looked in the phone book. Sure enough, there was a listing for a Jill McCall.' Marsh shrugged, as if it were no big deal.

China socked him in the arm. 'Whose idea was that, again?'

He grinned and jerked a thumb at the beautiful woman. 'China looked you up.'

'I see.' Jill sent a smile China's way, though she wasn't entirely grateful for her intervention. 'You mentioned Eunice. I hope she's doing okay.'

'She's fine.' Marsh had sat down slowly and now he kicked his leg out to the side, trying to find a comfortable position. 'Worried about you, though.'

'We talked.' Jill ran a fingernail across the formica of the table. 'I believe she understood my situation.'

'Did she, now?' He glanced around the apartment for a moment, his sheriff's eye missing nothing. 'This place is a dump, isn't it?'

Jill stiffened. It was brand-new, with a rent of a thousand dollars a month – more than most folks would want to pay. 'Not exactly. It's touted as one of the finer apartment complexes in Dallas.'

'Yeah, maybe. It's got no heart, though.'

She glanced at China, who merely shrugged and gave her another smile. Jill looked around the room, trying to see it through their eyes. Everything was white, of course. She and Carl had not planned on having children right away, with both of them being occupied with climbing the corporate ladder. The paint on the walls was white, the plush carpet was white, the heavy drapes were white. It was very contemporary, and nicely complemented the slate-gray leather sofas and chairs they'd purchased.

Jill's gaze swung to China's for a moment. The flame of her hair stood out against the white wall, vivid in the stark contrast. Marsh's face, browned by hours in the hot sun, looked the color of saddle leather next to the white curtains. Dustin's would look the same way. She thought about Carl and his rather pasty appearance next to Dustin. It showed a striking contrast in their lifestyles: corporate versus country.

She had agreed with Carl's selection of black lacquered furniture for their bedroom, which they had accented with large mirrors. A picture of her bedroom at the ranch blossomed in her mind: yellow-striped wallpaper and white eyelet curtains and the cabbage rose seat cushion in the window seat.

Marsh was right. This place lacked heart. Actually, her relationship with Carl had lacked heart, and it showed in the way they were planning to live their lives. She had gotten out in the nick of time.

'Perhaps Tommy means that your apartment will look much nicer once the furniture is in place, Jill,' China said kindly.

Jill looked at her and smiled. 'He means just what he said. And he's right. It's exactly why I went to Lassiter.' She leaned back in the wooden chair and tried to relax. 'I appreciate you two coming out here to check on me, but you can tell Eunice I'm fine.'

Marsh snorted. 'I think we better help you organize a garage sale. I thought you liked Victorian antiques.'

'I do,' Jill said softly. 'I mean, I don't suppose I did until I fell in love with Eunice's parlor.'

'Jill, let us take you back,' China pleaded. 'We can help you finish up what you're doing here, but you need to come back with us.'

She knew what they were trying to do, and it touched her heart. Unfortunately, she couldn't go back. 'It's not that simple, you guys. It's not really even me. Being the catalyst for Dustin losing Joey this week made me realize how much I'm irritating Maxine. She's just going to fight harder if I'm there. That's not fair to what Dustin and Joey are just now starting to enjoy with each other.'

'Did you know that crazy old woman's been poking around the Reeds' business most of their lives? I don't think Dustin's going to let her win now.' Marsh drummed his hand on the table.

'Don't you see, Marsh? Maxine was absolutely livid that I didn't have Joey ready on time. Even something that small irritated her about me. She said terrible things about me. And Dustin isn't going to ask me to leave because of Maxine, just like you said. With Eunice under the weather, they don't need any more stress at that ranch.'

'Eunice is going home. That gives the three of them something to be happy about.'

'The three of them? Did Maxine relent?' Jill couldn't believe that would have happened.

'Nope.' Marsh shook his head. 'Over my advice, of course, Dustin went to get Joey. Don't know that he managed it, but I know Dustin well enough to know

361

that when his mind is in that tactical mode, he's prepared for combat. Hope Joey's prepared for his daddy to lasso him and pull him up through the chimney if he has to.' Marsh sighed heavily.

'Oh, no! You don't really think . . .' Jill glanced at China. 'Is he breaking any laws? Can he get himself into any trouble doing that?' She couldn't bear to think of what Maxine's reaction to Dustin's determination might be. It was two strong wills going against each other – hard.

'I think Dustin will do anything he's put his mind to, and hang the consequences. The old lady was tired of Maxine jabbing at her all these years for no reason and told Dustin to go get her grandson. Actually, she didn't tell him to, since he was already going. But she gave her permission, never mind what *my* opinion was on the matter.'

'He's playing pissed,' China said, 'because he's afraid he's going to end up having to arrest Dustin.'

'Oh. I hope not.' Jill knew that would bother Marsh greatly.

'So, best as I can see it, Christmas is up to you, Jill. 'Cause it's pretty much gone to hell in a handbasket at this point.' Marsh looked at her expectantly.

'Up to me?'

He nodded adamantly. 'Joey wants you. Eunice wants you. Dustin wants you real bad. So, if they're gonna get any Christmas, you gotta get back where you belong.' He sniffed as he glanced around the apartment. 'Looks like you ain't gonna have much of one here, anyway.'

'I can't do it, Marsh. As nice as it is of you two to care, and Eunice, too, it's too heavy of a burden with the custody battle. I'm the worst possible thing for Dustin's chances of winning.'

'Yeah, but see, you gotta let the man decide how he wants to roll the dice. Did he ask you to leave?'

'No.' He'd never remotely hinted at it.

'Then you're doing him a disservice by not coming back. Why should Dustin be punished because of Maxine? My Lord, she's tortured Eunice all these years, now Dustin has to lose, too?'

'Maybe she'll cool off in a few years, Marsh. Maybe Dustin will find someone who doesn't upset Maxine so.'

'Why should he care if she cools off? After all these years, she needs to learn to mind her own business. But there's something else you should think about, Jill. Though I've stepped over the line in saying that, I'm also going to tell you that Dustin is not going to come here like we have and ask you to come back.'

Jill didn't reply, but she kept her gaze trained on Marsh.

'Right or wrong, Dustin has a bunch of pride. If he felt like you two had something special, and I believe he did, then you walking out on him is going to tear into that pride. He is not the kind of man to go chasing after a woman and do the "Honey, please take me back" thing.'

She closed her eyes for a second, wondering how to reply to that. It wasn't that she wanted Dustin to come after her at all. She hadn't discussed the problem with him because she knew him too well. He would have said 'to hell with Maxine' but Joey's grandmother was hell-bent for matters to turn out her way. Jill sparked that determination.

She shook her head. 'Marsh, I made the best decision I could under the circumstances. I don't want Dustin to come here. I don't need him to call me. I'm just as satisfied with my choice now as I was when I left. Yes, it hurts. Yes, I wish very much that it could have been different. But Dustin needs more than a housekeeper right now. He needs a huge amount of luck and a sympathetic judge.'

'Okay.' Marsh stood, slowly pulling his injured leg under him. 'You can't say we didn't try.'

'No. I can't. Please let Eunice know how much I appreciate her concern. It was awfully nice of you two to come out here to sweet-talk me on her behalf.'

China's eyes were distressed. Jill couldn't bear to look at her for long. She didn't think the woman agreed with her decision and that stung a bit. However, China swiftly leaned over and gave her a hug. 'I feel so sorry for you,' she said.

'You shouldn't. I'm going to be fine.'

'I know.' China broke the embrace and stood straight, but her large eyes were sparkling with unshed tears. 'I know you've made the only decision you can under the circumstances, but it's so hard to see this not work out. I don't think Dustin's ever had anyone love him just for himself before.'

Jill's jaw dropped. She remembered Dustin's

gratitude over simple things, and that she had once wondered the same thing.

She did love him, just for himself. In loving him that way, that deeply, she had to let him go.

Marsh wrapped an arm around China. 'What are you going to do with all these damn boxes?' he asked Jill.

'I'm about to call a truck rental company so that I can move the boxes to my parents' garage. The furniture will have to go into storage, but I'm not that far along, yet. Today, I'm just hoping to get the boxes moved.'

'Well, hellfire, Jill. Don't rent a truck for those few boxes. Let me put them in the truck bed and haul 'em to your folks. It's on the way to Lassiter, and your mom sure would like to give me another piece of her strawberry bread.' Marsh grinned winningly.

Jill would miss all these down-home people. She would miss Marsh's looniness. She would miss Eunice's strength. She would miss Joey's sweetness. Most of all, she would miss Dustin's honest loving.

'No, thanks,' she said quietly. 'You've got a sore leg. You don't need to be lifting anything.'

'Well, hell, what's in those boxes?'

'Clothes are in some. My china and day dishes are in others. All the things needed to start a new home.'

Marsh stared at her. 'We could save you a bundle of money and time if you'd just let us toss these boxes into the truck and drop 'em at your mom's.'

'He's right, Jill. Let us do this,' China said.

It would be such a huge piece of worry off her mind, though she hated to take advantage of their time. 'Heck, this isn't even that heavy,' Marsh said, carrying a box to the door.

'That one's got bed pillows in it,' Jill said, going to open the door with a grin. It was plain that Marsh had set his mind on helping her, so Jill decided to fall in with his offer gracefully.

'Here's the box marked "china". Let's not entrust it to Tommy,' China said. Jill stuck a box in front of the door to keep it open, then crossed the room to help China lift the box. Together, they carried it out the door and to the truck.

Fifteen minutes later the boxes were all neatly arranged in the truck bed. 'Well, that does it,' Marsh said. 'Guess will be on our way to Lana's. Boy, I hope she's cooking.'

Jill rolled her eyes and laughed. 'I think I'll go on out with you to Mother's. I'll call her and tell her we're coming.'

'Great! Let's lock this dump up – I mean this contemporary architect's dream – and get going,' Marsh said happily.

Jill found her purse, sending a last glance through the apartment. All that was left was the slate-gray leather furniture pushed over by the wall, which she now realized she had never liked anyway. That had been Carl's choice, and it showed. His things were still stacked around, but she wasn't going to move them out for him.

'Thanks,' Jill said, after locking the door and

hurrying to the truck. 'I would never have gotten that much done by myself.'

The three of them started to get into the truck's cab. 'I'll drive,' said Marsh.

'You can't with your leg,' China pointed out.

'I can. I can't exactly rest it at an angle like I was doing before, can I? So, I might as well drive.'

'Are you sure I'm not in the way?' Jill asked. She hadn't considered Marsh might have been resting his leg across the seat while China drove.

'You are definitely not in the way. Get in,' Marsh told her.

He winced as he pulled his leg inside. She didn't comment on it, knowing Marsh wouldn't have admitted his leg was bothering him. China placed her dainty, pink-tipped hand on his thigh, and Marsh perked up as he started the truck.

Good medicine, Jill thought. At one time she had thought she was good medicine for Dustin. Unfortunately, she had turned out to be toxic for him.

China and Marsh talked about mundane matters as he headed the truck north. They made sure Jill was included in the conversation as much as possible, but her heart wasn't really in it. Having repeated her feelings to them had only stressed why her decision to leave Lassiter had been the right one. Taking her things to store at her parents' underlined the finality of the situation.

'There's the turn-off to my folks up ahead,' Jill said, pointing. 'You'll want to go east, so you have to circle under the highway.'

Marsh nodded. He didn't ease his foot off the pedal. Jill watched them getting closer to the exit with some concern. If he didn't slow up soon, they were going to take the turn-off dangerously fast.

'Uh, Marsh, this is the turn-off.' They whizzed past it and Jill turned to stare at the sheriff. 'You just missed it. But up ahead there's a place where you can hang a U-turn.'

Jill's gaze met China's. The two stared at each for a second, as Marsh passed by the section in the highway. Then they looked questioningly at Marsh.

He looked sheepish. 'Well, hell. I can't let my best friend be a lawless renegade by himself, can I?'

'I think the sheriff has taken you into custody, Jill,' China said with a grin.

'Marsh, I hope you're turning this truck around. I don't want to go to Lassiter. You can't just shanghai me.' Jill froze him with a glare.

'Guess I'll have to arrest you, then,' he said cheerfully.

'For what?'

'Willful abandonment of a man's heart.'

CHAPTER 23

Marsh's blithe statement didn't set too well with Jill, never mind how truthful it might be. 'All I have to say to that is if you don't turn around and take me to my parents' house, I'm registering a complaint with your supervisor. Then I'll call a taxi from Dustin's house to bring me back home, at which point I will send the bill to the Lassiter police department.'

'You're kidding, right?' The carefree smile slid off Marsh's face.

'No, I'm not.' Jill shook her head. 'I'll be very upset with you if you do this.' She didn't know if the threats she'd thrown out would worry the sheriff, but it didn't matter. She couldn't to go to Lassiter.

'You'd better go back, Tommy,' China said softly.

'Aw, hell,' Marsh complained. He turned the truck around at the next break in the intersection.

'I appreciate the thought, Marsh, but there are some things you can't make happen, even for your best friend. Or his mother.'

Didn't he know it. 'I guess you'd say the word if you changed your mind. I'd be happy to drive out and give you a ride back, any time.'

She reached across China to pat him on the arm. 'Yes. I would tell you. Now, turn right at the next street ahead. My mother's is the red brick house with the white shutters.'

Marsh pulled into the drive. The front door opened almost immediately. Lana and Bob came out onto the porch, and once they saw who was getting out of the truck, they hurried over.

'Jill!' Lana threw her arms around her daughter's neck.

'Sheriff,' Bob said amiably. 'It's nice of you to come out.' He stuck his hand out for Marsh to shake.

'This is China Shea,' Marsh said, amazed by how easily he nearly tagged 'my girlfriend' onto the end of his sentence. He wondered how that would have gone over with her. 'China, this is Bob McCall, and his wife, Lana.'

'It's very nice to meet you, China. Please come in,' Lana invited.

'Actually, we can't stay. We loaded some of Jill's things up that she wanted to store in your garage. If you don't mind, I guess we should take care of that.'

'Oh, certainly.' Lana stepped to the side of the truck to examine the boxes inside. 'I can get the box of pillows, I believe. Bob, you get the sheets and towels.'

China and Jill reached for the box of dishes, smiling at each other as they slid it over the truck

370

gate Marsh had let down. He rubbed his leg before reaching in to grab another box. For a minute there he'd thought his plan was going to work. He hadn't counted on Jill's resistance. Sadly, Marsh realized there was nothing else he could do to make the old lady's wish come true. Maybe something more had happened between Dustin and Jill than he knew about. As China came around the corner to take another box, Marsh decided he wasn't going to make the decision Dustin and Jill had been forced to make.

Marsh wasn't going to let anything stop him from getting China Shea to the altar. He could just see himself pulling the wedding garter off of one of those long legs. He was going to take his time, nice and slow, doing it, too.

He wondered if she'd go for a Christmas wedding and a honeymoon in Bermuda. Seeing that woman in a bikini would probably kill him – but it sure would be worth it.

'We're so glad you're going to stay the night with us, Jill.' Lana smiled at her daughter and started putting cookies on a tray. Marsh and China had departed for Lassiter, leaving Jill feeling strangely out of sorts. A big part of her felt like she should have been in that truck, heading north with them.

The practical side of her nature knew she'd made the right choice, though it hurt. 'Thank you for letting me store my things here for a while, Mother. It shouldn't be for long. I'm planning on getting an apartment I can afford, and then I can get my stuff out of your way.'

Bob cleared his throat. Lana's hands stilled as she looked at Jill. 'There's no need for you to put yourself through that right now. For heaven's sake, Jill, it's only a few more days until Christmas. Can't you stay here until then, and wait until after the holidays to find something? Your father and I think you need some time before you go jumping into anything else.'

Jill started to shake her head. Then she thought about how devoid of love and warmth the place she'd rented with Carl had been. She wasn't going to find anything that measured up to what she'd had at the Reeds' house; everything she looked at was going to seem stark in comparison.

Maybe her parents were right. Maybe a little time would distance the way she felt about the household where she could not be. After Christmas, she could start all over. Again.

Dustin stopped in the middle of poking a needle through a piece of popcorn. This wasn't working. He was all thumbs at stringing, and his finger was getting sore from being pricked. This was a project for Jill. Leaving the needle and string on the kitchen counter, he carried the bowl out to the parlor, smiling for Joey's sake. His mother reclined on the antique divan, snoozing lightly while the fire kept her warm. Joey's eyes were huge when he saw the bowl of fluffy popcorn.

372

'What do you say we just eat this stuff, son?' Dustin sat cross-legged next to Joey and put the popcorn in front of them.

Joey looked a bit sorrowful for a moment, then he shrugged. 'Maybe . . . maybe you call Jill and ask her how.'

'Uh . . .' Dustin was trying to think of how to get himself of that trap as the doorbell rang. 'Just a second, son.'

Opening the door brought a chill in from the outdoors. The expressions on China's and Marsh's faces didn't warm Dustin's spirits too much, either.

'Well, look what the weatherman brought us, Joey,' he called, pointing China and Marsh into the parlor. 'Two human popsicles.'

'You did it,' Marsh said when he saw Joey. 'You brought him home.'

'Said I was,' Dustin said gruffly.

'Maxine didn't . . .'

'No.' Dustin didn't want Marsh to say anything more. No sense in Joey knowing that his father and grandmother had been locked in an emotional struggle over him. 'It went just fine.'

'I'm not going to have to arrest you?'

Dustin sat down on the floor next to Joey again, shrugging. He couldn't really have cared less what might have happened if his plan had gone awry. He'd been too desperate to worry about the consequences, and he sure as hell wasn't going to go over the what-ifs now.

'Hi, sheriff,' Joey said. Dustin patted his son's

little shoulders. It felt like heaven having him and Eunice back.

It would have felt even better if Jill could have rounded out their family circle, but that wasn't to be. The ornery woman had packed herself off, just when the going had gotten rough. He had asked her in the beginning if she was the type who fled when things got tough and Jill had given him that sassy smile and said he should just put combat pay in her stocking.

Well, she hadn't even hung around long enough to collect.

Eunice's eyes flew open. 'Goodness me,' she said, sitting up. 'Please pardon my manners. Sleeping in front of company. My mother would have sent me to my room for such behavior.'

China laughed as she sat down in the queen's chair next to the pie table. Marsh took the king's chair next to it. 'Don't worry about us, Eunice. We're not really company. At least, Tommy thinks he's part of the family.'

'Yes, I know.' Eunice's eyes gleamed brightly as she peered into the hallway. 'Did you bring me anything, my handsome, good-hearted, extra son?'

Dustin grunted at this exchange. He wondered what his mother thought Marsh might have brought her.

Marsh sighed, sticking the leg he favored slightly out in front of him. 'I'm afraid it's just you and Joey and your ugly boy, Dustin, for supper tonight.'

'Oh.'

374

At Dustin's puzzled expression, Marsh said to him, 'She invited me to eat today but I can't make it. I've got some paperwork to do to wrap up the Lynch case.'

Dustin was surprised by his mother's downcast expression. For heaven's sake, there was no reason to be sad just because Marsh was finally going to miss eating a meal at the Reed Ranch.

'Well,' China said brightly. 'I'm certainly glad to see you feeling better, Eunice. Joey, what is Santa going to bring you for Christmas?'

His son looked down. Dustin pressed his lips together. China was trying hard to dispel the sudden gloomy air in the room, but he knew what Joey was thinking when it came to Christmas presents. Seemed like he'd had only one wish – and that had been Jill.

When Joey didn't answer, China looked at Dustin. 'You still up for that hearing on Thursday?' At his nod, she said, 'Good. I know you're ready to get this thing over with.'

'You can say that again.'

'I'm ready to get home, China,' Marsh said suddenly.

'Is your leg bothering you?'

'No. I'm just ready to get home, if you don't mind taking me.' He got up slowly, and made his way to kiss Eunice's cheek. 'Sorry,' he murmured. 'Mind like a mule, you know.'

'It's okay. I know you did what you could.' Eunice laid her head back against the pillows. 'China, you come out here any time, all right? You're always welcome.'

'Thank you, Eunice.' She went to pat her hand. The shrug she made for Eunice's benefit confused Dustin. It seemed they were all talking a conversation he wasn't part of. Unfortunately, he had too much on his mind to give it much thought.

'Goodnight,' he called as China and Marsh walked to the truck.

They waved. A few moments later they were gone. Dustin stamped his boots on the porch, already feeling the cold stealing into his body. Telling himself that Monday night football would be a good thing to watch tonight, he went inside to join Joey and Eunice.

He wondered briefly if Jill liked football, then decided he wouldn't have cared if she hadn't. The woman was enough to make a man turn the television set off for good.

Unfortunately, he'd be looking at a twenty-seven-inch glass screen tonight, watching grown men chase a pigskin. He sighed, wondering how long it would take before he started enjoying the things again he'd always loved before.

Maybe after the custody hearing Thursday, his good mood would return.

The sun dawned bright Thursday morning, almost as if it were trying to warm the icy air blowing into people's coats as they walked into the courthouse. Dustin walked slowly, letting Eunice set the pace.

His mother was feeling better but still taking it easy. He hoped that a ruling in his favor today would cheer Eunice up. He wasn't sure her health could continue improving if the stress didn't let up.

Joey was being looked after by a friend of Eunice's from church. With all the wonderful innocence of a child, Joey'd had no idea his fate was being decided for him today. Dustin's heart had nearly broken as he'd said goodbye. All he could do was pray that everything would turn out for the best.

Inside the courthouse, Dustin sat down heavily on a wooden bench. His stomach felt tight, the muscles cramped until it was painful. He took a deep breath, trying to relax. Across the room, Maxine eyed him. He could feel her stare on him, as well as David's. He sat in his wheelchair in the aisle, looking like he didn't feel any better than Dustin did. Jeez. This bitterness of Maxine's had torn everybody apart – and practically obliterated the chance of anybody having a chance to mourn Nina.

Dustin's mouth twisted. Maxine had been right when she accused him of not thinking of Nina. He hadn't had half a chance to remember the good times before Maxine filed her lawsuit. The months after Nina's death had been spent worrying about Joey; Dustin hadn't possessed spare emotional energy to mourn his wife the way he might have if his mind had been free from the trap Maxine had sprung on him.

The judge entered, wearing black robes and an austere expression. Dustin saw his gaze flick briefly toward Maxine and David. Again, the fear pressed him that the judge might rule in favor of his friends. Certainly, nothing much had gone Dustin's way where Maxine was concerned.

The bailiff called the room to order. Out of the corner of his eye, Dustin saw Marsh enter the courtroom and take a seat, with China sitting beside him. People shuffled expectantly, waiting their turns for the judge to hear their cases; somewhere a baby wailed briefly. Dustin scanned the courtroom, his gaze instantly halting when he saw Vera Benchley and Sadie sitting on the far side. Sadie cradled Holly to her, feeding her a bottle. Dustin poked his mother to get her attention. She smiled when she saw them. Vera gave a small wave, which Eunice returned with a thumbs-up sign.

There were a few cases heard before theirs and Dustin let his mind wander as he pondered the fact that the Copelands didn't appear to have any friends who had come to sit with them in the courtroom. The two of them seemed very lonely as they sat listening. Dustin steeled himself not to feel sorry for their situation. If they could have their way, he would lose his son today – and it was nobody's fault but Maxine's if, over the years, she'd run off anybody who'd ever wanted to be their friend.

Their case was announced, and Dustin snapped to razor-sharp attention. At the same moment, the courtroom doors opened. Why that got his attention, Dustin didn't know, but he turned his head and instantly recognized the sweetly beautiful blonde walking in. She was wearing a white fuzzy sweater

378

with seed pearls scattered in flower shapes, and a white skirt. His immediate thought was that Jill looked like an angel. His heart hammered as he watched her take the seat beside Vera and Sadie, gently easing Holly into her arms. He saw Sadie smile gratefully at Jill, and that was the last thing Dustin's astonished brain registered before his mother prodded him toward the private hearing room.

He couldn't believe Jill had come back.

His lawyer took a spot next to him; his mother sat on the other side. Dustin barely listened as they went through the obligatory motions. Without realizing he did it, Dustin met Maxine's gaze. The judge asked her a question, but she didn't seem to hear him. Her lawyer touched her arm, but Maxine shook her head. Dustin's heart sank. It would be just his luck if Maxine took ill and they had to continue this another time. Dustin was afraid he'd explode if his fate wasn't decided one way or the other.

'We wish to drop the case, Your Honor,' Maxine said softly.

Dustin's eyes stayed riveted to hers. Her lawyer began frantically whispering in her ear. David reached out to lay a hand on Maxine's. She briefly squeezed his hand.

'We wish to apologize to the court for any undue trouble we have caused.' She turned her gaze from Dustin's to Eunice's. The two women watched each other across the table. There was regret and sadness in Maxine's eyes, but Dustin couldn't help wondering what had caused this new twist and where it was leading. He ignored the surprised acceleration of his heart.

'Although we love our grandson and hope we will be allowed to see him often, David and I have decided he belongs at the Reed Ranch with his father. There were many reasons I was convinced that I should have Joey myself, but the truth is – ' Maxine stopped, her voice breaking and her eyes filling with tears – 'the fact is, Nina is gone and nothing can replace her. I can't replace her. I didn't want to lose her, every bit of her.' She lowered her gaze to stare at her hand in David's. 'We just ask that you take good care of Joey and appreciate him and remember how swiftly you can lose your child, Dustin. We shouldn't have lost Nina so soon, but we did. Now we wish we'd spent more time loving her instead of trying to . . . protect her, I guess.'

Eunice moved quickly, going around the table to put her arms around the sobbing woman. 'Thank you, Maxine. You don't know how much this means to me.'

'I do.' Maxine nodded, her eyes streaming as she blew her nose into a tissue. 'Believe me, I do. I'd give anything to have Nina back. It's terrible to lose a child. It feels so empty.'

The judge looked at both the lawyers. He cleared his throat. 'Are there any further matters to resolve? It sounds like this case is going to wrap itself up, if Maxine is certain this is what she and David want.'

'It is, Your Honor.' Maxine's shoulders shook

with the effort not to cry. A tear sparkled in David's eye, but he met the judge's questioning look bravely.

'Yes.' David nodded his agreement.

The judge granted the case dropped. Dustin stood to make his way around the table.

'I expect you to be a big part of Joey's life,' Dustin said simply. 'You let me or Mother know and we can accommodate you.'

'Thank you, Dustin.' Maxine's eyes were huge with tears, making her skin look sunken and aged. 'That's very generous, considering what I've put you through.'

He looked at his mother who was hugging David. 'It's Christmas, Maxine. Let's let bygones be bygones.'

She nodded but Dustin barely noticed. Quickly shaking David's hand, then speaking a few words to his lawyer, Dustin hurried into the main room. Jill was gone, as were China and Marsh, and Vera and Sadie. He told himself that he was letting Jill's presence excite him too much; still he couldn't wait to tell her his good news.

He saw her standing outside on the sidewalk, with the Benchleys and Marsh and China, too. Eunice walked to his side, so Dustin moved slowly, telling himself it was for her sake, and not about to admit that he didn't want Jill to think he was hurrying to see her.

'How did it go?' Marsh called.

'Fast. Maxine did a clean reversal. She dropped the case complately.' Dustin found that the sound of those words leaving his mouth was very strange, as if he couldn't believe he was saying them.

'If I hadn't been there to see it for myself, I wouldn't believe it, either.' Dustin was feeling elated right about now. Eunice nodded, too.

'Well, heckfire. Come here, you old renegade.' Marsh slapped Dustin on the back, while Vera and Sadie hugged Eunice. 'That's kinda weird, though,' Marsh said. 'As glad as I was to hear it, what do you think changed her mind?'

'I have no idea,' Dustin said. His gaze had been holding Jill's during the entire conversation. She looked so adorable, with her cheeks rosy from the cold. Holly was bundled in her arms, and Dustin shook his head. 'I don't really care, either. My Christmas starts now, and I'm going home to my son.'

He took his mother's hand. 'Are you ready to go, Mother?'

She'd been hugging Jill. Now they pulled apart slightly but remained holding each other's arms.

'Just about. Sadie, will you be at the house in the morning? We'll surely need you now.'

'I will, Miss Eunice,' Sadie said with a smile. She took Holly from Jill's arms. 'I guess we better go put you down for a nap, sweetheart. It's been a very exciting day.'

Vera touched Eunice's arm. 'Well, good friend, I knew it wouldn't turn out any other way, though Maxine has certainly surprised me.'

'We're all getting too old to carry grudges, I suppose.' Eunice smiled as if she didn't mean the part about being old. Vera hugged her tightly.

'Thank you for letting your daughter work for us,' Eunice said. 'It's going to be wonderful having someone we can trust.'

Jill's heart dropped into her shoes. Sadie was going to be the Reeds' new housekeeper. Though she had come to Lassiter for the hearing to support Dustin and Eunice, and had intended to return to Dallas, it still felt strange to hear that they'd given her job away so soon. Jill lowered her gaze, unwilling to acknowledge the sudden pain shooting through her.

Final goodbyes were said, then Vera and Sadie left. Holly's eyes had closed contentedly, the cold weather not disturbing her serenity. China and Marsh drifted off, with promises to drop by later. Dustin nodded half-heartedly, his gaze on the elderly couple making their way across the parking lot to their car. A driver got out to help them in. Almost unbearably slowly, Maxine helped David in, then got into the car herself.

They were the loneliest people he'd ever seen. Their mistakes had cost them so much happiness, the price being not-so-golden years. At least they had discovered each other now, before it had been too late even for that. Somehow, Dustin thought they were probably very happy with that.

He turned, his gaze colliding with Jill's. She stood there, obviously uncomfortable.

'I'm glad everything worked out for you, Dustin,' she said softly.

'Not everything.' Jill's big blue eyes widened at his

words. 'I appreciate you coming out here today. It felt good knowing I had such a cheering section.' Dustin took a deep breath. 'But I hated the way you left earlier.'

'I'm sorry.' Jill's voice broke. 'I couldn't cost you . . .'

'Shh.' Dustin shook his head. 'I don't want to hear about it.' He looked around. 'Mother?'

Jill suddenly realized Eunice was missing. At that moment, China drove Marsh's truck by, both of them waving. Eunice was sitting securely in the middle.

Dustin grinned. Marsh thought he was being so sly. *He'd* show the sheriff sly.

'I guess it's just the two of us,' he said.

Jill nodded cautiously.

'What do you say we go back in and apply for a marriage license?'

Dustin's words were a shock. 'What are you saying?' she asked.

'I'm saying, we're here. The marriage license is in there. I love you, and I want to marry you. Jill McCall, will you marry me?'

She threw her arms around his neck. 'Oh, Dustin. Yes! I'd love to marry you. I love you so much.'

He pulled back to look at her. 'We haven't had much of a courtship. Are you sure you won't mind?'

'Are you serious? We've had more excitement in our courtship than most people ever get.' She gave him a teasing grin and slid her hands up his back.

'Besides, I hear that life slows down considerably once you're married.'

'Don't count on it. There's some aspects of life I intend to keep you very busy with. Dressing, un-dressing . . .'

For answer, Jill smoothed her lips against his. He kissed her thoroughly before saying, 'There's just one condition.'

She was returning his kisses with joy, but managed to ask, 'What's that?'

'No more of that running off stuff. I thought you didn't like me anymore.'

His face was boyish with happiness. Jill smoothed her hand along his cheek. 'I liked you too much. And I'm not going anywhere. You're stuck with me now.'

They kissed, long and deeply, before Jill pulled back to stare into Dustin's eyes. 'You gave away my position as housekeeper.'

He nodded. 'Mother and I knew Sadie needed a good job. We need a housekeeper. However,' he pulled her close against him, '*I* need a wife. And you fit the job description perfectly.'

'Perfectly?'

'Yes.' Dustin tweaked her nose. 'Let's hurry and fill out that application so we can go home. I want to hang the letters back up in the sign over the drive.'

'You mean it's going to say "REED" now, instead of just "RE"?' Jill laughed as he swooped her into his arms and carried her up the courthouse steps. 'I'll hold the ladder steady for you.'

'I like a woman who supports me.' Dustin quipped. Jill pinched his arm lightly, and he grinned. The Reed Ranch was back in business – no more regrets.

EPILOGUE

Tiny pieces of popcorn lay scattered under the tree on Christmas Day. Joey had enjoyed stringing it, but then he wanted to eat it, so occasional tugs on the string had left little pieces of the stuff lying on the carpet. Jill smiled at the mess, glad to be here instead of in the pristine apartment Marsh had said lacked heart. There was plenty of heart here.

Last night she and Dustin had performed their 'Santa Claus' duties, placing brightly-colored packages with fancy ribbons under the tree for Joey. His stocking bulged, especially the toe, where Jill had put an orange in the very bottom. She'd so enjoyed planning these surprises for the child; it was almost a miracle to her to be actually putting small toys and candy in his stocking. She had loved wrapping his presents.

She heard the pattering of Joey's pajamaed feet hurrying down the stairs. A smile automatically lifted her lips. 'Merry Christmas, Joey!' she called as he ran into the parlor.

He ran to squeeze her with a big hug. 'I was a good boy! You're still here!'

Her eyes instantly teared up. She hugged him hard, her eyes closed. 'Yes, I am,' she said solemnly. 'I'll be here every Christmas from now on.'

'You be my mother?'

Holding him close, Jill whispered, 'Yes, Joey.'

'Oh, boy.' At that reassurance, his gaze slipped to the tree. 'Wow!' Immediately, he sat down and grabbed a package.

Jill laughed and wiped the tears from her eyes. 'Dustin! Eunice!' she called up the stairs. 'I think Joey's ready to open presents.'

'Tell him to wait one second!' Dustin hollered back down. 'I gotta get dressed.'

Jill grinned. Yes, he had to get dressed this morning – she'd made sure of it last night. Christmas Eve had been a wonderfully romantic night to get married. It had been a dream come true for her. Jill gazed at the diamond engagement ring and wedding band Dustin had given her, still somewhat amazed. She had never thought she'd own anything so lovely. It had been a night to remember for everyone, even Joey, who had looked adorable in the wedding tux and little boots Dustin had wanted. Jill treasured the silvery memories floating through her mind, even more glad that her parents had seemed truly delighted for her and Dustin.

Eunice's door opened. A moment later, she came downstairs wearing a robe.

'You won't mind my informality, dear?' she asked.

Jill hugged her. 'If you won't say anything about me taking a nap this afternoon.'

Eunice nodded with satisfaction. 'I still wish you two had taken a honeymoon. It's what I want to give you for a wedding gift.'

'We will eventually. And I'm delighted with that idea.' Jill gave her a swift kiss on the cheek. 'But right now, this is all either of us wanted.'

Dustin walked into the parlor, coming to kiss Jill on the mouth and sweep his mother into a quick embrace. 'Merry Christmas,' he told them. Then he knelt beside his son with a hearty grin. 'Hey, Joey! What have you got there?'

'Santa brought me a train. And a ball!' His smile was huge. Jill reached for the camera off the mantel and snapped a picture of the two of them, not even bothering to try to smooth Joey's flyaway hair first. That was one of the things she loved best about the little boy she could now love as her very own.

'Open your gift from me, Dustin,' Eunice said, handing him a box. 'It's just a little something extra, but I think you'll be needing it.'

His expression was puzzled as he opened it. 'Thanks, Mother,' Dustin said, as he pulled a cellular phone from the box. He held it in his hand, then put it to his ear before he started reading the instructions.

She and Jill smiled at each other. 'I guess it's better than our old towel system,' Eunice told him. 'Technology is catching up with us.'

'This'll be great.' He really seemed pleased with the gift.

'You may not think so after we call you a few

times,' Eunice teased. 'So much for riding off into the distance to get some peace and quiet.'

'I've had all the peace and quiet I can stand,' Dustin stated. His gaze went to Joey. 'I'm looking forward to watching cartoons with my son again.'

'Here, Jill,' Joey said, blissfully ignoring his father's comment.

Jill took the small, soft package that Joey handed her, opening it to find a green and red wreath of his own handprints he'd pressed onto a woven cloth.

'Joey, I love it,' she said. 'Did you do this all by yourself?'

Joey grinned. 'Well, Daddy helped me. He's better at that than stringing popcorn.'

Dustin chuckled. 'But I'm learning.'

Jill scooted next to him on the floor, pressing her lips to his for a fast kiss. 'I always knew you could do it.'

'Yeah.' He swiped one more kiss before pulling a piece of silver tinsel from the tree and looping it over her ear. 'Luckily, I had a Christmas angel who believed in me.'

'I've always thought,' Eunice said from her place on the antique sofa, 'that Christmas is a time for believing.'

'I believe,' he murmured against Jill's lips.

'So do I,' she replied.

THE EXCITING NEW NAME IN WOMEN'S FICTION!

PLEASE HELP ME TO HELP YOU!

Dear *Scarlet* Reader,

As Editor of *Scarlet* Books I want to make sure that the books I offer you every month are up to the high standards *Scarlet* readers expect. And to do that I need to know a little more about you and your reading likes and dislikes. So please spare a few minutes to fill in the short questionnaire on the following pages and send it to me. I'll send *you* a surprise gift as a thank you!*

Looking forward to hearing from you,

Sally Cooper

Editor-in-Chief, *Scarlet*

*Offer applies only in the UK, only one offer per household.

Note: Further offers which might be of interest may be sent to you by other, carefully selected, companies. If you do not want to receive them, please write to Robinson Publishing Ltd, 7 Kensington Church Court, London W8 4SP, UK.

QUESTIONNAIRE

Please tick the appropriate boxes to indicate your answers

1 Where did you get this Scarlet title?
Bought in supermarket ☐
Bought at my local bookstore ☐ Bought at chain bookstore ☐
Bought at book exchange or used bookstore ☐
Borrowed from a friend ☐
Other (please indicate) _____

2 Did you enjoy reading it?
A lot ☐   A little ☐   Not at all ☐

3 What did you particularly like about this book?
Believable characters ☐   Easy to read ☐
Good value for money ☐   Enjoyable locations ☐
Interesting story ☐   Modern setting ☐
Other _____

4 What did you particularly dislike about this book?
_____

5 Would you buy another Scarlet book?
Yes ☐   No ☐

6 What other kinds of book do you enjoy reading?
Horror ☐   Puzzle books ☐   Historical fiction ☐
General fiction ☐   Crime/Detective ☐   Cookery ☐
Other (please indicate) _____

7 Which magazines do you enjoy reading?
1. _____
2. _____
3. _____

And now a little about you –
8 How old are you?
Under 25 ☐   25–34 ☐   35–44 ☐
45–54 ☐   55–64 ☐   over 65 ☐

cont.

9 What is your marital status?
   Single ☐   Married/living with partner ☐
   Widowed ☐   Separated/divorced ☐

10 What is your current occupation?
   Employed full-time ☐   Employed part-time ☐
   Student ☐   Housewife full-time ☐
   Unemployed ☐   Retired ☐

11 Do you have children? If so, how many and how old are they?
   _____
   _____

12 What is your annual household income?
   under $15,000   ☐   or   £10,000   ☐
   $15–25,000   ☐   or   £10–20,000 ☐
   $25–35,000   ☐   or   £20–30,000 ☐
   $35–50,000   ☐   or   £30–40,000 ☐
   over $50,000   ☐   or   £40,000   ☐

Miss/Mrs/Ms _____
Address _____
_____
_____

Thank you for completing this questionnaire. Now tear it out – put
it in an envelope and send it before 30 June, 1997, to:

Sally Cooper, Editor-in-Chief

USA/Can. address	*UK address/No stamp required*
SCARLET c/o London Bridge	SCARLET
85 River Rock Drive	FREEPOST LON 3335
Suite 202	LONDON W8 4BR
Buffalo	*Please use block capitals for*
NY 14207	*address*
USA	

Scarlet **titles coming next month:**

WILD LADY   Liz Fielding
Book II of 'The Beaumont Brides' trilogy
Claudia is the actress sister of Fizz Beaumont (heroine of WILD JUSTICE) and Gabriel MacIntyre thinks he knows exactly what kind of woman she is . . . the kind he despises! But Mac can't ignore the attraction between them – particularly when Claudia's life is threatened!

DESTINIES   Maxine Barry
Book I of the 'All His Prey' duet
They say that opposites attract . . . well, Kier and Oriel are definitely opposites. She is every inch a lady, while Kier certainly isn't a gentleman! And while Oriel's and Kier's story develops, the ever-present shadow of Wayne hangs over them . . .

THE SHERRABY BRIDES   Kay Gregory
Simon Sebastian and Zack Kent are very reluctant bridegrooms. So why is it that they can't stop thinking about Olivia and Emma? Emma and Olivia don't need to talk to each other about the men in their lives . . . these women know exactly what they want . . . and how to get it!

WICKED LIAISONS   Laura Bradley
Sexily bad and dangerous to know – that's Cole Taylor! Miranda Randolph knows she should avoid him at all costs – until she looks into his blue, blue eyes. Miranda is different to the other women in Cole's life and she's determined not to let him add *her* name to those already in his little black book!